NEARLY DEAD

URBAN FANTASY ROMANCE

MERELY MORTAL
BOOK FOUR

MICHELLE M. PILLOW

MICHELLEPILLOW.COM

ABOUT NEARLY DEAD

NOW COMPLETE AND READY TO BINGE!
READ THE FULL SERIES FROM BEGINNING
TO BLOODY END.

The final installment of the spellbinding first-person POV romantic urban fantasy series by NY Times and USA Today bestselling author Michelle M. Pillow.

I was supposed to stay dead. That's the one thing everyone agreed on.

One bite. One drink. That's all it took to rip apart what was left of my humanity. Now there's a war raging under my skin, werewolf venom battling vampire blood. I'm stuck in the middle, no longer mortal... and not quite anything else.

Costin says he saved me. That he did what he had to do. But what he really did was break his promise. He turned me into a monster.

And still, I want him.

Worse, I need him. His blood. His strength. His control. But every time I give in, I lose more of myself. The hunger is growing. So is the rage.

Everything's unraveling. My body. My past. The fragile peace holding the supernatural world together. And the only thing more dangerous than what I've become... is what I might do next.

Now, I'm out of time. If I don't figure out what I am, and fast, I'll destroy everything I've been trying to protect.

Including the master vampire willing to burn the world for me.

Tropes You'll Devour:
• Monster Girl Energy
• Transformation Gone So Wrong
• Enemies-to-Lovers
• Slow-Burn Dark Romance
• Forbidden Magic & Supernatural Politics
• Found Family, Deadly Betrayal
• Heroine Who Refuses to Die

To my cousin M's dog, Quincy Boy, who deserves all the treats and needs to know I'm the best. But not my cousin, M, who wouldn't let me take him home with me.

Just teasing, also to M, who's been a wonderful support on this series.

MERELY MORTAL SERIES

Merely Mortal

Mostly Shattered

Barely Breathing

Nearly Dead

Visit MichellePillow.com for details!

FROM THE AUTHOR

Now complete and ready to binge! Read the full series from beginning to bloody end.

Though this book can be read as a standalone if you really, *really* want to, the author recommends reading this series in the order of publication.

CHAPTER

ONE

Here is what I know.

I'm Tamara Devine. A mere mortal.

I'm twenty-eight.

My skin is on fire. Every nerve sparks straight into my brain, and I can't keep my eyes open. Someone keeps whispering my name. It's annoying. And I'm so fucking hungry.

Dammit, not again.

I claw at the bedding as I convulse, my senses too sharp like someone turned up the contrast on reality. I have to close my eyes. There's a metallic tang in the air. Blood. Old, powerful blood.

I want that blood.

Where the hell am I?

The last clear memory I have is of Draakmar's amulet. The ancient dragon's magic was the only thing keeping me alive. I reach for the magical amulet out of habit. It's my last line of defense. My fingers close around nothing.

Gone.

Of course. I gave it to Diana. She never should've been dragged into this supernatural nightmare. She should never have found out about monsters.

She's only six.

Paul's daughter.

Paul. I loved him. I still might. But knowing me destroyed his life more than once. I wanted so desperately to be normal and a part of their lives. I should have stayed away from them.

If I had the temperament to write it in a book, my story would be a tragedy.

I try to hold on to the memory, but it slips through my fingers like water. The fire. My family dying. Conrad framed me for their murders. Then time reset like some cosmic joke. It folded back on itself. Suddenly, they were alive again, none of them remembering they had died. Conrad took their place in death. Only I remembered. Only I carried that hell. Then I remember Conrad's ghost tormenting me.

No. Not now. That's over. Stay in the present.

I paw at my neck again. Please, gods, don't let the amulet have reset time.

No. Time didn't reset. Diana has the amulet now.

She's safe. Maybe giving away my protection was the final nail.

Maybe that's what happened.

Maybe I'm already dead.

A sharp pain tears through my stomach, and my mind screams with one truth. No. Definitely not dead. I feel every excruciating second.

I'm not human anymore.

Lord Constantine. Costin. Beautifully deadly master vampire who wants to possess me. I remember his silky voice and his cold hand. He's the flame to my moth. He pressed his wrist against my mouth while Alpha Thane's werewolf venom coursed like acid through my veins.

"Drink," he said.

I obeyed.

Sometimes I think it's love. Other times... I don't know. I think maybe it's all about control. Regardless, even now, in this agony, I want him.

Pain racks me. I need to think. Who am I now? What? The pieces are all scattered into a million broken shards. I have to figure this out.

My father is Davis Devine, a magic so powerful everyone he meets seems to bend to his will. I'm the byproduct of his affair with Lorelai, a human woman I just found out existed. She loved me as a baby, but my crib became a magnet for supernatural threats.

Goblins nearly killed me. So she gave me to my father and vanished.

Pain stabs deep, twisting through my gut. I scream, but the room swallows the sound. No one comes to save me. Why would they? I'm nothing.

I suppose I could say Astrid saved me once. Lady Astrid. Ice in pearls. She raised her husband's bastard. I used to wonder what kind of sadness you had to swallow to stay married to a man like Davis and raise his mortal shame. But Astrid? She doesn't show weakness. She sharpens it into knives.

The pain lessens, and I can thankfully breathe. Why won't I die?

That would make Conrad happy. He wanted me dead.

Conrad. My adopted brother. Human. Like me, or so I thought. They gave him to me when I was five, like a toy to keep me company. He died trying to kill us all. Then his ghost stalked me until the necromancer Leviathan trapped him. At least Conrad is finally silent.

I dream about him sometimes. Well, they're mostly nightmares.

I start to shiver. I'm not sure remembering any of this is helping to distract me. A surge of nausea twists up my throat. I taste bile and ash.

Fucking let me die.

Who else?

Anthony. My half-brother. Magical heir incarnate. He looks perfect from a distance. Gold-plated, carefully crafted. But I know the truth. He bleeds secrets. He gave up love to play their game.

And Paul... Sweet Paul. The only man who ever saw me without flinching. I wanted normal. He offered it. But I dragged monsters to his doorstep.

And then there's Costin.

Why does every nerve feel like it's on fire?

Why can't I keep my eyes open?

"Tamara..."

Ugh, shut up already! Who keeps whispering my name?

I'm so hungry.

I want...

I don't know what I want. I want everything.

Ravenous pain claws through my stomach, sharp and cruel, until it feels like my guts are on fire. Images of juicy hamburgers and giant rare steaks fill my thoughts. I want a giant food porn buffet of meat. Sizzling meat. Dripping red. Practically twitching. The desire is so strong I can smell it.

No. Not meat. Blood.

The realization hits me like a punch to the face. The very thought should make me gag. It doesn't.

The darkness around me is absolute. I open my eyes and see shapes dancing in the black. No, not absolute. I barely register where I am as I push up from a bed.

I concentrate on a shape and hear the harsh pants of my breathing drowning out all else. The wood grain comes into full focus as if my face is pressed against the wardrobe door. My fingers run over the bedding, feeling each individual thread woven into the fabric. All of my senses are sharply defined.

Have I been drugged? That might explain the bitter taste in my mouth and the strange traces of lights starting to dance across my vision.

Who would slip me acid? My brother Anthony comes to mind. Did we smoke a joint laced with magic again? I need to start saying no to him.

The pain is coming in waves along my body. My nerves are on fire, and I feel as if my skin is being peeled away from my muscles. I try to yell, but my throat is raw, as if I'd already screamed for hours. All I manage is a strange grunt.

None of this is right.

Something is catastrophically wrong with me.

A weird déjà vu nags me like I've forgotten this moment before, and I'm reliving the same morning over and over. I remember feeling Draakmar's magic being pulled out of my body like I was a supernatural conduit. I remember bright light and numbness. I remember being attacked by a... werewolf? Or was

it a vampire? In a bank vault? No gas station. No...
Subway tunnel?

I grab at my bare neck. They're puzzle pieces that don't fit neatly together.

For the love of everything, please don't tell me my amulet reset time again. I can't take another trip down a parallel universe with multiple timelines in my head when no one else can remember what happened.

Wait no. I've already been over this. I'm cycling. Time didn't reset again. Diana wears the amulet.

Draakmar wants to be with the six-year-old. Her innocence calls to the dragon. Being raised in my supernatural family, innocence is not a word I'd use to describe me when I was Diana's age. I like knowing she'll be taken care of. Conversely, I'm scared to be without my protection. The amulet saved my life more times than I can count. Now I'm defenseless.

Is that what happened to me? I gave away my protection, and that sacrifice killed me?

Is this what death is? Floating in confusion from moment to moment?

It must be Hell. Heaven wouldn't hurt so much.

No, wrong again. This is Costin's home. I smell him like a fine cologne lingering on the sheets. It stirs inside me a curious mix of desire and rage. Behind that is the copper tang of blood.

Why am I so hungry?

I breathe deeper, trying to connect the dots of the last several days. Time is a mindless blur that makes no sense.

A memory of Elizabeth performing a ritual with the werewolf Alpha comes trickling back. They tried to harness all the world's magic, redistributing power to themselves. Thankfully, they failed, but their attempt came at a great cost. It won't go unnoticed. Ancient powers don't like it when you fuck with their shit.

I see a flash of light, and I close my eyes tight. I don't know if it's a memory or actually happening.

I remember Elizabeth and Thane standing on the altar of blood and moonlight. The memory feels like it belongs to someone else or perhaps a movie I watched long ago. The image has been haunting my thoughts since I entered this newest supernatural nightmare.

Elizabeth is Costin's vindictive vampire sister. She's never pretended to be anything other than what she is, a power-hungry bitch who'd sacrifice anyone for her own ends. At least she's honest about her intentions, unlike half the people in my life lately. She wanted all the power for herself, and when Thane tried to take some of the control, she didn't hesitate to kill the Alpha.

But not before he bit me.

I run my hand over my shoulder and chest. My body is healed. It shouldn't be.

This is all wrong.

I *was* dying.

Fuck, this is confusing.

We are born, we live, we die.

That is how it's supposed to be for humans.

That's normal. That's mortality.

I've always had the sense that there isn't much time. Life is short. Live for the moment. I have an expiration date. That's how we mere mortals think. We're on a finite timeline.

But mortality should never have been in the cards for me. Not with the Devine legacy hanging over my neck like a guillotine. Not with Uncle Mortimer constantly shoving supernatural suitors at me to continue the bloodline like some broodmare.

Everything is becoming clearer now.

A week ago was my expiration date. I was ready. I even looked forward to the eternal calm. And then... Costin.

Costin, with his ancient eyes and cold hands. Costin, who promised he wouldn't let me become a monster. Costin, who broke his word to save my life. I can still taste his blood on my lips.

Hot tears stream down my cheeks.

I'm not a mere mortal. I'm a mere monster.

I don't want to be a monster.

I don't know what I am, but I'm clearly no longer human. There's so much pain. My lungs are filled with glass shards, and my blood has been replaced with magma that should turn me to ash.

There is a reason monsters like me don't exist. Vampires and werewolves don't mingle in any capacity. They can barely stay in the same room together, let alone the same body.

My stomach clenches with a need so intense I curl into myself. It's not just hunger. It's starvation, desperation. And beneath the feeling is a thirst so raw it burns my throat.

I need to feed.

The thought comes unbidden in a voice that doesn't quite sound like mine. Feed. Not eat. Not drink.

Feed.

The fire in my veins intensifies, and my back arches involuntarily. A howl builds in my chest, fighting to escape my parched lips. What the fuck is happening to me?

"Tamara."

Costin's voice cuts through the painful haze. I try to focus on it, to use it as an anchor, but it sounds wrong. It's too loud, too textured like I can hear each vibration of his vocal cords in slow motion.

"Tamara, love, you need to stay calm."

Stay calm? Is he kidding me? I want to laugh, but

it comes out as a growl. An actual growl that vibrates through my chest and throat.

It feels good, so I do it again. Louder.

"The transition is difficult under the best circumstances," he says, closer now. I can smell him. Gods, I can smell him. His scent is an intoxicating blend of blood and power. It calls to me on a level I don't understand.

"What," I rasp. "What did you do to me?"

I remember fragments. The ritual. Thane's altar. Elizabeth's betrayal. The werewolf bite burning through my system. Costin's wrist at my mouth as everything went dark.

"I did what I had to," he says. There's an edge to his voice I've never heard before. Desperation? From Costin? "I saved your life."

"I'm hungry." The words scrape out of me. "So hungry."

"I know." His hand touches my forehead, cool against my burning skin. "You need blood."

Blood. Yes. The word resonates through me like a thunderbolt. Blood. Feed. Blood.

A howl builds in my chest, and this time, I can't suppress it. My spine tries to reshape itself, bones cracking and muscles tearing.

"You have to fight the wolf," he urges. "Resist it, my love. Don't let it out."

"Hurts," I grunt, my muscles going stiff as I arch back.

"You're caught between transformations." His voice is strained. "The werewolf venom is trying to trigger a shift, but the vampire blood is fighting to heal you instead."

He should tell me something I don't know. I have a front-row seat to this shitshow. The opposing powers war beneath my skin like primordial enemies. Something wild and feral tries to claw its way out while the vampire blood attempts to subdue it. My body wants to change, the bones pushing to crack and reshape, while the vampiric virus' need to heal its host pulls me back. I stay human-shaped while my insides tear themselves apart.

"Resist, my love."

I want to argue with him, but my contorting body won't let me.

"Make it... stop," I beg, hating how weak I sound. "Please, Costin, end it."

I want him to end me. He should have let me die. I want to remind him of his promise not to let me turn into a monster.

"I'm sorry. I can't." He's a master vampire who rules all the North American territories, and he sounds so helpless. "We don't know what you are now. Or what you'll become."

My fingers dig into the sheets, tearing through

them like paper. I feel my nails lengthening, hardening into something else. Claws. I have claws.

I feel something wet on my face and realize I'm crying. But when I touch my cheek, my fingers come away red.

"Blood will help. It will strengthen the vampire side." Costin sits on the edge of the bed and pulls back his sleeve. "Take mine. It will help fight the werewolf infection."

He offers his wrist. The gesture isn't lost on me, even with the intense hunger.

"No," I try to say, but my body betrays me. I can hear his blood pumping, and the smell of ancient power calls to me. I'm moving before I can stop myself, grabbing his arm with a strength that should be impossible. He falls back under my weight, tumbling off the bed and onto the floor. We land with an ugly thud, but I don't care.

His skin gives way easily beneath my new fangs. The taste of him hits me like a drug, pure electricity flowing into my mouth. Primal energy enters my system, and with it comes clarity. And rage.

I'm no longer content with his arm, and I attack like a feral animal. My fangs sink into his neck, and I feel him tense beneath me as I tear at his flesh. He's stronger than me—*he's always been stronger*—but he doesn't fight back as I drink deeply.

The monster inside of me takes over. It's not just

a vampire or a wolf, but a terrifying combination of both. I want to consume him, to claim him, to tear him apart until I devour every piece, bones and all.

"Tamara," Costin gasps, and I feel his hands on my shoulders, no longer gentle, as his sharp nails bite into my skin. "Tamara, stop."

I don't want to stop. I can't stop. The blood is all that matters.

His grip tightens, and he rips me off him. Suddenly, I'm flying across the room, slamming into the wall with enough force to crack the plaster. I land in a crouch, a snarl ripping from my throat, my body coiled and ready to spring.

The rage feels almost as good as the new blood pumping through my body.

Astrid stands in the doorway, her eyes wide with surprise. Behind her, Anthony's familiar face contorts with an emotion I can't name.

But it's Costin who pulls my gaze. Blood—*my blood, his blood, I can't tell anymore*—stains his throat and shirt. The wounds I've made ooze. He's not healing.

"What have you done?" Anthony whispers in horror.

I look down at my hands. Claws extend from my fingertips, and dark fur has sprouted along my forearms. I feel the sharp points of fangs pressing against my lips.

"What have you made me?" I ask, my voice a distorted growl that doesn't sound real.

No one answers. No one has to.

Their eyes say it all.

I'm a monster.

And I'm still hungry.

I launch at Astrid, fury in my veins. She's always made me feel like the family shame. Her husband's mortal mistake.

"Tamara," Anthony shouts, raising his hand. Blinding light slams into me. "Stop!"

TWO

I jerk awake, which is a stupid way to describe how I wake up because it implies I can actually move. I can't. Cold metal clamps bite into my wrists and ankles. I'm chained to a bed like a horror movie cliché about to be exorcized of demons, which would be funny if it wasn't so damn tragic. The kind of demon I carry now can't be expelled.

"You're awake," Anthony says from somewhere to my right.

I turn my head. My brother stands in the corner of the room, far from the bed. His hands are raised with a faint shimmer of magic dancing between his fingers. He's defensive. Ready to strike.

Anthony is afraid of me.

I can't say I blame him. I've calmed a little, but

there is that nagging feeling of rage still lingering inside me.

"Where's Costin?" My voice sounds raw. The taste of his blood is still metallic and sweet in my mouth. I run my tongue over my teeth, relieved to find them normal again. But how long will that last?

"Recovering," Anthony says, not moving any closer. "You did quite a number on him."

Shame burns through me. I wanted to tear him apart without thinking of the consequences.

"Calm yourself," Anthony states, his tone strained. The magic around his fingers brightens. "I can see you spiraling. Your eyes are changing."

I force myself to take deep breaths in through the nose, out through the mouth. The meditation technique helps a little.

"There you go," Anthony encourages. "Stay with me, Tam."

"Astrid?" I ask.

As if to answer, the door opens, and Lady Astrid sweeps in. She appears composed as ever in a sleek black pantsuit. Nothing in her expression betrays that she witnessed me transform into a beast.

"What's happening to me?" I ask.

She cautiously approaches the bed, though her face remains composed. I remember being irrationally angry when I attacked her, like beyond what I normally feel at my lowest emotional points.

"We're not entirely sure," she answers. There is some comfort in her familiar calm. I used to think her distant and cold but have come to learn she's pragmatic out of necessity. Without her the entire Devine empire would have crumbled decades ago. "The combination of werewolf venom and vampire blood is unpredictable."

"Unpredictable?" I laugh, and it sounds more like a growl. "Fucking hell! Why are you fucking sugarcoating things? It must be fucking bad."

"Yes, I'm sugarcoating it to keep you calm," she answers. "And there is no need to cuss. You're still a Devine. I expect you to hold yourself to that standard."

"Sorry if my vocabulary doesn't meet your standards while *I'm chained to the fucking bed!*" I jerk violently against the restraints, hearing the metal creak.

Anthony's hands glow brighter with protective magic. Astrid doesn't flinch, but she takes a step back.

"The restraints are necessary." She studies me. "Until you can control yourself."

"Control myself?" I want to fight. If they won't let me throw punches then at least I can yell. "Look at me! I'm a science experiment gone wrong."

Something shifts inside me, a strange resonance

that directs my attention to the door. I feel Costin before he enters.

He moves with a slight stiffness. His neck scabbed where I tore into him as if he's struggling to heal. That isn't right. He's a master vampire and should recover faster than this. I must have really done a number on him.

Gods, what if I had killed him?

His eyes meet mine, and something electric passes between us. It's a pull so magnetic I feel a physical reaction.

"What is that?" I whisper, my anger momentarily receding as this new sensation washes over me.

"The sire bond," Costin approaches quietly. "It's part of the transition. It should have happened before now, but..."

Of course there's a bond. Nothing about me gets to be mine anymore.

"Sire bond?" The words seem strange to say. "Like what you have with Elizabeth?"

His face tightens at the mention of his sister. She's the vampire who turned him centuries ago as an act of revenge. That bond has kept him tethered to her for hundreds of years, fueled by his guilt over choices he made as a human in the medieval period.

"Similar, but not the same," he says, approaching the bed like I'm a wild animal he's trying to tame. To a degree that control is working. "Every bond is different."

"So I'm cosmically linked to you? Forced to feel this..." The chains rattle as I strain against them. This time I'm not trying to escape but needing some physical outlet for the storm inside me. "This pull to obey you?"

"It doesn't have to be like that with us." Costin reaches for my hand. His fingers brush mine, and the contact sends a jolt through my system. It's comfort and rage and need and resentment all at once.

I try to jerk away from him, but my movement is limited. I don't want him looking at me. I feel my body is transformed and can only imagine what I look like. My face doesn't feel right, and I saw the furry patches on my arms. "You promised."

I'm a monster.

Pain flashes across his face. "You were dying, Tamara. Thane's bite was killing you."

"So you made this choice for me?" My voice breaks. "To make me this... this...?"

"I made the only choice I could." His voice is low and urgent. "Life or death. I chose your life."

"That wasn't your choice to make. I told you I didn't want this." The rage bubbles up again. The magma of it is right beneath the surface ready to erupt through any fissure in my emotions. My vision sharpens, and I feel my canines lengthening against my elongating mouth.

"Costin," Anthony warns. "Step back."

Costin doesn't move. His beautiful, unreadable eyes hold mine. "I can't let you go."

The sire bond pulses between us, a living thing with its own demands. Part of me wants to surrender to it, to let it soothe the chaos in my blood. Another part, the part that's always valued my independence and humanity, recoils.

"I hate this," I whisper, tears welling. "I hate feeling like I'm not my own anymore."

Astrid clears her throat. "Tamara."

I turn my attention to her.

"We need to discuss practical matters," she says, ever the pragmatist. "Although we have tried to keep this quiet, there are rumors circulating in the supernatural community, and the elders will need to be informed. Mortimer and your father are already asking questions."

Great. Just what I need. Uncle Mortimer, the family doomsayer, who spent years warning me that mortality was a curse and who tried multiple times to marry a powerful supernatural to ensure the survival of the Devine bloodline. I can just hear his condescending voice bemoaning this new embarrassment I have brought onto the family name.

"Let them ask," Costin says sharply. "Tamara's condition isn't up for debate by the council."

"Tamara's condition," I repeat, letting out a bitter laugh. "Is that what we're calling this? Not abomination? Not freak of nature?"

"You're not an abomination," Anthony puts forth, finally stepping closer. "You're my sister."

The simple declaration nearly breaks me. A sob builds, but it comes out as a strangled growl. My body tenses against my will, and that awful shifting sensation comes over me again, my bones wanting to crack and reshape.

"Something's happening," I groan. "I can't... I can't stop it."

"Her eyes," Anthony says urgently. "They're changing again."

The room spins as pain lances through me. I arch off the bed, straining against the chains until the metal cuts into my skin. Blood wells from my wrists, the scent intoxicating even though it's my own.

"Hold her down!" Astrid commands. "We can't have her breaking free again and attacking the staff."

Hands press against my shoulders and legs. The bond I have with Costin intensifies as his touch lands on my chest, right above my heart.

"They're probably how the council found out about this," Anthony adds. "I'm sure one of them talked about her condition."

"I'll handle my staff," Costin answers.

"The council won't order her destroyed, will they?" Anthony asks.

The fact no one answers him worries me.

"Tamara, listen to me," he says, his voice compelling. "Focus on my voice. You can control this."

But I can't. The beast inside me surges up, drowning out reason and humanity.

Costin's hand slips onto my cheek and I snap at him, fangs fully extended now. He jerks back just in time.

"Astrid," he says. I hear the fear in his voice. Real fear. "This isn't working. We need to sedate her again."

"No!" I try to say, but it comes out as another inhuman sound.

Astrid steps forward with a syringe filled with red liquid.

"I'm sorry, Tamara," she whispers. Genuine emotion cracks through her icy facade. "Until we understand what you are, this is the only way."

That shot is why my thoughts keep cycling and I can't concentrate.

"She's dying, isn't she?" Anthony sounds far away. "No one has ever survived the mixing of were-wolf and vampire bloods."

The needle plunges into my arm. I feel the cold

spread through me, a momentary relief from the burning.

As consciousness starts to fade, I lock eyes with Costin one last time. The sire bond swirls between us, a connection I can't escape.

I sink into a magic-induced haze, completely paralyzed. I hear a familiar voice whispering along the corners of my mind.

"Poor little Tam-tam... always someone's puppet."

Whatever was in the shot causes me to shiver.

"And you thought I was a monster. Look what they've made you into."

Conrad?

I try to answer but can't.

This isn't happening. Leviathan has him trapped. Conrad can't be here. My vision is blurry as I look for him in the room. My head won't turn.

"Did you really think a necromancer could keep me locked away forever? I'm coming for you, sister dear."

His mocking laughter echoes through my fading consciousness. I want to warn the others, but no sound comes out. I'm trapped in my own mind with my dead brother's ghost.

I pray it's just the drugs. Maybe I'm going insane from the transformation. Maybe the wolf and vampire parts of me are creating hallucinations.

Conrad can't be back. He can't be.

Can he?

Costin touches my cheek, stroking it as he leans over me to kiss my forehead.

"I'm sorry," Costin whispers.

I want to tell him that sorry isn't enough. I want to rage at him for taking my choice away. I want to beg him to never leave me alone with the monsters inside.

Darkness reclaims me before I can force the words, and as it swallows me completely Conrad's whispers follow me into oblivion.

"Poor little Tam-tam..."

THREE

I'm no longer restrained. Thank the gods for small victories.

The hunger pains are still there. The constant gnawing makes my stomach feel like a hollow bottomless pit. At least the cravings are manageable. For now.

I sit up slowly, inspecting my limbs, half expecting claws or fur. There's nothing. Just my regular arms and legs.

I'm in one of Costin's guest rooms, not one I demolished during my last feral episode, or the one before that. This one is decorated in muted grays and blues with heavy curtains pretending to keep out the fake sunlight since we're safely underground. I remember getting a peek of this particular bedroom once. A vampire was feeding on a willing human in the chair next to the bed.

Is that my future? Drinking people?

The thought makes me want to gag, even as I salivate.

I keep staring at the curtains wondering if I'll ever see the sun again. I think about walking out into daylight and letting it turn me to ash. During the worst of the pain it's a persistent fantasy I can't stop. There is something beautiful to the idea of just blowing away.

"How are you feeling?"

I jerk my head toward the voice. Anthony sits in a corner chair, his phone grasped in his hand like he's been scrolling. He looks like he hasn't slept in days.

"Like I've been hit by a truck, then the truck backed up and parked on my chest." My voice is rough. "How long was I out?"

"Three days this time." Anthony leans forward. "We've been taking turns watching you."

Three days. Fuck.

He hesitates like he's going to say more. His thumb brushes his phone screen, lingering there a second too long. I catch a flicker of something unreadable in his expression, like he's thinking about something that has nothing to do with what's happening.

"Is something going on that I should know about?" I ask.

"Boy crush drama," he dismisses with a small shake of his head. He puts his phone down. "That sedative our mother gave you is pretty strong. It's the only thing that keeps both the vampire and werewolf sides dormant."

"Lovely." I swing my legs over the side of the bed, testing my balance. I feel stronger than I should after three days unconscious. "I don't suppose I can convince you to sneak me out of here? That idea you had to hop on a cargo container to South Africa is looking good about now."

"Sorry, Tam. No can do." He doesn't come close, and I wonder if he's scared of me.

"Any chance of getting some food?"

He looks back at his phone screen and asks, "Staff member or pedestrian off the street?"

It takes me a moment to realize he's trying to make a joke. The corner of his mouth lifts a little.

"Shut up!" I launch a pillow at his head, surprised by how hard it smacks against his arm when he blocks the attack.

Anthony's expression falls and he stands. "There's a special diet Costin has prepared for you. I'll let him know you're awake."

"Special diet. Great." I have a feeling I know

exactly what that means, and it doesn't involve ordering pizza.

Before Anthony can leave, the door swings open and our father strides in. I recoil as Davis Devine fills the room with his commanding presence. I don't want him to see me like this.

My father has always been larger than life. People are drawn to him, especially women. He's charming and handsome, with silver-streaked dark hair and the kind of face that belongs on a statue. Behind him, like a particularly persistent dark cloud, is Uncle Mortimer.

Perfect. The Devine patriarchy has arrived to save the day.

"Tamara." My father's voice is carefully neutral as he looks me over. "You're finally awake."

"Don't sound so disappointed," I mutter, touching my face to feel if it's malformed.

His eyes narrow slightly. "That's not fair. I've been concerned."

"About me, or about what I've become?" I stand up, pleased to find my legs steady beneath me. Someone has put me in silk pajama bottoms and a tank top. I try not to think about who has been taking care of me while I was unconscious.

"There were delicate matters to attend before—" my father begins.

"Both are valid concerns," Mortimer interjects.

He's thinner than my father, with sharp features and more calculating eyes. Where Davis commands through presence, Mortimer manipulates through precision. "The council has heard about the unfortunate events you were engaged in and is demanding answers."

"The council can go fuck itself." The words come out harsher than I intended, with a growl underneath that makes everyone in the room tense.

"She's clearly disturbed," Mortimer mutters, waving a dismissive hand, as though he's already written me off.

"Watch yourself," my father warns. "The supernatural council isn't something to dismiss."

I can't remember a time when my father was really angry with me. He was often more dismissive than annoyed. Normally Astrid was left to discipline. My father was always the fun one. As a kid, I idolized him. The older I get, the more I realize his flaws. Astrid is the real family glue.

"I wasn't engaged in any activities," I tell them. "I was kidnapped and made to participate in a werewolf ritual."

"They've called an emergency session specifically about you." My father doesn't appear to be listening to me.

"Lucky me." I cross my arms.

"They want assurances that you're not a threat."

Mortimer's tone is clinical. "No one has ever survived being bitten by both a wolf and a vampire, let alone an Alpha and a master vampire. The combination has been known as incompatible with continued existence."

I take a deep breath, and it occurs to me that vampires don't need to breathe, yet I do. "Yet here I am. Existing. Sorry to disappoint."

"This isn't a joke, Tamara." Davis runs a hand through his hair in a rare display of frustration. "The political ramifications are significant. The Devine family has always stood for order in the supernatural world. Now my daughter is an unprecedented hybrid at a time when the werewolf hierarchy has collapsed after their Alpha's death, a death you were present for."

"Their Alpha was killed by Elizabeth," I remind him. "While she was trying to steal all the magic in the world. Maybe tell them to focus on that instead of me."

"Elizabeth has gone underground," Mortimer says. "The council is looking into those accusations. And she is not in question at the moment. Vampires are known equations. You are an…"

He hesitates.

"Abomination?" I offer to help him.

"Anomaly," Mortimer corrects, but I can see he agrees more with my answer than his.

"So what's your solution? Lock me in the basement until I learn to heel?"

"That would be the simplest approach," Mortimer agrees, missing my sarcasm. Or maybe he simply ignored it. He turns to his brother. "Davis, it is an accepted practice to lock away troubles until they can be resolved. We could keep her comfortable while we determine the extent of her condition. The council might agree to this, and it will show we're handling the problem."

"I'm not a condition." My fingers curl, and I feel a prickling sensation as my nails begin to sharpen. I bite back the growing rage, but it's difficult to control. "I'm not a problem to solve."

"Tamara," Davis says, his voice softening slightly. "We're trying to protect you."

"Are you? Or are you trying to protect the Devine reputation?" The anger continues to bubble, rising up in my throat.

"That's enough." My father's voice hardens. "I understand you're struggling but remember who you're speaking to."

"I know exactly who I'm speaking to." I step closer to him, feeling a surge of power that's new and intoxicating. "The question is, do *you* know who you're speaking to?"

The tension in the room is broken by Astrid's

arrival. She sweeps in like a cool breeze, assessing the situation with one glance.

"Davis, Mortimer," she nods to each, then turns to me. "Tamara, I see you're awake. Good. You're looking better."

"I was just explaining to our daughter that she needs to cooperate with the council's investigation," Davis says.

"Was that before or after suggesting she be hidden away?" Astrid's tone is ice.

"It would be best if we moved her to the country estate," Mortimer says.

"Tamara is a Devine. We will not hide her away like cowards. That is to imply we're ashamed or scared. I am neither. Tamara is our daughter, and we will stand beside her."

I blink in surprise. Astrid openly defending me to them is new territory.

"The council—" Mortimer begins.

"Will be managed," Astrid cuts him off. "As it has always been managed. By me." She turns to me. "You have visitors. The werewolf delegation is here to speak to you."

"Werewolves? Here? At a vampire's home to speak to my daughter?" Davis looks incredulous. "Without asking me for permission first?"

"You were gone. I gave them permission," Astrid

says simply. "Get dressed, Tamara. They're waiting in the west drawing room."

"Wait," I say, as everyone moves to leave. "Why do they want to see me?"

Astrid pauses at the door. "Because their Alpha is dead, and you, my dear, are the closest thing they have to a connection to him."

"The hell they..." my father's voice tapers off.

"You can't be serious," Mortimer exclaims.

Astrid pushes him out of the room and shuts the door on the men before turning to me. She pulls a shot out of her pocket. "You need a small dose. It'll help suppress your anger. Don't tell those two you need it. They'll use it as an excuse to chain you up."

Astrid jabs the shot into my thigh. I feel the cold flowing through me from the injection site. It calms me.

"I thought the wolves would be here before your father and uncle showed," she says. "Werewolves are hot-tempered, especially without their Alpha to keep them in line. You don't want to rile them up. I'm worried Davis and Mortimer will make things worse."

"Why are they here? What does it mean?" I ask.

"It means," she gives me a slight smile that doesn't reach her eyes, "that supernatural politics just became even more complicated."

She goes to a drawer and pulls out a silk robe.

"Costin should have let me die," I tell her as she holds the sleeves so I can thread my arms inside. "It was always my fate."

Her hard eyes snap to mine. She reaches for my face and grips it tight. I feel her fingers digging in. "You are a Devine."

She doesn't say more but she doesn't have to. I feel the weight of that statement and everything it means to her. I'm no longer the mortal girl child she raised. I'm supernatural, whatever that means in my case. Her expectations for me are higher now.

She lets go and proceeds to cinch the belt around my waist. "We can't do anything about your hair, but they're only wolves. They won't notice. There are slippers by the chair."

I do as she commands, putting them on. We don't speak as we leave the room. I watch her move in my peripheral. She's so calm. I only remember seeing her worried once, and that was when I was supposed to be dying. She gave Costin permission to do this to me, but I don't blame her. I blame him. He is the one who broke his promise.

The west drawing room of Costin's underground mansion is a study in controlled tension. Three werewolves are on one side, my father and uncle on the other, with Costin between them standing on an invisible line that no one crosses. I see him trying to meet my gaze and I look away. I feel the sire bond growing and it makes it hard to be mad at him.

Magics, vampire, and werewolves stand in a room. It sounds like the start of a bad joke. Fuck, I don't have the capacity to deal with this. I want to turn around and go back to bed. The animosity is so thick I could cut it with my newly acquired claws. I look down at my hands. They appear normal, but they feel numb.

I feel a slight tremor as I look at the wolves. They radiate a raw energy that seems to thread between us. It stirs the feral creature inside of me.

They're dressed in biker leather and t-shirts. The clothes act almost like a badge of rebellion in the vampire master's refined home. Out of the three, I recognize Sully. He acted as our escort the first time I ventured into the werewolves' city territory. He is a giant mountain of a man with a beard the color of dark iron that would make Vikings jealous. It's braided in places, like he put effort into his menacing appearance. His crossed arms and wide stance are almost regal, but the kind of royalty earned in blood, not birthright.

I can't stop staring. His eyes glow with recognition and something else. Not deference. Not challenge. Consideration? Like he's taking measure of the mess fate dropped in his lap.

I wonder what they want with me.

Beside him stands a woman with cropped blue hair and scars that speak of a hard life. The third is a stocky man who looks stuck in a half-shift. His elongated mouth opens to show sharp teeth.

"Tamara Devine," the woman speaks first, her voice gravelly. "I am Rhea, first lady of Alpha Thane."

"I'm sorry about Thane," I say automatically, though the truth is more complicated. The Alpha tried to kill me, after all.

"Are you?" the stocky wolf growls. "His blood is in your veins, vampire-wolf. Some would say you stole his power."

"James," Sully warns quietly.

"One of us should be next in line," James says to Sully, clearly not my biggest fan. "Not this—"

"Careful," Astrid states, her tone crisp compared to the werewolves.

"Absolutely not," Mortimer blurts at the same time in obvious disgust.

They think I'm Thane's potential successor? The realization takes me by surprise, and I can't speak.

"Tamara, tell your guests they're mistaken and send them on their way," my father orders. He refuses to look at the wolves directly. In fact he seems to be having a hard time looking at me.

"I didn't ask for this," I manage, my voice steady. "Elizabeth killed Thane, not me."

"Yet you benefit from his death," James challenges.

"Benefit?" I snort holding back a laugh. I feel the emotions bubbling to the surface. "You call this a benefit? I'm at war with my own body. I'm hungry all the time for things I don't want to crave. I attacked people I love. How exactly am I benefiting?"

Astrid grasps my elbow to get me to stop talking. Costin is staring at me as if trying to communicate the same.

"You're not a human," Rhea says matter-of-factly. I see the smirk she tries to suppress. "I would call that a benefit."

"Alpha blood runs in your veins," James adds. The statement gives him no pleasure. There is a wildness to the way he is looking at me, like he wants to tear my limbs from my body and watch me bleed out.

I should tell him the Alpha can go fuck himself, but it seems wrong to speak ill of the dead to his sycophant.

Sully steps forward, as if to unnecessarily draw attention to himself. He looks at me expectantly, eyes all glowing hot as the beast within is barely contained. "If I may have a word in private."

"Absolutely not," Mortimer says.

"Of course," I answer, for no other reason than to get away from this gathering from hell.

"Tamara," my father warns.

A growl rumbles in the back of my throat. I don't know where the sound came from, but it seems to shock my father into silence. Astrid gives my arm a little squeeze as if to remind me of my place.

"We forbid—" Mortimer begins.

Astrid holds up her hand. "Relax, gentlemen. It's a conversation, not a coronation. Tamara can handle herself."

"I'll join you." Costin walks toward me, not giving me a choice as he threads his arm through mine and leads me from the room.

"I'll come too," Rhea says.

"No," Sully denies.

Sully follows behind us. I feel him moving, as if each step sends a current of warning across my back. The predator growing inside of me knows the danger Sully represents and it doesn't like it.

Costin takes us to his library. A fire bursts in the fireplace when we enter though I didn't see anyone light it. Just being back here makes me tremble. My eyes go to the table, expecting to see the prophecy book that led me to my current situation. Everything is clean, the books back in their places on the floor-to-ceiling shelf like it never happened.

Costin gestures toward the chairs before leading me to one side and standing between Sully and me. After Sully takes his seat, Costin sits between us.

"The pack is in chaos," Sully states. Some of his tension is gone now that he's away from the others. "We need leadership. Without an Alpha, we're vulnerable." He shoots Costin a pointed look. "The vampires already look at us as lesser beings. The magics treat us like junkyard dogs. After what Thane and Elizabeth tried to pull, the council isn't pleased. They, of course, blame the wolves. We need someone to negotiate on our behalf."

"What does that have to do with me?" I ask, though I know where this is heading. I'm the last person who should be negotiating with the council. Most of my interactions with the elders has been hiding in the protected wing hoping they don't see me while they meet with my parents.

"There are those in the pack who believe you should lead us, despite you being... *you*," Sully says. "They see your attack as a sign. Some believe we need a new approach and an alliance with the Devines through you would send a powerful message to the other supernaturals."

I look between the two men, waiting for the punchline I know is not coming. This is insane. I'm not even a real werewolf. I'm... What's another name for a hot mess monster?

"But not you," I surmise. "You don't think I should lead."

"I'm less superstitious and more pragmatic,"

Sully agrees. "Your wolf is too new. You have no experience with pack politics."

That's an understatement.

He sighs, studying me in a way that makes me uncomfortable. "At best you would be a figurehead I'd have to manage. If I must do the work, I might as well take the position. Also, the one time I saw a werewolf-vampire hybrid it did not end pretty. Or sanely."

"Don't pull your punches on my account," I mutter.

"That said, you're stronger than a regular werewolf." Sully's tone still makes it clear he doesn't agree with the idea of me being in charge. "You have Alpha venom in your blood. You have master vampire blood. You're a Devine by blood, one of the most powerful magical families. And you tamed an ancient dragon. That kind of powerful leader excites some members of our pack."

I know he's describing me, but it feels like a glossy interpretation of what I am. I don't feel powerful. I feel like a science experiment gone wrong.

I'm hyper-aware of Costin sitting next to me. His presence is both comforting and infuriating at the same time. The sire bond pulses between us like an unwanted heartbeat, making it hard to think clearly when he's so close. I'm not sure if I want to feed on him or screw him.

I force my eyes away from him.

"I didn't tame Draakmar," I manage. It's a lie. "We came to an understanding."

"Semantics," Sully dismisses with a wave. "The point is you represent power. And right now, the pack needs power."

I want to tell him I don't know what I am. I might not be a wolf. Or a vampire. Or I might be both. Or I might be some kind of new monster that can't be controlled. I feel insanity whispering at the edge of my thoughts. Ironically, it sounds like the late Conrad. It figures my brain would choose that voice to torment me. He represents every insecurity I have— my mortal inner child raised in a supernatural family, my love for a brother who betrayed me, my best friend who tried to frame me for murder and kill me.

"Sully, I appreciate you coming here and the offer, but I'm still figuring out how to not kill people when I get hungry. I can't lead the pack. Please tell the others I decline."

"It may not be that simple." Sully glances at Costin as if worried by what the vampire might do. "You will be expected to try for the position. If you don't, the new Alpha will always be doubted. A clear path is the best."

My knowledge of werewolf culture isn't strong. Most are horror stories ending in disaster. I know they're feral beasts. What I saw of their territory gave me outlaw biker gang vibes. Sure, I know I've been through a lot. I've proven that I am strong, can stand supernatural trials, and all that self-empowered whatever. But mostly I'm tired. I just want to be invisible to the supernatural world again. I want to crawl back into my gilded cage that was the protected wing of my family's country estate. I want to watch the supernatural world from the safety of my balcony.

I spent so many years pushing at those bars wishing to be free. I touch my neck, not finding my amulet.

Ego sum avis stultus.

I'm a stupid bird.

I look to Costin, who has been surprisingly quiet this whole time. "Tell him I can't do this."

Costin's face is carefully neutral. "It's not my place to tell werewolves what to do. Our treaties do not give vampires the authority to dictate terms over such things. This is their internal matter."

"Then if I'm vampiric, I can't have a say," I reason.

Sully's eyes gleam. "You are also a wolf, so it does concern you, whether you want it to or not. The full moon is in two weeks and, by tradition, that's when a new Alpha must be named. Any longer, and other packs will sense our discord. You do not want them coming to solve our problems."

"Why?" The second I ask, I regret it.

"Because it is easier to exterminate a problem than to try to absorb orphan wolves into another pack," Sully answers.

"Tamara is not entering the competition," Costin says. "You asked, she refused. She doesn't want to be Alpha. That should be enough for the others."

"Good," Sully answers, "because if she did want it, I would have to challenge any claim she might make." He leans forward, his massive frame filling the chair and causing it to creak under his weight. "I was Thane's right hand. I am the strongest wolf. I should be Alpha."

"I'll back whoever keeps the peace," I say firmly.

Sully stands to tower over us, and I feel something stir inside. The wolf part of me responds to the natural challenge of his stance. "Peace is a luxury we can't afford right now. Elizabeth is still out there spreading her lies about what happened. The magic she tried to harness is unstable. The supernatural world is changing, and werewolves won't be left behind again."

"What does that mean?" I ask, not liking the edge in his voice.

"It means," Sully's eyes flash gold, "that whether

you accept the role or not, you're part of this now. Thane's blood made sure of that. You'll be expected to make an appearance when the time comes."

"I didn't ask for his blood." I stand but it does little good. I feel small next to him. My skin itches and I feel my emotions churning as they heat my blood. My grip on sanity is slipping.

He smirks as if I amuse him. "No one asks to be bitten. There is no middle ground anymore, Devine. Not for creatures like us."

The way he says "creatures like us" sends a chill through me.

"I need time to think," I step back, trying to deescalate my unintentional challenge.

"Two weeks," he reminds me. "You'll feel the call."

That timeline doesn't feel right.

"You've said what you came to say." Costin's voice drops to that dangerous tone that sends an involuntary shiver down my spine. I hate how my body reacts to him, especially now these new senses pick up every nuance of his scent, and every subtle shift in his posture as he moves protectively closer to me.

As he turns to leave, Sully pauses. "One more thing."

"What?" I ask. What more could he possibly want to say?

"Watch yourself."

"Is that a threat?" Costin is suddenly standing next to me. I never saw him move.

"No," Sully says, his eyes staying on mine. "It's a warning. From one wolf to another. The council is talking about putting you down as a precaution." His gaze flicks to Costin. "I'll see myself out."

After he leaves, I collapse into a chair, my mind racing. "I never wanted any of this."

Costin reaches to touch my cheek. "Supernatural politics are never easy, but we'll get through it."

"They're insane if they think I'd make a good leader." I would laugh if it wasn't so dire. Tamara, Alpha of the Werewolves? "Six months ago I wasn't allowed near them. A few weeks ago was my first time in their territory and I needed you to escort me. Now I'm a psychotic mess you need to restrain to the bed to keep from eating your staff."

"Which is exactly why they want you," Costin leans closer, his eyes searching my face.

I wonder if I look like a monster. I feel my skin prickling. Is my mouth ugly and elongated like James'? Are my eyes glowing? I run the tip of my tongue over my teeth. They feel sharper than usual.

"You're unpredictable," he continues. "Danger-ous. And, right or wrong, they believe you're powerful enough to elevate their status."

"And what do you think?" I ask him.

He studies me for a long moment. "I think you're more than you realize. I think you've always been more than any of us have realized. And," his lip curls up at the corner, "I think when you say you want to eat my staff—"

I smack his shoulder. "I meant servants."

"As you wish." He nods, appearing disappointed I didn't flirt back. "Do you want me to take you back to your parents?"

I grimace, shaking my head. I don't want to deal with Uncle Mortimer right now.

I run my hands through my hair, trying to process everything while keeping my emotions under control. "I can't be responsible for a pack of werewolves. I can barely be responsible for myself right now."

"The choice may not be entirely yours," Costin says gently. "Sully was right about one thing. The council is nervous."

"Great. So I'm either wolf queen or dead. Fantastic options."

"There's a third option," Costin says, his voice taking on that careful tone he uses when he knows I won't like what he's about to say. "You could let me claim you officially as my progeny. As a master vampire, I have certain protections I could extend to you."

Is he serious? Our relationship is already all

kinds of messed up. This would only give him a new layer of control over me.

"At what cost?" I ask.

"I publicly claim you. The sire bond you already feel would be formalized to the council. You would be under my authority in the eyes of supernatural law."

"So I'd be your pet." The anger surfaces and I have a harder time pushing it down. Soon it's going to explode. I hear it grumbling in my voice when I add, "Trading one leash for another."

"You would be my official responsibility," Costin counters. I hate that he sounds reasonable and calm. His eyes swirl with red as they travel over me, and I catch a flash of possessiveness that makes my pulse quicken despite my anger. He reaches toward me but stops just short of touching my face. I would much rather he yell and fight me. "Nothing will change between us. I will always protect you."

"Protected and controlled. No thank you." What I don't say is if I fail to get myself under control, it would be left to Costin to deal with me. He wouldn't be able to. He couldn't watch me die after he promised me he would. I doubt he could kill me if the council demanded it of him.

"Think about it, Tamara. Please." His eyes hold genuine concern.

I wish I could figure out what I am and what I

want, not what everyone else wants me to be. I close my eyes and take a deep breath. My blood is rushing around in my veins.

"Why does it matter what I want?" I ask. "Everyone will just make the decisions for me anyway."

"You're slurring your words. Here, drink this."

When I open my eyes Costin is standing in front of me with a goblet. I instantly smell the blood, and my senses focus in on it. I don't think as I grab it and pull it to my mouth. The liquid slides past my tongue, as I gulp so fast I don't taste it.

A drop escapes the corner of my mouth. Before I can wipe it away, Costin's thumb is there, swiping the blood. Our eyes lock as he brings his thumb to his own lips. The gesture is so intimate that heat floods through me, momentarily drowning out the hunger with a more desperate kind of need.

"Careful," he whispers, his voice low enough that only supernatural hearing could catch it. "Drink too fast and you'll make yourself sick."

I want to tell him I'm already sick. Anger and confusion swirl inside my brain. My hands tremble from the unwanted connection that makes me want to simultaneously throw myself into his arms and rip his throat out.

I lick my lips, watching his eyes track the movement.

"Don't look at me like that," I say.

"Like what?" He doesn't pull away.

"Like nothing has changed between us. Like I'm the same. Like this is normal."

Costin holds still for a long time, and I try to imagine all the things he's not saying. Is it guilt keeping him next to me? Pity? Does he still think he loves me? Has he admitted to himself that I'm a monster?

"Anthony and I will speak to Davis and Mortimer on your behalf." Costin takes a step back. "They're worried about the council."

"The menfolk to the rescue," I drawl. It would be laughable if it wasn't so awful.

"Do you really want to deal with them on your own?" he asks.

I sigh, shaking my head.

"Your color is better. Tell a servant to bring you blood from my food supply if you feel the slightest bit hungry. Don't let yourself get hungry." He starts to reach for me but then threads his hands behind his back. "I'll find you when we're done. If you need me before then, I'll know."

I watch him leave and find myself alone in the library.

FOUR

Something's wrong with the shadows.

I've been pacing Costin's underground mansion for hours, trying to walk off the restless energy that surges through me. My senses are on overdrive. The blood he gave me has settled uncomfortably in my stomach, making me feel nauseous and full. I watch servants press against the walls every time they fall into my eyeline, trying to be invisible. One of them has fresh puncture marks on his neck. The sight makes me both sick and hungry. I can't say I blame them for avoiding me. I don't trust me either.

My eyes focus too closely on the floor, and I smell damp rocks, like moisture is seeping into the underground walls, but I can't find the source. The search gives me purpose, and my mind becomes obsessed with finding the damp.

"What are you doing, Tam-tam?" Conrad's voice whispers to torment me. I whip around, looking for him, but he's not there. My shoulder joint pops. It's only my mind playing tricks as insanity takes hold.

I don't know when it happened, but I've stopped pacing and now find my body pretzeled on the floor sniffing the run of carpet like some kind of ghoul.

But none of that is what's bothering me.

The shadows are moving wrong.

At first, I thought my new vision was playing tricks on me. Everything appears different, like the camera on my phone zooming in to create a sharper, clearer image with details my human eyes couldn't see. This is something else. The shadows aren't just dark spaces where light doesn't reach. They're shifting in ways they shouldn't.

"Don't be paranoid," I mutter to myself, watching a particularly dark corner where two walls meet. The shadows seem to pulse, like they're breathing.

I'm not being paranoid. I see movement.

I crawl slowly toward it, trying to make out shapes in the darkness. I've found the source of the smell.

My gaze meets the smaller eyes of a creature lurking in the dark. For a moment, neither of us moves. My breath catches in my throat, like something is pressing against my neck, preventing me from pulling air into my lungs in an attempt to weaken me.

I think of the story Lorelai told me about when I was a baby. Goblins had come to my crib and tried to steal my breath. The supernatural attacks were one of the reasons she gave me to my father and Astrid for protection, before disappearing from my life.

I take a step back, crawling backward as my new instincts scream danger. My shoulders pop as I straighten my spine, moving to slowly stand while focusing on the darkness. Tension rolls through me.

I start to call for Costin, wanting his protection, but stop myself. I can't bitch about his control and then call for it the second I feel scared. I don't have the excuse of being mortal.

"What do you want?" I ask the creature in the shadows. I hate how weak my voice sounds.

A clawed hand swipes out of the darkness.

I leap backward, clearing half the hallway faster than should've been possible. My new reflexes are a surprise, but the shadow creature is faster. I only see a small streak as it comes at me. Razor-sharp teeth come into focus encased in sickly skin the color of old bruises. Claws anchor into my arms. Its wide smile and gnarled body remind me of the creature Costin and I saw in the graveyard outside the mausoleum entrance to the underground supernatural city.

Goblin.

Fear trickles through me and, though I know I have strength, I remain frozen. It's hard to breathe. With each struggle to draw air, the goblin's black veins rise and pulse beneath its flesh as if it's gaining energy from my struggle. Its beady eyes are wide, and the damned thing is smiling.

I feel the wolf inside me bristle, even as the vampire blood surges. Rage and hunger fill me, bringing with it a mindlessness I can't control.

"Tasty hybrid," the goblin taunts. Its voice crackles like stepping on fall leaves. "Not so power-ful, not so pretty, not so special."

I rasp in response trying to tell it to fuck all the way off.

More shadows emerge from the darkness, surrounding me with fangs and claws. They swarm my body. The first goblin attacker lunges for my neck. Claws bite into my arms and legs. The sharp stings propel me into action. I move on pure instinct. *Bam, bam, bam,* I strike one goblin after another, sending them flying. They land in the distances with sickening thuds.

My hand wraps an arm, stopping it mid-strike, and I feel a bone crack against my palm. There's a loud shriek of pain. The sound gives me a perverse pleasure and I try to do it again.

A drumming sounds in my ears. At first I think

my heart is the cause of the chaotic rhythm, but then I realize it's coming from the goblins. I hear their heartbeats calling to me. Their blood smells of rotting tree roots in a decaying forest. I see it sludging through their veins just beneath the skin.

I keep fighting, hitting one after another. Rage and hunger. It's all I know. It's all I care about.

A goblin cackles, as it perches high on the wall sconce like a gargoyle. Its black tongue lolls out of its mouth as it chatters commands in a language that mimics nails on a chalkboard. The others respond instantly, their attacks becoming more coordinated and vicious.

My senses focus on the leader. A wild darkness takes completely over, drowning out every human thought. Everything fades but that cackling face. I see every detail of its twisted expression. I smell the rot in its blood like a fine wine. The savage rhythm of its heart pounds like a drum.

The monster inside me wants to tear it apart.

Correction. The monster inside me *needs* to tear them apart.

I shake off the attacks and launch myself at the wall. My claws dig into the stone as I scale my way toward the ceiling. Fur ripples along my arms, and my bones crack as my body reshapes. The vampire and wolf war for control, but for once, they want the same thing.

Blood.

"Show them what a real monster looks like," Conrad's voice urges.

I have never moved so quickly or with so little thought. The other goblins try to pull me down, but I kick them away without looking. All I see is my target.

The leader's smile falters. Its taunting laughter turns nervous.

Good.

I swipe at the sconce, knocking it off the wall, but the goblin is quick. It leaps to another fixture. I growl in frustration and my rage intensifies. Copper flavors my mouth. My fangs stab into my lip, but I don't care.

I chase the creature along the wall, stone crumbling beneath my grasp. I leap to catch it mid-jump, and we fall, crashing down into the swarm of goblins. They scatter away from us to form a circle. The chatter intensifies as I clutch their squirming leader in my hands.

I growl, my voice a guttural sound I barely recognize. The goblin's eyes widen as I bare my fangs.

Time becomes a frenzy of moments. I feel pressure in my mouth as my teeth tear into the goblin's throat. Black blood sprays across my face. The blood tastes like it smells, of earth and decay, and I don't drink. Instead, I rip and claw. Tissue separates under my hands. Bones snap.

Screams turn to gurgling, then silence.

I don't stop.

I can't stop.

I need to—

"Tamara!"

Costin's horrified voice cuts through the red haze. I look up, still gripping a lifeless body in my hand while straddling what's left of the goblin leader. I open my mouth, and another goblin falls to the ground. It crawls away from me. The other goblins lucky enough to have escaped my wrath have vanished back into their shadows, leaving me alone with my massacre.

Costin stands in the doorway, Anthony and Astrid beside him. The horror on their faces brings me crashing back to reality.

I release the goblin in my hand and slowly stand. I look down to find my hands covered in black blood, chunks of flesh cling to my nails. My silk robe is shredded and soaked. I can feel goblin blood cooling on my face and sticking to my hair.

"I..." My entire body shakes.

The bitter taste in my mouth gags me. I don't want to move.

"They attacked me," I try to explain, more to

myself than to them. I step toward Costin. "They were trying to—"

"Don't move," Costin says, but his voice isn't steady either. He takes a step toward me, hands raised like he's approaching a wild animal. Which I suppose he is.

My breathing is ragged. "Costin, I—"

"She's lost control," Anthony whispers. "We need to chain her again."

"No!" I stumble backward, leaving bloody footprints on the carpet. "I'm fine. I'm in control now. I was protecting myself. I don't want to hurt anything."

Astrid moves next to Costin and touches his shoulder. If she says something, I can't hear it.

Even as I say it, I feel the monster inside me stirring, wanting more. I look at the horror on the floor. It's not just the carpet. It's splattered on the walls and staining my skin.

The violence has awakened something that won't easily be put back to sleep.

"This isn't me," I say, wishing I could make it true. I stare at Costin, begging him to stop this. "Please, this isn't me..."

"Tamara." Costin takes another careful step closer. He doesn't seem to be listening as he stares at my face.

I catch my reflection in the polished metal of a

shield on his wall. Black blood covers my distorted features. I lean closer to look at the monster I've become. My eyes are a swirling mix of vampire red and werewolf gold, and there's nothing human left in me at all.

I see movement coming at me but before I can turn I feel a sharp jab in my arm. I try to fight it off, but Costin holds me tight. I look down to see a spent syringe sticking out of my arm. I fall limp.

"I'm sorry, Tamara," Costin whispers as he catches me against him. "Forgive me for what I've done to you. I never meant for you to become this."

I wonder if this is what Elizabeth felt when she was first turned by her husband, this overwhelming urge to destroy. Is that why she attacked her brother and turned him? Why she's so desperate to harness more power? Is this why she is like she is? Is it why Costin has been so ready to forgive her, because he knows what we become?

Maybe that's what we all become in the end. Monsters.

"I'm so sorry," he whispers. "So sorry..."

I can't answer him as I fall into oblivion, hoping I never wake back up.

FIVE

Dammit.

I'm awake. Darkness recedes, giving way to unwanted consciousness. There isn't even a moment of feeling like I'm normal. I know I'm a monster, and this is my hell.

I'm back in the guest room, on the same bed, with the same thick bands of metal shackling my wrists and ankles. My throat is raw, like I've been screaming for hours, though I don't remember making a sound.

I remember blood.

I remember death.

I remember Costin's face, watching me with horror and regret. Or was it pity and guilt?

I flex my hands, remembering the feel of bones cracking and the squish of...

Oh, gross, what have I done? That's not me. It can't be me. I didn't...

I try to lift my arms, but the chains stop me. I lift my head, half-expecting to find my hands still covered in goblin blood, but they're clean. Someone has bathed and dressed me in a white cotton gown. White? That seems like a bad joke. I'm hardly pure and at the rate I'm going it'll be stained the second they release me.

At this point being handled while unconscious is the last of my worries. It's better than waking up drenched in the evidence of my brutality.

"Kill me," I whisper, not expecting an answer.

"I remember that feeling. Don't worry, it passes."

The voice doesn't belong to Costin or my family. It's smooth and feminine, with a slight European accent I can't quite place. I turn my head to find a woman perched elegantly in a chair near the window, her posture so perfect it makes my spine ache just looking at her.

Costin's bitch sister, Elizabeth.

"Soon you'll just want to kill everyone else," she continues. There is a resignation to her sad tone. I don't buy it. I doubt the vampire feels such things. If she's sad, it's because her scheming didn't work out.

The last time I saw Elizabeth was at the failed ritual. Diana had launched her into a column by channeling Draakmar's magic. Costin used the opportunity to subdue his sister by her throat. He had the chance to end her schemes, to avenge everyone she'd hurt. I remember her taunting him through bloody lips, *"Do it. Finish what you started all those centuries ago."*

But he couldn't. He couldn't kill her. Just like he couldn't let me die.

Now she's sitting here in Costin's house like she's the guest of honor at a blood-soaked tea party.

My teeth sharpen in response to her presence. The mortal in me wants to give up, but the monster fights to live. "Come to finish the job?"

"Is that any way to greet family?" Her smile doesn't reach her eyes. "After all, you are from my bloodline now."

"You're not my family."

"Ah, now, don't be like that." She stands and lifts her arms to the side. "Give grandma a hug."

"Fuck off." I pull at the chains, feeling the metal cut into my skin. She tried to kill me. She tried to kill Diana and Paul.

Elizabeth drops her arms and laughs. She waves a dismissive hand. "Calm down. I'm not some goblin you can tear apart. Besides, I'm here to help."

"Help?" I snort in disbelief. "The only thing you could offer is to leave and never come back. How did you get in here?"

"Good servants are so hard to find." She touches

the corner of her lip before rubbing her fingertips together.

"Where's Costin? He wouldn't let you anywhere near me."

She walks to a small table and lifts a wine bottle from a bucket of ice. She stabs her fingernail into the cork and pulls it out. Sniffing the top she smiles before pouring red liquid into a glass. I instantly smell the blood and hunger curls through me. "My dear brother is busy cleaning up his mess with the council. Well, technically, it's your mess, but since he made you they'll blame him. Seems they don't appreciate hybrid monsters tearing apart other supernatural creatures, even ones as lowly as goblins."

I remember what Costin told me about their shared past. Elizabeth was only fourteen when he arranged her marriage to a nobleman who turned out to be a vampire. Marcus killed her after forcing her to watch him impale her lover. She was nineteen and pregnant when she was turned. No fetus would survive the transition. Afterward, she sired Costin as revenge or perhaps as a twisted way to keep her only family with her forever.

Their history is a tragedy that's played out over centuries. No wonder he can't bring himself to destroy her, despite everything she's done.

"My dear simple brother..." Elizabeth muses,

watching me over the rim of her glass as she swirls the blood. "First he sold me to a monster, and now he's turned you into one. Being a female in his orbit isn't exactly the safest place, is it?"

"At least he didn't mean to hurt me," I say, defending him despite my anger. "Unlike you, who tried to sacrifice me on an altar."

"Next to an altar, not on it," she corrects. "Don't be so dramatic. It's the past."

"It was days ago," I grumble, gritting my teeth. I ball my fist and wait for her to come close enough to grab.

"You survived. We shook up the supernatural world. Tell me you don't feel all the released magic floating around in the air just waiting to be claimed? Admit it." She grins. "You're having fun."

"Nothing about this is fun."

Her smile drops in annoyance. She sets down her glass of blood. "Stop whining. You survived. We shook up the magical world, which desperately needed a transformation."

I stare at her.

"I'm here to talk about the future," she says.

I wait for the punchline.

"He couldn't kill me when he had the chance," Elizabeth continues, "just as he couldn't let you die. That's my brother's greatest weakness."

"Love?"

"Sentiment." Elizabeth smiles and again takes the glass of blood to sniff it. "He will spend the rest of his days trying to atone for his sins. You may find it romantic now, but soon the remains of your humanity will fade, and you will grow to resent how weak he truly is."

"Why are you here, Elizabeth?" I pull at my wrist, only managing to cut myself on the edge of the shackle. It doesn't release me.

She downs the blood in one gulp and gives a small sigh. "He always did stock the clean stuff."

"What do you want?" I enunciate.

"I'm going to offer you a way out of your," she leans toward me and gives me a once over, "predicament."

My stomach twists. I should tell her to take a flying leap into a vat of acid but can't force the words. I want to hear what she has to say.

She sits next to my thigh, keeping just out of my reach. "I can undo what's been done to you. Unchecked, it's unlikely your sanity will survive what's happening. I can purge the vampire blood from your system or neutralize the werewolf venom. I can do both and make you human again, though I have no idea why anyone would choose option number three. Humanity is so... messy."

"Go away." I avert my gaze from her. She's lying. This is just another game for her to alleviate her centuries-old boredom.

"I'm serious," she insists. "I've spent centuries studying blood magic. I understand the transformation process better than anyone."

"Why would you help me?" I shouldn't play along. She's lying. She has to be. There is no cure. Everyone knows that.

"Perhaps I see myself in you." Her eyes hold mine. "Another of Constantine's mistakes. Another woman he's failed."

She holds up her hand and lets it hover. I feel a pull. It's not like what I feel with Costin. It's not sexual or romantic, but it's ancient and it's there. My blood recognizes her as an authority. My sire's sire. With Costin, the bond feels different. It's warmer and more intimate. Even now, angry as I am at him, I can sense him nearby, feel the invisible thread connecting us. It's both comforting and infuriating, that unnatural connection that makes me want to please Costin, to obey him even as I hate the impulse. As my transformation progresses, will I start to feel obedient to Elizabeth? She's the last person I'd want to give control.

Something shifts inside me, and I try to fight the flicker of hope. It's so fragile I'm afraid to acknowledge it. "You expect me to believe you would do anything to help me?"

"Believe what you want." She stands, smoothing her immaculate dress. "But remember this. The sire bond isn't just about blood. It's about control. It's about ownership. He will never truly see you as his equal. To him, you'll always be his creation, his responsibility. A pet."

The words hit like a slap.

"So you're looking for ways to control Costin," I counter. "That's all this is."

"The council interfered with the natural order." She waves her hand in dismissal. "It's not the same for women. If you haven't learned that lesson by now, I can't help you."

"He doesn't see me that way," I say, but uncertainty creeps into my voice. I remember the gentleness in his touch when he thought I was asleep, the way his voice breaks when he says my name. The monster in me wants to hurt him, but some part of me, the part that still remembers loving him, aches at the thought.

"Doesn't he?" Elizabeth's smile is knowing. "Ask yourself why he keeps you chained. Why he makes decisions for you. Why he couldn't respect your wish to die rather than become this hybrid monster. Costin will always do what is best for Costin."

The door opens before I can respond. Costin

stands in the threshold, his face tight with controlled fury.

"Get out." His voice is dangerously soft.

"I was just leaving." She glides toward him, pausing as she passes. "She deserves to know all her options, brother. Even if you're too selfish to tell her."

I watch the muscles in Costin's jaw work as he restrains himself. Even now, even after everything, he can't bring himself to truly harm her. The woman who turned him, who bound him to her for centuries. I understand now more than ever that it might not be something he can help. She made him. Vampiric blood holds great power.

"Think about my offer, Tamara," Elizabeth calls over her shoulder.

When she's gone, Costin approaches me slowly, his eyes moving over my face. "What did she tell you?"

"That she can make me human again." I study his reaction. "Is it true?"

"It's not a real option." He sits heavily in the chair Elizabeth vacated. "Blood magic is unpredictable at best. Deadly at worst."

"That's not an answer."

"It's unlikely."

"But possible?"

"Possible," he admits reluctantly. "But Elizabeth's magic comes at a price. Always."

"Maybe her price is worth paying." I look away. "Maybe being human again is worth any cost. What's the worst that can happen? Death? I turn into a bigger monster than I already am?"

"You don't mean that."

"Don't I?" I meet his gaze. "You made this choice for me. You decided I should live as a monster rather than die human."

Pain crosses his face.

"You promised me you wouldn't turn me."

"I promised your grandfather I would always protect you." He stands, running a hand through his hair. "I couldn't lose you, Tamara. Not like that."

His voice catches on my name, and for a moment, I feel past the rage to the raw pain underneath. He reaches toward me, his fingers stopping just short of touching my face. I feel myself instinctively leaning toward him, my body remembering what my mind wants to forget. I crave the comfort of his touch, the safety I once felt with him.

"So instead you made me like your sister?" The anger rises, hot and sudden.

He flinches as if I've struck him. "You're nothing like Elizabeth."

"Aren't I? We're both monsters now. Both bound to you by blood." The words pour out, fueled by a bitterness I didn't know I harbored. Even as I say it I don't fully believe everything coming out of my mouth. The monster inside me lashes out just to be mean. "That's the real reason you can't kill her, isn't it? Because every time you look at her, you see your failure."

"Stop." His voice is barely audible. "I saved your life."

"You saved my existence," I correct him. "It's not the same thing."

"Tamara—"

"And now when you look at me, what do you see? Another monster connected to your bloodline? Another failure to atone for?" The words don't sound like my own. They're not reasonable.

"I see the woman I love," he whispers.

"The woman?" I repeat. "That woman is gone."

He turns away, but not before I catch the sheen of red liquid in his eyes.

"Release me," I say, softer now.

"I keep you restrained because you're danger-ous," he says. "Because you're still learning to control your new nature."

"At least let me sit up."

He moves to unlock the cuffs on my wrists. I notice he leaves my ankles bound. Still not trusting me completely. Smart.

I rub my wrists, feeling the indentations where

the metal bit into my skin. Already the cuts are healing thanks to my vampire blood. Costin watches the wounds close, and I catch a flicker of something like relief in his eyes. Despite everything, something inside him likes what I've become. I hate how much that matters to me. "If there's a chance Elizabeth's ritual will work, I have to consider it."

Costin frowns, centuries of pain in his eyes. "You don't understand my sister's games. There is always a cost."

We stare at each other, the gulf between us wider than it's ever been. My emotions seem dulled, distant. Is this part of becoming a vampire? This cold removal from human feeling?

"I'll consider Elizabeth's offer," I say finally.

"Tamara, please—"

"You made your choice." I look away. "Now I'm making mine."

Costin appears like he wants to argue, but instead, he just nods and glances at the empty wine glass. "I'll have food brought to you. Something more substantial than what I've been giving you."

"You mean blood."

"And meat." He moves toward the door. "The wolf in you needs both."

I hate the reminder, but my stomach growls in response. "Fine."

"Tamara," he pauses, his hand on the doorknob.

"Whatever you decide about Elizabeth's offer just be careful. My sister never gives anything without taking something more valuable in return."

After he leaves, I test the shackles on my ankles. They're stronger than the ones on my wrists had been. The chains are longer and I'm able to stand up. I'm still a prisoner, just with slightly longer chains.

Hours pass and I feel every ticking second of them. A dull ache settles over my body, like a flu virus zapping my energy. At least it's not the sharp agony of before. My hip and shoulder joints ache and there is no comfortable position.

I pace the length of my chains, testing the boundaries. I can just reach an ensuite, and I have to wonder at the thought given to the preciseness of my restraints. The mirror is old, more polished metal than glass, and I don't like the chaos I see staring back at me. My eyes move over the walls, following grooves between the stones, imagining they are little trails leading to better places. Anywhere but here.

A servant brings a tray with a carafe of warm blood and a plate of rare steak. He seems scared of me, and I hear the soft clatter of his shaking hands as he sets the food down. Funny, since he works for a vampire, and I see puncture wounds healing in several places on his skin. Not funny, because there is a chance I really would try to eat him given half a chance.

I devour both blood and steak like a feral animal, happy no one is watching, and disgusted with myself even as I savor the taste. Afterward, I feel stronger. The room sharpens. Colors become more vivid, and sounds are more distinct.

Including the whispers that seem to come from inside the walls.

I follow a groove with my finger, letting it travel slowly along a wall until I reach a corner. I remember that road trip I took with Paul and Diana. Monsters were chasing us because Conrad told everyone I started the birthday fire that killed my family and others. It feels like a lifetime ago. I guess it was. That trip, those stolen moments with Paul, the innocent perfection of Diana's childhood, they were the most human I'd ever felt. And just like mortality, the memory is so fragile. I feel like I have to bury it inside of me to keep it safe from the ugliness whispering to get in.

I press my cheek to the stone, trying to hear its secrets. At first, I think the whispers are simply my imagination, maybe the stressful aftermath of the goblins, or just my mind playing cruel tricks as sanity slips. The artificial lights dim behind the curtains to the fake windows to mark the evening in this underground fortress. I can see how it might trick someone who hasn't seen a sunset for five hundred years, but to me the light looks off.

"*Tam-tam...*"

I stiffen. The whispers grow clearer and more insistent. I still can't wrap my head around how even death doesn't silence my brother. I thought it was over when the amulet killed him. But I didn't know then what I know now. His spirit didn't just disappear.

"*Miss me?*"

"Conrad?" I stay pressed against the wall, afraid to turn around to where the voice originates.

He doesn't answer me, and I release a slow breath. It's all in my head. I move to look at a dark corner to prove he's not there.

I'm wrong. I see Conrad's face. The familiar smile mocks me. I wait for it to fade. He can't be back. The necromancer has him imprisoned. Conrad shouldn't be haunting anyone.

"*Death becomes you.*"

I lean against the wall, liking the protection of it behind my back. "You're not real. This isn't real."

"Time off for good behavior." His voice is more corporeal now and I see his lips move. His eyes are two hollow dark pits in his transparent body.

The shadows writhe in impossible ways, and I smell the musk of old books and ash. The scents don't belong in the room.

"This isn't happening." I can't deal with a Conrad hallucination right now. It's too much. "The necromancer would not have freed you without telling us."

"Call it work release then," he answers.

Apparently, even in death, he still isn't done trying to ruin my life.

"I heard what you did to Leviathan's goblins." Is that pride in his voice? Amusement? "I wish I could have seen their faces when they found you among all the entrails."

I don't ask him whose faces he's referring to. "I didn't want to kill anything. I don't."

He laughs. "But you did, want to, didn't you?"

A knock at the door makes me jump in surprise. The shadows instantly return to normal, and Conrad vanishes like smoke.

"Come in," I whisper, my voice shaky.

Costin enters, looking exhausted. Vampires don't get physically tired, but the weight of the meeting seems to have worn on him.

"Feeling better?" he asks, noting the empty food tray.

"Sure. Yeah." I don't mention Conrad. I don't know what I saw or heard, and the last thing I need is Costin knowing I'm hallucinating my dead homicidal brother on top of everything else.

I cross back to the bed, the chains rattling with each step to remind me of my situation.

He sits at the edge of the bed, careful to keep space between us. "The council wants to meet you."

"Meet me or execute me?" I mutter.

"It's not like that."

I can see he's sugarcoating the truth.

"Let me guess, they want to blame me for your sister's ritual, since I was there, and they tried to use Draakmar's magic through me. Clearly, that makes it my fault." I sound grumpy but I don't care.

He sighs. "They're curious about you. A hybrid has never survived this long before. They want to understand what you are."

"They want to lock the monster in a dungeon," I counter, crossing my arms over my chest. I'm tired of being treated like a science experiment gone wrong.

"You're not a monster, Tamara."

"Tell that to the new goblin painting in your hallway."

His expression darkens. "That wasn't entirely you. The attack was provoked."

I arch a brow. It sure as hell felt like me. I remember the feel of bones breaking under my hands and the sick satisfaction I got from each crack.

"Goblins don't come into the home of a master

vampire on their own. It's too bold and it goes against their need for self-preservation. The fact that they were here says someone sent them."

"Like when I was a baby," I say.

Costin frowns and walks toward the corner where I'd seen Conrad's ghost. He runs his hand through the air and turns to me with a frown. "Who was here?"

A chill runs through me. I don't want to answer.

"Tamara?" he insists.

I say nothing. I don't want it to be true.

"I smell necromancy magic," he insists.

"Is that what that is?" I whisper, not meeting his gaze.

I should tell him about Conrad. About the whispers. But what if it's just my damaged mind playing tricks?

Please let it be my damaged mind.

"Leviathan?" I ask, hoping he tells me I'm wrong.

"Possibly." Costin moves closer, and he touches my cheek, forcing my eyes to meet his. "Did something happen to make you think of him in particular?"

"He's creepy." A tremor works over me from his touch. "At my birthday, he gave me this eyeball-shaped ring. He told me I should wear it and that it's enchanted with an old family recipe."

The jewelry would have let him watch me like a

supernatural spy cam. Thank the gods I never put it on. I wonder if he's still trying to spy on me, if that's how he knows what's happening.

"He did what?" Costin looks as if he wants to go defend my honor.

I find myself reaching for him, needing contact, needing to feel something other than fear and confusion. I stand from the bed. My fingers brush his cheek, and he goes utterly still.

"Tamara," he warns. "We need to talk about this."

"Shh," I answer, brushing my fingers over his lips. "Let me remember what it felt like before all this."

I want the world to fade. I want to lock us inside this room and never leave.

Costin hesitates, then leans into my touch. His skin is cool beneath my fingers, familiar yet strange now that my own temperature has dropped.

"Everything is so..." I explore the subtle texture of his skin, the faint stubble on his jaw, details my human senses had missed.

"Heightened," he finishes for me with a nod.

I pull him closer, and he comes willingly. He rests his forehead against mine. I breathe him in, noticing his stillness in comparison. I hear his heartbeat.

I'm not sure what to make of us.

Vampire and hybrid.

Sire and progeny.

Lovers caught in an impossible situation.

"I hate what you did to me," I say, my lips hovering close to his mouth. "But I can't hate you."

He cups the back of my neck, gentle yet possessive. "I will find a way to make this right."

I want to say there is no making this right. Even as I think it, I close the distance between us, pressing my lips to his.

The kiss is different now, hungry, wild. My hybrid senses make the sensations more intense. I can taste the lingering traces of blood on his lips, can hear the unnecessary breath he draws in. The sire bond surges between us, a living thing that both connects and divides.

When we break apart, his eyes are filled with red. "We shouldn't—"

"I know." I can't pull away, even as reality crashes in. "Nothing's changed."

I'm still a freak.

"Everything's changed." He steps back to put distance between us. "Except for my feelings."

I snatch his forearm before he can retreat. My strength surprises both of us and he stumbles into me. The chains on my ankles rattle to remind me I'm a prisoner. I don't care. Not in this moment. A primal need is taking over me. It's hunger and rage and desire, all blended in an implosion I can't control.

"Don't leave me." The growl in my voice sounds deadly and not entirely human.

Red fills the whites of his widening eyes in response to my aggression. A rumble starts in my chest as I sense his predator rising to meet mine.

I smell his desire. It swirls around us. His pulse quickens like drumbeats in my ears.

"Tamara, stop. You're not in your right—"

I silence him by dragging him to me. My fingers dig into his silky shirt, and I feel it rip under my extending claws. The destructive sound excites the emotions raging inside me. I like it so I rip more.

I don't hesitate.

I don't wait for permission.

I want this and I'm going to take it.

I press my mouth to his. My fangs nick his bottom lip, and the taste of his blood ignites something feral in me. I tear off his clothes, growling into our kiss.

He tries to pull away and presses his hands against my arms as if to calm me. "Tamara, wait—"

"No." I push him toward the bed, blocking his path to the door. The chains limit my movements but not my resolve. "I'm through waiting."

I slide my tongue down his jaw and throat, over the exposed vampiric-pale skin beneath his tattered shirt. My teeth tease the skin over his collarbone, and I can't resist pressing hard enough to leave marks. Drops of blood stain my hostile seduction. The monster inside me wants to claim him, to make him mine as thoroughly as his blood has made me his. I want to control him.

No. It's more than that. I want to possess him.

"If you want me to stop," I pant against his skin, "make me."

He doesn't even try to fight.

A groan escapes him, and suddenly, he's matching my aggression. My cotton gown rips like tissue paper in his hands, leaving me exposed and trembling. He grips my hips, lifting me off the ground. The chains jingle and I feel the weight of them pulling at my suspended legs. There is something very seductive about being both powerful and vulnerable.

"Is this what you want?" he demands.

"More," I answer, wrapping my legs around his waist. I claw his back, feeling the skin break under my touch. I want him to make me forget what I am.

The monster wants to tear him apart.

We fall onto the bed in a tangle of limbs and torn clothing. The chains rattle with each movement, a strange melody behind our growls. Our lovemaking is as much a battle as it is an embrace, and there's nothing gentle about the desperate way we come together.

It takes little effort to tear the remaining tatters

of his clothes from him. My claw marks heal on his flesh as soon as I make them. When he's finally naked, I crawl over him, pinning him down with my newfound strength. I straddle him.

The vampire in me wants to consume.

The wolf wants to dominate and tear apart.

The woman doesn't get a say.

"Tell me to stop. You're not yourself." His eyes are so red they almost look black.

"I'm exactly what you turned me into," I snarl, bending to bite at his chest.

The last of his control snaps. With a ferocity that matches my own, he flips me onto my back and pins my wrists above my head. The sire bond rises between us, a living current of power I can't resist. It makes me want to obey him. I feel his hunger resonating with mine, amplifying everything I have become.

The bed frame creaks under our supernatural strength. His eyes capture mine and force me to look at him. When he enters me, it's not sweet and gentle. It's war.

The force of our lovemaking would have damaged my mortal body, but I'm not human anymore. I meet his thrusts with my own, body arching off the bed, chains tangling our legs. A cry of half-pleasure, half-challenge escapes me.

The chains anchor my movements. I wrap my

legs around his waist the best I can, forcing him deeper and harder. My nails score down his back, leaving bloody trails.

Through our bond, I feel flashes of his emotions. There's guilt tangled with desire and fear mixed with pride over what I've become. The flow goes both ways. I know he senses my rage and confusion, and my desperate need to feel anything other than fear.

My hybrid monster howls for release. My body shifts subtly, fangs lengthening, muscles coiling with supernatural strength. Costin responds in kind, fully unleashing his own vampire nature.

Climax hits hard. Violent. Relentless. My body convulses around him, and I scream his name. Without conscious thought, I clamp my mouth down on his shoulder. The taste of his blood pushes me over another edge, as waves of pleasure crash through me.

Costin follows moments later. His fangs find my neck. He drinks deeply, completing the circuit between us. The double bite intensifies everything, the sire bond pulsing with power and possession.

For several heartbeats, we remain locked together, blood and bodies joined. Gradually, awareness returns. I release my bite, licking the wound closed as instinct dictates. He does the same, his tongue gentle against my neck.

When I look around, I see the destruction we've caused. Our clothes and the bedding are in shreds. The headboard is cracked. One of the anchors holding my chains is bent from the force of our pulling at it, but magic keeps it intact.

Costin brushes blood-matted hair from my face. His expression is a complex mix of satisfaction and concern. "Are you back?"

I blink, realizing how far gone I'd been, how completely the monster took control. "I... I think so?"

He doesn't ask if I'm all right. We both know I'm not. Instead, he presses his forehead to mine, a gesture that feels more intimate than what we just shared. "I'm sorry."

I feel closer to normal than I have since this change started. I don't need to ask him what he's sorry for. His guilt and shame linger inside me. It hums through my veins.

I look at the destruction. It's the perfect representation of my life—everything broken and in shambles.

Costin rises and disappears into the bathroom. He returns wearing a robe and holding a second one for me. He drapes it tenderly around my shoulders, his movements are careful. It's a stark contrast to our violent coupling. He touches my cheek, stroking me gently.

"I have to go," he says, his voice low. "The

council is waiting for me. I don't want to give them another reason to be irritated with us."

Reality crashes back. The council. My fate. Elizabeth's offer.

But that's not all.

I catch his arm as he turns to leave, my grip firm but no longer brutal. "Costin. There's something else I need to tell you."

His expression remains serious.

"I think something bad is coming."

He gives me a long look. "I know. I can feel it too. But we'll handle the council and the werewolves and anything else that comes for us."

I give a small shake of my head.

"I saw Conrad." The words feel heavy. "Here, in this room. He spoke to me."

Costin goes still. "That's impossible. Leviathan has him imprisoned in an orb. Your brother's spirit could not escape necromancer magic."

"Either it was him, or my sanity is completely slipping." I tighten my grip on his arm. "He made a joke about being out on work release. You said you could tell something was here. What if Leviathan isn't containing him? What if he's using him?"

A shadow crosses his features, and I can feel the stress radiating from him. "What else did he say?"

"He heard what I did to Leviathan's goblins." I

can't look him in the eyes. My fingers flex, still able to feel the squish.

Costin touches my cheek, turning my eyes to meet his. "If that's true, we're in more danger than I thought."

As if summoned by our conversation, the shadows in the corner begin to shift. Costin drops his hand. The temperature drops, and the air grows thick with a musty scent.

"*He's coming for her, vampire.*" Conrad's voice echoes, though his form remains hidden. "*You can't stop him. Don't try. This was always her path.*"

Costin moves toward the voice, fangs bared. He puts his body in front of mine like a shield. "Show yourself, coward!"

My brother's presence fades, leaving a lingering chill. I hear the echo of his mocking laughter.

Costin turns back to me, his expression grim. "I need to speak with Astrid."

"Why Astrid?"

"She's the one who wanted Leviathan to capture Conrad." He moves to the door, pausing with his hand on the knob. "She might have an idea as to what the necromancer is planning, or why he's letting Conrad escape."

"I thought you chose Leviathan," I counter, confused as I try to remember how it all happened.

"Lady Astrid made the decision to have the

necromancer contain Conrad's spirit so he wouldn't keep wreaking havoc. She had me reach out to Leviathan."

"She chose Leviathan?"

Costin frowns. "I believe so? I can't remember who mentioned his name first. He is the natural choice. He's an elder. He doesn't handle small jobs, but he would take satisfaction in making sure Conrad's spirit couldn't escape. Plus, he seemed to like the idea that I would owe him a favor."

I didn't know how to feel about Conrad's imprisonment at the time. I still don't, honestly. I know it was the right thing to do. Conrad is dangerous, even as a ghost. But another part of me can't shake the guilt. No matter how messed up he is, he's still my brother.

"We're going to figure this out, Tamara," Costin promises. "Try to remain calm. Don't let your emotions take over."

After he leaves, I pull the robe tighter around my body, shivering despite the heat still lingering from our encounter. The shadows seem to watch me.

"Why won't you leave me alone, Conrad?" I whisper.

Conrad's faded voice answers, *"Poor little sister. You're on borrowed time. Costin can't save you from your true fate. No one can."*

SEVEN

"Remember who you are." Astrid circles me like a predator, her hand smoothing indiscernible wrinkles from my dress.

I feel like a human sacrifice about to be led to an altar.

Well, minus the human part.

I watch her hands, remembering how many times they've tugged at my clothes just like this. When I was a kid, I always felt an air of disappointment in the gesture, like if she could just make me presentable enough, it might hide the fact I was the family's mortal embarrassment.

My eyes move to study her beautiful, perfect face. Am I still an embarrassment? The family's monster? A hairy beast dressed up in silk and heels?

Like usual, her steeled expression gives nothing away.

Maybe I've been too hard on her. I've seen the moments of caring. She did take in the bastard daughter of her philandering husband when my birth mother couldn't protect me. She's stood by me since the supernatural hits started coming.

People are complicated.

Life? Even more so.

"You should have let me go," I tell her. "It would have made everything easier."

I don't know if I'm talking about now or when I was a baby.

Her hands stall, but she pretends like she doesn't hear me.

Costin's home feels like an endless maze of rooms. Just when I thought I'd seen it all, I find myself in a new underground wing. Astrid has led me down a winding staircase to the antechamber of a formal meeting hall where we will face the council members. Ornate sconces cast a warm glow that does little to dispel the chill emanating from the marble floors. I smell the gas fueling their fires.

The air feels like we're standing inside a giant tomb. Under the staleness, I detect a hint of old blood emanating from behind the doors. I imagine layers of it season the walls like a testament to those who died here.

Is this where I will meet my end?

As much as I say I want to die, there is a part of me that rebels from the idea.

The walls are black stone, and there are no fake lights behind fake curtains to make me feel like this place is anything other than the bottom of a deep pit. Ancient tapestries hang over the stone depicting supernatural histories, their colors still vibrant despite centuries of existence.

I miss the daylight.

"I hate these old meeting halls," Astrid grumbles. "They somehow manage to make the gothic style feel both claustrophobic and cavernous at the same time, with none of the beauty and all the charm of the gates to hell."

I see her point. I don't think it matters. A tomb is a tomb.

The dress Astrid brought me is the color of burgundy wine. In the shadows, it looks black until a thread of dancing light hits it just right to reveal the deep undertones. It reminds me of dried blood. Maybe if I make a mess massacring some creature, the material will hide the stains better.

I wish that were a joke.

The fabric feels like cool liquid against my legs as it falls to the floor. Long slits move up the sides, and I can only imagine they're for freedom of movement in case I need to fight. It seems silly. If my body shifts, I'll tear the material. The bodice looks elegant but feels like it's reinforced with steel panels. Armor beneath elegance or an attempt to keep me from changing forms?

"The council will be looking for any sign of weakness," Astrid says as she pats my hair. She's tamed the curls back into a slick style. I think it makes my cheekbones look sharp and my eyes even more feral. In my opinion, the heavy-handed makeup doesn't help.

Her own attire is equally formal. She wears a slate gray suit with silver threads that catches the light like tiny knife blades. I see blue threads of magic twirling over her fingers before she reaches into her pocket. She pulls out a silver pendant and places it around my neck. The metal burns slightly against my skin, and I automatically reach to pull it off.

"Leave it," Astrid orders, producing one of her syringes. She grabs my arm and unceremoniously injects me with it. "The magic will help regulate your wolf side. They will be watching for any hint that you can't control yourself."

I think I might be better off if they had left me chained. I flex my wrists. The shackles are gone, but I can still feel their phantom weight. My skin has healed completely, leaving no trace of the marks they'd made. Another reminder of what I've become.

"They want to see what you are." Astrid's ice-blue eyes meet mine. I've never noticed the depth of that color until now. It's like looking at the walls of a snow cave. "Show them strength, not savagery. Remember, you are a Devine. You can control this. You are more than the forces inside you."

She seems so confident in me. I don't know why. She's never expressed this level of surety when I was human. The odds of my disappointing her feel greater now.

The shot Astrid gave me forces my mind to become clearer than it's been in a while. I feel the fog lift.

Three days have passed in a blur since Conrad's ghost appeared in my room. Three days since Costin went to the council about Leviathan. Three days of blood and meat brought on silver trays, of servants who won't meet my eyes, of staring at shadows and waiting for them to speak again.

Three days. No news. No contact. Just shadows and silence.

Three days of cycling between madness and sanity.

Three days of trying to claw Costin's clothes off him whenever he comes to my gilded prison room.

The last one causes my lip to twitch up in the corner.

"Have you spoken to Lorelai? What about Paul

and Diana?" The questions fall out before I can stop them. "I tried to ask earlier, but you didn't answer me. Are they safe? Does Lorelai know what's happened to me?"

A flicker of something crosses Astrid's face. Annoyance, perhaps? She probably doesn't think I should be thinking of my human birth mother and my mortal friends at a time like this. "We'll discuss it later. You're getting emotional. You need control, Tamara."

"Please. I must know," I beg.

"Lorelai is kept informed through appropriate channels," she says, her tone clipped. "She's been calling daily but bringing her here to see you is unsafe. We have not told her where you are. It would be best if she went back to California. As for Paul and his child, they are under constant protection. The girl's connection to Draakmar makes her valuable, and thus a target."

That's not what I want to hear. I gave my amulet to Diana to keep her safe. The child must be terrified after everything that's happened.

"Are they...?" I feel the hybrid inside me stirring at my agitation. I don't know what I'm asking, or if I can handle the answer. Happy? Safe? Mad at me? Do they hate me? "Are they well?"

"The child is resilient." Astrid's expression softens slightly. "But yes, they are well. We've moved them to a secure location outside the city. Your, uh, *friend* Paul was reluctant, but he understood the necessity once the situation was explained."

I wonder what explanation they gave him. Sorry, but Tamara's turned into a bloodthirsty monster who might eat your daughter if she gets too close?

Guilt eats at me. I also wonder if they gave him a choice before they moved them. I doubt it. Supernaturals aren't an ask-for-permission type of crowd. Paul and Diana's lives would have been so much better if they'd never met me. No matter how I've tried to fix it, that fact never changes. Out of all my regrets, that one stings the worst.

I feel tears threatening. The monster inside me doesn't like the emotion, and it starts to push itself to the surface as if it can protect me from the pain.

"What happens if I lose it in front of the council?" I ask, changing the subject.

"Then we'll all pay the price." She hands me a small vial filled with dark liquid that seems to absorb rather than reflect the light. "Drink this. It will help keep the wolf calm for a few hours."

I take the vial, rolling it between my fingers. The glass is warm, as if the liquid inside generates its own heat. Magic around my neck, a shot, and now a vial. I worry it won't be enough. "And the vampire?"

"That's up to you." She steps back, giving me a

final assessment. "You are not a mortal anymore, Tamara. Don't act like one. Don't think like one."

Footsteps interrupt us. Anthony joins us, dressed in formal robes of deep blue that mark his status as a high-ranking magic. His expression is tense, a small furrow between his brows that I've learned to recognize as trouble.

"They're ready for us to go in." He hesitates, glancing at Astrid.

"But...?" I prompt, uncorking the vial and downing its contents in one swallow. It tastes like ash and copper, burning all the way down as it coats my throat with a film that seems to mute the constant hunger.

"There's been a complication." Anthony's eyes dart toward the stairwell. "The werewolves have arrived."

I see them crowded in the corridor leading into the antechamber.

"The werewolves were not invited." Astrid's perfect composure cracks slightly.

"Try telling them that." Anthony steps aside. A group of five werewolves enters, led by Sully's imposing figure.

While we are dressed in formal attire befitting a council summons, the wolves have come in a deliberate display of their nature. Sully wears leather pants and a vest that leaves his muscular arms exposed, showing off intricate tribal tattoos that seem to shift subtly across his skin. Silver chains hang from his belt like a challenge. He fears no traditional werewolf weakness.

I touch my neck. The necklace stings and I want to tear it off.

Behind Sully is Rhea with her blue-cropped hair, dressed similarly but with the addition of a long coat made from what appears to be wolf pelts. Morbid, but whatever. There is also James with his permanent snarl. That feral wolf has gone even further. His half-shifted state displays elongated teeth and claws. Two others that I don't recognize flank them. One, a tall, willowy woman with unnaturally golden eyes, and the other a stocky man whose massive shoulders strain against his leather jacket to the point that the seams look ready to pop.

Sully's eyes find mine, and instantly light with a challenge. "Miss Devine."

If ever I heard subtext in someone's tone, this is it. The way he greets me sounds like a warning not to fight him. I don't know why he thinks I want to be Alpha. I can barely manage my own life. Like I'd want a shot at running werewolf politics.

"Ready to face judgment?" Sully asks, smirking.

"This council meeting is not about judgment," Astrid says coolly. "It's about assessment. There is nothing for you to do but leave."

"She's a wolf. That makes it our business," Rhea puts forth. Her stance changes as if she's ready to brawl. Sully puts a firm hand on her shoulder to stop her.

"She's not a wolf," Astrid counters. "She's something special. She's a Devine. You have no blood claim."

Sully's lips curl, but he's not smiling. I can feel the tension building. The emotions cause my monster to respond. It tries to push its way to the surface. Claws and fangs feel so much more appealing than silk and niceties.

I fight the temptation to shift.

Sully chuckles like he knows what I'm going through. "Call it what you want, Lady Astrid. She's a wolf."

"What are you doing here, Sully?" I ask, feeling the potion beginning to work. A cool stillness spreads through my limbs, dampening the wolf's instinct to respond to his challenge.

"Making sure werewolf interests are represented. If they're deciding your fate, then they're deciding ours." His gaze sweeps over me, taking in the elegant dress, the controlled posture. "Playing dress-up won't fool them, you know. They'll still smell what you are."

"And what am I?" I step closer, ignoring Astrid's warning glance.

"I know what you should be." His voice drops, meant only for me.

The heavy undertone doesn't go unnoticed.

Before I can disagree, Mortimer appears behind the werewolves. My uncle's face is pinched with his usual disapproval. His traditional council robes are charcoal gray and embroidered with silver sigils, marking his position as a senior magic representative.

"Your presence is highly irregular," he scolds. "The council called for the Devine family, not a pack of—"

"Careful," Sully warns, not bothering to look at him. "We have every right to be here. This concerns werewolf succession."

"Werewolf succession is not on the council's agenda tonight," Mortimer snaps, though I notice he doesn't step any closer to Sully.

"It is when one of your family carries the blood of our Alpha." Sully's eyes never leave mine. "The full moon is in eleven days. By then, Tamara Devine will have made her choice. She'll stand with us, or against us."

"Enough." Astrid moves between us, easily commanding the space. "The council is waiting. We will sort this out inside."

She threads her arm through mine and pulls me along with her to the nearby doors. The short corridor we walk through is a study in ancient power. I feel as if modern time is fading into the carved stone walls inlaid with protective spells that make the air shimmer. My likeness shines up from the polished obsidian floors, which reflect our procession like a dark mirror.

My heart is beating fast and hard. Where is Costin? I wish he were with me.

I see the glimmer of ancient symbols in the stone as we pass. Contemporary notions don't belong in this historical world. They won't care about my rights as a person, or my feelings. None of this is about what I want. There is no fairness. The council is about power and control. They don't abide by human laws.

"Through the looking glass," I mutter, wishing the Tamara walking with me in the floor would offer to switch places.

"Shh," Astrid scolds, her grip tightening on me.

The air is still down here. Sconces hold eternal flames to light our way, the fire neither flickering nor producing smoke. I don't smell the faint trace of gas that I did in the other rooms. We pass alcoves with artifacts of supernatural significance. Some I've seen in books, others I just guess at. There are crystallized dragon tears in a bowl, the preserved hand of a creature still clutching a wand under a dome of glass, and a goblet that emits a smell I don't want to investigate.

My heart beats faster. I hear it in my ears, making everything else sound far away.

I don't want to do this.

I don't want to be here.

I don't want to be this... this *thing*. This monster.

This corridor looked short when we started, but it keeps going, as if we're not crossing any gap and the doors stay the same distance away. Sully falls into step beside me. I feel his energy, wild and barely restrained, calling to something similar inside me. Astrid tenses and keeps hold. I glance back to see the other werewolves forming a loose perimeter behind us, as if they're both escorting and containing me.

"You feel it, don't you?" Sully murmurs. The tiny hairs along my neck stand on end and I shiver. "The pull of the pack. The call of your true nature."

"I don't have a true nature," I reply. "I'm just me. I don't want to be your Alpha. I don't want any of this."

How many times do I need to say it?

"That's where you're wrong." His hand brushes mine, the brief contact sending a jolt through me that has nothing to do with attraction and everything to do with awareness. "You're stronger than you know. And after today, you'll have to decide which side you're on."

"We're here," Astrid says.

I glance forward to see the massive doors to the council chamber rising above us. We finally made it to the end of the magical corridor. The doors loom fifteen feet tall, carved from oak and inlaid with iron and silver. My skin itches in warning not to touch the metal.

I catch Costin's scent on the other side of the door. He's not alone, but he's all I can focus on. I desperately want to be with him, but I fear my feelings are a manifestation of the sire bond.

"What's in there?" I can't help but ask. I don't want to go in.

"Welcome to Amphitheater Subterraneum," Sully mutters.

"Like gladiators?" I look at Anthony for help.

Sully chuckles. I wasn't making a joke.

I don't want to fight. Well, fine, I do, but I'm trying hard to suppress that rage.

Anthony places his hand on my shoulder and squeezes. "It's just a meeting place. Neutral territory."

Astrid lifts her hand and pushes magic at the doors. They swing open silently despite their massive size, revealing the council chamber beyond. She leads me forward, forcing me to step in front of Sully to cut him off.

The room is circular and vast, with a domed

ceiling painted to resemble the night sky, complete with luminescent stars that twinkle. Tiered seating surrounds a central floor of white marble inlaid with a complex pattern of gold supernatural symbols.

Around the underground amphitheater, sitting above where I stand in what I can now only think of as a gladiator pit, are the most powerful supernatural beings from North America and the Old Country. Their collective power makes the air feel thick and charged. Or maybe it's my imagination. Either way, I find it hard to breathe. I slowly turn, looking my judges over.

I recognize some of the North American contingent. Of course, Costin is there, master vampire and my sire. He's not meeting my gaze. Madam Britannia, the witch whose botanical shop in Maine disguises her role as head of the Eastern Seaboard covens' alliance. Elder Birch, the gruff wizard representative from the Appalachian mountains who's been to our estate for my father's hunting parties. He carries potion bottles he calls moonshine, but I don't think they're filled with liquor by the way he always smirks when he says it. Conrad once told me Birch is a prison warden, locking away the worst supernatural criminals. I have no idea if that's true.

The Old Country representatives are, largely, unfamiliar to me. I might have glimpsed their faces at formal gatherings, but I was never introduced to them. A pale woman with hair so blonde it appears white, her eyes an unnatural violet, watches me with clinical interest from what I can only assume is the vampire section, since she's close to Costin. She parts her lips to show fangs. Beside the vampires sits a man whose features seem to shift subtly, as if he can't decide which face to wear. I have no clue what he is.

My father sits with Birch and the other magics. He's dressed in a formal charcoal suit designed to project authority and command respect. Mortimer leaves our group to join him. Next to them is an elderly man in elaborate robes covered in moving constellations. His beard almost reaches the floor, and his skin is like parchment stretched over bone, with eyes milky with age yet somehow piercing.

My eyes turn back to Costin, his face unreadable as he finally looks at me. He's dressed in formal attire befitting his station as Master Vampire, a deep black suit with subtle crimson embroidery at the cuffs and collar. I feel the sire bond pulling between us, a silent acknowledgment of our connection.

A chill sweeps through me. I didn't see Elizabeth enter, but she's suddenly there. She's in a gown of blood-red velvet that clings like a second skin, the plunging neckline more tease than fashion. The color makes her luminous pale skin look like she was sculpted from moonlight. Her hair is twisted into some obscenely perfect updo with rubies (at least I think they're rubies) woven through the strands. She looks like a queen from some ancient, bloodthirsty empire, the kind that didn't bother with trials before executions.

She takes a seat beside her brother as if it's the most natural thing for her to do. Costin stiffens at her presence but doesn't move. I wait for him to throw her across the room, to do something, anything to show he disapproves of her being here. He doesn't. Elizabeth smiles a predator's greeting, and I realize whatever game she's playing has already started.

I feel the sire bond with Costin. I don't think I could really hurt him even if I wanted to. Is that part of what keeps him from attacking his sister? Simple vampire biology? Some ancient bloodline magic rule to keep children from devouring their vampire parents?

The silence in the chamber feels deliberate, a pressure against my ears as all eyes focus on our unusual procession. All eyes but my father's. He looks at the floor in front of me. He's ashamed of me. I don't fit the narrative he's made for himself. Having a human bastard was quaint. Forgivable. Having a hybrid monster with werewolf blood... not so much.

I never asked for any of this.

I feel the rage stirring inside me. Astrid leans

closer. I feel the tension in her, though her face betrays nothing.

The milky-eyed wizard by my father stands.

"I, Decimus, will speak for this council," he intones, his voice surprisingly strong despite his fragile appearance. "We recognize the Devine family and," he pauses, his blind eyes somehow finding me, "the hybrid."

The word ripples through the chamber, causing a stir among the supernatural elites. I hear whispers in languages I don't recognize. I see pointed fingers and raised eyebrows.

Anthony appears at my other side. His hand hovers near his ceremonial dagger. It's a gesture that would look casual to most, but I recognize it as preparing for trouble.

His eyes meet mine, and I give a slight shake of my head. I don't want him fighting for me.

"Anthony, go take your place by your father," Astrid says.

He frowns and starts to protest.

"Go," Astrid insists under her breath. "Now."

Anthony moves toward the seats, dragging his feet.

"We did not, however..." Decimus' gaze shifts to Sully, who stands his ground without flinching. "... extend an invitation to the wolf pack."

"With respect, Elder Decimus," Sully responds,

his tone sounding anything but respectful, "the hybrid carries Thane's blood. Any judgment of her is a judgment of werewolf interests. Since there are no wolves present on your council, we demand our historic right to be here."

"Is that so?" Madam Britannia demands, her accent thick with an Old World cadence. "And do you speak for all werewolves now, young one? The Alpha is dead."

I find it amusing anyone would call Sully young when he's clearly been around a long time.

"I speak for those who matter," Sully replies. "Until the Alpha is chosen, I command the wolves."

"Enough," Decimus orders.

Before Decimus can continue, the marble floor trembles and opens. A wizard ascends from below onto the central dais. Zephronis.

His robes move like oil poured over starlight. The shifting constellations sewn into the fabric undulate as though alive. The gold inlay beneath his feet pulses once in acknowledgment, as if serving as an introduction of his importance.

I feel a small glimmer of hope to see him.

His long, silver beard nearly brushes the floor and is exactly as I remember it. His skin is pale but not frail, and his eyes glow with a faint violet. It's the same haunting hue that once bore into my soul before he called off my forced engagement to Chester Freemont with a single word: *impossible*.

That day, Zephronis had overridden every power in the room, including Uncle Mortimer. He literally saved my life. I could never have survived Chester.

I found out later that the wizard is older than most of the council's bloodlines. A true neutral. A high arbiter of balance. He doesn't play politics. He doesn't take sides.

Except he did.

He took *my side*.

And then he vanished.

To see him now gives me hope.

His presence commands the chamber like gravity. Some of the council members seem surprised to see him.

Decimus says in a patronizing voice, "Old friend, we did not expect—"

Zephronis lifts one hand. That's all it takes. Decimus shuts up and sits down.

The air tightens. Silence deepens.

Zephronis sighs. The sound releases slowly like a frustrated parent trying to compose himself before scolding his children.

"Balance," Zephronis says, his voice smooth as glass. The one word reverberates in a way that makes me think of an echo through time. The wizard had seen much in his life, and I wonder at how tired he must be of the endless supernatural chaos.

As if hearing my frantic thoughts, he turns toward me.

"This Council convenes under ancient law, guided not by politics or blood, but by the eternal need for balance. And balance," he pauses, and those glowing eyes lock on mine.

A ripple of tension passes through the tiers, but no one speaks. No one dares.

I feel their eyes. Their skepticism. Their judgment.

"Balance is not a struggle between mortals and gods," Zephronis continues, "or werewolves and vampires, or magics and monsters, but an agreement amongst us all. It is a pact to share all that we have, all that we are, and all we can be."

Zephronis turns toward Sully.

"We're not leaving," Sully says before he can be kicked out.

"This session concerns the hybrid's nature and the potential threat she poses. It's not an open forum," Decimus counters.

"The werewolves may stay as quiet observers," Zephronis decides, as he gestures toward the empty seats.

Sully motions for the wolves to follow him. They make their way above to watch. I'm left alone with

Astrid, and naturally lean closer to her. I don't want her to leave me too.

"My daughter poses no threat," Astrid states firmly, remaining in the pit with me. "She is a Devine, and as such falls under our responsibility. We will take care of her."

"Your daughter," Elizabeth interjects, looking down at us, "tore apart three goblins with her bare hands and tried to consume a fourth. All within my brother's residence. I think it's obvious she can't handle her new powers."

I feel rather than see Costin's reaction through our bond as he quickly suppresses a flicker of rage. "Goblins who wouldn't normally dare enter a master vampire's home. Goblins who, I suspect, were sent to attack her just as they were when she was a baby. She was defending herself, as any of us would have."

"Sent by whom?" Decimus demands.

A moment of silence follows his question. I can feel Costin's reluctance to speak the name aloud in this chamber.

"Davis?" Decimus forces the attention onto my father. "What do you know of these attacks on your daughter?"

"Nothing but speculation," my father answers. He glances at me but doesn't keep my gaze.

"We have reason to believe Leviathan is

involved," Astrid puts forth, causing another ripple of murmurs through the assembly.

"The necromancer?" Decimus scoffs. "He has been quiet for centuries. Why would he concern himself with a hybrid?"

"Perhaps because she is unprecedented," Elizabeth offers. "A successful hybrid of vampire and werewolf has never existed before. Such a creature would naturally attract attention."

"Why is the vampire whore allowed to speak?" Madam Britannia asks. "She is the cause of this magical imbalance."

"It was a werewolf spell," Elizabeth dismisses the accusation. "I'm the one who stopped Thane. You should be thanking me."

I start to call out the lie, but Rhea beats me to it.

"Liar! Murderer! It was your spell!" Rhea jumps to her feet and tries to charge toward Elizabeth. Sully restrains her, struggling as she snarls and starts to shift. He growls loudly and throws her so hard against her seat that it cracks beneath her weight. He points his finger in warning, forcing her to stay on the ground.

The chamber erupts in chaos as everyone begins to argue. Energy ripples in warning from the magics while the vampires push up from their seats and bare their fangs. The witch holds up a bottle of green potion as if ready to throw it. Decimus materializes a long staff.

Zephronis again lifts both hands, and everyone instantly stops. I feel a subtle ripple of magic wash over me from the gesture. He waits for everyone to settle before slowly lowering his arms to rest at his sides.

"If I may," I speak for the first time, my voice steadier than I expected. All eyes turn to me, some curious, but most openly hostile. "I didn't ask to be turned. I didn't ask for any of this. But I'm standing before you, in control of myself, willing to answer your questions. That's why we're here, right? To see if I'm a mindless monster?"

Elizabeth smirks. She's enjoying herself. I can practically see her mind calculating ways to push my buttons. I remember her offer for a cure. Is that her plan? To force me into a corner so I have to beg her for help?

Madam Britannia holds her potion but no longer threatens to throw it. She leans forward. "Control is relative, child. My sources tell me you've been restrained for days. That you attacked your own sire."

"It wasn't..." I think of sex with Costin and can't bring myself to explain. I mean, come on, my parents and every elder on the continent are right here staring at me. "It wasn't an attack."

It wasn't *just* an attack, but something far more primal.

Heat rises to my cheeks, remembering in exact details what happened between Costin and me. Even now, the bond between us pulses when his eyes meet mine.

"I was newly turned and confused," I answer carefully. "I've since learned better control."

"With the aid of suppression potions," Decimus notes, his eyes flicking to Astrid. "Not true control. What happens without it?"

"We were all young once," Elizabeth says with a laugh. "Who here hasn't gone on a violent sexual rampage?" She laughs harder and points at Madam Britannia. "Well, clearly you haven't. Even a dead goblin wouldn't fuck that sour—"

"Enough," Decimus orders.

"Vampire whore," Britannia grumbles.

"Dusty spinster prude," Elizabeth answers.

"Lord Constantine," Decimus demands, "control your sister."

Elizabeth's eyes narrow, and her smile becomes stiff.

Zephronis raises a hand, calling for silence. He looks weary. "Lord Constantine. You are her vampire sire and well-respected by this council. I would hear you speak as to her nature."

"Her true nature," Costin says softly, "is

complex. She is both vampire and werewolf, and something more entirely. She saved the lives of many. She tamed Draakmar and kept him from ending the world. She faced the labyrinth as a mortal. She stopped magic from being stripped from the world—"

I watch Elizabeth's stiff face and frozen gaze. I can practically feel her invisible rage.

"—and redistributed to those who would destroy centuries of tradition. And she survived death to become something magnificent." Costin's lip twitches subtly, breaking his stoic demeanor. It was slight, but I can tell I'm not the only one who caught the expression.

Zephronis looks at Sully. "Since Thane is not here to claim his place as her maker, I would hear from his second. Sullivan, speak."

Sully stands, his chest puffing up with his own importance. "Thane bit her before the vampire. The wolf blood in her is strong. Alpha blood. It calls to her true nature."

"She is an abomination," a voice calls from the far side of the chamber. It takes me a moment, but I see Birch is the one talking. "She should be imprisoned."

Anthony glares at him as Mortimer holds my brother by his shoulder to keep him seated.

"Such hybrids have been forbidden for good

reason," Birch continues. "They cannot maintain the balance between natures. They inevitably go mad."

"Yet here she stands," Astrid counters, her voice cutting through the growing tension.

Zephronis looks toward Birch, Mortimer, Anthony, and my father before turning to where Astrid stands beside me. "Lady Astrid, speak on behalf of the Devines."

"I will speak for my family," my father says, standing as Mortimer pushes him up by the arm.

"Lady Astrid," Zephronis prompts, dismissing his interruption.

"My daughter has always defied expectations." The way she calls me her daughter carries weight. "She should not belong to the vampires or the werewolves. She is a Devine. We take care of our own. She belongs with us."

"She is a wolf," Sully protests.

"She belongs with me," Costin says, his voice smooth as it carries over the chamber.

Zephronis raises his hand, and again the chamber immediately quiets. He steps off his raised platform and comes toward me. Touching my cheeks, he holds my face as he looks into my eyes. I feel a steady pull of magic from his fingers. I have no clue how long I stand there, being studied, but when he lets go he lowers his head for a long moment. "We have not gathered to cast judgment, but to assess the threat to balance. The hybrid will be tested."

"Tested how?" Anthony asks.

"Her control. Her loyalty. Her nature." Zephronis gestures to the center of the floor, where the marble pedestal he just abandoned pulses with light. "Step forward, Tamara Devine. Stand in the circle of truth."

I hesitate, looking at my father, at Astrid, at Costin. None of them seems surprised by this request.

Sully gives a small growl to get my attention. He lowers his jaw and slightly shakes his head as if to tell me, *"Don't do it."*

Astrid takes me by the shoulders, blocking Sully from view. Very softly, she explains, "The circle strips away all magical influence, including the potion you took."

I swallow nervously, understanding the implication. Without the potion suppressing my wolf side, with all the heightened emotions of this chamber, I might lose control. Exactly what the council wants to see.

"If I refuse," I whisper back. "They'll assume the worst?"

She nods. I can hear her words echoing in my head, *"Remember who you are."*

Taking a deep breath, I step forward. My silk

dress whispers against the marble as I walk toward the platform. I feel their eyes on me, the weight of their judgment, their curiosity, their fear, their need for control.

When I approach the circle, I see the symbols more clearly. The ancient runes represent all supernatural factions, intertwined in a complex pattern that vibrates with power. When my foot crosses the boundary, I feel a sharp tingle that races up my leg and spreads throughout my body.

The suppression potion burns off like water on fire-heated stone. The itchy necklace breaks and falls. Suddenly, every sense is heightened. I can hear heartbeats around the room. I smell the distinct scents of different supernatural beings. Power presses against my skin like heat before lightning. The wolf inside me stretches, no longer muted, and the vampire responds in kind.

I am fully myself for the first time since the attack, both natures present and demanding attention. And I am standing in front of the most powerful supernatural beings in the world, expected to prove I'm not a monster.

EIGHT

I stare at Costin, able to recall the texture of his skin against mine. I feel the air entering my lungs. I smell his blood. I taste the memory of it. His very presence calls to me, a bond so thick I don't know that I could ever deny him.

He's always been there. A constant. My constant.

At first, he was my protector, lurking in the shadows of my childhood, keeping me safe as a promise to my grandfather. I always saw him as another monster, a nice-enough monster, but a monster. I was wrong. It took me twenty-eight years to see what he could be to me. I fought it. Part of me still fights it, because this is not the path I wanted. I never wanted to be a supernatural, not like this. I've seen what power does to people.

I wanted to be normal. Human. I wanted to want

Paul. But Paul is only an idea, a representation of all my disappointments and secret dreams. Life has proven that path would never work. Death. Prophecies. Fires. Labyrinths. A near apocalypse. Claws and fangs. The images of all of it swirl in my mind. I was born to this destiny, to these horrible moments, this monstrous reality. A mere mortal could never survive it.

I can't look away from Costin's eyes. They draw me in. He's been so much of my timeline, and I'm barely a blip on his. He's controlling and frustrates the hell out of me. Still, I feel our deep connection like a thread pulsing between us. Suddenly, I realize he's trying to influence me and give me his calm.

I try to focus on him, but I hear the chorus of heartbeats from those in the room. They call to my monster like raining chaos to demand my attention. Each beat is like a drop of water on the floor, one after another, too many to focus on.

The magic takes away all of my safeguards. I hear the ugly crack of my bones. Pain rolls through me, but I ignore it. Both natures are present and demanding attention. This is my full self, the one we've been trying to stop.

The chamber falls silent as I stand in the circle, my body humming with barely contained energy. My gaze slips from Costin's hold to move over the most powerful supernatural beings in the world.

They expect me to prove I'm not a monster, and I can tell most of them think I'll fail the test.

I feel the dual natures inside me, vampire and werewolf, struggling for dominance. The wolf wants to fight, to assert itself before these predators. The vampire wants to calculate, to manipulate the situation to my advantage.

Great. My choices are dog or bat? One wants to pee on the floor to shock them as I mark my supremacy, and the other wants to skulk away into the shadows to plan.

Both want to feed.

"Look. She's smiling," Anthony says. He's not talking loudly, but I detect the hope in his voice. "She's in control."

"That's not a smile," Mortimer whispers. "She looks insane."

I remain still, forcing both sides of my nature into an uneasy truce.

"Interesting," Decimus says, coming down the stairs toward me. "She maintains control even without the suppression."

"For now." Elizabeth's smile doesn't reach her eyes. She lifts her hand, and I see the glint of metal. "Fetch."

She throws the coin in the air. I twitch as I track it to where it lands. It clinks on the marble floor, and my nerves jolt at the sound.

"But for how long?" Elizabeth asks.

Zephronis approaches the edge of the circle, his foot coming to stand on the coin to break my concentration. I feel the magic surrounding me is connected to him. He's doing this.

"Tamara Devine," his voice intones, though I don't see his mouth move. *"Do you understand why you are here?"*

"Because I'm unprecedented?" I whisper. It's the nicest way I can think to describe what I am. "Because you need to decide if I'm a threat."

"Yes." He nods, his magical eyes seeming to see through me. He's in my head, listening to my thoughts. My eyes dart to Costin, trying not to think of the last time we had sex. Dark, bloody images instantly emerge.

Fuck. Did Zephronis see that?

He nods his head.

Fuckety fuck fuck.

Okay, I need to think of something good. A benign memory. Diana's giggle. Her stuffed dog named Plop. Donuts with fairy sprinkles. Sunshine coming through the car window to land warm across my hand.

My heart aches. I'll never see sunshine again.

"What is happening?" Decimus asks. "What do you see?"

"Tamara in the circle," Zephronis answers wryly,

not revealing my thoughts even though I still feel him in my head.

"The circle you stand in compels truth and reveals nature," Decimus states as he appears behind Zephronis. "We will ask questions. You will answer. Your responses and your control will determine much."

I nod.

"Does she agree?" Decimus stares in my general direction but doesn't see me.

"I understand," I answer.

Decimus taps his staff. "First, we must establish baseline facts. Are you a wolf or a vampire? Which faction has claim on you for you cannot belong to both."

"She's mine," Costin states.

"Thane bit her first," Sully says at the same time.

"She's a Devine," Astrid states.

Zephronis whips his hand up for silence. I feel his irritation with the process growing.

"What do you remember of your transformation?" Decimus demands.

The question seems simple enough, but as I open my mouth to answer, memories flood back with visceral intensity. I remember Thane's fangs tearing into my shoulder, the ritual circle, the moonlight pouring through the glass dome, Elizabeth's knife, Costin's wrist at my mouth as darkness claimed me.

"I was bitten by Alpha Thane during his and Elizabeth's ritual attempt to steal all the magic for themselves," I say, the words pulled from me by the circle's magic.

"Liar!" Elizabeth shouts.

"Silence!" Decimus yells. Then to me he orders, "Continue."

I try to keep my words in, but the circle compels honesty. "I was dying. Costin turned me against my wishes to save my life."

"Were you dying or turning?" Decimus asks.

"Against her wishes," Sully rumbles. "We wouldn't even be here if the vampire hadn't intervened. There would be no questions as to her true nature. She's a wolf. Death is part of that process. She belongs with us."

"The ritual made me too weak. I wouldn't have survived the bite." I believe it, even if I don't know if it's true.

"But you did survive," Sully counters.

"My family is here as a courtesy," Astrid states. "The council needs to ask its questions of her, or we're leaving."

I look at my father. He doesn't speak. His expression says he just wants this to be over.

"You were saying, Lord Constantine bit you," Decimus prompts. "Are you sure you weren't just trying to pick your future as a vampire rather than a wolf?"

I can tell most of the people in this room would easily believe that. The wolves are treated as the lesser of the human-originated supernatural beings.

"I didn't want to become a vampire, either," I state. "I had made him promise me not to let me turn. He didn't honor that."

A murmur ripples through the chamber. I see Costin's jaw tighten and feel a pulse of complex emotions through our sire bond. Regret, defiance... pain?

I don't like that he's hurting. I should never have said such a thing. My hybrid stirs. I start to move toward Costin.

"Yet here you stand," Zephronis says, demanding my attention. He's staring at me, and I wonder at the intensity of his look. It doesn't match the calmness of his tone. "Neither fully vampire nor fully were-wolf. What do you feel when the moon calls to you?"

The question triggers something primal. Even underground, I can feel the approaching full moon. It's a distant pull on my blood that grows stronger each night.

"Hunger," I admit. "Rage. The need to run, to hunt." I swallow hard. "To tear things apart."

"And what of your vampire nature?" Decimus asks. "Do you feel the thirst?"

"Always." The word escapes before I can consider it. Damn this stupid truth circle. "But it's different from the wolf's hunger. Colder. More calculating."

"And which is stronger?" asks Elizabeth, her voice deceptively gentle. "The wolf or the vampire?"

I feel both sides surge at the question, as if responding to the challenge. My fingernails lengthen slightly, my canines pressing against my lower lip. I force them back with effort.

"They... take turns," I manage, breathing heavily. "It changes. Sometimes minute by minute."

The white-haired vampire seated near Costin rises, her movements so fluid she seems to float. "May I approach the circle, Elder Zephronis?"

The old magic nods, and she glides down to the center floor to join us, her violet eyes never leaving mine. Up close, I can see the true age in her face, not in wrinkles or gray hair, but in the depth of her gaze, the subtle way her skin seems almost translucent.

"I am Elder Vasilisa," she says, her accent thick. At the sound of her voice, I feel a violent pull toward her. "I have lived five centuries and seen many curiosities, but never a successful hybrid." She circles me slowly, studying me intently. "Your sire," she gestures to Costin, "comes from my bloodline. I can sense his power in you. But there is something else too. Something... unexpected."

She stops directly in front of me, her head tilting

slightly. "The wolf blood in you is not just any Alpha's. It is old blood. Ancient."

Sully steps forward, ignoring the warning glances from several council members. "Thane's lineage traced back to the first packs."

"So he always claimed," Vasilisa says, though her tone suggests doubt. "Or perhaps there is more to this story than we know." She turns to the council. "I would request a private examination of the hybrid."

"No," Costin and Sully say simultaneously, then glare at each other for the agreement.

My father clears his throat and finally speaks. "My daughter is not a specimen to be studied."

"She is an anomaly that threatens our entire world," Birch counters. "If she cannot control both natures, if she exposes us to humans—"

"That's not going to happen," I interrupt, feeling both sides of my nature bristling at the accusation. "I understand what's at stake."

"Do you?" Vasilisa asks. "You haven't even experienced your first full moon since the transformation. What makes you think you can control yourself when it comes?"

Before I can answer, Sully strides forward, stopping just short of the circle. "That is what I've been saying. The moon is coming. Eleven days. By then, she needs to be with the pack. We can help her."

"She is not one of yours," Costin says coldly. "She is mine."

"She carries our Alpha's blood," Sully counters. "She belongs with us when the moon calls."

"She belongs with those who can contain her if necessary," Elder Decimus cuts in. "Your pack is in disarray, Sully. No Alpha, no clear succession. How can you protect her or others from her?"

A low rumble builds in Sully's chest, a sound I feel more than hear. "I can handle her."

Sully's challenge snaps something inside me. The wolf surges forward, responding to the dominance play.

"Can you?" I snap.

Before I can stop myself, I'm at the edge of the circle, teeth bared, a growl building in my throat.

"You think you can handle me?" The words come out distorted as my mouth begins to reshape. "You have no idea what I am."

The council chamber erupts in a flurry of movement—vampires rising to their feet, magics raising defensive shields, werewolves leaning forward with interest. Rhea cackles, the sound oddly joined by Elizabeth's chuckle.

I feel my body starting to shift, not fully wolf, not fully vampire, but something in between. Claws extend from my fingers, tearing through the silk of my dress. My chest presses against the metal bodice as it tries to expand. My vision sharpens. Colors become more vivid as my eyes change.

"Tamara." Costin's voice cuts through the chaos. The sire bond resonates with it, not forcing obedience but offering support. "Control it."

I want to snarl at him, to challenge his authority too, but something in his steady gaze reaches past the monster to the part of me that's still Tamara. I take a deep, shuddering breath, focusing on pulling my warring natures back into balance.

Slowly, painfully, I force the transformation to recede. My claws retract, my teeth return to normal. The room comes back into focus as the red haze of rage dissipates.

The silence that follows is deafening.

Finally, Elder Zephronis puts his hand on my shoulder. He looks sad. "The hybrid shows potential for control but is clearly unstable."

"She needs training," Astrid says firmly. "Time to adjust to her new nature. She should be with her family. We can deal with this."

"Time we may not have," Birch counters. "The full moon approaches, and if what the werewolf says is true, her control will be tested severely."

"Then let her prove herself," Elizabeth suggests, her voice silky. "Let her demonstrate whether she can be trusted with freedom or whether she requires more permanent containment."

I don't like the gleam in her eye, the way she makes *permanent containment* sound like something worse than a death sentence.

Before I can respond, Vasilisa raises a hand. "I believe I can offer a solution." Her violet eyes fix on me. "A trial period. The hybrid will remain under observation until the full moon. If she can maintain control through the lunar cycle, she proves herself worthy of continued existence."

"And if she can't?" Anthony asks, his voice tight.

Vasilisa's smile is cold. "Then the council will take appropriate action."

"What does that mean?" I ask, though I already suspect the answer.

Vasilisa's gaze doesn't waver. "If you lose control, the council will act. Swiftly and permanently."

"Who will observe her?" Astrid demands. "Where will she be kept?"

"Neutral territory," Zephronis decides. "Neither vampire nor werewolf domain."

"The Devine country estate," my father suggests. "It's warded and secure."

A snort of derision comes from the werewolves.

"Hardly neutral," Sully growls.

"I have a better suggestion," Birch says smoothly. "The hybrid will be kept in council territory, with representatives from all factions present to observe."

"Prison," I mutter. "You're talking about putting me in prison."

"Safety," he corrects. "For you, and for others."

I look to Costin, seeing the carefully contained rage in his eyes. He doesn't like this any more than I do, but I can tell he's calculating, trying to find the best way forward.

"I accept," I say before anyone else can speak. "But on one condition."

The chamber falls silent again, every eye on me.

"I want information about Leviathan and why he's coming after me," I continue. "And about what he's doing with my brother Conrad's spirit."

A ripple of surprise moves through the council members.

"Conrad?" Decimus repeats, his eyes narrowing. "Your adoptive brother who died?"

"Whose ghost has been haunting me," I clarify. "A ghost that Leviathan is supposedly keeping contained, except he isn't. He's using him for something. I want to know what."

"How do you know this?" Vasilisa asks.

"Because Conrad told me." I straighten my shoulders, forcing confidence I don't entirely feel. "Three nights ago, he appeared in my room. He said Leviathan had given him work release. And then he said he's coming for me."

The council members exchange glances, some

skeptical, others concerned. I notice Elizabeth's face has gone carefully blank, giving nothing away.

"Necromancers are not council business," Birch says dismissively. "Their practices are their own, so long as they maintain discretion."

"Do you not believe me because he's an elder from the Sacred Delegation and I'm—?" I start to ask.

"A Devine," Astrid inserts. "She is a Devine, and it becomes council business when they target a Devine."

Vasilisa chuckles. "The Sacred Delegation is just a meaningless title we gave lesser creatures centuries ago to make them feel special."

"Thane was part of the Sacred Delegation," Sully interjects.

Vasilisa smirks as if it proves her point.

"If she's being targeted at all," Elizabeth interjects. "We have only the word of a hybrid who, by her own admission, is unstable. Perhaps these visions are simply manifestations of her fractured mind."

I feel a surge of anger at her dismissal, but before I can respond, Costin stands.

"I was there," he says, his voice carrying easily through the chamber. "I smelled the necromancy magic in the room. He was there."

Decimus taps his staff, thinking. Finally, he nods.

"Very well. The council will investigate these claims regarding Leviathan. In the meantime, the hybrid will be taken into council keeping for observation until the full moon. If she maintains control, we will reassess her status."

Zephronis' thoughtful gaze flicks to me.

"And if Leviathan comes for her while she's in your custody?" Sully asks, his voice hard. "Will you protect what belongs to the pack?"

"Tamara Devine belongs to no one," Astrid says sharply. "She is a Devine, first and foremost."

"She carries my blood," Costin says quietly, but with unmistakable authority. "She is under my protection."

I want to scream at all of them that I belong to myself, that I'm not a possession to be claimed. But the circle keeps me rooted in place, revealing the uncomfortable truth. I am bound to all of them in different ways. By blood, by family, by supernatural politics I never asked to be part of.

"I have heard enough. I will decide where she is held. The hybrid will be protected," Zephronis states. Decimus and Vasilisa look as if they want to protest but no one dares contradict him. "Now, step out of the circle, Tamara Devine."

As I step across the boundary, I feel the suppression snap back into place, not as strong as the potion, but enough to dull the warring natures inside me. Astrid is immediately at my side, her hand on my arm in a silent show of support.

"This is temporary," she murmurs. "We will find a way through this."

I wish I shared her confidence. As council guards appear to escort me away, I catch Sully's eye. His gaze makes me uneasy.

"Eleven days," he mouths, so others don't hear.

His meaning is clear. When the full moon rises, I'm either pack or problem. And Sully doesn't seem like the type to leave problems unsolved for long.

The last thing I see before they lead me from the chamber is Costin and Elizabeth, locked in what appears to be a tense conversation. His face is cold with fury and hers alights with satisfaction.

I wonder if she still thinks I'll take her up on her offer to help. That smile on her face says she already believes she's won.

Whatever game is being played, I'm certain of one thing. I'm not just a player.

I'm a prize.

NINE

I never expected I'd be brought back to the Devine Country Estate, but here I am watching the sprawling stone walls covered in ivy through the car window. Night has fallen over the manicured gardens now dormant in winter's tight grip. It snowed at some point when I was underground. It makes everything white and peaceful, very unlike my turbulent soul. Behind us, I hear the familiar groan of the heavy wrought-iron gates closing. They have kept the mundane world at bay for generations. I've taken this drive so many times I can't remember each trip.

I do, however, remember feeling like a prisoner returning to my cell.

Sorry, "protected wing" of the house.

I can't complain, though. Things could have

ended up much worse. This is not the prison I thought Zephronis would choose for me. Honestly, I'm still confused by how this happened. When my father suggested it, they'd said no.

I'm sure I have a sarcastic thought about misogyny or patriarchy or something profound, but I'm woozy from Astrid's constant injections. They're keeping me calm for the trip. Otherwise, I might have tried jumping out the car window to run in the moonlight. I don't protest as I feel another jab in my thigh.

Three days have passed since the council meeting. Three days of being shuttled from Costin's underground fortress to the council's holding cell to this gilded cage under Zephronis' watchful eye. The old wizard simply appeared in the cell, took one look at the arguing factions trying to get in to see me, and declared, "She goes to the Devine Estate. I will oversee her myself."

No one dared object, not Sully with his pack ambitions, not Vasilisa with her clinical curiosity, not even Elizabeth with her venomous schemes. Zephronis is too ancient and powerful to be challenged directly. Even now, I can feel his magic saturating the estate, reinforcing the spells that have protected it for centuries. Whatever his reasons for choosing this place, they're his own. The only explanation he offered was, "Their arguing does my head in."

The car slows. I can't see the driver through the dark window separating us. My father and Mortimer stayed behind. They barely spoke to me when they came to visit me in my cell. My father looked ashamed, like he was embarrassed I'd done this to him.

My head wobbles as I turn to look at Astrid. "Costin?"

"You don't remember? He'll be here. He's overseeing your blood supply," Astrid answers.

I nod. My head bounces against the seat as I stare at her beautiful face. "You're so pretty."

Astrid smirks. "I see the potion is working."

"You're better than him," I persist, knowing I should shut up but not caring. I feel the need to say it, and the words tumble out. "You shouldn't put up with his infidelities."

"He's my husband," Astrid says. "Your father. Choices were made that can't be undone."

"It's not the 1500s. You can divorce him. Take half of everything. He'd be too scared to deny you."

"You know better. This is the supernatural world. It is very much still the 1500s." Astrid pats my cheek. "Don't dwell on things that cannot be changed. Life has put enough before us."

"He hates me now. I see it on his face," I mutter.

"No, he hates anything that ruins his plans," she corrects. It's a small difference, and it doesn't make me feel better.

"You should at least take a lover." I chuckle and turn back to the window as we stop in the front drive. "Or twelve. No one would blame you."

"Who says I haven't?"

I whip my head back in surprise.

She schools her expression. "We need to get you inside before the sun comes out. There is no way to know how the light will affect your vampire blood. You'll be safe inside as long as the windows are closed. The glass is coated to be vampire-safe, well safe-ish, but you don't want to be in front of it too long. Daylight is daylight, and it can still harm vampires through the glass, as well as drain energy faster than normal. We'll see about getting you a suite built underground."

The car door opens, and I'm ushered inside beneath a cloak. The potion keeps me weak, and the driver helps me walk. They lead me to my bedroom in the protected wing. The curtains are drawn, casting it into shadow. I can still see perfectly, though, in the dark. He releases me so I drop on the bed, and I stare unmoving at the same ceiling I contemplated as a mortal. There's comfort in familiarity, but the feeling doesn't last. It never does. Yet for a few minutes lying here in the quiet, I can almost trick myself into feeling safe. Like I never left. Like everything's simple.

I remember spending hours wondering if I'd ever fit into this supernatural world. The irony isn't lost on me. Now I'm too supernatural to fit anywhere.

It seems I'm always marking the passing of time, moving from one cage to another. Is this what my life has become? An eternity of new prison cells?

It's fitting I'm here, in my childhood home, confronted by the memories of my mortal life. Never in all my years did I guess this would be my fate.

My bedroom feels like a time capsule, stuck between childhood and adulthood. I guess I am too, in some ways. This place never quite figured out what it was supposed to be. Kind of like me.

I'm hit with the old scent of lavender and wood soap. There is a distinct mustiness that develops when windows are kept shut for too long. I used to throw them open just to feel the breeze on my face, desperate for some connection to the outside world. Now they stay locked closed, heavy curtains pulled tight, as if the room itself wants to block out reality.

I find a tiny glow-in-the-dark star that I had slapped on the wall when I was eight. I had stubbornly refused to take them down even after Conrad teased me about them. All but that one have fallen, leaving behind little flecks of glue.

Astrid has always kept pristine homes. She likes control, and I imagine it gives her some happiness to keep things familiar and perfect. My bed smells faintly of cedar from the storage chest where they keep my bedding. When I sleep, I find myself pulling the covers up to my chin like I did as a kid. I'm too old to hide from monsters with a blanket, but the habit sticks. Though, to be honest, even as a kid I knew blankets did not ward off evil intent. If a monster made it into the protected wing, I wasn't going to be able to stop it.

Now I am the monster.

The small bookshelf is overflowing with old books. These human fairy tales were not kept in the library with the literature on real magic. Human children weren't allowed to read the real stuff.

The mirror over the dresser is slightly crooked. I keep meaning to have it fixed, but somehow never do. Seeing my reflection off-kilter feels right. I glance at myself now, hair a tangled mess and eyes rimmed with exhaustion, and for a second, I almost don't recognize the woman looking back at me.

When I peek outside, the early morning light

filters through the frost-covered windows. I put my hand in the light, holding it to see what happens. At first, I'm fine, but after a minute, my skin starts to itch and turn red. After three minutes, it burns, and I can no longer bear the pain. I do it multiple times, just to watch my skin heal itself.

Unlike the werewolves, who enjoy basking in sunlight, vampires are forced to retreat from the day. It seems in this instance, I'm more vampire than wolf. Another fundamental difference between the two sides of my nature.

Costin visits daily, bringing blood and staying for hours at a time. More often than not, we end up in bed. Sex is easier than talking. I'm not sure we have much to say to each other. He's still my sire, and I'm still a messed-up headcase.

Astrid remains at the estate, brewing potions that help keep the warring natures inside me in a tentative truce. My father and Mortimer make appearances, though they always seem to be rushing off to "handle" some aspect of the fallout from my transformation. I see the blame in their faces. Mortimer mutters accusing things like, *"If only you had married Chester like we planned..."*

As if being the wife of smarmy Chester Freemont would have been a better fate. The guy tried to sacrifice me on an altar to help Elizabeth steal all the magic in the world. Seriously? That is who Mortimer wants in the family?

Anthony comes with them. He wants to stay, but my father keeps dragging him away. It's like he's worried my monster-ness will rub off on the family golden boy. Or that I'll eat him.

I'd rather they keep him away. I don't want to hurt Anthony.

A knock at the door interrupts my brooding. Astrid enters without waiting for a response, carrying a tray with a steaming mug and a small glass vial.

"Breakfast," she says, setting the tray on my bedside table. "Both kinds."

I don't need to ask what she means. The mug contains a thick, red liquid that makes my fangs ache, and the vial holds today's dose of her suppression potion. I've come to think of the combination as my new balanced diet.

Astrid must love this. She always tried to control my diet as a child.

"I'm not hungry," I lie, even as my stomach clenches with need.

Astrid fixes me with her ice-blue stare. "Tamara, we've been through this. You need to maintain your strength for your visitor."

Right. Visitor. The first potential breakthrough in this whole mess that is my life.

"Is she here yet?" I ask, sitting up and reaching for the mug, no longer pretending I don't want it.

"Downstairs. Zephronis is…" Astrid gives a small wave of her hand, "prepping her. They'll be done soon. You should go meet them."

I frown at the idea of my mortal, bohemian birth mother being interrogated by the ancient wizard. Part of me wishes Astrid had never told me about the woman. I lived nearly twenty-eight years not knowing I had a human birth mother. Then Lorelai would be safe in California, and I'd be blissfully ignorant.

"She's been calling daily since your transformation." Astrid's voice is carefully neutral. "Lorelai may have given you up as a baby, but she never stopped being your mother."

The statement hangs between us, loaded with unspoken complications. Astrid raised me, but Lorelai birthed me. Both women have a claim to the title of "mother," and neither seems entirely comfortable with the arrangement that there are two of them.

"What about Paul and Diana?" I ask. "Did you ask Zephronis? Can I see them?"

"Drink," Astrid orders, as if holding the answer hostage.

I down the blood in three long gulps, feeling the immediate rush as it hits my system. The suppression potion follows, bitter and burning all the way down. The combination makes me light-headed for a moment, before settling into a strange clarity.

"Better?" Astrid asks, watching me closely.

"Clearer," I admit. But not better. Never better.

I glance toward the window and flex my hand. All it would take is a three-minute walk in the sun.

She sighs, collecting the empty containers. "Zephronis believes Lorelai may have insights about the goblin attacks from your infancy that could help understand why they're targeting you now. Costin told us what Conrad said, but it doesn't make sense that Leviathan would use them to attack you as a baby. Necromancers are lesser magics. They have their place, and it's not at the top of any hierarchy. Leviathan knows that. Conrad, however, is a known troublemaker. He can't be trusted."

"I already know why they targeted me as a baby," I say, standing and moving to my closet. "Lorelai told me. They were trying to steal my breath as some kind of test or something."

"They tried to kill you," Astrid corrects. "Stealing breath was their means. But there may be more to it, especially now that you're changed." Astrid hesitates at the door. "Costin will be here this evening. He wanted to be present for this, but council business required his attention."

I nod, pretending I don't feel the pang of disappointment. The sire bond makes his absence physically uncomfortable, like an internal itch I can't scratch. Even with the suppression potion, I'm constantly aware of our connection, the invisible tether that pulls me toward him. I could find him anywhere in the world without being told where to look.

"Vampire or not, you're lucky to have him, Tamara," Astrid says. "Not every man would be willing to go up against the elders for you. Especially not an elder from your vampire line. Vasilisa is not pleased with his refusal to turn you over to her, but Costin does have rights as your sire. Vasilisa doesn't usually leave her home. For her to be in the United States means you've piqued her interest."

That's high praise coming from Astrid.

Also, it's somewhat terrifying to think that Vasilisa wants me as some kind of new pet.

What's that saying? I'm not going to borrow trouble. I'll deal with that if it happens. There is too much else needing my attention.

"Wait. What about Paul and Diana?" I insist when she starts to pull the door shut.

"We had to move them before we brought you here. It's best if you don't know how to find them. I sent them away with most of the servants. You're dangerous enough without tempting you with snacks," she says. "But yes, we're bringing them back if they agree to come."

She doesn't like the idea, but Draakmar's amulet protects Diana. She'll be safe around me. As long as Paul is with her, she can keep him safe.

My future is uncertain. I don't know what is coming, but I want a chance to say goodbye to them. And I'm sorry.

"I'll be down in ten minutes," I tell her.

After Astrid leaves, I pull out a sweater and jeans from the closet. No point dressing up for this reunion. Lorelai has seen me at my worst already. No amount of glamor and lip gloss will cover the monster.

I dress quickly and move to the mirror. The reflection that stares back is both familiar and foreign, like an AI filter gone wrong. It's my face, but with subtle changes. My eyes seem more intense, my cheekbones sharper from the weight loss. My skin has an almost luminous quality. I look predatory. Even at rest, there's something lurking beneath the surface, waiting to emerge.

I turn away from the mirror and head downstairs. The wooden floor creaks under my feet. I don't remember the sound being so loud. Or maybe the house is too quiet. The protected wing feels abandoned, even though I know it's warded with spells for my safety.

The pulled curtains block the sun, but through the hall lights, I see dust motes dancing in the air. I glance toward Conrad's old room. My memory stirs with an image of him sneaking toward his bedroom with a stolen book from the family library tucked under his arm. It hasn't even been a year since his death, but so much has changed that it feels like an eternity since I thought of him as an ally.

I worry that Conrad's ghost will appear, summoned from my thoughts, so instead I focus on the runner under my feet. The rug is ancient, but it doesn't show the faded tracks of everyone who walked over it.

I breathe deeply, steeling myself, before heading toward the main staircase, following the scent of coffee and incense. The smell brings back memories of my first meeting with Lorelai, when I discovered her living in California.

My senses are on high alert. Everything is vivid and in sharp focus. The foyer sprawls below me, and the chandelier catches a thread of light, throwing fractured rainbows onto the polished marble floor. The stairs themselves curve elegantly, like a dramatic stage entrance. I grip the railing, feeling the smooth, cold wood under my palm. I've taken these stairs a thousand times, *tens of thousands*, but something about them today feels different. The house seems to be holding its breath.

Which is nonsense because houses don't breathe.

My skin prickles, the nerves raw and electric. Everything feels like a warning. Instinct tells me to retreat underground, to escape the sun.

I look toward the front doors. What would happen if I ran out into the sunlight?

"Don't." Costin's voice whispers in my head. I gasp, coming out of my deep focus to look for him. He's not there.

"Costin?" I whisper.

He doesn't answer, and I'm unsure whether he actually spoke to me or if I just imagined it.

"They can't help you. No one can help you," Conrad's voice taunts. It's followed by the sound of children laughing and the hammering of running footsteps.

Again, I don't know if it's real.

I force myself to keep moving. I follow the smell of essential oils that I associate with my birth mother. At the bottom of the stairs, I turn left, moving through the main corridor. It's broader here. The ceilings are arched and painted with elaborate frescoes depicting ancient family triumphs. A line of marble figures frozen in stern contemplation stands guard along the wall. I feel as if their heads move to follow me. My footsteps echo too loudly, despite the thick rugs laid down at intervals.

No, not my footsteps. That's a heartbeat.

Ahead, the conservatory doors loom. The ornate wrought iron is set within glass panels. Morning light filters through the intricate patterns, spilling a lattice of shadows onto the stone floor. I hesitate, one hand reaching for the iron handle. Through the glass, I see the lush, almost chaotic greenery within. Palm fronds brushing against tall windows, tendrils of ivy spilling from hanging pots. The air in there always feels thick with humidity and the earthy scent of soil. Today, it looks scarier, like splashes of deadly light have taken root alongside the plants.

My fingers bounce on the metal handle, and it burns me. I jerk my hand back.

Without me pushing them, the doors creak open to let me pass.

I immediately find Lorelai and Zephronis, sitting on a wicker chair surrounded by dormant plants. I remain in the doorway. Winter sunlight streams through the glass walls, casting long shadows across the tiled floor like the first warning shot from the heavens. Zephronis stands nearby, examining a withered fern with apparent fascination. He touches the leaf, and the plant instantly perks up.

Lorelai rises when she sees me, her long curly hair loose around her shoulders. A bohemian skirt swirls around her ankles. Her face is so similar to mine in structure but weathered by years of California sun. Thanks to my predator eyes, I can now see the texture of it in more detail. It's her heart I've been listening to, thumping away like a dinner bell.

"Tamara," she breathes, moving toward me with arms outstretched.

I step back instinctively deeper into the shadows, keeping out of the sunlight. I hold up a hand. "Don't. I'm not stable."

Her arms drop, but her expression doesn't change. "I don't care. You're my daughter. I'm not scared of you."

"I'm dangerous," I insist. "I killed goblins with my bare hands. I attacked Costin. I'm not safe."

"All the more reason you need a mother's care," she says, stubbornly stepping forward again.

Before I can retreat further, Zephronis speaks. "You will not harm her, Tamara. The potions are working, and my presence adds an extra safeguard."

I hesitate, torn between hunger for comfort and fear of myself. Lorelai doesn't wait for me to decide. She closes the distance between us and wraps her arms around me.

The hug is warm. Solid. Real. For a moment, I'm transported back to the first time I can remember her holding me. It was only a few months ago, but I was human then. I feel the monster inside me quiet at the comfort, just a little.

When we pull apart, I see tears in her eyes.

"Look at you," she whispers, touching my face. "My beautiful girl."

I laugh without humor. I'm a monster. A hybrid freak that shouldn't exist.

Her smile seems a little too plastered on. A tiny tremor works over her hands. She's trying. Hard. But I know she sees the changes in me, and they're not beautiful.

I again focus on her heart thumping faster now.

"Let's move to another room," Zephronis says, placing a guiding hand on Lorelai's back to usher her away from me. "Tamara will be more comfortable away from the sun."

He leads us past a series of closed wooden doors before waving his hand to open the library.

There is comfort in the scent of old leather and parchment. Dark wood gives the space a somber, almost oppressive feel, but there's consolation in the familiarity. I spent endless hours here as a child, but it feels different now. I'm different.

The floor-to-ceiling shelves are filled with ancient tomes and family records. As a child I was told I wasn't allowed to touch them or bad things would happen, as if their magical secrets would poison my human mind. That never stopped Conrad.

My eyes land on the old leather armchair by the fireplace, and a knot forms in my stomach. I can still see Conrad sprawled in that chair, a spell book braced on his stomach, his limbs draped lazily over the sides as if he owned the place. I'd usually find him there whenever I managed to sneak away from my tutors, his nose buried in some ancient text, trying to learn the secrets that the adults wouldn't teach us.

He used to tap the book absently with his thumb while muttering about the unfairness of being born mortal. Even now I hear his voice.

"They should be teaching us what they're teaching him," he once grumbled, glancing at Anthony's empty seat. *"This is our world, too. It's like they want us to be helpless."*

I hadn't known how to answer him back then, so I just shrugged and listened, not sure how to make him feel better. Part of me wanted to argue that we couldn't change what we were, but I knew that would only make him mad.

I close my eyes, fighting the urge to sit in the chair myself. The memory feels too raw, too close to the surface. I still remember his voice, low and determined.

"I'm never going to be helpless again. No one is going to hurt me. You watch. I'm going to do what I want when I want."

He had said it so many times I should have believed him. Little did I know...

"Tamara?" Lorelai asks, shaking me from the memory. She appears worried, and I realize I'm frowning.

I glance back at the chair, half expecting to see my brother there, looking up with that defiant spark in his eyes. It's strange how a place can feel haunted even when there's no ghost.

At least, I hope there are no ghosts.

"I need a moment." With a deep breath, I force myself to cross the room, tracing my fingers over the shelf in front of the forbidden books. Conrad had been relentless in his quest to understand magic, memorizing languages and glyphs. I should've been there, learning beside him, but I was too busy trying to be normal, to fit into a life that was never really mine. Those lessons would have come in handy now.

I try not to hear Lorelai's heart beating.

I pull a dusty volume from the shelf and let it fall open in my hands. I trace the faded ink with my finger. The words swim on the page, jumbled and indecipherable. I'll have to bleed onto the page to unlock it.

"Tell me about that night," I say, not turning away from the shelf as I put the book back in its place. "Everything you remember about the goblins."

Astrid seems to think it might help us understand why they're coming after me now.

Lorelai's bangle bracelets jingle as she sits. I glance back to see her fussing with her skirt. "It's like I told you. They came when you were in your crib to steal your breath."

"Tamara, take a seat," Zephronis urges.

"I need more details," I insist. "Why me specifically? Was it random, or was I targeted? And why did they run from a butterfly mobile? Did Leviathan send them? Who else attacked?"

Zephronis glides closer, his robes shimmering. "Your mother has agreed to share her memories directly. It will be more comprehensive than verbal recounting. But I need you to sit."

I give in and sit in the armchair. It creaks under my weight. I tighten my grip on the armrests, the leather cool under my palms. I glance at Lorelai. "You've agreed to this?"

She shrugs, the gesture so casual it seems out of place in this serious conversation. "I'd do anything to help you, butterfly. Besides, I've done plenty of mind-melding in my day. This way is just more magical."

Mind-melding? Great. My mother is an acid-tripping pothead.

I can't say that I'm surprised.

I wonder if she'll share. I could use some forgetting.

"I will create a bridge between your memories,"

Zephronis explains. "You will experience your mother's recollection as if you were there. It will be disorienting."

I've been down this road before, reliving memories. I can't say I'm a fan of the process.

"Will it hurt her?" I ask.

"No," Lorelai answers before Zephronis can. "He's already explained it all. It's like a guided meditation, but with magic instead of visualization."

I look between them, uncertain. "And you really think this will help?"

"Your demands in the council chamber were clear. You want answers. This is how we get them," he says. "We need more proof before we accuse Leviathan of dark deeds."

He means more proof than the word of an unstable hybrid monster who might be hallucinating.

I resist pointing out that necromancers probably only perform dark deeds. I mean, angry spirits, zombies, controlling the dead? These don't sound like passive "nice" activities to me.

Come on. He calls himself Leviathan after a primordial sea serpent. His real name is probably Lester Wigglesworth or something. What kind of person decides their immortal life path is playing with dead things?

"Why can't everyone just leave me alone?" I

grumble, only realizing I said it out loud after it's out of my mouth.

"Fate is not a choice," Zephronis says. "It is a duty."

I think the word he's looking for is burden.

"The goblins' fixation on you is not in itself unusual. They're curious, mischievous creatures, but not stupid. They don't go against their own self-preservation," he continues. "Their daring to enter a master vampire's home to attack you after you have transformed is strange behavior. Understanding the original connection may reveal why their interest has intensified."

I take a deep breath. I'm tired of talking about it. "Alright. Let's do it."

Zephronis moves to stand behind us, placing one hand on my shoulder and one on Lorelai's. "Close your eyes," he instructs. "And remember, Tamara, you are observing only. You cannot change what has already happened."

As I close my eyes, I feel Lorelai reach for my hand to give it a reassuring squeeze. There is a strange pulling sensation, as if I'm being tugged sideways through reality. I open my eyes to peek, but I'm in darkness surrounded by the sound of soft breathing.

TEN

Lorelai's Apartment, Twenty-Eight Years Ago...

The magic is cold, coming from where her hand touches mine.

It latches onto my skin like smoke trailing from a dying candle, sinking into my pores. I can't feel Zephronis' touch on my shoulder, but his magic pulses like a tether between then and now. His magic's warmth contrasts with the icy pressure traveling up my arm, pulling me deeper into Lorelai's memory.

I blink, and I'm no longer in the library.

The world reforms around me in disjointed pieces. A cluttered apartment. Cheap baby furniture. A bassinet. The air smells like essential oils, lavender and vanilla. Moonlight filters through thin curtains, catching the edges of a butterfly mobile spinning lazily above a crib. The wings are glass, delicate and glimmering, each one casting tiny rainbows on the walls like protective spirits doing their best in a world that doesn't believe in them.

And there sits Lorelai, rocking in the chair beside the empty crib.

She's younger with dark hair. Her face is unlined, but she wears exhaustion like armor. She rests a hand on her pregnant belly.

"I tried to keep you," Lorelai whispers. The words don't come from her mouth, but instead they come through the memory like echoes, vibrating against the air like meditations. *"Davis gave me support, but he couldn't give me time. He had a family. Responsibilities."*

The memory shifts, and suddenly I *feel* her pain. Her stomach drops, the pregnancy vanishing. I don't just see it, I absorb it. Her love. Her regret. Her loneliness and frustration. Her absolute terror. She reaches through the slats of the crib, resting gently on the chest of the fussy baby inside.

Me.

Tiny. Mortal. Vulnerable. Pink and flailing with infant fury. I'm not in my body. I hover just above the scene, a ghost in a memory that shouldn't exist.

"They came after you," her voice continues as if she's meditating like the wizard told her to do. Her voice cracks. *"The werewolves in the park. The*

vampires... One offered me a million dollars. When I said no, she threatened to rip you from my arms and drink you dry. Necromancers sent spirits to watch you sleep."

The walls of the apartment shudder slightly, like the memory itself is reacting to the wizard's command. I can't hear Zephronis, only her. Her hand drops from the crib, and mother and baby are both sleeping.

I've heard this story. Lorelai told me as she zoomed through California traffic. But hearing is different than *feeling* it.

The air thickens. The kind of thick pressure that forces itself against the skin before a storm hits. The hairs on my arms stand up. The silence shifts.

Something is coming.

At first, it's just a flicker at the edge of the room. A ripple of shadow that doesn't match the moonlight. Then, like spilled ink, the darkness spreads, crawling up the walls, slipping under the doorframe, pooling in the corners.

Shadows slip under the door. Small, twisted creatures with wrinkled skin the color of bruises.

Goblins.

I instinctively turn toward the crib, my feet weightless and floating. I see the goblins crawl from the shadows like mold come to life, hunched and skeletal. Their clawed hands wrap the slats of the crib as they slowly crawl to where baby me sleeps.

More skitter across the ceiling in jerky lurches. One drops down inside the crib, and I feel a sudden pressure in my chest.

Lorelai doesn't move. Her breath is slow and deep, like she's enchanted.

My heart races. I want to stop the creatures. I know this is a memory. Fear is not rational. I survive this. Yet, I still feel the helpless terror building inside of me.

The baby in the crib whimpers softly, sensing something is wrong.

A goblin places a gnarled hand over baby Tamara's nose and mouth. Others start to chant, their voices like bones cracking in a fire. At first, I can't understand their language, but then the translation whispers magically into me.

"Life force, bright and new. Magic untapped, power subdued. Feed the master, feed the need. Take the breath, plant the seed."

I freeze.

What the fuck?

No, *seriously*, what the ever-living fuck?

Baby me begins to struggle. Her tiny limbs flail weakly as the goblin draws out a shimmering thread of breath. It glows faintly as it's pulled toward the goblin's mouth.

My throat suddenly tightens. I can't breathe

either. I pull at my neckline and lift my head back to gasp.

In the chair, Lorelai's fingers twitch. Her eyes flutter beneath her lids. She's fighting the spell, but it's too strong. She can't wake up.

I wheeze violently. My lungs burn. Baby me doesn't make a sound, but I see the thrashing.

I fall helplessly to my knees, my head dizzy as it hits the edge of the crib. I swing my arm weakly toward Lorelai but can't reach her. My vision begins to fade.

Then, one of the goblins pushes another out of its way, and they begin chattering in an argument. The other fights back, and they roll in a tangled mass before crashing into the mobile.

Butterflies spin. Glass wings catch the moonlight and scatter rainbows across the room, throwing the sharp prismatic light like a disco ball made of lightning.

The goblins shriek a high-pitched, feral sound. They stagger back, clawing to escape as the rainbows slice through the darkness. In their panic, they hit the mobile again, spinning it faster. The one taking my breath recoils from the crib as the rainbow light cuts through the dark close to it. The breath-thread snaps, recoiling like a whip into baby Tamara's lungs. I inhale sharply, finally able to breathe again.

"Lorelai!" I grunt instinctively, forgetting my mother can't hear me. I try to pull myself to my feet, but I'm weak.

The baby gasps and lets out a powerful, soul-piercing cry.

The sound cracks something in the room. Lorelai jerks in the rocking chair. She screams, but it's muffled. A magical gag pulls tight across her mouth as unseen ropes pin her to the chair. Her panic is so tangible, and she thrashes violently to be free.

The goblin cackles and returns to infant me, its mouth opening far too wide, as it tries to resume its task amid the chaos. The baby quiets, and I feel my throat tighten once more. I try to reach into the crib to knock the creature away. It's no use. The creature can't feel me.

This time, a shimmer of green light coils from the baby's lips, and I want to vomit. My body, my *soul*, is being tugged out of me. The goblins want to capture me for their necromancer master.

I don't know how, but the invisible gag finally slips from Lorelai's mouth.

Lorelai bolts upright, screaming. The goblins hiss and scatter into the shadows. The mobile above the crib continues to spin. The air still stinks of burnt magic and rot. Before she reaches her daughter, the memory breaks like glass.

CRACK.

I stumble into the next scene like pages flipping in a nightmare. I have no idea how much time has passed, but my lungs still ache. The mobile is still. The rainbows are gone.

Lorelai clutches her baby to her chest, pacing and crying softly as she mumbles, "I'm sorry. You're okay. You're okay. I'm sorry, butterfly…"

All I can do is watch as I try to catch my breath.

Her words are only stopped by the sound of heavy footsteps pounding from outside the apartment. I lean to watch as the door bursts open. My father appears, accompanied by two bodyguards flanking him.

"Davis," his name leaves my mother like a sigh of relief, and I imagine she's glad not to be alone with a helpless baby.

"What happened?" Davis demands. I recognize that annoyed tone.

"Creatures were in her crib," Lorelai says. "They were trying to do something to her mouth."

My father sniffs the air and frowns. "Goblins."

"They were making it so she couldn't breathe," Lorelai continues, her panic a stark contrast to my father. "I was in the rocking chair, and I woke up and—"

"You fell asleep?" Davis says coldly, scanning the room. "After everything we discussed."

"I didn't fall asleep. I was *enchanted*," Lorelai

snaps, holding her baby closer and bouncing in her agitation. I see the exhaustion etched on her face. "They were stealing her breath."

"I detect necromancer magic," my father says, not moving to comfort his lover.

"I can't be alone here. You said you'd send someone." She eyes the guards who stand still by the door, pretending not to hear. Her voice lowers, "Why can't you move in with us? She's your daughter, too. You said when I got pregnant that—"

"Enough." His voice cuts through the room like a blade. Louder than necessary, he says, "I'm not leaving my wife. That was never the deal."

Lorelai shakes her head. "No. That's not what you—"

Astrid appears, her face tight. Unlike Lorelai, Astrid looks exactly the same. Time has not taken a toll on her features.

"As-Astrid," Lorelai stutters. "I didn't know you were here."

Astrid arches a brow with a look that says, *obviously*. She looks around the cheap apartment and frowns. She crosses over to the window where I just now see the salt line drawn along the windowsill. Her tone cuts like ice. "The child is not safe with you, Lorelai. You can't protect her here." She swipes at the salt before dusting her fingers. "Not with these mortal charms."

I'd heard that tone a thousand times.

My father's voice is calm but firm. "Tamara will live with us. We can protect her."

"She's my daughter," Lorelai whispers, pressing against the edge of the crib like it might anchor her to the child being taken from her. Her eyes burn. "She needs her mother."

"She needs to survive," Davis states. "You know who I am, Lorelai. You know why they want her. I can't let them use her to control me. I won't let a necromancer use her spirit to curry favor."

"Her humanity makes her a liability," Astrid's tone softens slightly, patting Lorelai's arm. "You can't take care of her. We can. She'll be given a life you..." She again looks around the apartment. The place would be beneath Astrid's discernible tastes. "She'll be protected."

Lorelai breaks. I see the grief crashing over her as tears slip down her face.

"She's just a baby, Davis, please," Lorelai whispers. I feel her heartbreak as if it's my own.

"She'll never be just a baby," Davis replies, more to himself than anyone. "She might be a mere mortal, but she's Devine blood. That puts her in danger."

"She's perfect," Lorelai breathes. "She's mine. Don't let her forget me."

Astrid gently pries me from Lorelai's grasp, and for a shaking moment, Lorelai doesn't let go.

"You know that isn't how this will work," Astrid says. "At least not any time soon, but someday, when she's old enough."

The figures start to dissolve until only Lorelai remains.

I sense her pain at the loss, but beneath it, I feel a thread of relief. She's glad it's over, and that makes her feel guilty.

Life is complicated.

The silence in the memory is louder than screaming. Lorelai collapses beside the empty crib. "I'm sorry, little butterfly."

I try to hold on, to stay in that moment to explore what it all means, but the memory slips through my fingers like smoke.

Pressure against my shoulder makes me aware of Zephronis' touch. I fall back into my body like a kite being yanked from the sky.

ELEVEN

I find myself back in the library. Tears wet my cheeks. I didn't realize I had been crying. Lorelai's eyes mirror my own, haunted by the memory she just shared.

"I'm so sorry," she whispers, her voice breaking.

She still holds my hand, only now she's clutching it hard like she's scared to let go. The hybrid monster inside of me doesn't like the emotions pouring through. It's hard to remain calm when I feel like I was just attacked.

"Take a breath," Zephronis says, removing his hands from our shoulders.

Lorelai appears as if she wants to hug me, but I give a slight shake of my head and pull my hand away. Her heart is hammering in her chest, and it's taking everything in me not to reach for it to make it stop.

"Life force, life force, bright and new," Zephronis recites the chant, his tone grave despite its singsong cadence. "Magic untapped, power subdued. Feed the master, feed the need. Take the breath, plant the seed."

A chill works over me and I stand from my chair. The room spins for a moment as the memory's effects linger. "Stop saying that."

"Do you know what it means?" Lorelai asks.

"I haven't heard it for centuries. It sounds like a version of an old necromancer binding spell." Zephronis remains calm. Frankly, it's annoying when all I want to do is scream and tear shit up. "It's a mark to claim you when your time comes."

"What do you mean when her time comes?" Lorelai demands.

"He means that when I die, the necromancer has dibs," I answer. My hands tremble. I keep hearing the sound, and it's hard to concentrate.

Thump-thump. Thump-thump. Thump-thump.

"But..." Lorelai shakes her head. "Why? She was just a baby."

"I think time has shown Tamara was never just anything," Zephronis says. "I don't think a necromancer could have known what you would become, but his goblins could have sensed the value in you."

"My father knew," I say, anger rising in my chest. "All this time, he knew exactly what was happening, and he didn't say anything."

"Davis knew about the supernatural threats, but I don't think even he understood what the necromancers wanted specifically. He just knew you weren't safe with me." Lorelai tries to reach for my hand, but I jerk back. Why is she defending him? "This wasn't the only threat. Werewolves and vampires came for you, too. And other magics. It was chaos."

Thump-thump.

I begin to pace. I feel the monster inside me begging to be unleashed.

"From what I saw, Davis believed the threat centered around manipulating him," Zephronis says. "He never heard the spell."

What the wizard isn't saying is that my father is a selfish person, and it probably never occurred to him that I could be in danger for any other reason.

"So what am I supposed to do now? Leviathan has been hunting me my entire life, and—"

"We don't know that for certain the necromancer is Leviathan," Zephronis cautions.

"Oh, come on," I snap, not caring that yelling at a powerful elder isn't exactly prudent behavior. But really, what's he going to do? Lock me up some more? Kill me? "The goblins tried to steal my breath as a baby, chanting about feeding their master my soul. Now he's using Conrad's ghost to torment me. My brother might be a dead liar who can't be trusted, but we all know who has his spirit entrapped. He sent goblins to Costin's home to attack me again after I've transformed into this... this... this *thing*." I gesture at myself in disgust. "It can't be a coincidence."

"You present a logical argument," Zephronis says, surprising me. "But we need more information before confronting a necromancer as powerful as Leviathan. He has allies. Magical balance has already been disrupted. We cannot risk more turmoil until the mess with Thane and Elizabeth's ritual is cleaned up."

I pace the library, the floorboards groaning beneath my feet. The late afternoon sun filters through the seams in the curtains, creating pockets of light I instinctively avoid.

"Tamara?" Lorelai's voice is gentle. "What are you thinking?"

"I'm thinking I want this to be over," I mutter. "I didn't ask for any of this. I didn't want to be a hybrid. I didn't want to be hunted my entire life by some power-hungry necromancer. I don't want to play in goblin entrails. I don't want to eat people or tear them apart. I don't want to avoid the sun. I don't want—"

"Few of us choose our path," Zephronis states, his ancient eyes following me. "But we can choose how we walk it."

I'm about to respond with something appropriately sarcastic when a chill sweeps through the room. The temperature drops so suddenly that Lorelai's breath becomes visible in small, frightened puffs.

"What's happening?" she asks, wrapping her arms around herself.

I know before Zephronis can answer. I've felt this before.

"Conrad," I whisper, my eyes scanning the shadows.

The wizard moves to Lorelai's side, one hand raised defensively. "Are you certain?"

The lights flicker, and the books on the shelves begin to vibrate, some sliding out to crash to the floor. A familiar voice that has haunted me since his death fills the room.

"Run, little sister. Run while you still can."

Unlike before, Conrad's voice doesn't sound mocking. He's afraid.

"Conrad?" I call out, turning in place. "Show yourself."

"He's coming. He's already there."

The windows rattle in their frames. The door to the library slams shut with such force that Lorelai yelps in surprise.

"Who's coming?" I demand, though I already know the answer.

"Leviathan." Conrad's voice seems to come from everywhere at once. *"He wants what you are. What you can become."*

"Zephronis," I say, my voice tight. "Get Lorelai out of here."

The wizard nods, taking my birth mother by the arm. "Come," he tells her. "This is not a battle for mortals."

"No," Lorelai protests. "I won't leave her!"

"Your presence will only distract her," Zephronis insists.

"But—"

"I will return," Zephronis promises me. "Remember, balance is key."

Zephronis taps Lorelai on the forehead, and they both disappear into a spark of white light.

As they disappear, a shadow detaches itself from the ceiling, pooling on the floor like spilled ink. I back away, feeling both my vampire and wolf natures stirring in response to the threat.

"Conrad," I call again. "What does he want from me?"

"What all necromancers want. Power over life and death." Conrad's voice sounds strained, as if he's

fighting to speak. *"But he can't control me much longer. I'm fighting him, Tam-tam."*

The shadow on the floor begins to take shape, rising into a hooded figure. The temperature drops further, frost crystallizing on the bookshelves and walls. My breath clouds in the air.

I don't take my eyes off the forming apparition.

"Don't let him take you," Conrad warns, his voice echoing into silence.

I know I can't trust my brother, no matter how earnest he sounds. It all feels like a manipulation meant to confuse me.

"How beautifully touching," Leviathan mocks. His voice slides over my skin like poisoned silk. His dark form seems to eat the light. "The devoted brother, trying to protect his little sister. After he tried to kill her and frame her for mass murder, of course."

Every cell in my body recoils, but I stand my ground.

The cloaked form steps forward and solidifies into an imposing figure. He's lean and elegant, and disturbingly fluid, like he's a half second from turning into smoke. His unremarkable features are neither handsome nor ugly. Honestly, if I'd met him on the street, I wouldn't have remembered him.

"What do you want?" I demand.

He tilts his head. His voice lowers. "There is no

reason to be defensive. I'm not here to hurt you, my little lotus flower."

I snort. "Yeah, right. And I am not anyone's flower."

"Sure you are," he answers. "It's the flower of purity, of rebirth and transformation. That is exactly what you are. Beautiful. Delicate. Pure. A true supernatural queen."

"Yeah, and no." I frown.

"You've grown, Tamara. Or perhaps fractured is the better word for it. All those little pieces inside you, so many flavors of power fighting for dominance. Mortal soul. Vampire. Wolf. Suppressed magic. Your blood sings to me."

I clench my fists, trying to hide the tremor. "Back off."

He smiles slowly, and his look appears indulgent. "You were so much easier to reach when you were screaming in a crib."

I flinch before I can stop myself.

"You failed," I counter. "You'll fail again."

His smile widens, and he chuckles. "You weren't necessarily supposed to die as a baby, you know. I knew it was a possibility. And the innocence of babies is," he sighs in pleasure, "delightful."

"Gross."

He continues as if I didn't speak. "Goblins are loyal, but not terribly smart. You're lucky the butterflies interfered. But they did mark you, so I could track you. Though I am hurt that you never wore my birthday present. I wouldn't have needed Conrad to watch you if you had just put on the ring. Such a waste of good craftsmanship."

I think about the eyeball ring he gave me for my birthday. Conrad had called it a "Peeping Tom". It's still wrapped in a washcloth, buried in the back of my drawer at the penthouse where I'd hidden it. The thought of him watching me through that thing makes my skin crawl.

Leviathan leans in slightly, and the shadows curl at his feet like pets.

"Let my brother go," I say, surprised by the steadiness in my voice. "Release him. Send his spirit on."

Leviathan's cold laugh is his only answer.

"I'll never cooperate with your plans," I say. "You've lost. I'm immortal. You can't claim me when I die."

"You think?"

"I belong to no one," I growl, feeling my fangs extend. My claws push at the skin of my fingertips, eager to emerge.

"Fascinating," he says, circling me slowly. "You've maintained more control than the others. A true success at last."

"Others? What others?"

"You didn't think you were the first hybrid, did you?" He sounds amused. "I've been experimenting with hybrids for centuries. Werewolf-vampire. Vampire-magic. Magic-shifter. So many failures. So many unstable abominations that tore themselves apart from the inside. A regular Island of Dr. Moreau."

"Island of what?" I frown.

"H. G. Wells?" He tsks when I don't respond. "Old book. Hybrid monsters. You should read more. You'd appreciate the irony."

"You should take a flying leap off a skyscraper," I counter. "Why would you possibly want a hybrid?"

I can think of a million reasons why something like me shouldn't exist.

"Because the creature with the most power wins," he says simply. "Think of what we could do. With your blood we could create a super army. Creatures with the strengths of multiple supernatural species but none of their weaknesses. Imagine vampires who can walk in daylight, werewolves with the cunning of vampires, magics with the raw power of shifters. Following you, the great Devine hybrid. Born of a master vampire and werewolf Alpha. Loyal to us."

"And what?" I laugh, but there's no humor in it. "I'm supposed to be your general?"

"No." He steps closer, close enough that I can

smell the grave-dirt and decay on him. "You are to be my queen."

I recoil. "Go to hell."

"I've been," he says conversationally. "It's overrated."

"Aren't you married?" I back up, trying to put distance between us, but he matches me step for step.

Rumor has it Leviathan's wife passed years ago, but he summons her nightly to his bed.

"Like such things have ever stopped the supernaturals," he says.

"Gross," I whisper under my breath.

"You're different, Tamara Devine," he continues. "From the moment you were conceived, I sensed your potential. A mortal child born to a supernatural father and a human mother, carrying dormant abilities that just needed activation."

"You sent goblins to kill me," I remind him. "That doesn't really say, hey, I want to marry you, does it?"

"Not kill you," he corrects. "Test you. Prepare you. The goblins fed your life force directly to me, creating a connection that would make your transformation easier to control. And you've transformed beautifully. Your hybrid nature is stable, more or less." His eyes gleam. "You just need guidance. I can help you."

"I don't want your guidance." I recoil. "And I definitely don't want your control."

"Don't you?" he asks softly. "I can feel your struggle, Tamara. The constant war between vampire and wolf. The hunger that never quite leaves. The rage that simmers just beneath the surface. I can help you master it all. Look at you. Tethered to a vampire. Hunted by werewolves. Half-lit with a power you barely understand. Your own family's ghost rotting on your shoulder. You're unraveling, Tamara. And you don't even know which thread to pull first."

My pulse pounds in my ears, but I keep my spine straight.

"I know who I am."

"Do you?" he whispers.

For a moment, *just a moment*, I'm tempted. The promise of control, of understanding what I've become, is seductive. Just like when Elizabeth offered her version of it.

"And all I have to do is what?" I ask. "Become your weapon?"

"My queen," he corrects. "My equal."

"Bullshit." I give a short, humorless laugh. "You don't want an equal. You want a lacky."

His expression hardens. "I'm offering you a choice, Tamara. Join me willingly, and I'll teach you to harness your true potential. Refuse, and I'll take what I want anyway. But it will be much more unpleasant—"

"I'll take unpleasant," I say, feeling my wolf nature pushing forward, eager for battle.

"—unpleasant for everyone you care about," he finishes.

Conrad's voice breaks through again, weaker now. *"Tamara, don't fight him. He's too strong."*

"Listen to your brother," Leviathan says. "He's learned the hard way what happens to those who defy me."

"Let Conrad go," I demand. "You don't need him."

"He's mine," Leviathan says simply. "Just as you will be."

I lunge forward, my hybrid speed taking him by surprise. My claws slash across his face, drawing blood that looks black in the dim light.

Leviathan staggers back, touching his cheek. He looks at the blood on his fingers with something like wonder. "Impressive. No one has managed to wound me in a very long time."

Before I can press my advantage, he makes a sharp gesture. The air between us thickens, and I'm thrown backward, crashing into a bookshelf that collapses under the impact. Heavy books drop around me.

"I'd rather not damage you," he says,

approaching me as I struggle to my feet. "But I will if I must."

I snarl, feeling my body begin to shift. Fur sprouts along my arms, my jaw elongates, and my senses sharpen to predatory focus. The vampire in me is there too, calculating, cold, patient beneath the wolf's rage.

Leviathan watches with evident fascination. "Remarkable. You can partially shift without losing your mind. The others never managed that."

I don't waste time responding. I launch myself at him again, faster this time, my hybrid strength propelling me across the room. But he's ready. He speaks a word in a language I don't recognize, and pain erupts through my body, stopping me mid-leap. I crash to the floor, every nerve on fire.

"I've studied your kind for centuries," he says, standing over me. "Did you really think I wouldn't know how to subdue you?"

I try to move, but the pain intensifies. It feels like my blood is boiling inside my veins. Tears stream down my face and a cry rips from my chest.

"This is your last chance," Leviathan says. "Join me willingly."

Through gritted teeth, I manage one word, "Never."

He sighs, almost disappointed. "Very well. We'll do this the hard way."

He reaches into his cloak and pulls out a small crystal orb similar to the one that he had used to trap Conrad's spirit. This one is empty. "I had hoped to avoid doing things this way, but you leave me no choice."

As he begins to chant, the orb glows with an eerie light. I feel something tugging at me, not my physical body, but something deeper. My essence. My soul.

"Stop," I gasp, fighting against the pull.

"Use both sides," Conrad's voice cuts through the pain. *"Vampire and wolf!"*

I close my eyes, focusing through the agony. Conrad is right. I've been treating my dual nature as separate parts fighting for dominance. But what if they're meant to work together?

Balance.

"Remember, balance is key," Zephronis had said.

I reach inside myself, not suppressing either side. The vampire's cold calculation and the wolf's primal strength.

The hunger and the rage.

The predator and the pack hunter.

Power surges through me, different from anything I've felt before. The pain recedes, and I feel my body responding to my will, not just shifting, but transforming in a controlled way. Strength flows into my limbs. My senses sharpen beyond anything I've experienced.

Leviathan's chanting falters.

"Impossible," he whispers.

I rise to my feet, my body a perfect blend of vampire and werewolf. My claws are extended, my fangs bared, but my mind is clear. For the first time since my transformation, I feel good. I'm in balance.

"Get out," I growl, my voice deeper than normal but still recognizably mine. "Get out now."

Leviathan backs up a step, genuine uncertainty in his eyes. "This isn't over, Tamara Devine. You can't run from what you are. You can't run from our destiny. It's been foretold."

Foretold. Destiny. Fate. Prophecy. How many times have I heard this spiel already?

"I'm not running," I say, advancing on him. "You are."

He makes a gesture, and the shadows around him begin to swirl. "We'll meet again," he promises. "And next time, I'll be better prepared."

The crystal orb in his hand pulses, and Conrad's voice rings out one last time, "...*fight.*"

Then Leviathan is gone, melting into the shadows, taking Conrad's voice with him.

The frost remains.

So does the silence.

The temperature in the room gradually returns to normal, the frost on the windows melting away.

I stand alone in the destroyed library, my body slowly regaining its human form. But something has changed. I can still feel both sides of my nature, no longer at war but existing in an uneasy alliance.

Light flashes and Zephronis reappears. His eyes immediately take in the destruction.

"I don't care what you say. I have my proof. Leviathan has been hunting me my entire life," I say, my voice hollow with exhaustion. "He wants to use me as some kind of breeding stock for a hybrid army."

Zephronis nods gravely. "This is not good news. Necromancers have always sought to control life and death, to twist the natural order to their will. To know Leviathan has gotten this far in his plans—"

"He said I'm the first success," I say. "That all his other hybrids destroyed themselves."

"Which means he will not give up easily," Zephronis concludes.

I look around the room. "Where's Lorelai?"

"Safe. I've sent her away from the estate with protection." He studies me carefully. "You're different."

I flex my fingers, feeling the power humming beneath my skin. "It's like you said. It's about balance."

A rare smile crosses the wizard's face.

Before I can respond, the door to the library bursts open. Costin stands there, his face a mask of barely contained fury and concern. His eyes sweep the room, taking in the destruction before landing on me. Red swirls in his eyes.

"Tamara," he says, crossing to me in an instant. "What happened? I felt…"

"Leviathan," I say simply. "He was here."

Costin's face darkens. "Are you hurt?"

"No." I look down at myself, realizing my clothes are torn from my partial transformation. "Not physically, anyway."

He pulls me against him, his arms protective. The sire bond hums between us, less like a leash, more like a thread. "I shouldn't have left you."

"I handled it," I say, pulling back to look at him. "I found a way to control both sides. At least temporarily."

His eyes search mine, surprise evident. "How?"

"By not fighting it," I explain. "By accepting what I am." I glance at Zephronis, but he's gone. "By finding balance."

"Leviathan will be back," I continue. "He thinks I'm the first successful hybrid he's created. He wants to use me to create some kind of supernatural army."

"Created?" Costin repeats, his brow furrowing. "He didn't turn you. Thane and I did."

"He's been manipulating things from the beginning," I explain. "Since I was a baby. He sent goblins to steal my breath, to create some kind of connection. He's been waiting for this, Costin. For me to become this."

Costin's expression hardens. "He won't touch you again. I swear it."

"You can't be with me all the time," I point out.

"Then we'll find somewhere safer," he insists. "Somewhere he can't reach you."

I shake my head. "There is no such place. You know that. Not for long. And I'm tired of running and hiding."

CHAPTER

TWELVE

My mouth tastes like blood. Not a metaphor. Literal blood.

It covers my tongue, fills my nostrils, and makes me want to drink. I try to open my eyes, but they're locked shut with what I can only assume is more blood. My blood? Leviathan's? I'm not sure.

I remember standing my ground. Finding balance. Costin arriving. For a moment, everything was fine.

Then... *nothing*?

This seems to be a pattern in my life lately. Consciousness, unconsciousness, rinse, repeat. I wonder how many more times I'll wake up not knowing what happened to me or how much time has passed.

I swipe at my eyelids with trembling fingers.

Flakes are crusted along my lashes. They sting as I peel them apart. I manage to pry one eye open. The destruction looks worse than I remember, like a bomb went off after Leviathan fled. Broken shelves. Scattered books. Shattered glass from a mirror.

No. It wasn't this bad.

Pain radiates through my body as I try to move. It's not the sharp agony of a spell, but a bone-deep ache, as if I've been pushed beyond my supernatural limits. Each muscle screams in protest as I force myself into a sitting position.

"Easy."

Costin's voice comes from somewhere to my right. I turn, wincing at the stiffness in my neck. He sits in a chair a few feet away, watching me with careful eyes. There is a bloody rip in his shirt sleeve.

"Did I do that?" I ask.

He waves a hand in dismissal. "It's nothing."

Costin doesn't rush to help me. Doesn't try to lift me or support me. He just waits, giving me space to find my own strength.

That's new.

"How long was I out?" My voice sounds like I've been gargling gravel.

"A few hours." He passes me a glass of blood without touching my hand. "You collapsed shortly after I arrived."

I drain the glass, letting the warm liquid soothe

my parched throat. Even my fangs ache, retracted but tender against my gums.

"Leviathan came back?" I ask.

Costin's jaw tightens. "You don't remember?"

I look around at the devastation, trying to force a memory. "Astrid's going to be pissed about her books."

His lips twitch with a ghost of a smile. "I believe her exact words were irreplaceable first editions and centuries of magical knowledge."

Someone had given me a pillow and blanket, but I'm on the floor. I try to stand, but my legs buckle. I expect Costin to catch me, to sweep me up in his arms with vampiric speed. He doesn't. He watches me struggle, his body tense with the effort of restraint, but he lets me find my own balance.

When I finally manage to stand, swaying slightly, I see something in his eyes I didn't expect. Pride.

"You're giving me space," I observe.

"Yes."

"Why?"

He considers his answer carefully. "Because you need it."

I wait for more, for the lecture about safety, for the possessive concern, for the sire bond to pulse between us with demands of obedience. None of it comes.

"That's it?" I press. "No, 'Tamara, you shouldn't have faced Leviathan alone'? No, 'you could have been killed'?"

"Would it change anything if I said those things?" He raises an eyebrow. "Would you do anything differently?"

I think about it honestly. "Probably not."

"Then what would be the point?" He stands, keeping his distance. "You made your choice. You survived. You even found a way to balance your natures," he gives a pointed look around, "if only temporarily."

I follow his gaze. "Are you saying I did all of this?"

Costin nods. He's so refined and composed, like we're discussing the weather.

I shake my head. I don't remember. "No, I... Really?"

"From what we can gather, you expended too much energy fighting without properly feeding and went into a rampage. That, Zephronis' little time travel memory spell, Leviathan's magic, and the sunlight. Your vampire side has not built a tolerance to daylight. That comes in centuries, not days, and you will never be able to handle more than this."

Centuries. The word sends a chill through me. No longer a mortal. I'm going to live forever... well, forever or until I'm killed.

And then what? Leviathan gets my marked soul? That means even death won't free me.

I look to the closed curtains, knowing there is protection on the glass. Someone has thrown an extra blanket over the small stream that had been peeking through. It's only now I realize we're in the dark and I can see almost perfectly.

"Did I hurt anyone this time?" I smell for fresh blood and detect a hint of it. I look at his arm, and clarify, "Anyone else?"

"No. You started to, but you showed restraint. You attacked the books instead." He gives a small laugh as if trying to hide a smile.

"You're not angry?"

"I'm furious," he says calmly. "But not at you. At Leviathan. At myself for not being here when he came."

I take a tentative step toward him, testing both my physical strength and the strange new dynamic between us. "I expected you to be..."

"Controlling?"

"To use the sire bond to keep me in line."

He tries to hide his emotions from me. "Is that how you see me? As someone who would use that connection to control you?"

I don't answer immediately. The truth is complicated. He did turn me against my wishes. But if he hadn't I'd be a prisoner of Leviathan. He has used the sire bond, intentionally or not, to influence me. But I also know he's been trying to give me freedom within the supernatural constraints that bind us.

Maybe fate is really in charge of my life.

"I don't know what to expect anymore," I admit. "Everything keeps changing."

"Including us." He takes a step toward me, then stops, as if remembering his commitment to give me space. "I trust you to figure this out, Tamara. Your way. Not mine or your father's. Not the council's. Yours."

The words hit me like a physical force. Trust. Such a simple concept, yet so foreign in my current existence. Everyone wants to contain me, study me, use me, tempt me. No one trusts me. Not even me.

Well, apparently one person does. Costin.

"Why now?" I ask, genuinely curious. "What's changed?"

A hint of awe creeps into his voice. "You found balance between your natures. You did what no other hybrid has ever done. And..."

I'm not sure how to process his admiration. It feels dangerous, like believing in it might lead to disappointment later. "And?"

"And I..." He hesitates. "I care for you."

That's not what he was going to say. I can see it in his eyes.

"What if the balance was temporary? I don't

know if I can do it again. You see what happened afterward. I blacked out. I don't remember doing any of this."

"But you did it once." He takes another careful step closer. "That's more than anyone thought possible. You're getting better."

"Including you?"

He hesitates, then nods. "Including me."

His honesty stings, but I appreciate it. There's been too much manipulation in my life lately. Too many half-truths and hidden agendas.

"I need to sit down," I mutter, feeling suddenly exhausted.

Costin gestures to the loveseat along the wall that miraculously survived my destruction. I make my way there slowly, my muscles protesting with each step. When I finally sink into the cushions, the relief is immediate and overwhelming. In the wall behind me is a secret passageway. I lean my head back, listening

Costin remains standing, as if unsure whether to join me or maintain his distance.

"You can sit," I tell him. "I won't bite. I don't think."

A wry smile touches his lips as he takes a seat at the opposite end of the couch. "Wouldn't be the first time if you did."

The memories of our violent couplings flash

through my mind. I recall the feel of my fangs in his neck, his in mine, blood and desire mingling in a primal dance of possession. I look away, embarrassed. "I haven't exactly been myself."

"You were exactly yourself," he counters softly. "Just a different part of yourself."

I turn back to study him, trying to reconcile this measured, patient Costin with the possessive vampire who claimed me as his.

"The sire bond," I begin hesitantly. "I feel it all the time. This pull toward you. This need to please you, to obey. It scares me."

He nods, unsurprised by my admission. "It's meant to. It's a survival mechanism. It ensures new vampires remain loyal to their sires, learn control, don't expose our kind."

"But it feels like..." I struggle to find the words. "Like I'm losing myself. Like what I want doesn't matter anymore."

"What you want matters very much," he says firmly. "The bond exists, but you are still your own person. I won't force you to stay with me."

I blink, surprised by the declaration. "You won't?"

"No." His voice is quiet but resolute. "If you choose to go, I won't stop you. Though I hope you choose to stay."

"Even if it would hurt you?"

"Even then."

I search his face for signs of deception, for the subtle tells that have marked so many conversations in the supernatural world. I find none. Just open vulnerability. It's a rare sight in a centuries old master vampire.

"Where would I even go?" I ask, more to myself than to him. "The wolves want to use me as their Alpha. Elizabeth wants to experiment on me. Leviathan wants to make me his necromancer queen and breed a hybrid army. The council wants to study me like a lab rat."

"You have options," Costin says.

"Do I? Because it feels like I'm just trading one cage for another."

He's silent for a long moment. "What do you want, Tamara? Not what others expect. Not what duty demands. What do *you* want?"

The question hits me harder than it should. What do I want? Has anyone ever actually asked me that?

"I want..." I start, then falter.

The truth is I don't know. What I want has never really been an option. Not in my whole life.

I know what I thought I wanted. I fantasized of being normal, away from the supernatural with others like me. I thought I wanted a life with Paul and Diana, but that was a mistake. Our time together only led to disaster.

Even if I wanted to take that path, it's no longer an option. It's never been an option. I realize that my wanting to be normal is like a turtle wanting to be a bird. Sure it might be able to come to the surface, breathe air, and look at the sky, but a turtle will never fly.

Even when I was human, I would never be normal.

The truth seems too simple, naïve even. "I want to be free. To figure out who I am now. What I am. I want to make my own decisions."

"Then that's what we'll work toward." He says it like it's that easy, like we can just decide to change the rules that have governed supernatural society for millennia.

"And how exactly do we do that?" I can't keep the skepticism from my voice.

"One moment at a time," he answers. "Beginning with trust."

I laugh, the sound brittle. "Trust isn't exactly in abundance around here."

"Then we build it." He shifts slightly closer. "I trust you, Tamara. Now you need to decide if you can trust me."

The sire bond pulses between us, a living reminder of our unequal connection. But beneath it,

I feel something deeper and more genuine. The feeling was there before I turned, in the way he looks at me.

"I want to," I admit softly. "But I'm afraid."

"Of what?"

"Of being wrong. Again." I gesture vaguely at myself. "Look at my track record. I trusted Conrad, and he tried to kill me. I thought I could protect Paul and Diana, and I almost got them killed. I trusted my own judgment about what I wanted, and now I'm this monster. And now I think I can beat centuries of supernatural will and my destiny?"

"You're not wrong for wanting freedom," he says firmly. "You're not wrong for fighting against a destiny others tried to force on you. I have seen enough of your life to realize that fate is just a course we have been put on. All these prophecies, all these things you've had to overcome, and look at you. You beat them all. You're going to beat this. I have never seen a stronger being."

His words touch something raw inside me. A wound I didn't know was still bleeding. I look away, blinking back unexpected tears.

"Or more beautiful." Costin moves closer, slowly, giving me time to object. When I don't, he reaches out, his cool fingers brushing my cheek. The touch is gentle, respectful, nothing like the possessive grasp I've come to expect.

I want so many things in this moment. The wishes fill my heart with hope and dread at the same time.

"I can't undo what's happened," he says quietly. "I can't change what you've become. But I can promise you this, whatever comes next, whatever you decide, I will stand with you. Not as your master or your sire, but as your equal."

I look into his eyes, searching for the truth. The sire bond hums between us, but it feels less like a leash and more like a connection. A bridge rather than a chain.

"Equal," I repeat, testing the word. "Is that even possible with this between us?"

I gesture to the invisible thread I feel linking us.

"I believe it is," he says. "If we choose it to be."

Choice. Such a simple concept. So much of my life has been dictated by the machinations of beings more powerful than me. The idea that I still have choices feels like a fantasy.

I lean into his touch, making my own choice. His palm cups my face, cool against my skin. I close my eyes, allowing myself this moment of vulnerability.

When I open them again, Costin is watching me with an intensity that steals my breath. Not the predatory hunger I've seen before, but something deeper and more honest. The mask of the master vampire has slipped, revealing the man beneath. It's a man who has waited centuries for something he never thought he'd find.

"Did you mean what you said to me?" he whispers.

"When?"

The mask doesn't come back. His eyes search mine. "When you were dying, you said that you loved me. That you always have, even when you were trying not to."

I vaguely remember.

"You haven't said it since. I don't blame you. I know you can't forgive me for what I've done to you." He strokes my cheek, caressing me softly as if he's scared I'll pull away.

"I'm still angry about what you did," I whisper. "Breaking your promise and turning me against my will."

"I know." He doesn't try to defend himself. Doesn't make excuses. Just accepts my anger as valid.

"But I'm trying to understand it," I continue. "Trying to see beyond my own pain to what you were feeling in that moment."

His thumb traces the curve of my lip. "I was selfish, terrified of losing you. I won't apologize for saving your life, but I am sorry for taking your choice from you."

The honesty in him breaks something open

inside me. For the first time since my transformation, I feel the full weight of what I've lost, what I've become, what still remains an uncertainty.

He puts his forehead against mine, and I feel him tremble. There is something to the moment calling me into my memories. All of his careful control and centuries of power mean nothing. He's as broken as I am.

"I've loved you your entire life. And I will love you for the rest of mine." His lips don't move, but I hear his voice echoing from the past. The agony in it breaks my heart. "I can't watch you die. Not like this. Not when I've finally found the one soul in centuries who makes me feel human again."

How could I have forgotten those words? I had begged him to let me die. The pain had been overwhelming. I feel echoes of it now as I look into his eyes.

"You could never be a monster."

My heart stutters in my chest. The wolf venom had been taking over. I wasn't going to survive the transformation. I was too weak from Elizabeth's spell and losing the amulet.

"*I love you,*" Costin had whispered as he lifted his wrist to my lips to give me his blood.

I should resist the memory. Should maintain my independence, my anger. Instead, I let myself collapse into him.

"I love you," I repeat what he said in the memory as I died. The emotions I felt in that moment come back to me. They had been so pure, untainted by the monster I now carry. How could I forget that moment?

Costin pulls me against his chest, his arms encircling me in a hold that's protective.

"Do you mean it, Tamara?" he whispers. "Only me?"

I can sense he's trying hard to be possessive, but it goes against his nature. He wants to know if I still have feelings for Paul.

I care for Paul. He'll always be that fragment of a dream.

"Only you, Costin," I say. The vulnerability terrifies me.

I should feel embarrassed by this display of weakness, but I don't. Instead, I feel lighter, as if poison has been drawn from the wound in my heart.

"Thank you," I murmur against his chest.

"For what?"

"For not trying to fix me again. For just being here."

His arms tighten fractionally around me. "Always."

The word hangs between us, weighted with promise. I lift my head to look at him, suddenly very sexually aware of how close we are, of the current of energy flowing between us. But it's different from the desperate, violent need that has driven us before. It's deeper, built on more than the sire bond and physical hunger.

I reach up to touch Costin's face, mirroring his gesture. His skin is cool beneath my fingers, familiar yet strange to my heightened senses. He remains perfectly still, letting me set the pace.

"What happens now?" My voice is barely above a whisper.

"Whatever you want to happen."

For once, I believe him. The choice is truly mine. I could pull away, maintain the distance between us. Or I could bridge it, on my terms, driven not by supernatural compulsion, but by my own desire.

I choose the latter.

When I kiss him, it's nothing like our previous encounters. No violence, no struggle for dominance. Just a gentle meeting of lips, a question asked and answered in the same perfect moment.

He responds with equal gentleness, his hand coming up to cradle the back of my head, fingers tangling in my hair. The bond sings between us, but beneath it runs something more fundamental, more human despite our supernatural natures.

The kiss deepens slowly, like ice melting into warmth, revealing what was always beneath his frozen surface. My hands slide up his chest to his shoulders, feeling the strength contained in his lean frame.

When we finally break apart, his eyes have shifted, red bleeding into the iris. But there's control there too, a careful balance between the vampire and the man.

Are you sure?, his eyes seem to ask.

I nod, more certain than I've felt about anything since my transformation.

"I'm choosing this," I say. "I'm choosing you."

He lowers his mouth to mine once more.

This time, there's no restraint from either of us. The kiss builds into a desperate hunger. Violent but not destructive.

His hands roam my body, relearning the terrain, finding places that make me groan into his mouth. I do the same to him, exploring the planes of his chest, the hard muscles of his arms and shoulders. When my fingers find the buttons of his shirt, he lets me undo them one by one, not rushing and never taking control.

The destroyed library fades into insignificance. All that exists is us. My werewolf blood keeps my temperature naturally warmer than his. When my torn shirt joins his on the floor, the air raises goosebumps on my skin.

I don't fight the new parts of myself. The bond is always there, humming beneath my skin like a second heartbeat, even when I pretend to ignore it. The change I feel inside when he touches me is not the painful, bone-breaking change of the wolf or the driving hunger of the vampire. It's deeper and more fundamental.

It's balance.

Costin's love centers me.

We take our time. Every touch feels like a conversation. When he lowers me onto the couch, his body covering mine, I feel no fear about losing myself. There is only anticipation and desire.

Our bodies join and I can't help the loud sigh of relief that escapes me. His body moves within me, gentle at first, then building to a more furious rhythm as I urge him on. My nails dig into his back, not to draw blood but to anchor myself as pleasure builds.

The sire bond amplifies each sensation into a kaleidoscope of feeling. I can sense his pleasure as well as my own, creating an endless loop of desire. But unlike before, I don't lose myself to the beast within.

Perfect balance.

The pleasure is too much. Our climax builds and when release finally washes through us, it's a revelation. I cry out softly.

Afterward, we lie tangled together on the couch, my head on his chest, his arms around me. Neither of us speaks, content to exist. I float on the edge of reality, not wanting to come back. I listen to his heart, the slow, steady rhythm different from the frantic pulses that have haunted me since my turning.

"What are you thinking?" he finally asks, his fingers tracing patterns on my shoulder.

"That I should be more worried about having sex in my parents' library," I reply, surprising a laugh out of him.

"Is that all?"

I crane my neck to look up at him. "I'm just taking your advice and facing one moment at a time."

THIRTEEN

The full moon is a week away. Sully was right. I can feel it pulling at my blood like an invisible tide, calling to the wolf part of me. The sensation is strange, not painful exactly, but an insistent dull ache. There is the constant awareness that something primal and unstoppable is coming.

As if my urges weren't bad enough, now I have the moon fucking with my hormones. This takes my "monthly visitor" to a whole new level. Too bad there isn't a pill to stop the cramping.

I stand near the edge of the woods on the Devine estate, far enough from the main house that I can see the stars clearly in the night sky. The snow has melted, leaving behind dormant grass and mud. Magical protection shimmers faintly throughout the property, visible now to my enhanced senses. It's faint, like glowing dust in the moonlight. I've spent my entire life inside these barriers, safe from the supernatural world that now courses through my veins.

Or so I thought. Being supernatural, I don't feel the magic holding me back. It seems more like something to keep things out. It occurs to me my human childhood wasn't as protected as I assumed.

A twig snaps behind me. I don't turn. I already know who it is by scent, earthy and wild, with an undertone of leather and pine.

"You're trespassing," I say.

Sully chuckles, the sound low and rumbling. "The Devine wards don't keep out those who are invited. I've heard rumors of your family's parties. And you call us the animals."

I turn to face him. He looks different tonight, more contained. The wild energy that usually surrounds him is focused. He wears a simple black t-shirt that stretches across his massive chest and shoulders, and dark jeans. His beard is trimmed shorter, and his eyes gleam with purpose.

"And who invited you?" I ask, though I already suspect the answer.

"Your brother." Sully nods toward the main house, where lights still burn in several windows. "Anthony seems to think we should talk before the moon rises."

Nope. That's not who I would have guessed. I would have said Mortimer did it in hopes that Sully would kill off the family problem.

"Anthony should mind his own business," I mutter, but there's no real heat in my words. I know my brother means well, even if his methods are questionable.

"He's worried about you. Enough that he met with me in a dark alley." Sully takes a step closer, his movements measured as if he's trying to intimidate me. "He's worried about what will happen when the call comes."

The call.

"You already feel it starting, don't you? The pull of the full moon on your werewolf's blood. What will happen when it reaches its peak? Will you be able to control yourself, or will you become the monster everyone fears?"

I swallow nervously at his telling words. I've felt echoes of it already, growing stronger each passing second.

"I'm handling it," I say, more confidently than I feel.

Sully gives me a knowing look. "Are you? Do you think the goblins would agree?"

"That was different." I cross my arms defensively. "Leviathan sent them to attack. I didn't go looking for them. I was defending myself."

"Ah, yes. The necromancer." Sully's lips twist in distaste. "Another complication we don't need."

"We?" I raise an eyebrow. "Last I checked, Leviathan was my problem."

"He's a problem for anyone who stands with you." Sully steps closer, his massive frame blocking out the stars behind him. "And whether you like it or not, that includes your pack. A threat to one is a threat to all."

I sigh, looking past him toward the distant tree line. I'm trying to look brave, but I am very aware of where he is standing. His speech about pack loyalty is all well and good, but I've learned nothing comes free. For that loyalty I would have to give up my freedom and control to run with the gang.

"I've told you I'm not interested in leading your pack."

"*Our* pack. The sooner you accept that you're one of us, the better it will be for you. And whether you want it or not, some still believe you're our best hope."

"Tell them to take a number," I drawl sarcastically. "My dance card is full."

He frowns.

"What the hell is a dance card anyway?" I wonder. "And why are they always full?"

"Hey, this isn't a joke." His voice drops lower.

"The Alpha's blood runs in your veins, Tamara. That means something to werewolves."

"It means he tried to kill me," I counter. "It means I'm a hybrid freak that shouldn't exist."

Sully's eyes flash gold, shining eerily in the darkness. I wonder if my eyes are doing that.

"It means you're powerful," he says, "and power is what the pack needs right now."

I turn away, frustrated by his persistence. "The pack needs a leader who understands them, who knows their ways and their traditions. That's not me."

"Some would disagree."

"Some would be wrong."

A howl cuts through the night, distant but clear.

I shiver and rub my arms. "Sully, tell me, honestly, what happens when they realize my loyalties will always be split between vampire and wolf? That I feel the pull to my vampire sire as strongly as I feel the pull of the moon and tides? Sometimes more so."

My words seem to have an effect on him, and I know he gets my point.

"If werewolves don't want to be the bottom of the rung of the supernatural hierarchy, they don't need an Alpha whose blood demands obedience to a vampire."

"We're not in disagreement," he says.

The first howl is joined by another, then several more, until the air vibrates with their call. The sound stirs something inside me, an answering hunger that makes my skin prickle and my teeth ache.

Sully watches me closely, noting my reaction. "They're gathering. The leadership trials begin tonight."

I try to ignore the pull to join in, focusing instead on keeping my breathing steady. "Good luck with that."

"Normally we'd wait for the full moon, but the council's... We'll call it their *interest* in werewolf politics. It has demanded we do this now before they arrange another fate for you. Otherwise, there are some in the pack who will doubt the new Alpha and will think we were robbed of our true leader."

What he's saying makes sense. I can see why he'd be so persistent about it.

"You need to be there," he says. "Even if you don't intend to compete, your presence matters. The pack needs to see what you choose."

"I've already made my choice clear."

"Have you?" He circles around to face me again. "Because refusing to show up sends its own message. It says you think you're better than them. Above their concerns. Do you really want your own pack turning on you?"

"That's not—"

"It's how they'll see it," he puts forth. "Were-wolves respect strength, Tamara. They respect those who face challenges head-on, not those who hide behind spells and potions in mommy and daddy's dollhouse."

The accusation stings because there's truth in it. I have been hiding, trying to control my new nature with Astrid's concoctions and Zephronis' magic. But the full moon won't be denied, and neither will the wolf in my blood.

"What exactly happens at these trials?" I ask, my concern getting the better of me.

A smile spreads across Sully's face, revealing teeth that seem just slightly too sharp for a human mouth. "Come and see for yourself."

"I'm supposed to be imprisoned," I look back at the house nervously. "I don't think the council wants me to leave."

Sully's grin widens and he leans closer. "Do you see the council anywhere? Do you see guards? Come on, Tamara, the only way to lock up a wolf is to chain it to the floor and even then those chains better be strong as hell."

The abandoned steel mill on the outskirts of some backwater town seems an unlikely gathering place for supernatural creatures. Though it's close to the family estate, I've never been here. And yet it's somewhat fitting for werewolves battling it out to be Alpha.

Sully's motorcycle rumbles beneath my ass as he drives us toward the rusted structures looming against the night sky. They're like the skeletal remains of some industrial beast lit by its funeral pyre. Orange flames glow through broken windows that gape like missing teeth. As we enter one of the buildings, I see the tangled remains of conveyor belts and machinery sprawled across the grounds. There is also a strong stench of dust and burnt oil.

"Romantic spot," I grumble as Sully stops inside the massive warehouse building.

"This isn't a date. You smell too much like vampire for my tastes," he answers. "Besides, you're not my type."

I think of Costin. I know he'll come if I need him. I feel his constant presence through our bond. It gives me comfort... kind of. I don't want him coming here. Not with the sound of wolves flooding in the building waiting for us to join them. Costin would try to fight every one of them to protect me. He's strong, but there are too many wolves.

"We're not here for the ambiance." Sully pushes open a heavy door that groans in protest. "We're here because it's remote and the humans avoid it. The locals know to leave us alone."

The moment we step inside, the atmosphere changes. Like the werewolf den Costin took me to in the city, this one is a façade. The abandoned building is transformed into a ceremonial stronghold. Torches line the walls, casting dancing shadows across the vast space. The floor has been cleared, creating a circular arena surrounded by scaffolding. Werewolves climb the various levels, perching to watch our entrance.

The air hums with a wild, barely contained energy that makes my skin tingle. The scent of sweat, blood, and excitement fills my nostrils and makes my heartbeat quicken. My inner wolf stirs in response, pushing against the vampire for control.

"Easy, girl," Sully soothes, noticing my tension. "They're just saying hello. No need to tear someone apart just yet."

I look at my hands seeing the claws and fur pushing toward the surface. I feel the stares like physical weight pressing down upon my head, most hostile, a few intrigued.

Whispers follow us as we move deeper into the arena. I can't tell who's speaking. There are too many of them.

"So this is the hybrid?"

"...that's no queen of..."

"Thane's blood…"

"What's she doing here?"

"*That* is our salvation?"

I keep my chin proudly lifted, refusing to show weakness even as the unease crawls along my spine. The vampire in me calculates escape routes. My eyes dart around, trying to assess the number of threats. The wolf wants to assert dominance in the bloodiest of ways. I force both instincts down, trying desperately to maintain my fragile balance.

Rhea detaches herself from a group near the center of the arena. Her fading blue hair seems like it's on fire in the bright torchlight, and her scars stand in stark contrast against her pale skin.

"Why did you bring her?" She doesn't sound pleased.

"She needs to be here," Sully answers simply. "She's one of us by blood."

Rhea's eyes narrow as she gives me a disgusted once-over. Her voice rises as she sermonizes to the others. "She may have our blood, but she's not one of us. She's an abomination. Besides, she's made her choice."

Some of the wolves cheer. Others boo. It's diffi-cult to tell if any are on my side. They could just not like Rhea.

"Have I?" I challenge, tired of being talked about as if I'm not standing right there. "Because everyone seems awfully concerned about decisions I suppos-edly made. How about you ask me?"

"You chose vampire," Rhea spits the word like a curse. "You reek of him and his preserved blood stores. You flaunt your sire bond with that blood-sucker while denying the call of your wolf."

I step closer to her, ignoring Sully's warning hand on my arm. "I didn't choose either. Both were forced on me. And I don't need to flaunt anything. Can you say the same?"

"Your scent says otherwise." Her nostrils flare.

I feel my fangs lengthen in response to her hostility. "And you smell like wet mutt. We all have our cross to bear."

A tense silence falls over us. From the predatory stillness that settles over the gathering, I've crossed a line.

Rhea's lips pull back in a snarl, her face begin-ning to elongate as her partial shift takes hold. "You dare—"

"Enough!" Sully's voice cuts through the tension like a blade. He steps between us, his massive frame blocking Rhea from my view. "This isn't why we're here."

"Then why are we here?" I demand. The need to argue and yell seep out of my pores. It would be so easy to let go and pummel Rhea to the ground to wipe the annoying smirk off her face. "Because so far all I've gotten is attitude and accusations. I thought this is supposed to be my pack. If this is how you treat a sister, then Rhea is right, I don't belong here."

Sully turns to face me, his expression grave. "We're here because in seven days, the moon will rise full in the sky. When it does, every werewolf will feel the pull to shift, to run, to hunt. Including you." He gestures around at the gathered wolves. "Without an Alpha to guide the pack, that energy becomes chaotic. Dangerous. Those who want the position will be compelled to battle to the death. In the old days, we'd let that tradition play out. Unfortunately, that path will result in our strongest warriors dying. With the misbalance of magic and power right now, we can't afford to be so careless with our numbers."

"We can make more!" James yells inciting laughter.

I see how their rowdiness feeds off each other. It would be so easy to fall into the frenzy, letting the mindlessness take over until all I am is rage and instinct. I take deep breaths and force myself to calm down.

"We need our center," Sully shouts before turning to tell me, "This needs to be decided."

"I understand that," I say quietly to him, more subdued now. "But I don't see how my presence helps."

"Because some still believe you should lead us." He nods toward a group of werewolves standing together on the far side of the arena. Their hopeful gazes make me deeply uncomfortable. Among them is Peter, Anthony's childhood friend who had a crush on me. He tries to smile, and I have to look away. "They see your hybrid nature as strength, not weakness. They believe you could elevate the pack's standing in the supernatural world."

I follow his gaze back to them. They don't understand what they're asking. They see power not the constant struggle that comes with being a hybrid.

"And you?" I ask Sully. "What do you think?"

His eyes meet mine, unwavering. "I believe the pack needs a leader who understands what it truly means to be a wolf. We need someone who has lived it, breathed it, fully embraced it." He frowns. "That's not you, Tamara. Not yet. Maybe not ever."

His honesty is refreshing after so many hidden agendas and manipulations. "What do you need me to do?"

"They need to hear it from you." He nods toward the expectant faces. "They need to know where you stand."

A hush falls over the warehouse as more werewolves notice our conversation. They gather closer, forming a loose circle around us. I see James with his permanent snarl, standing with a group that clearly supports Sully. There's Rhea and her followers, hostile and suspicious. And Peter and his wolves, looking at me with that uncomfortable mix of hope and expectation.

I take a deep breath, balancing myself.

Sully steps back, giving me the floor. The torch-light flickers across the sea of faces watching me, waiting for my words to either unite or divide them further.

"I didn't ask for Thane's bite," I begin, my voice unsteady. "I didn't ask for any of this."

"No one is asked!" a voice shouts.

"This life chooses us!" another adds.

I feel their irritation.

"Boo-hoo I didn't pick this," Rhea taunts. "She whines like a little bitch."

They're laughing at me now.

Fuck. It pisses me off, but she's right. I do have a tendency to be all poor me and feel sorry for myself.

Also, fuck Rhea.

"Thane's blood runs in my veins now," I shout, "alongside vampire blood and my own human heritage. I am what I am. I'm something new, something that hasn't existed before."

Murmurs ripple through the crowd, but I press on.

"Some of you think that makes me special. That

it makes me your destined leader." I shake my head. "It doesn't."

I could tell them that I'm still learning what I am, still finding balance between the different parts of myself. Or that I can barely lead my own life right now, let alone a pack. All of those things will sound weak. There is only one language wolves seem to understand. Strength.

"I will not compete for Alpha. I will not lead you." My voice grows stronger with conviction. The hopeful faces begin to fall. I feel a pang of regret but push through it. "But I will stand with you. I will fight alongside you if needed. I will honor the wolf blood in me, even as I honor the other parts."

Silence follows my declaration. I can feel the disappointment from some, the relief in others. Sully watches me with an unreadable expression.

"So that's it?" James calls out, his distorted mouth twisting in a sneer. "You just walk away from responsibility? From your potential place in our world?"

"I'm not walking away," I counter. "I'm choosing my own path. Just as each of you should choose yours."

"Pretty words," Rhea scoffs. "But it changes nothing. We still need an Alpha before the full moon."

"Then choose one," I say simply. "Choose the

one who understands you best, who can lead you through whatever challenges lie ahead. That's not me and pretending otherwise would only hurt the pack in the long run."

"Coward!" a woman yells.

"Liar!" another adds. "This is a trick!"

Sully steps forward, commanding attention. "The trials will proceed as planned. Those who wish to compete for Alpha will face each other in tests of strength, cunning, and leadership. The strongest will emerge to lead the pack through the coming moon and beyond."

"And what of the hybrid?" someone calls from the scaffolding above. "Where does she stand if not with us?"

Did I not just say I'd stand up for them? I try to hide my growing annoyance. They're like talking to a drunk who doesn't want it to be last call. Nothing I say seems to get through their addled brains. My emotions are only making the wolf in me edgy.

I meet Sully's gaze briefly before addressing the crowd. "I stand as what I am, not fully wolf, not fully vampire, but something of both. I won't pretend to be something I'm not just to fulfill your expectations or prophecies."

"You abandon us," a young female accuses, her voice breaking with emotion. She doesn't look old enough to be here but then looks can be deceiving in the supernatural world.

The warehouse erupts in discussion, some angry, some thoughtful.

"I'm freeing you to find a leader who truly knows what you need," I try to tell them, but no one is listening. I don't bother to add that I'm freeing myself from expectations that were never mine to begin with.

Sully raises his hand, and gradually the noise subsides.

"The trials begin," he announces, leaping into the arena. "Challengers, step forward."

A wolf leaps into the circle to face Sully with a snarl. His actions prompt several werewolves to move into the arena. James stands aggressive and eager. Rhea is confident and calculating. Three others I don't recognize, each carrying themselves with the surety of born leaders.

I step back, staying on the outer edge of the circle. This isn't my fight.

The first battle is chaos. Cheers echo so loudly from the gathered crowd that I can barely hear the punches land. It's more a display of raw strength than bloodshed. The challengers circle each other in the center of the arena, partially shifting to their wolf forms. Muscles bulge, bones crack and reshape, fur sprouts along limbs as each competitor embraces their beast.

I hear the beating hearts around me. It's like a song calling me into the wild. The sight stirs my own wolf. I find myself eager to join, to test myself against the others. I resist the urge. I'm here to observe, not to participate.

Sully's transformation is something to behold. He flows smoothly into the partial shift, his body expanding with raw power. His face elongates into a wolf's muzzle and his eyes blaze gold in the torchlight. He towers over the challengers, a perfect blend of man and beast.

The contest itself is controlled brutality. Blood flows, but not freely. This isn't about killing. It's about proving superiority.

Sully charges at several competitors, throwing them out of the ring. I hear their thuds as they crash into the warehouse walls behind me. The gathered werewolves watch in rapt attention, occasionally howling encouragement to their preferred champion, and taunting those who don't do well.

I have a feeling this night is only going to get worse. Thank goodness I'm not competing.

I find myself strangely fascinated. This is part of my heritage now, this primal display of power and dominance. The wolf in me understands it on a level my human mind never could.

One by one, the lesser challengers yield until only James, Rhea, and Sully remain. They circle each other, growling and snapping, looking for weaknesses to exploit.

"Get in there, hybrid!" A hand shoves me hard against my back. I fall forward into the circle, stumbling before landing on my hands and knees. Pain shoots up my unshifted limbs. Springing to my feet, I instantly try to back out.

"Alpha! Alpha!" they chant. They tighten their circle around the arena, pushing at me whenever I try to get out. "Alpha! Alpha!"

A loud roar comes at me like a warning. Sully crosses his arms, and I swear his shifted face smiles, as if this was all planned.

My heart is beating faster now. This is not what I agreed to.

FOURTEEN

"Show us what you're made of, hybrid!"

James is the first to strike, lunging at me with extended claws. I dart out of the way, diving onto the hard ground. I hear my bones crack as pain rolls through me. Fear causes my heart to pound. But there's something else behind it. Excitement? Exhilaration? Violence?

I hear James' feet slide on the dirty cement, claws scraping as he stops his momentum. I have no choice but to defend myself.

I roar, the sound ripping from deep inside. The vampire in me tries to calculate, but the wolf rips forward, uncaring of strategy. I'm forced into a full shift. Fur sprouts over my body and I feel as if I'm being ripped apart from the inside. My spine arches with a snap, and I feel my ribs crack. My vision sharpens. I hear James' harsh breath and count his every footfall like thunder in my ears.

My clothing tears and hangs off me in shreds. James doesn't let up or give me time to adjust. He crashes into my side, rolling me onto my back. The shouts of the crowd rise up. I feel their frenzy tearing through me.

I defend myself against his attack. Claws bite into my side and it only inspires me into action. I act on pure instinct. James expects brute force. I give him precision and savagery, claws raking across his chest as we collide again.

There is no balance, only survival.

But even in the chaos, I feel the pull of both beasts inside me. The wolf howls for dominance, the vampire craves blood, both demand I kill the man who dares attack. It would be so easy to lose myself, to snap James' neck and let the bloody taste of victory fill my mouth. My last thread of humanity anchors me. I won't be the mindless monster they fear I am.

The fight continues, a savage dance of claw and fang. We crash and roll until finally I get lucky and manage to catch his arm. I use his momentum to throw him across the arena. James crashes into scaffolding but recovers quickly, snarling in fury.

He wobbles as he tries to return running in a curved line that doesn't quite reach me. Sully pushes him down when he comes close to his side. James falls against the ground with a moan.

Sully roars and several hands dart out to drag James away.

They don't give me time to regroup or protest.

Rhea's attack is more patient, more tactical. She circles around me as if waiting for an opening. I glance toward Sully, trying to keep him in my eyeline when Rhea darts in with surprising speed. She rakes her claws across my arm. Blood wells from the wounds. The pain is immediate and sends an electric jolt of awareness over my body. I flinch in surprise, trying to reach after her. She eludes my claws.

The look in her eyes hits harder than any physical strike. She *wants* this battle, thirsts for it. She wants me broken beneath her. My blood marks her like a trophy.

I know all of this because I want the same thing from her. I want to crush her smug face beneath my heel and tear her limbs from her body. I remember the goblin squish as I defended myself. I will defend myself again.

I snarl, the sound guttural and low. If she wants a monster, I'll give her one. I didn't start this fight, but I'll end it.

The warehouse echoes with growls and the impact of bodies colliding. Fights are breaking out in the crowd, fueled by our show. The energy turns feral. Snarls and yelps echo off the walls. The pack is unraveling, stirred by our violence, hungry for blood. It's not just a fight anymore. It's a challenge to every wolf watching. My presence is waking something dangerous in them.

She darts for me again, weaving close before jumping away. Several males bark and howl, their taunts toeing the line between challenge and flirtation. Laughter rumbles beneath the playful sounds.

At least I hope they're playful. I'm not given too much time to process as Rhea darts at me a third time.

Rhea's fight lasts longer. Unlike James, she doesn't ram full on, but her cunning makes up for what she lacks in raw power. She darts and weaves, trying to tire me out.

She closes in again, and this time I don't wait. I fake a stumble, drawing her near. The moment her claws flash, I pivot, slamming my shoulder into her ribs with enough force to lift her off the ground. We crash into the concrete, teeth snapping. She slashes my chest. I drive my shifted fist into her jaw. We roll. Snarl. Tear. There's no technique now. Just instinct. Just war.

Rhea recovers faster than I'd like. She kicks out with both legs, catching me in the gut and sending me flying backward. I hit the ground hard, the impact knocking the air from my lungs. My vision blurs. Everything tastes like blood and rage. I rise to one knee, snarling.

She's already circling again, blood dripping from her mouth.

"You hit like a human," she taunts, but I can see that I'm taking my toll on her.

I answer by lunging.

We collide midair. Claws tear across my back, and I bite into her shoulder, feeling the give of muscle under my fangs. She screams and draws her claws across my face, scoring my cheek.

Everything around us fades.

There's no pack. No audience. No torches or concrete or Sully shouting at us to end it. Just her. Just Me. And the animal fury that binds us.

I catch her arm, twist, and throw her again. She slams into a metal wall with a sickening clang and drops. I fight for breath and will her to stay down, but she's already scrambling to her feet.

We rush each other one last time.

My claws slice across her side. Her knee slams into my ribs. We fall again, tumbling in a tangle of limbs and fur. I smell her pain. She tastes my blood. Neither of us yields.

But then momentum shifts.

I end up on top. My hand wraps around her throat, claws pressing into the vulnerable skin just beneath her jaw. She freezes. I stretch my mouth wide and press my teeth by her throat, ready to bite. I pause, eager to move my hand and clamp down my teeth.

Rhea goes limp, turning her head away and yielding with a reluctant growl which I take as a wolf's way to surrender.

Sully gives a short growl. He stands with his arms crossed watching to see what I'll do. I feel the ripple of attention as the crowd realizes what's happened. Silence spreads like a crack in the earth.

I don't know what to do.

Every instinct in me screams to finish her, to rip, to rule, to *win*. But the part of me that's still human refuses.

I force myself to release her. I step back slowly, watching to see if she does something stupid.

Rhea gasps and rolls away, coughing. She's lucky. Her pride is more wounded than flesh. It could have been so much more brutal.

I stagger back, panting, blood-slicked and trembling, barely clinging to myself.

I turn slowly, meeting the wide, stunned gazes of the gathered pack.

A hush settles over the arena, thick with tension and anticipation. Then the crowd begins to stir. In my heightened state I expect jeers and taunts, but instead it's the low, pulsing chant building in volume.

"Alpha! Alpha! Alpha…"

I look at Sully who gives nothing away. They're not chanting for him.

They're chanting for me.

My stomach twists.

Across the fighting ring, Sully's expression hardens. The half shift has faded from him, and he looks human. Well, scary human but human. He steps forward, his movements unhurried but sure. He doesn't need to posture.

The crowd senses it too. The energy shifts again, rising toward a crescendo.

The final challenge isn't about James. Or Rhea. Or bloodlines.

It's about me and Sully.

He stops a few paces away. Our eyes lock.

"You should have let them take you down early," he says quietly, so only I can hear.

"Would you have?" My voice is raw. There is a deep part of me that's having fun and wants to keep fighting.

"Now you have to fight me."

"I told you I didn't want to be in the contest."

"You still don't get it. We weren't asking. Being a wolf isn't about you. It's about the pack. They need you to fight. They need to *see* it." He waits a beat. "And so do you."

He shifts. It's not flashy. Not showy. Just raw control and brutal grace.

Sully's muscles ripple. His face elongates into a half-wolf, half-warrior. It's like watching inevitability take form.

This was the plan all along. He lured me here to make me fight.

I think of Costin, of tugging at the sire bond to bring him to my rescue. I resist. This isn't a vampire battle, and I'm no longer the damsel in distress.

I shift, too. Not because I want to, but because the natural response is pulled from me at the threat of danger.

We circle each other, silent and calculating. Sully is not like the others. He has control. There's no bloodlust. No chaos. Just the immense pressure as the crowd holds its breath.

He strikes first with a right hook to my face. My head snaps to the side in surprise, but I hold my footing.

The bastard actually hit me!

I growl in response and counter. I punch at his side. He dodges, barely, and my claws skim his ribs. His fist clips my jaw, and I bite my tongue. The blood fills my mouth.

We trade blows. He's strength and werewolf tradition. I'm speed and unpredictability. (Thank you, Astrid, for all those childhood trainers.) For a breathless moment, the crowd sees my awesomeness.

I could take him.

He knows it.

I know it.

I could rule the pack. Alpha Tamara. How do you like my merely mortal ass now?

I make my choice.

As he charges again, I feint, letting him tackle me to the ground. I don't resist as I let him pin me just long enough for them to see.

Then I shove him off and roll away, springing back to my feet with a snarl.

He hesitates. So do I.

I go still.

A silent moment of understanding passes between us.

He charges. His howl splits the air, primal and wild, echoing off walls. I lift my arms to put on a show for the others, but I don't stop him.

The crowd erupts in a fury of sound.

Sully knocks into me, and we fly several feet into the air before dropping to the ground. The back of my head strikes concrete, and my vision swims.

Sully raises his head and howls.

"Alpha! Alpha! Alpha…"

The sound of the chants anchors my consciousness and keeps me from going under. I feel Sully's weight lift off me.

He rises, his massive form silhouetted against the torchlight. Blood drips from various wounds. He raises his head and lets out a victorious howl that shakes the warehouse.

The pack joins him, their voices rising. The sound washes over me, calling to my wolf blood. Before I realize what I'm doing, my head is tilted back, a howl tearing from my own throat to join theirs.

The sound startles me back to awareness. I clamp my mouth shut, embarrassed by the instinctive response. But no one seems to notice or care. They're focused on Sully, who has shifted back to his human form, standing over me.

He reaches out his hand. I ignore the offer to help and push to my feet.

I stand before them, bleeding, shaking, and proud.

Let them see me.

Let them feel what I am.

Not their Alpha.

Not their monster.

Just me.

Hybrid. Survivor. Something new.

One by one, they get on all fours bowing their heads toward Sully. He doesn't move except to turn to look at me. His wounds are already healing, the blood drying on his skin.

Bowing to any man feels wrong, but I move to hands and knees. I stare at my bloody hands as I acknowledge our pack leader. Let him take the position. He can have it.

It seems like an eternity before Sully orders, "Go. Feast!"

I hear the others leaving, but I don't get up right away. Sully's feet come near my head, and I sit back on my legs. Despite our shared violence, there's a calm assurance about him that's undeniable.

"The trials of strength are complete," he says. "They need to know their Alpha earned the position, that I'm strong enough to protect them and smart enough to lead them. Especially with the tensions between our kind and the vampires. The mental trials are tomorrow."

I scowl. "You're not going to make me do more tests."

He laughs and reaches down. "No. The next trials are only mine. True leadership is more than physical power. It is wisdom, strategy, and foresight. Though if I fail, they'll come back around to you."

I let him pull me to my feet. "Then you better not fail."

He studies me for a long moment. "You surprised me tonight."

"How so?"

"I expected that once you got a taste of the wolf you'd want to hold on to being Alpha." A faint smile touches his lips. He begins to walk through the warehouse toward the door. "Most would, given how intoxicating the power can be. I'm not saying you could have beaten me, but I know you could have put up a harder fight."

"I'm not interested in power." I meet the gazes of those we pass, but they don't try to interrupt us. "This was never my dream."

"Then it might be the pack's loss. The ones who seek power rarely deserve it."

"And you?" I challenge. "Do you seek it?"

Sully doesn't answer immediately. He holds open the door to let me pass. When we're away from the others, he appears resigned. "I seek what's best for the pack. If that means taking power, then yes, I'll take it. But not for its own sake."

I nod, believing him. I absently trace the handle of his motorcycle. Whatever else Sully might be, he's not driven by ego or ambition alone. I mean, sure, he has plenty of both, but that's not all he is.

"You'll pass tomorrow," I say. It's not a question.

"Probably." There's no arrogance in his tone, just certainty. "You realize since you've proven yourself, I'm required to name you as a member of my Chosen Guard. You're not done with us."

I arch a brow. "I'm not looking for a job."

"You can't refuse your Alpha." He grins. "Think of it as being part of my brain trust."

I grumble even as I understand the politics at play. "I meant what I said. I don't want your job, but I will stand with the pack if needed."

"I know." Sully's expression turns serious. "That goes both ways. The necromancer's interest in you concerns us all."

"Leviathan is my problem," I say.

"Your problems became pack problems the moment Thane's blood entered your veins," Sully continues. "Besides, I have no love for necromancers. They disturb the natural order."

I nod. "Let me handle Leviathan my way. I'll call on you if I need you."

"And what way is that?" He raises a skeptical eyebrow.

I bristle at the question. "I'm still figuring it out."

"Figure it out quickly. You should be preparing for the transformation, not distracted by everything else." His tone softens slightly. He looks toward the broken windows. "The full moon waits for no one, Tamara. And neither will your enemies."

Before I can respond, the door opens, and Rhea approaches. Although her wounds are already healing, she still moves with a slight limp. She stops a few paces away, her expression guarded.

"The pups want to know if you're staying for the hunt," she says to me, though her eyes slide to Sully as if seeking his approval.

I blink in surprise. "Hunt?"

"It's tradition after the trials," Sully explains. "A way to bond as pack, and to release the tension built up during competition."

"I wasn't planning to—"

"You should come," Rhea interrupts, surprising me further. "If you meant what you said about standing with us, even if not leading us."

I look between them, sensing there's more to this invitation than simple inclusion. "What exactly does this hunt involve?"

"Nothing you can't handle," Sully says with a hint of challenge in his voice. "Unless you're afraid your vampire side won't let you embrace your wolf nature."

It's a transparent attempt to provoke me, but it works, nonetheless. The wolf in me bristles at the suggestion of cowardice. "I'm not afraid."

A smile spreads across Sully's face. "Good. Then you'll join us."

Part of me wants to refuse on principle, to show I can't be manipulated so easily. But the wolf part is curious. What would it be like to run with a pack, to let that side of myself free?

"What are you hunting?" I ask, stalling for time to think.

"Nothing sentient," Sully assures me. "We're not monsters. The thrill is in the chase, not the kill."

I glance at his motorcycle. I could probably steal it when he's not looking and ride back to the safety of the estate. Going back means more potions from Astrid, more endless *talk-talk-talk* about control and balance. It means safety, but also constraint. Joining the hunt means risk, but also the chance to under-stand a part of myself I've been fighting against.

"I'm not killing anything," I say by way of a decision.

"Fair enough," Sully agrees. "Just run with us. Feel what it means to be in a pack, even if only for one night."

Rhea stares at me. I sense her begrudging respect before she turns away to rejoin the others.

When she's gone, Sully says, "This is the right choice, Tamara. You can't control what you don't understand."

"I'm not doing this to control it," I clarify. "I'm doing it to know it."

"Same thing, different words." He strides toward a side exit. "We leave in ten minutes."

The thought of running with a pack sends a ripple of anxiety through me. I've fought so hard against the changes in my body, against the pull of both vampire and werewolf natures. Deliberately embracing one seems counterintuitive.

But maybe that's been my mistake all along. Fighting against what I am instead of working with it. Balance doesn't mean suppression. It means harmony. Every time I give up the inner fight, things seem to get better.

Until I black out and destroy the family library.

Well, nobody is perfect.

I draw my fingers across his motorcycle as I follow Sully outside toward the waiting pack. For so long, I've been defined by what others want me to be. The Devine's human daughter. Conrad's pawn. Draakmar's keeper. The vampire's progeny. The werewolves' Alpha.

Tonight, I reject those imposed identities. I claim the right to define myself.

Sully takes his rightful place at the head of the pack. A feeling of relief comes over me to know that it's settled. I have a feeling I'm not the only one feeling this way. There's no resentment in me, no sense of missed opportunity. That role was never truly mine.

The wolves begin to shift. The air fills with the sounds of transformation. Bones crack. Bodies reshape. Groans turn into howls.

Peter comes up next to me, grinning in welcome. He doesn't speak as he lets his body change.

I close my eyes, reaching inside myself for the wolf blood that now swells in my veins. I don't try to suppress instinct. Instead, I invite it forward.

The change begins slowly, then accelerates. There's pain, but also exhilaration as my body reshapes itself. I become attuned to the night around me. My senses sharpen beyond even their vampire-enhanced state. I can sense the excitement of the pack, smell the distant trees beyond the steel mill, hear the rapid heartbeats of tiny creatures in the woods, feel the cool night air against fur that now covers parts of my body.

When I open my eyes, the world looks more vivid. The pack is no longer a collection of individuals but a single living organism, bound by invisible ties of loyalty and shared purpose.

Sully, now in his massive half-wolf form, meets my gaze across the gravel drive. There's approval in his golden eyes. He throws back his head and howls. The sound echoes off the metal building. The pack joins him, our voices blending into a primal chorus.

As the howl fades, Sully leads us toward the woods. I hesitate only briefly before sprinting alongside them. We move as one.

This is freedom.

I've rejected a destiny others tried to force upon me. I've chosen my own way.

And for the first time since my rebirth, that feels like enough.

FIFTEEN

Dawn threatens the night sky with pale light along the horizon as I make my way back to the Devine estate. The vampire side urges me to seek shelter from its rays. My body aches from the night's hunt, but it's a good pain, the kind that comes from intense exercise.

The pack ran for hours through dense forest, tracking deer and small game. I didn't kill anything, but I ran alongside them, feeling the wind in my fur, the earth beneath my paws. For the first time since my transformation, I had found peace. Or at least something close to it.

As the sun threatens to breach the horizon, the wolf in me is sated, tired but content. Vampire and wolf blood are no longer at war. They're two sides of an ancient coin that somehow landed on its edge.

I slip through the magical protection surrounding the estate, feeling it shiver around me like chiffon drapes. My heightened senses catalog my surroundings as I run up the drive on all fours. There is the new scent of unfamiliar supernaturals. Someone has arrived at the estate. Tension hangs heavy in the air like pressure before a storm. It's a palpable oppression. The wolf wants me to turn around and go back to the safety of the pack. I resist the instinct.

Beneath it all, a familiar presence pulls deep inside me.

Costin.

I latch on to the feeling, letting the vampire's logic soothe the wild tendencies of the wolf. Changing course, I find him waiting in the shadow of an ancient oak that stands sentinel near the edge of the property. He doesn't move to approach me, just watches with those ancient eyes that seem to see more than I want to reveal.

I stand on all fours, letting him see this hairy version of me. I wait for a repulsion that doesn't come. If anything, he looks sad.

I latch on to my feelings for him, letting them calm the beast. They flow through me, helping me to return to my human form. I cry out as my bones snap. The pain is intense but short-lived. When it's over, I'm crouched completely naked on the ground.

"I don't think I'll ever get used to that," I say with a deflective laugh. He says nothing as I stand. I nervously come within a few paces of him. Crossing my hands over my breasts, I glance around the empty yard. "You're still here."

"Did you think I wouldn't be?" His voice is carefully neutral.

I shrug, wincing slightly at the pull of sore muscles. I think about saying I didn't think about it, but that would be a lie, and I don't want lies between us. I'd agonized over it while I ran with the pack, wondering if he could sense what I was doing through our bond, if he was worried, or perhaps angry that I was embracing my wolf side.

"You ran with them." Not a question. He'd be able to smell the forest on me, and the lingering scent of the pack.

"Yes." I lift my chin slightly, ready for judgment or possessiveness.

Instead, he just nods. "Did it help?"

The simple question catches me off guard. "I think so. It was..."

He waits for me to finish. I sense more than see the struggle in him as he tries to control his jealousy.

"It was freeing," I finish.

A tight smile crosses his lips. "Good."

I study him in the growing light, noticing the

tension in his jaw. His hands clasp behind his back as if he doesn't trust himself not to touch me.

The threat of daylight causes my skin to prickle in warning and I look to the threat of the horizon.

"We need to get inside," he states. "You need blood."

"You're not angry?" I study him wishing he'd talk about the fleeting emotions I'm picking up through our bond.

"Would it change anything if I were?" He echoes his own words from our conversation in the library.

"No," I admit. "But I still want to know."

He considers this, his eyes never leaving mine. "I watched you leave with him."

My breath catches. "You followed me?"

"Only to the edge of the property. I sensed him here and wanted to make sure you were safe." His expression shifts, revealing a glimpse of the struggle beneath his composed exterior. "I wanted to follow further."

"But you didn't."

He shakes his head. "You asked for freedom. For trust. I'm trying to give you both."

The admission touches something in me. I know what it costs him. He's a master vampire accustomed to control, to possessing what he considers his.

I'm his.

The possessive thought doesn't upset me as it once did.

The connection vibrates between us, warm and alive. It's a seduction of my senses, a lure calling me to him, but he's not using it to influence me. He's fighting against its very nature.

"Did you...?" He stops himself.

"Ask," I urge. The sun is so close. I can feel it threatening to burn me. The dawn causes my skin to itch.

"Did he touch you?" His tone cuts deeper than it should. I know he's fighting the vampire instinct to claim.

I think of the battle, of the surge of adrenaline. It could easily mimic sexual attraction.

"I didn't sleep with him," I answer. "We fought in the trial thing. Sully is the new Alpha." I shrug. "And apparently I'm on the werewolf board of directors, whatever the hell that means."

"I think they call it the Chosen Guard."

"Whatever." I shrug again. The itching is beginning to burn, and I'm propelled to walk toward the side door. He whips past me almost faster than I can track only to hold open the door to let me pass.

"Thank you," I say softly. "Very gentlemanly of you."

He inclines his head slightly, accepting my gratitude. "You should get cleaned up. The estate has been active in your absence."

The careful way he says it puts me on high alert. I remember picking up the new scent on my way in. "What kind of active?"

"Your uncle has been gathering allies."

I sigh. Of course he has.

"My uncle is an asshole," I grumble under my breath. "Mortimer never misses an opportunity to manipulate a situation to his advantage. Let me guess. He's trying to convince everyone I'm too dangerous to be allowed to roam free?"

"Among other things."

I run a hand through my tangled hair, highly aware that I'm roaming the house naked. "I should have expected this. He's still pissed I didn't want to marry Chester Freemont and pop out magical babies like a broodmare."

Costin flinches. He takes a step closer, his eyes softening with concern. I feel his nearness pulling at me. I can think of several things I'd rather be talking about than Mortimer and Chester.

Or not talking about.

I start to reach for his waist, thinking only of pulling him against my naked body.

"Freedom," he says.

The word takes me by surprise. It's not what I expected him to say.

"You resisted becoming Alpha. You will learn your vampire side. I will help and I will never try to control you." He touches my cheek. "When you face your uncle, remember your ultimate goal. Freedom."

"You're not coming?"

"The sun rises," he reminds me. "I'll be in the guest sanctuary beneath the east wing unless you call for me. Astrid's coverings on the windows help, but I cannot be at my full strength if I stay in the light for too long. If you need me, I want to be able to fight for you."

I nod. "Wait, we have a guest sanctuary under the east wing?"

Figures. This house has more secrets than a Devine family reunion.

He grins. "This house is full of surprises."

"Maybe I should go down there with you?" I suggest. It's not all pragmatic. I'm feeling a little amped after the run. "I notice the light affects me too."

"A vampires curse." He pushes my hair back behind my ear. "I was hoping that was one thing you'd inherit from the wolf."

I shake my head. "No."

I press against him. The firmness of his body makes me shiver. Every nerve is raw and the feel of him sends a ripple of pleasure over me. I can't help the small moan as I rock my hips forward. Cool hands move along my hips.

"I find my nighttime habits lean toward the vampire," I whisper, trying to kiss him.

He chuckles, stopping me. "What does that even mean?"

"It's seductive!" I slug him on the arm.

He glances down where I hit him. "That temper would be the werewolf in you."

"You're lucky you're cute, Costin. Otherwise I wouldn't bother." I don't pull away. I can't. My heart is pumping too fast, and he feels too good. His cock rises in an invitation I won't refuse.

"You should stop looking at me like that," he says, glancing down to my lips.

"You should do that speedy thing where you zoom me through the estate to your lair," I say. Then pushing back to look at him. "Can I do that speedy travel thing? It never occurred to me I can do cool vampire tricks. What else can I do? Turn into a bat? To be honest, I've been so focused on maintaining control and trying to come to terms with my new liquid diet, it never occurred to me that I'm super badass."

I close my eyes and focus on being a bat. It doesn't work. I stay human.

"Tamara Devine!" Astrid scolds. "What on Earth are you doing?"

I stiffen and lean to look down the hallway toward her. I give a weak smile.

"Go put some clothes on," Astrid orders. "Now!"

"Allow me," Costin says. He puts his arms around me and the hallway blurs sideways as he carries me with him. I'm just along for the ride, held to him tighter than gravity. Unlike the time I traveled this way as a human, the motion doesn't make me sick to my stomach. Suddenly, the inertia stops and I'm standing in my room in the protected wing. The sound of my door shutting punctuates my regained vision.

Costin smiles.

I gasp in desperation, reaching between us for his waistband. I don't wait for permission as I yank open his pants and push them down his hips to free the length of his arousal. Turning so that my back is against the door, I lift my leg in offering.

He doesn't disappoint. His body slides into mine and it feels like home. This is where I belong. With him. How could I ever doubt that?

He loves me. I feel it more deeply than I feel my own emotions. Sure, it's dark and a little twisted, and more than a bit domineering at times, but then again he's a master vampire. To love him is to love all of him.

Our hearts beat in time with each other. His eyes swirl with red as he stares into me. Climax comes too fast, but I can't stop it. I cling to him, not wanting to let go.

Costin is the first to release me and step back. My leg drops to the floor. There is light trickling into the room from the edge of the curtain. His skin is looking paler than normal. The light might affect me, but the allergy is worse for him.

"I need to go," he says.

"Will I see you tonight?" The question comes out more vulnerable than I intended.

His expression warms. "If you wish it."

"I do."

His hand rises to my face, hovering just shy of touching my cheek. I lean into his palm, accepting the connection. He steps back, pulling me away from the door.

"Be careful today," he murmurs. "Mortimer is desperate."

"I can handle Mortimer."

"I know you can." His thumb traces the curve of my cheekbone, and he turns me slowly as if in our own private dance. "But even cornered rats can be dangerous. Don't underestimate him."

"I'm more worried about the necromancer."

"One problem at a time. Don't forget to drink the blood." With that, he fades into the shadows next to the door. The room feels colder without him, emptier. I instantly want him back.

I open the door, hoping to catch a glimpse of him speeding away, but he's already gone. My heightened senses immediately pick up movement somewhere downstairs. I close my eyes and listen to the multiple heartbeats and the low murmur of faraway voices. There's a faint scent of burnt magic and something else... Fear? Anger? I'm having a hard time deciphering the smell of different emotions, but I'm beginning to see patterns. It's not like being human.

"Tamara..." I hear Conrad's voice whisper from the direction of his old bedroom.

I shut the door, refusing to engage with my dead brother.

I smell blood and find a large goblet full on my nightstand next to a decanter. It's tepid but I don't care as I gulp it down. It coats my mouth like a fine wine and instantly makes me feel more focused.

I catch myself drinking in the mirror and lower the goblet. A trail of blood runs down my chin before dripping onto the floor. I swipe it with the back of my hand. I'm dirty with patches of dirt and dried blood from the night's activities. My hair is a wild tangle around my face. I'm in no state to face anyone, least of all whatever gathering Mortimer has assembled.

I give a soft laugh. My questionable state didn't seem to bother Costin.

SIXTEEN

"...historical precedent cannot be ignored! The Queensland Incident. The Philadelphia fires. Pompeii." Mortimer's nasal tone is pitched higher than usual with what sounds like righteous indignation. "All triggered by unstable hybrids which took decades of meticulous magic to cover up."

"I thought wizards were responsible for Pompeii," a man counters. I recognize the voice and try to place it.

"A hybrid's body was discovered there at the base," Mortimer says, as if that is evidence enough for whatever nonsense he's spouting.

"Wasn't that creature chained?" a woman asks.

I stand in one of the lesser-used corridors, not wanting to join them and knowing I should.

"We've all heard the legends, Mortimer," the

man says, sounding bored. "But legends are often exaggerated."

I picture the man in my head. He was at the council meeting. Elder Birch, supernatural prison warden.

I follow the sound, moving silently down the hallway until I reach one of the smaller meeting rooms. The door is slightly ajar, allowing me to peer inside without being seen.

"The evidence is irrefutable," Mortimer continues, gesturing to a stack of ancient scrolls spread before him. "Hybrid creatures are inherently unstable. The competing supernatural bloodlines war within the host until the resulting madness manifests in destruction."

"But Zephronis must see something we don't," Birch says. "He brought her here instead of a secure facility."

Mortimer stands at the head of an oval table, his thin frame vibrating with self-important intensity as he addresses a group of solemn faced supernaturals. I recognize a couple from the council. Elder Birch with his perpetually narrowed eyes sits close to Madam Britannia. There are several others whose names escape me.

"Zephronis," Mortimer begins only to visibly stop himself. "He is respected, to be sure."

The others glance at each other.

Mortimer seems empowered by their silence. "I can't help but wonder if none of this would have come to pass if he would have upheld the marriage agreement between the Devines and Freemonts. So much could have been avoided. The Freemonts would never have been tricked into joining Thane in his misguided attempt to rebalance magic."

Yeah. That's not what happened. No one was tricked. The Freemonts are treacherous, greedy assholes. No wonder Mortimer likes them.

"Or if he'd let you take her under your care, Birch," Mortimer adds.

"We need more than suspicion if we're going to go against Zephronis," Birch insists. "I'll say it again. Legends are often exaggerated. They cannot be used as evidence."

"Are they? Then how do you explain this?" Mortimer unfurls a larger scroll. I focus my vision as he reveals what appears to be a detailed illustration of a city in ruins. "Queensland, after the hybrid Daina de Silva lost control. Over three thousand supernaturals murdered." He touches a book. "The Philadelphia fires inventory listing magical artifacts that were never recovered all because a hybrid couldn't be contained any other way. There is a reason why hybrids should be forbidden."

A murmur passes through the assembled guests.

"But you're right. Let's look at more recent

events," Mortimer presses, "my own niece's destruction of invaluable magical texts. The library incident is merely a prelude to greater violence. The pattern is clear to anyone willing to see it. Werewolf and vampire natures are not meant to be contained in one body."

My hands curl into fists at my sides. The library incident wasn't a sign of my inherent instability... or not *just*. It was the result of being attacked by Leviathan. A fact Mortimer conveniently omits.

"Speaking of her werewolf nature," another voice interjects, "are we not concerned that she spent the night running with Thane's former pack? If she's forming alliances with werewolves while maintaining her vampire sire bond, she could become a nexus of power that threatens the established order."

How do they know where I was? Has someone been watching me?

"Fair point," Madam Britannia puts forth. "She is already positioning herself at the center of a potential power struggle. The hybrid's very existence disrupts the balance we have maintained for centuries."

"Your concern is noted," a deep voice says from somewhere I can't see. "Davis what are your thoughts? She's your daughter."

I can't breathe. My father is here? I lean forward, trying to see him even as I want to stay hidden.

"I love my daughter," Davis answers. I strain my ears, not wanting to miss a word. "However, I am not ignorant of the fact she was born human and was not prepared for such a fate. As a father, I hate to see her tortured in such a way. It breaks my heart. She's too delicate for the supernatural world. I tried to protect her. I tried."

"Of course you did, Davis," Madam Britannia soothes, as if this conversation is all about my poor, suffering father. "We all know the trials you have faced and how wonderful of a father you've been. None of us doubt that."

I clench a fist. Do I charge in and let them know I'm listening? The urge to fight is strong. I could tear apart the room, squish them like goblins and prove them all right.

Fuck. I can't prove them right. I have to focus on my goal. Freedom.

"She was never meant to be immortal," Mortimer justifies. "As a human, she would only have had a few more years. In fact, for her last birthday she chose the mausoleum that she wanted me to have commissioned for her."

Yeah. That would be inaccurate as well. I did not choose a mausoleum. He gave me a catalog and told me to pick one. It was morbid as fuck.

"It's sad, but these are facts," Mortimer continues. "If it comes to it. That is how we restore order."

"What exactly are you proposing?" Mr. Deep Voice asks.

"Containment," Mortimer answers promptly. "For her own safety and ours. A specially designed chamber where both her vampire and werewolf natures can be suppressed until we determine if balance is possible. Tests need to be run in a controlled environment. Magics would be in control of her. Not the wolves. Not the vampire. Her mausoleum is almost complete. We can keep her there. It is the place she chose."

"And if it isn't enough?" Madam Britannia asks, tapping her nails on the table close to the scroll as if to draw attention to the other hybrid's deeds.

Mortimer's pause speaks volumes. "Then more permanent measures for the hybrid may become necessary."

My blood runs cold. He's talking about killing me. My own uncle is calmly discussing my execution with his supernatural cronies as if it's a regrettable but necessary step.

And my father is saying nothing.

"The hybrid has a name." Astrid's voice cuts through the room like ice.

I shift slightly to see my adoptive mother standing in the doorway opposite my position. She's dressed in a tailored gray suit that makes her look like she's stepped into a board meeting rather than a supernatural gathering. Her hair is pulled back in a severe bun, emphasizing the cold fury in her eyes.

Mortimer falters momentarily before recovering. "Lady Astrid. I didn't expect you to join us."

"Clearly." She steps into the room, her heels clicking sharply against the hardwood floor. Her eyes glance in my direction but don't linger. I don't know if she knows I'm there. "Otherwise you might have waited until I was present before discussing the fate of my daughter."

"Your stepdaughter," Mortimer corrects. "And this is a matter of supernatural security that transcends family sentiment. Davis is the Devine patriarch, and she is his blood."

"Supernatural security." Astrid arches one perfect eyebrow. "How curious that your concerns about security align so perfectly with your personal ambitions."

A tense silence falls over the room. Mortimer's face tightens. "I don't know what you're implying—"

"Don't you?" Astrid moves to the table, placing a slim folder before the assembled council members. "Perhaps these documents will refresh your memory."

Elder Birch reaches for the folder first, opening it

with a frown that deepens as he scans the contents. "What is this?"

"Evidence," Astrid says calmly, "of Mortimer Devine's correspondence with known necromancers over the past twenty years. Including, as you'll note on page seventeen, arrangements regarding the possible acquisition of Tamara's essence upon her death."

Gasps and murmurs ripple through the gathering. I press a hand to my mouth to stifle my own shock. Mortimer has been planning my death for two decades? I try to think about what I might have done to him as an eight-year-old that would have caused this.

"These are fabrications," Mortimer protests, but his voice has lost its conviction.

"Are they?" Astrid produces another folder. "Then perhaps you'd care to explain these financial records showing transfers from your accounts to known associates of Leviathan? It's ironic that something as simple as human email and financial records are what revealed your intentions when you apparently loathe all things mortal."

The room erupts in chaos. I watch as Mortimer's face drains of color, his thin hands trembling as he reaches for the documents.

"You've been working with Leviathan?" Elder Birch demands, rising from his seat. "The very necromancer who threatens the balance you claim to protect?"

"It's not what it appears," Mortimer insists. "These were research grants—"

"For research into hybrid creation," Astrid finishes for him. "Specifically, research into creating a controllable hybrid that could harness multiple supernatural bloodlines. One you could reproduce."

"She's just a human," Mortimer tries to explain. "The family embarrassment. This way her existence could have real meaning."

My mind reels with the implications. Mortimer wasn't just trying to get rid of me. He's been studying me. Using me as a template for something worse.

"You've overstepped, Mortimer," Madam Britannia says coldly. "The council does not look kindly on those who play both sides."

"I was protecting our family's interests!"

"Were you?" Astrid opens a third folder. "Or were you positioning yourself to assume control of Tamara once she was contained? These documents outlining a transfer of power in the event of her incapacitation suggest otherwise."

"That was to take the burden off my brother," my uncle insists as he glances around the room.

One by one, those gathered rise from their seats, their expressions ranging from disgust to fury.

Mortimer stands alone at the head of the table, his carefully constructed alliance crumbling around him.

"This meeting is adjourned," Elder Birch announces. "Mortimer Devine, you are suspended from council activities pending a full investigation into these allegations."

"You can't—"

"We can," Birch cuts him off. "And we have."

Still my father says nothing.

"Astrid, you will send us copies," Birch states.

I take a quick step back and press myself against the wall as they file out of the room from the main door, none of them noticing my presence in the shadowed alcove. Only Astrid remains with Mortimer and my father, gathering her folders with methodical precision.

"You've ruined everything," Mortimer snarls once they're alone. "You have no idea what you have done. What this would have done for our family. All of this has been for the power of the Devine legacy, in service to—"

"No, Mortimer," Astrid replies calmly. "You ruined everything yourself. Did you really think I wouldn't discover your schemes? That I would allow you to sacrifice my daughter for your ambitions?"

"She's not your daughter," he yells. "She's the bastard spawn of your husband's infidelity. A reminder of his betrayal that you've been forced to tolerate."

Astrid goes very still. When she speaks, her voice is barely above a whisper, but it carries a weight that makes even me shiver.

"I pity you, Mortimer. How lonely your life must be, spent clinging to the coattails of your older brother, trying to find meaning in nothingness. You have never understood family, have you? You see only power and position, calculations and advantages. You've never comprehended what it means to love someone beyond yourself. To take responsibility and do the hard things in service to another's well-being." She closes the distance between them, looking down at him with cold contempt. "Motherhood is a choice. Tamara has been my daughter from the moment Lorelai placed her in my arms, just as Anthony is my son by birth. I chose to be a mother, Mortimer, her mother, their mother. I continue to choose her. Can you say the same about anyone in your miserable existence?"

Mortimer has no answer. He stands there, diminished, as if Astrid's words have physically reduced him.

"You will leave this house today," she continues. "Your personal effects will be sent to you. If you attempt to contact any member of this family again, I will ensure the council receives the complete record of your dealings, not just the excerpts I shared today. Think about that. Think about all those letters and emails and scrolls. Centuries worth of evidence."

"Davis, you won't allow this," he says, but there's no conviction in his voice.

"Mortimer, I think Astrid..." My father's voice trails off.

Astrid gives a soft laugh. "Davis has never been the one making these decisions, have you darling?"

Astrid's smile is thin and sharp as a blade.

My father stays quiet.

"We just let the world believes he is," Astrid continues. "The magics do so love the idea of their perfect patriarchy."

With that, she turns and walks toward my door forcing me to quickly retreat down the hall and around the corner. I sag against the wall, my mind racing with everything I've just heard.

Mortimer's betrayal hurts but it doesn't surprise me. He's always treated me as a burden. But Astrid's defense of me, the ruthless efficiency with which she destroyed him, the blunt revelation that she's been the true power behind the Devine name all along shakes me to my core. I mean, I've assumed as much, but to hear it confirmed as a cold hard fact...

All my life, I've been led to believe my father is the central figure in our family's power structure. Davis Devine, the charismatic patriarch whose decisions shaped our world. But it was Astrid, working from the shadows, making the real choices that kept our family secure.

And she chose me. Not out of obligation or appearances, but because she wanted to. She claimed me as her own, defended me as her own, even knowing I wasn't her blood.

I hear the sound of the door closing, followed by the sound of Astrid's heels moving toward me. I try to put distance between us, but her voice stops me. "I'm sorry you had to hear that."

I hang my head and take a deep breath. When I turn to answer, she's gone.

I find myself moving down the hallway in a daze, my mind full of worry. The sun has fully risen, its light filtering through the sides of curtains in golden streams that I instinctively avoid.

I don't know where to go or what to do. I start to head back to the protected wing only to stop in the foyer.

"Costin," I whisper, my heart aching. "I think I need you."

The world tilts and suddenly I'm pulled toward a study in the east wing. This house has so many rooms that I've barely spent time in this one. I'm standing on the red carpet. I turn ready to put my arms around Costin, but he's not there.

"Costin?"

The floor begins to vibrate and a tile near the fireplace lifts from the ground and slides to the side. Costin's hand reaches out of the darkness. It's then I realize I traveled with vampiric speed on my own. I'm too hurt and tired to be pleased by the revelation.

I go to the hole in the floor and sit to drop my legs in. Costin's hands grab my hips and help me down. I drop to the floor in the darkness. It's cool here in the secret room. The ceiling is low but I'm able to stand. I see Costin's face in the shadows as he pulls the tile back into place to hide the light.

His arms wrap around me, and he doesn't speak. For a moment, he holds me. Then, sweeping his arms around me he lifts me into his embrace and carries me to a bed. I feel sleep pulling me in, the kind of deep sleep that makes me think of the dead in their graves. My breathing stops and I wait to see if my lungs will burn for air. They don't. I don't resist the needs of my vampire to find respite from the day.

Costin holds me against him as my thoughts drift.

I am Tamara Devine, daughter of Davis and Lorelai by blood, but Astrid's daughter by choice. Hybrid, vampire, werewolf, mere mortal, all of these things and none of them completely.

Whatever comes next, I'll face it standing firmly on my own two feet. Not because I'm alone, but quite the opposite. Because I finally understand what it means to be loved. It's not all sunshine and roses and happiness. Sometimes it's darkness. It's having those around you willing to make the tough choices, to push you to do what you don't want to. It's support and understanding. And, yes, sometimes it feels like control... but only when I let it.

Tomorrow will bring new challenges, new battles. But for now, in this moment of clarity, I know who I am. Today, that is enough.

SEVENTEEN

"He's coming. He's coming for you."

A nightmare pulls me from my dead sleep with a violent jerk. Sweat slicks my skin as I gasp, panting until I realize I don't need to breathe. My heart hammers against my ribs. In the darkness of Costin's underground sanctuary, I can still see the lingering image of Conrad's face from my dreams. Though, now it's not the mocking ghost who's haunted me since his death, but my brother, desperate and afraid.

"Tamara." Costin's voice cuts through my panic, his cool hand finding mine in the darkness.

The image of my brother fades like it was never there. "I'm sorry. I didn't mean to wake you."

I feel Costin shift beside me on the bed, his body pulling me into reality. "What is it?"

"Conrad," I manage, my voice steadier than I feel. "He was scared and trying to warn me."

Costin doesn't dismiss it as just a dream. Instead, he sits up, instantly alert. Even in the pitch darkness, I can feel the intensity of his gaze. "What did he say?"

Before I can answer, a piercing scream echoes through the estate, followed by the sound of breaking glass. The sanctuary's ceiling trembles, dust raining down on the silky sheets.

Costin is on his feet in an instant, moving with supernatural speed. I'm only a heartbeat behind him. My hybrid reflexes nearly match his vampire quickness as I ready for battle.

The echoes of the scream fade.

"What is it?" I whisper.

"Stay close," Costin orders, as he reaches for the ceiling.

"What about the sun?" I ask. "That sounded like glass. It's not safe."

"It's night," he answers. "Can't you sense it?"

I look up at the ceiling. The prickling warning that came with dawn has faded.

Costin pushes open the hidden door leading up to the study. He jumps up, moving with elegant grace. I try to follow his example, but my foot is less sure, and I stumble a little.

The rancid scent hits me first. It's the copper

tang of old blood mixed with the putrid smell of decay. The study is intact, but chaos unfolds elsewhere in the house. Panicked shouts and breaking furniture mark the unmistakable sound of combat.

He leads me through the corridors. My wolf senses are alert to every sound. My vampire instincts calculate threats. I sense the carnage waiting for us before we enter the main foyer.

Three servants lie dead on the marble floor, their bodies strewn in unnatural angles. My heart breaks to see them. We weren't close, but they were always kind and didn't deserve this fate.

Anthony stands at the base of the grand staircase, his hands glowing with defensive magic as he faces off against the open front door. Beside him, fallen back on the stairs, looking terrified, is Paul.

Paul. Here.

My heart stutters at the sight of him, and I look for Diana. I can't see her. This is no place for a human. I should know better than most.

"Get back!" Anthony shouts, hurling a burst of magic through the front door. I hear something gurgling in the night. "I can't hold them all!"

"Tamara?" Paul's voice is a mix of relief and horror. There's no time to process his reaction.

"Diana?" I yell, looking for where the girl might be hiding.

"She's not here," Anthony answers as Costin and I rush toward them.

"Walking corpses?" Costin asks, scowling.

"They're coming up the drive from the old grave-yard," Anthony says. "We almost didn't make it to the house."

I see the front door isn't open, it's torn off the hinges. Rotting creatures amble through it toward us. The first one wears a coat that might've been red for his burial but is now the color of mold. His hat is smashed against a crooked skull, the kind of lopsided triangle you see in paintings of powdered men posing with muskets.

A woman in a collapsed mobcap limps behind him. Her dress hangs open at the throat, and her arms are nothing, but clawed bone wrapped in paper skin peeling like old bark. Her petticoats drag like a bridal train from hell, barely hanging onto her naked hips. It's something I could have gone a lifetime without seeing.

"Zombies?" The word sounds like a curse. I cover my nose and mouth. The smell is horrible, enhanced by my preternatural senses. I can't look away as I watch the dead walk. Why does it have to be zombies?

Anthony throws magic at them, knocking the creatures back only to have more clamor to get inside. They stumble into each other in a grotesque dance to reach the door.

"Aim for their heads," Costin instructs Anthony.

A moan sounds from one of the servants on the floor and I automatically go to her to help. "Mina?"

"Tamara, no!" Costin shouts. He zooms into me just as I'm reaching to touch the woman's shoulder. The momentum knocks me back.

I struggle against his tight grip. "Costin, what the hell are you—?"

A gargle cuts me off as Mina lifts her head. Half her face is missing and she's oozing blood. Her shoulder juts at odd angles as an arm hangs limp at her side. She jerks violently as she comes at us. What is left of her mouth opens like she wants to bite me.

I don't hesitate. The wolf surges forward. I strike her face propelling her across the foyer. The other now-undead two servants begin struggling to their feet to join the others.

Paul looks terrified as he grabs a marble bust from its stand. I hear his human heart calling to me. He lobs it at undead Frankie at the bottom of the stairs, subduing him. Poor Frankie. The servant was a low-level magic and has only worked for us a couple of years.

Paul's eyes meet mine and I see the moment my new look registers. He stiffens and gives a small shake of his head. There's no time to ease him in.

This is not how I wanted to introduce him to my changes. I wonder if he sees me as a monster now. There's no time to soften the blow.

They won't stop coming. Buttons from a militia jacket clink softly as a soldier emerges, the brass dulled by centuries but still attached. He leads others like a commander. They groan incoherent threats, biting the air as if that is their only driving need.

I come between Anthony and an attacking corpse soldier, my claws already extended. With one savage swipe, I separate its head from its shoulders. The body takes a few trembling steps, hands grasping blindly before dropping to the ground. The disembodied head keeps trying to bite.

Costin is a blur of movement. He grabs reanimated Micah and carries him toward the door. The servant used to hide in the various rooms pretending to clean, so he didn't have to work. He might have been lazy, but he didn't deserve this fate.

Costin bowls over the zombies as he makes his way out of the home. I hear thuds. He's clearing the front steps of attackers before they make it inside. The flow of corpses slows. Moments later, Costin reappears, hands bloody. He grabs Frankie, who is still squirming to get to his feet near Paul and carries him out. I see them go upward only to have Frankie's body drop to the lawn.

"How have zombies breached the property? There are spells protecting the borders," Anthony says in confusion. "We're protected by family magic."

The realization hits me like a slap.

"Mortimer," I growl.

"Why would...?" Anthony shakes his head in confusion.

"Long story short? He's in league with Leviathan," I say. "There was a meeting here earlier. Astrid humiliated him in front of his friends and kicked him out of the family. He has access to the estate's defenses. He knows the blood keys, the structure of the spells, and where the weak points are. If he wanted to hand the house over to Leviathan, it wouldn't be difficult."

Costin materializes beside me, his movements a blur as he tears through three more undead with efficient brutality. He tosses them out the door as soon as he dispatches them. "Zombies are necromancer puppets. Leviathan is here."

"Zombies," Paul whispers. We all glance at him.

"Yeah, man, zombies," Anthony says. Blue magic swirls my brother's fingers as he lifts them toward the door. The broken wood fits itself into place before glowing red. "Fucking necromancers. Of course Leviathan would have a stash of Colonial corpses lying around like wine he's been aging for a special occasion."

"Come on, Paul," I grab his arm and lead him down the stairs. We need to find a safer location. He stares at my clawed hand on his arm, and I try to retract the shift, so I don't scare him.

"You're..." he manages.

"I know. I won't hurt you," I try to sound reassuring. I'd never hurt him.

A cold laugh echoes through the foyer, seeming to come from everywhere and nowhere. Leviathan's disembodied voice fills the space. *"Sorry about my pets. They're not housetrained."*

I hear the corpses outside, banging against the side of the house trying to get in.

"Why are you here?" I demand, positioning myself protectively in front of Paul. Anthony moves to my side, his magic crackling at his fingertips.

"I don't like how we left things unfinished, my little lotus flower," Leviathan's voice replies.

"Ew." I grimace at the nickname.

Costin places his bloody hand on my shoulder and squeezes. I feel the possessiveness through our bond that he tries to hide when he looks at Paul.

"Conrad?" Anthony takes a step forward in surprise.

Conrad's ghost steps from the shadows as if he's been watching the whole time. His eyes are dark pits reflecting the obscurity inside his spirit, but his movements are sluggish as if he's struggling to stay manifested.

"What the hell happened to you?" Anthony demands. I hear the anger and confusion tinging his words. I can't say I blame him. Before his death, Conrad had almost succeeded in killing all the people in this room.

Conrad doesn't speak, but his face turns toward the floor.

Paul cries out in surprise. I turn, but before I can process what's happening, the marble floor beneath Paul's feet ripples like water. A stone hand with a missing finger bursts upward. It grabs his ankles and pulls him downward.

"Paul!" I dive for him, catching his wrist as the stone liquefies around his legs. His face is contorted in terror, eyes wide and pleading.

"Hold on!" I strain against the supernatural pull, my new strength locked in a tug-of-war with whatever magic Leviathan has conjured. Costin is there in an instant, his hands joining mine, but the magic is too strong. Paul is wrenched from our grasp and pulled under, the floor solidifying once more as if nothing had happened.

I beat my hand repeatedly against the marble. "Paul!"

"The old church. Come alone, hybrid," Leviathan says.

"Like hell she will," Costin snarls, his eyes blazing crimson.

"Conrad," Anthony yells, but the ghost fades, not speaking.

The sound of the remaining zombies suddenly stops. I look out the window to see them collapsing into limp piles of decaying flesh. The foyer falls silent except for Anthony's ragged breathing.

"Anthony," I turn to my brother, "why did you bring Paul here?"

Anthony runs an irritated hand through his hair. "You asked him to come. Zephronis sent me to get him from the safe house. You wanted closure. He refused to let Diana come, thank the gods." His eyes dart to the window where the corpses litter the yard. "We arrived just as these things started stumbling onto the property. They crowded the car. I tried to get him out, but—"

"It's not your fault," I cut him off, my mind already racing ahead. "Leviathan was waiting for an opportunity to draw me out. He's been watching the estate with Mortimer's help."

"Yeah, what the hell is up with that?" Anthony frowns. "I'm going to need someone to catch me up."

"Costin can. I have to find the church." I start for the door.

"I know it," Costin says, his voice tight with controlled rage. "It's a deconsecrated site surrounded by a colonial graveyard on the far north edge of the property. You can't go there. It's not safe. It'll be a necromancer's playground. His magic will be stronger there." He motions to the floor. "You saw what he was able to do."

"He said to come alone," Anthony puts forth. "You can't be considering it."

"I won't abandon Paul," I say.

Guilt crushes down on me. In my selfish need for closure with Paul, I dragged him once again into harm's way. When will I learn just to leave him and his daughter be? I'm no good for them. All I do is cause them grief.

"Diana is safe?" I ask Anthony.

"She wears the amulet and is in a safe place," he assures me. "If something happens to her father, she'll be looked after."

I meet Costin's gaze, seeing my own determination reflected in his eyes. "Since when do we do what necromancers tell us to?"

A ghost of a smile touches his lips. "Never."

"We need to move fast." I head for the door. "Paul's human. He won't last long with Leviathan."

Anthony hesitates. "I should tell Astrid—"

"I think she'll get the picture when she sees the

bodies on the lawn," I cut him off. "Call her from the car. Tell her to alert the council."

Outside, the night is unnaturally still. I feel the full moon's approach like a crisp sting in the air. I keep an eye on the corpse piles. They don't move. Anthony's sleek black car waits in the circular drive, engine purring and door hanging open. I see the driver dead on the ground with bite marks.

"Poor Gary," Anthony whispers.

"Leviathan is going to pay," I swear. "It's time he was stopped. Permanently."

Costin takes the driver's seat. I slide into the passenger side while Anthony climbs in back, already dialing Astrid.

"Do you have a plan?" Costin asks as we tear down the driveway, gravel spitting beneath the tires.

"Save Paul. Don't die. Make Leviathan regret being born." I flex my hands, feeling the hybrid strength flowing through me. "I'm making this up as we go."

"Good plan." Costin nods and presses the accelerator to the floor. He drives down an overgrown dirt road that looks like it hasn't felt tires in decades.

EIGHTEEN

The car eats up the miles. Costin drives with the reckless confidence of someone who can't die in a crash. Anthony speaks in rapid, hushed tones to Astrid, explaining the situation. I tune him out, focusing instead on preparing myself. The wolf and vampire inside me seem unusually aligned, both ready for the upcoming battle.

"There," Costin points as we crest a hill. I lean forward to see. I haven't had reason to go to the north end of the property before.

Beneath the cold light of a waxing moon, stands the silhouette of a crumbling church. Its steeple is partially collapsed, and the graveyard surrounding it stretches into the darkness like a sea of crooked headstones. The wrought iron gates are chained shut, but they look ancient and brittle.

Costin brings the car to a sliding stop in front of the fence. The scent hits me first. It's damp earth and the old decay of rotting wood from the church, which makes me wonder how the structure remains standing. One push and the termite temple is likely to crumble.

"Look at the ground," I say quietly, stepping out of the car. My shoes sink in the loose soil, and I feel the sponginess of it underfoot. The land has recently been disturbed. Overturned grave dirt reveals the source of the zombies.

"The veil between worlds is thin here." Costin comes beside me. His nearness steadies something wild inside me that's been coiling tighter with every mile. I wouldn't want to be here alone. Even so, the hairs on the back of my neck lift, and my wolf blood is already bubbling in warning. "It's why necromancers are drawn to places like this. There is easier access to the dead."

Undead, my mind corrects thinking of zombies. And then it hits me. I'm undead now. Does that make us like supernatural cousins or something? Gross.

I'm going to try to not think about it.

"If we don't handle Leviathan, Astrid will." Anthony joins us at the gate. "I wouldn't want to be him or Mortimer tonight after the damage they caused at the estate."

I wrap my hands around the rusted chain and pull. The metal groans, then snaps with surprising ease. The sound is sharp like a starter pistol going off. My stomach clenches. I wait for someone to answer it. Nothing does. Tension knots my shoulders. The gate creaks open, vibrating in my bones like a string pulled too tight.

I step onto the cemetery grounds, and a chill runs through me that has nothing to do with the night air. I sense movement all around us, subtle shifts in the shadows and the soft crunch of dead leaves where nothing visible walks.

"I feel like we're being watched," I murmur.

"We probably are. Focus all your senses," Costin replies, his voice carrying a predatory edge that reminds me he's not just my lover but a centuries-old master vampire. "Nothing is insignificant. Attacks can come in the most unexpected of forms."

My nerves prickle. Invisible eyes track our every step. The magic is heavy here, exerting a gravity that pulls us under.

We move deeper into the graveyard, following a winding path between the tombstones. Magic crackles around my brother's hand, casting a blue light. The glow shimmers off headstones and bones left behind in the churned earth. Wet stone and broken marble carve out grotesque shadows. They're thicker and move against the light.

Giant statues loom among the gravestones. An angel with outstretched wings and a missing finger lords over robed figures with faces worn smooth by time. I point at the hand. "I think that thing grabbed Paul."

"When we were kids, we used to dare each other to spend the night in places like this," Anthony tells Costin. "We brought Conrad here and scared the shit out of him. He would have been, oh, eleven or twelve? Anyway, he broke the hand off that angel, and we convinced him he was cursed."

"I never..." I look around, shaking my head. "I don't remember any of that."

"You were never invited. Sorry, Tam-tam," Anthony says.

"Though, to tell you the truth, if we had known what really lurked in the dark," he continues, "we would have never slept with the lights off."

"You still don't sleep with the lights off," I tease, trying to keep my voice light despite the tension coiling in my stomach.

A twig snaps to our left. We freeze, all senses alert.

Nothing moves.

Then, a low sound rumbles the dirt at our feet. The vibration hums up my legs, a slow-building chill that climbs my spine. The ground begins to crack and bulge, as something beneath the surface struggles to break free. The wolf snarls. The vampire tenses.

"Move!" Costin orders, grabbing my arm and pulling me back just as a bony hand erupts from the soil near where I was standing.

All around us, the earth pulses and heaves. Rotting hands claw their way up from disturbed graves. Corpses in various states of decay begin to emerge, their hollow eye sockets somehow fixing on us with hungry intent.

"Come on, seriously? More fucking zombies? This seems excessive," I mutter, backing up until I'm standing between Costin and Anthony. I didn't think the smell could get any worse, but I was wrong. Thankfully I don't have to breathe. I can't say the same for my brother. Anthony clears his throat and presses a hand to his face.

Dirt rains down from the reanimated bodies as the dead drag themselves free. They lock onto us with predatory need.

"Next time I get to pick the activity," Anthony grumbles. "Beheading zombies is not my idea of a good time."

The first zombie lurches toward us, its movements jerky but surprisingly agile. I don't wait for it to reach us. I launch myself forward, my hybrid speed turning the world into a momentary blur. My claws extend and I tear through the corpse with a violent blow, separating its torso from its legs. The top half keeps coming, pulling itself forward with determined arms.

"Head!" Anthony shouts, sending a blast of magic that obliterates the zombie's skull. The body finally collapses, lifeless.

More rise, forming a shambling wall between us and the church. I bare my fangs. The wolf and vampire are in perfect agreement for once. These walking stink bombs need to die... again.

Costin moves like air, flowing between the undead with deadly grace. He tears through rotting flesh and brittle bone with ease. He doesn't waste energy or motion, each strike precise and fatal.

I find myself trying to follow his lead, but I lack his elegance. I move more like a beast trampling a field than air. I sense a zombie before I see it, and spin to remove its head. The hybrid strength flows through me.

Anthony provides support, his magic blasting paths through the thickest clusters of undead. But for every zombie we destroy, two more seem to rise from the earth.

"How many people could they possibly bury here?" Anthony yells.

As if answering him in the most horrific way possible, a large mound begins to rise under the angel. The stone creature tips over and crashes down as a mass grave is unearthed. A tangle of bodies fights to the surface, climbing over each other. Anthony tries to contain it with magic, but it doesn't seem to have an effect. The sound of their fury is deafening.

"We need to get to the church," I shout, ducking under a swinging arm and retaliating with an upward slash that splits a zombie from groin to crown.

"This way," Costin calls, clearing a path toward a narrow gap in the growing horde.

We make a break for it, fighting our way through. The stench is overwhelming when I breathe out of old habit, but I push through, focusing on the church. Paul is in there. I have to reach him.

A skeletal hand catches my ankle, its bony fingers digging into my flesh hard enough to draw blood. I stumble, nearly going down amid the grasping dead. But before I fall, Costin is there, ripping the skeleton apart and hauling me back to my feet without breaking stride.

"Thanks," I gasp, immediately back in the fight.

"Always," he replies, his eyes briefly meeting mine with an intensity that steals my breath. My heart is beating fast and I'm ashamed to realize I'm partly enjoying myself.

We reach the church steps, battling through the

last ring of zombies. Costin shoves himself against the heavy wooden doors, which fly open with a crash. We tumble inside. Anthony immediately turns to slam the doors shut behind us with his magic. Undead hands thrust through the gap, but he forces the doors closed with a final surge, dropping a heavy beam across them as a makeshift barricade.

The banging starts immediately, dozens of fists pounding against the wood. I look around half expecting the building to fall down on top of us. It's surprisingly stable, more so that it looked on the outside.

"That won't hold them long," Anthony pants, leaning against the wall. Dirt and blood mar his body. He pushes up his dirty sleeve and swipes his forearm at the blood on his face. "You so owe me a spa package after this, Tam."

I take stock of our surroundings. The church interior is a ruin of collapsed pews and fallen rafters. Moonlight streams through holes in the roof, casting eerie patterns on the dusty floor. At the far end, where the altar would have been, a faint glow emanates from beneath the slatted floor.

"There." I point. "Underground."

We pick our way through the debris, alert for traps. The glow leads us to a section of the floor that has been cleared of rubble. In its center is a stone slab with a metal ring.

"A crypt," Costin says, his voice tight. "How uninspired."

"Allow me," I say, bending to grasp the ring. The stone is heavy, but my new strength makes lifting easy. It swings upward, revealing a set of narrow stone steps descending into green-tinged darkness.

The stench of rot is stronger here, mingled with something else.

"What is that?" I ask, glancing at my brother.

"I had a class that smelled like that. Alchemical compounds," Anthony says. "Alchemy. The basis for most necromancer magic."

I wrinkle my nose but can't hesitate. Paul needs me.

"I'll go first," I say, already placing my foot on the top step.

Costin catches my arm, his grip firm. I nod. He blurs as he disappears into the hole to scout ahead.

Anthony and I descend side by side.

"I know men and that one is crazy in love with you," Anthony whispers. I didn't need him to tell me that, but I like hearing it.

"The feeling is mutual," I admit, keeping my voice soft to match his. "Thank you for coming with me. Thank you for being my brother and always protecting me."

"Stop thanking me. It sounds too much like a goodbye," he answers with a wry grin. "Tokens of appreciation will be accepted in the form of spa vacations and hot escorts named Hans."

I can't help but smirk at his deflective humor.

The stairs lead to a vast underground chamber that bears no resemblance to a simple crypt. It's more like an unholy laboratory, with glass containers lining the walls, each holding floating specimens I can't bear to examine too closely. Many look like the orb I saw Leviathan carry Conrad's spirit away in. Arcane symbols cover the floor and ceiling. They glow with that same eerie green light.

And at the center of it all, chained on his back to a stone altar, is Paul. I see bruises forming on his cheek and neck.

"Tamara," he calls, struggling against his bonds. "Run. It's a trap!"

"Of course it's a trap," Leviathan's voice echoes through the chamber before he steps from the shadows. He looks exactly as I remember him. Unremarkable features somehow convey ancient malice. His simple black clothing is a stark contrast to the elaborate setup around him. "But that doesn't make the invitation any less sincere."

"Let him go," I demand, stepping forward. Costin moves with me, his presence at my side a reminder that I'm not facing this alone.

"You brought uninvited guests. How rude,"

Leviathan tsks though he hardly looks surprised. Or concerned.

"Paul has nothing to do with this," I insist.

"On the contrary," Leviathan smiles, the expression never reaching his eyes. "Your human pet is the perfect bait. He is your weakness. And look, here you are, right on cue. He'll make a nice first soldier for our army, don't you think?"

"Tamara, get out of here," Paul yells, struggling against his restraints.

"Hush," Leviathan draws his hand down and Paul instantly gasps and passes out.

"If you wanted me here, you could have made it a little more welcoming," I growl. "No need for the zombie apocalypse upstairs."

I glance at Paul to make sure he's still breathing.

Leviathan chuckles. "Where's the fun in that? Besides, my friends needed the exercise, and I needed to see what you are capable of."

He gestures toward the shadows on his right, where more figures begin to emerge. These aren't simple zombies. They're Egyptian mummies straight out of a museum. They hold spears and look ready to pounce. They move to stand behind us, forcing us deeper into the main chamber of the crypt.

Then, almost reverently, Leviathan gestures to his left. "Come say hello to your new queen. Don't be shy."

The creatures who come forward are the worst yet. They move with purpose, their bodies twisted and malformed. Some have extra limbs and misshapen features. Others seem to be amalgamations of different creatures entirely. All of them watch us with intelligent, hungry eyes.

"Do you like them?" Leviathan asks, pride evident in his voice as he motions toward the mutants. "Some of my earlier experiments. Not as elegant as you, of course, but serviceable in their way."

"You're sick." Anthony spits on the ground.

"I'm a visionary," Leviathan corrects. "And soon, I'll have the final piece I need."

His gaze fixes on me with uncomfortable intensity.

"I will never be your queen," I swear.

My words seem to upset some of the mutants who groan incoherently in protest. Leviathan lifts his hand as if to calm them.

"This crap never works," I press on, glancing around the crypt for an advantage. "Thane and Elizabeth tried to rebalance power by stripping it from the world. They failed. Draakmar tried to rise up. That dragon's been tamed. Conrad tried to kill everyone. He failed. What makes you think you'll be any different?"

I'm not really listening to what I'm saying. I'm

just trying to buy time. I don't know how we're going to get out of this. Zombies are blocking the way up. We're able to take them down one on one, but as a horde they'll easily overrun us by sheer force. I don't see another way out of the crypt. Who knows how many more creatures Leviathan has hidden around here.

My eyes fall on the red orbs holding spirits. Leviathan let my brother out of his cage, but who else does he have in his collection? He's called on to captured vengeful ghosts.

"I told Elizabeth she couldn't trust the wolf, but you know women, always wanting more." Leviathan looks at Costin as if he'll agree with him.

Costin says nothing. I feel him through our bond. He's biding his time until we start fighting again.

"Draakmar rising was a surprise. Your grandfather kept that prophecy close to the chest. I was worried he'd ruin my plans, but then my prophecy was stronger." Leviathan waves his hand in dismissal. "And sweet, stupid Conrad. He was a useful tool, but he's served his purpose. I don't have much use for him anymore. He doesn't have much essence left."

Anthony's magic flares in warning.

Leviathan turns a sharp eye on him and lifts his own hand. The mummy guards take a menacing step forward. Anthony smothers his magic.

As if summoned, Conrad's spirit materializes beside the altar. He looks different. I can see his eyes through the black pits of his sockets. He appears less monstrous, and more like the brother I remember. His form flickers, as if he's struggling to maintain it.

"What are you doing to him?" I demand.

"Consider it a coronation gift." Leviathan spreads his arms. "I'll let you kill him."

Conrad stares at me. His mouth moves but there's no sound.

I know what he's done. Conrad brought this fate on himself. Asshole or not, he's still my brother.

"*Ego sum avis stultus,*" I whisper.

"Uh, Tamara?" Anthony looks at me in concern. "That doesn't make sense."

Costin places his hand on my shoulder. I can feel he wants me to let this go. I can't. Anything would be better than this purgatory.

"Release Conrad," I order. "Send him to his afterlife."

"Him for you," Leviathan says. "Your power. Your potential. Your very essence. You're the perfect vessel, Tamara. A successful hybrid vampire and werewolf, with latent magical ability in your bloodline. Do you have any idea how rare you are? How valuable?"

"You can't have her," Costin's voice is deadly.

We're not going to make it out of here alive.

Conrad's spirit is flickering. I stare at Paul's eyes as they flutter open. He doesn't stand a chance. The mutants will tear him apart before we can fight our way to him. I hear the zombies break into the church. Their fumbling becomes louder.

"Me for them," I negotiate.

"Deal," Leviathan snatches the offer.

"What?" Anthony gasps. "No!"

"Tamara," Costin warns. I feel his anger surging through our bond like lightning.

I turn to Anthony, pleading with my gaze. "Take Paul. Get him to his daughter and send them far away from me. Somewhere safe."

He wants to argue but instead he nods once. The flash of understanding in his eyes tells me he knows I have a plan. Or at least I hope he thinks I do.

"How touching," Leviathan mocks. "The hybrid sacrifices herself for the humans she loves." He waves his hand, and Paul's chains fall away with a clatter. "Take him and go. We'll find a new test subject."

Costin steps closer to me, his body tense. "I'm not leaving you," he whispers, his voice so low only I can hear it.

"You have to," I reply just as quietly. "Get Anthony and Paul out safely. I need you to protect them. Do this for me. You owe me."

The mention of his broken promise hits him like

a slap across the face. It's a low blow to call in the debt now, but it's a manipulation I need.

"I've lost too many people I love," Costin says, his voice cracking with emotion. "I won't lose you too."

I reach up to touch his face. "Trust me."

The conflict in his eyes is palpable. The master vampire who's lived centuries, who's controlled and commanded and conquered, now faced with the one thing he can't dominate. My choice.

"I'll come back for you," he promises, his eyes burning red with intensity.

"I know."

Leviathan gestures impatiently. "Enough with the tearful goodbyes. I have an empire to build and a queen to crown."

Anthony helps Paul off the altar. He looks disoriented, his eyes glazed with confusion and fear.

"Tamara, don't do this," Paul pleads weakly. "Whatever he wants—"

"Go," I tell him firmly. "Live your life. Take care of Diana. Forget about me. Forget about all of this."

He stops near me, searching my face. His eyes are so kind. They remind me of all the things I can never have. The man has the biggest heart of anyone I have ever met. A part of me will always love him.

There is so much he wants to say, but he slowly

shakes his head. He doesn't need to say goodbye. I know.

"Call off your zombies, Leviathan," Anthony says.

The zombies above give one last series of thuds and suddenly go silent.

Anthony leads Paul toward the stairs. The mummies part to let them pass, spears held at the ready in case they try anything. Costin hesitates, his eyes lock with mine.

"If you truly love her," Leviathan says to him, "you'll respect her choice. Isn't that what you've been trying to learn, vampire? That love means letting go?"

The necromancer chuckles at his own wit.

The words hit their mark. Costin's jaw tightens, but he takes a step back. "This isn't over," he tells Leviathan, his voice deadly. "If you harm her—"

"You'll what? Kill me?" Leviathan laughs. "Death is my domain. I walk its borders as you walk through night. There is nothing you can threaten me with that I don't already command."

Conrad's spirit flickers more violently now, his form becoming increasingly transparent. He looks at me with eyes that somehow seem clearer, more present than they've been since his death. His body contorts in pain.

"Tamara," he manages to say, his voice a ghostly whisper.

"Go," I tell Costin one last time. "Protect Paul and Anthony."

Reluctant, he turns and follows them toward the stairs. Once they reach the top, Leviathan closes the stone slab with a flick of his wrist, sealing me in the crypt with him and his grotesque collection of failed experiments.

Conrad's fading spirit looks as if it's crying as he clutches his stomach. I can't hear him, but I see his pain increasing.

"And now," Leviathan's smile makes my skin crawl, "let's begin."

"You promised to release my brother," I remind him, stalling for time. I got Paul and the others out of here. That's about as far as my plan went. I need to know what I'm dealing with before I make my move.

"Did I?" Leviathan tilts his head. "I don't recall making that specific promise. Are you sure? After all he did? I've watched his sins. He's not worthy of your compassion."

Conrad's mouth moves like he's begging me for help. I might be a fool. I know Conrad betrayed me, but I can't leave him like this. I'm also not about to start taking life advice from a necromancer.

"Send his spirit somewhere nice," I answer.

Leviathan reaches into his pocket and pulls out a

small crystal orb, much like the one I saw him use to capture Conrad's spirit. "A gesture of good faith to prove I'm not such a bad guy."

He holds the orb up to Conrad's flickering form. Conrad's spirit begins to disintegrate, particles of his essence streaming toward the crystal.

"No!" I lunge forward, but two of the mummy guards block my path with crossed spears. "That's not release. You're trapping him again!"

"I'm preserving what's left of him," Leviathan corrects. "His essence is nearly depleted from all the times I've called on him to do my bidding. He doesn't have enough left to maintain form much longer."

Conrad's eyes find mine as his spirit continues to dissolve.

"I'm sorry," he mouths, the words barely audible. "For everything."

Something inside me breaks. Despite everything Conrad did—*the betrayal, the attempts on my life, the pain he caused*—he's still my brother. The boy who played with me when no one else would. The friend who understood what it meant to be human in a supernatural world. And despite everything, I can't let him go like this.

I feel a surge of power unlike anything I've ever experienced. It's not just the vampire's cold strength or the wolf's primal fury, it's deeper.

"No!" I roar, the sound echoing through the chamber with supernatural force.

The mummies falter. The mutant creatures back away.

I focus every ounce of my power on Conrad's fading form. I don't know if what I'm attempting is possible, but I have to try.

"Conrad," I call to him, reaching out not just with my voice but with something profound, something tied to blood and family and shared history. "I forgive you. I release you."

For a moment, nothing happens.

Then Conrad's spirit flares with sudden brightness, momentarily stabilizing. His eyes widen in surprise, then understanding. A smile, a real smile not the mocking grin of his ghost, spreads across his face.

"Thank you, Tam-tam," he whispers.

Conrad's ghost suddenly explodes in a blinding flash of light. Not dissolving into Leviathan's orb, but expanding outward, filling the chamber with radiance. The force of it knocks Leviathan backward, the crystal orb flying from his hand and shattering against the stone wall. The other orbs clank together under the current, some rolling from their displays to smash onto the floor. The red lights are pulled toward Conrad.

Leviathan screams in anger, waving his arms as the lights zip past him.

The spirits trapped inside the remaining orbs surge together, gaining strength from each other, breaking free of their containers all around the room. Glass shatters everywhere as orbs explode, releasing their captives.

Lights coalesce into a swirling vortex above the altar, and within it, I catch glimpses of the souls that Leviathan has trapped over the years. Their expressions are a mixture of surprise and relief.

"No! What have you done?" Leviathan screams, his composure breaking. He raises his hands, dark energy gathering at his fingertips as he tries to contain the escaping spirits. He crawls onto the altar after them, swiping his hands through the air as he tries to catch them. "I will see to it you pay for this!"

He flings his hands, but nothing happens. It's as if his magic is gone.

The vortex of souls descends on him like a hurricane, enveloping him in whirling light. I hear his cries for help as the spirits he's tortured and imprisoned for centuries take their revenge.

I back away toward the stone slab, searching for a way out. But before I can reach it, the vortex suddenly expands, engulfing the entire chamber. The light is blinding, the noise deafening.

Then, silence.

When my vision clears, I find myself alone in the crypt. Leviathan and his creatures are gone, as are the spirits. Only broken glass orbs and scattered alchemical equipment remain.

Conrad is gone too, truly gone this time. I don't know why, but I feel it deep inside. That hard knot that's been sitting inside my stomach since I discovered the truth has finally eased. It doesn't feel like loss. It feels like closure.

I move to the stairs, but before I can ascend, the ground begins to shake violently. The church above is collapsing, the crypt beginning to cave in. Dust and small stones rain down from the ceiling.

I race up the steps, pushing against the stone slab. It won't budge. Something heavy has fallen on top of it from above.

"Costin!" I scream, hoping he's still nearby. "Anthony!"

No answer comes. Just the growing rumble as the church continues to collapse.

I press my hands against the stone, feeling panic rise in my throat. I'm trapped underground as the building falls, with no way out and no one to hear me.

Unless...

I close my eyes, focusing on the bond I share with Costin. I've never tried to use it this way before, never tried to send a message through it rather than just feeling his presence.

"Costin," I project, pouring all my strength into the connection between us. *"Help me."*

The rumbling grows louder. A large crack appears in the ceiling of the crypt. Time is running out.

And then, like an answer to a prayer I didn't know how to make, I feel him. The warm pulse of recognition, the tug of the sire bond responding to my call.

He heard me.

But will he reach me in time?

The first section of the ceiling caves in, and I throw myself against the wall to avoid being crushed. The rest won't hold much longer.

As the world collapses around me, one thought fills my mind.

Conrad is free.

And soon, one way or another, I will be too.

NINETEEN

Costin doesn't reach me.

Darkness, complete and absolute, surrounds me. Rubble pins my arms at my sides. The weight of the collapsed church presses down on me from all directions, dust filling my lungs with each unnecessary breath I take. Old habits die hard, even for the undead. I cough, the sound muffled by the tons of stone and wood entombing me.

Had I needed to breathe, I'd be suffocating. Instead, I lie trapped and hacking in my grave. My heart beats faster as I start to panic. Wouldn't this be a fitting end to my new immortal life? Trapped in a location everyone has forgotten for centuries?

No. Costin would never leave me down here. I have to stay calm.

The crypt's ceiling has partially collapsed, but the ancient stone walls have held, creating a pocket of space barely large enough for me to move. I try to find my bearings so I can dig out.

I push against a beam that's pinning my leg, feeling the wood splinter under my hybrid strength. Pain shoots through my calf as blood flows back into the crushed muscle. The shift in wood makes my tiny room unstable and the beam cracks in half. Another section of ceiling gives way with a sickening thud. The space is getting smaller by the minute. I roll to avoid being crushed, pressing myself against the cold stone wall.

I close my eyes, trying to calm the panic rising in my chest. The vampire in me wants to conserve energy and wait patiently. The wolf wants to dig, claw, and fight its way out. And somewhere between them, the girl I used to be just wants to scream.

My tomb ceiling continues to crumble. The falling stone shifts the broken beam in my direction. I cry out, pushing my hands up to stop it from dropping on me. A thick splinter aims its sharp edge at the center of my chest only to hover inches away like a stake. This looks a lot like how you kill vampires, and the only thing between me and death is my werewolf strength locked in a bench press.

"Costin," I whisper, focusing on our bond. It's

been a long night of fighting and I haven't fed. My arms are already trembling a little. I'm not sure how long I can hold this position.

I feel him frantically coming for me, but I don't think he will reach me beneath the rubble in time.

"Costin," I insist, hoping he can hear my words. "I need you to do something for me."

"I'm coming," he says.

"No, listen, I need you to make sure Paul, Diana, and Lorelai are protected without them knowing. They've had enough supernatural interference in their lives. I need to know they're safe from—"

"Tamara," Costin interrupts. I feel his irritation. *"We can talk about this later."*

My arms shake and the stake drops closer to my chest. "Tell Anthony that Conrad's spirit has moved on. It's over. Tell him thank you. He's the best brother I could have asked for. Tell him to forget about everyone else and find his own happiness. He'll know what I mean."

"You tell him," Costin counters.

The beam is getting heavier.

"Costin, I love you. I..." The stake is touching my chest now. I can't wiggle right or left with any significance to avoid its threat. *"Just, I forgive you and love you."*

I think of Costin. His face, solemn and watchful, as he looked after me my whole life. I know it started as an obligation to my grandfather, a promise to his old friend to protect me and guide me through a prophecy. He looked at me like I was an annoying kid. I looked at him like he was an old monster. But these last months it evolved into something more. It's like he finally saw me as a capable woman, and I saw the man hiding in the vampire's shadow. That night everything changed between us, when the dam broke and we came together for the first time, it was angry and raw, and I still feel his skin against mine. I wouldn't change that moment for anything.

The memories give me strength. I focus on our bond, pulling on it like a lifeline. "Hurry."

I push against a fallen beam, muscles straining. It doesn't budge. I push harder, summoning every ounce of hybrid strength. The wood groans but holds fast. I feel it press into my skin. Blood trickles down between my breasts. My heart hammers violently.

Frustration boils over, and I shove hands against the beam as hard as I can. "Move!"

To my shock, the beam trembles, then slides sideways as if pushed by invisible hands. It wedges itself next to my thigh, bracing the ceiling just enough to allow me to rest. I drop my hands to my legs and look down at the spreading bloodstain on my shirt. That was too close.

I stare at my hands in disbelief. Did I just...?

No. It can't be.

I focus on a chunk of stone near my feet. "Move," I whisper, concentrating.

Nothing happens.

I close my eyes, thinking of how it felt when Conrad's spirit exploded in light, when all those trapped souls broke free. The raw power that surged through me in that moment. I reach for that feeling, that connection.

"Move!"

The stone skitters across the floor.

Fucking hell.

I did that. I just moved something with my mind.

Before I can process what this means, dust rains down from above as something heavy impacts the debris. I hear muffled voices, and the scrape of stone against stone.

"Tamara?" Costin's voice, closer now. "Tamara, answer me!"

"Here," I shout, hope surging through me. I look at the staked beam next to me as I press a hand over the wound in my chest. My fingers are covered in blood. I'm not healing. "Careful! It's unstable."

The sounds of digging intensify. I hear Anthony's voice now too, and others I don't recognize. They're arguing about the best approach, worried about causing another collapse.

A shaft of moonlight suddenly pierces the darkness as a hole appears above me. Dust motes dance in the silver beam, and I've never seen anything so beautiful in my life.

"I see her!" Costin's face appears in the opening, his eyes glowing red with intensity. He reaches into the hole, but his hand is several feet away. "Can you get to me?"

I close my eyes and try to make my vampire body travel like I did once before, but I feel too weak.

"Tamara, hold on. We're almost there."

"I'm not going anywhere," I reply, with a wry laugh.

Costin's voice becomes distant as he says, "I smell blood. She's badly hurt."

My head drops back weakly and all I can do is watch. The hole widens as they clear more debris. I can see Costin working frantically, his movements a blur of supernatural speed. Anthony's hands glow blue with magic as he stabilizes the remaining structure around us. And to my surprise, I see Sully's massive form, his werewolf strength making short work of the larger pieces of rubble.

"Careful," someone warns as the structure groans.

"I've got it," Anthony replies, his magic creating a web of support.

Finally, the opening is large enough. Costin reaches down, his hand extended toward me. I move to my knees and stretch up a bloody hand, our fingers almost touching. Just a few more inches…

The rubble shifts beneath me, and I fall. Costin doesn't hesitate. He leaps down into the hole, landing beside me with catlike grace. There's barely enough room for the both of us but he manages to wrap his arms around me, pulling me tight against his chest.

"I thought I'd lost you," he whispers, his voice rough with emotion.

"You can't get rid of me that easily," I reply, burying my face in his neck as I drop weakly against him. I close my eyes and take in his scent.

He pulls back just enough to look at me, his eyes scanning my face, my body, cataloging every scratch and bruise. His hand cups my cheek, thumb gently wiping away a streak of dust. Then his mouth is on mine, desperate and hungry, as if he needs to physically confirm I'm alive.

I kiss him back with equal fervor, uncaring of our audience above. In this moment, nothing exists but us and the solid reality of his body against mine, the taste of him on my lips, the pulse of our bond flowing between us stronger than ever.

Someone clears their throat above us. Reluctantly, Costin breaks the kiss.

"Perhaps we could continue the reunion somewhere less likely to collapse?" Anthony suggests dryly.

Costin smiles against my lips.

With little effort, he pushes me toward the opening. I start to protest that I can climb out by myself, but the truth is, my leg is throbbing, my arms are weak, and I'm not sure I can support my weight.

Anthony and Sully help pull me out. A few wolves are with him, but I don't know their names. Once I'm clear, Costin scoops me into his arms and carries me past the rubble before setting me down gently on the ground. Corpses are scattered around the graveyard, a reminder of what Leviathan did.

"Paul?" I ask, looking around. "Is he okay?"

"Safe," Anthony assures me, dropping on the ground next to us. "He's passed out in the back seat of the car."

Relief floods me. At least I didn't get him killed. Again.

"We should go," Sully says, his massive form silhouetted against the moonlight. "This place is unstable, and there could be more of those things."

He means zombies. I glance around the graveyard, but the undead are truly dead once more. The ground is torn up where they emerged, but nothing stirs in the moonlight. Whatever power animated them died with Leviathan.

Or at least, I hope it did.

"Thank you," I tell Sully.

He nods. "I told you. A threat to one of us is a threat to all of us."

With a sharp whistle, he tilts his head and orders the wolves to leave. The werewolves take off across the graveyard. A part of me jolts, instinctively wanting to follow them, but I'm too exhausted.

"See you at the full moon," Sully says to me with a grin.

As he heads for his bike, Anthony goes next to him as the Alpha pulls on his driving gloves. He whispers something low, then reaches to shake Sully's hand.

Sully looks at him, and for the briefest moment, something unspoken passes between them. Sully's gloved hand comes up to take Anthony's, and his eyes flash with gold. My brother doesn't flinch, just gives a small nod.

Sully climbs onto his bike, starts the engine, and peels off into the night without another word.

Anthony watches him go.

"Can you walk?" Costin asks, his arm slipping around my shoulders.

I test my injured leg, wincing. "I'll manage."

"You don't have to," he says softly, brushing back my hair. The tenderness in his voice makes my chest ache.

I turn my face into his palm, pressing my lips against his skin. "I thought I was going to die down there."

"I would have torn the world apart to find you," he says, and I know it's not hyperbole. The master vampire who's lived through centuries would have reduced the church to dust with his bare hands if necessary.

"I know," I whisper.

He leans forward, his forehead touching mine. "I'm sorry I left you."

"You had to. I made you."

"Never again." His voice is fierce with promise. "I won't leave you again, Tamara. Not for anything."

The words settle between us. I close the distance, capturing his lips in a kiss that's gentle at first, then deepens with building hunger. His hand slides into my hair, cradling my head as if I'm something precious.

The bond pulses between us, but it feels different now. It's less like a chain and more like a bridge connecting two equal forces. I don't feel dominated or controlled. I feel understood, as if Costin is my missing piece that makes me whole.

Motorcycle engines rev in the distance, interrupting us.

When we break apart, his eyes have shifted to deep crimson, betraying his need. I feel an answering hunger rise inside of me. It's not just for blood, but for him. For the deep connection we share.

"Home," I say softly. "Take me home."

I lean into him, accepting his support as we stand.

We make our way slowly through the graveyard, past the broken iron gates to where our vehicle is parked. Anthony waits by the car. The sleek black vehicle somehow survived the zombie apocalypse unscathed.

"Let's get back to the estate," my brother says. "We need to report to Astrid and have her check on Paul before we send him back to his daughter."

"You need blood," Costin says, his eyes flicking to my injured leg and chest. "I'll go ahead and get it ready."

I start to answer but Costin is already stepping away.

"Get her home," he tells Anthony.

My brother waves his hand in dismissal before sliding into the driver's seat. I glance in the back window to see Paul laying on the seat, eyes closed. Once I'm in the car, the adrenaline that's been keeping me going finally ebbs. I slump in the passenger seat, exhaustion settling into my bones.

"Hell of a night, huh?" Anthony starts the car but doesn't immediately drive away. Instead, he turns to face me fully. "What happened down there, Tamara? After we left?"

"Later," I reply. "Right now I just need a moment to process everything."

Anthony sighs and stares at the church. "I can't believe Mortimer was helping Leviathan this whole time. I heard about necromancers fueling their power with the dead, but did you see how many spirits he had trapped? Do you think our uncle knew what he was doing to Conrad?"

"Drive," I insist. "I don't want to be here anymore."

The car pulls away from the church.

I can see Anthony isn't going to stop asking questions until I tell him. I take a deep breath and tell him everything about Conrad's final moments, the release of the trapped spirits, and Leviathan's apparent destruction.

"There's something else." I hesitate before mentioning my new ability. "When I was trapped, I moved things. Without touching them."

Anthony gives a small smile, but I sense his surprise. "Telekinesis?"

"I don't know what to call it. It just happened. Like the power that freed Conrad somehow stayed inside me."

He's quiet for a moment, processing. "I mean, maybe the spirits Leviathan had imprisoned transferred their residual power to you when you freed them."

"Really? How is it even possible? I've never been able to harness my own magic."

"In the supernatural world, many things are possible that shouldn't be. You're a Devine. Our blood was made to carry magic." He reaches out to tousle my hair and I swat him away. "About damn time, if you think about it. We always knew mortals were slow on the uptake but talk about a late bloomer."

"You know, this is the first time I've ridden in a car with you driving. This feels more dangerous than fighting zombies."

"What are you implying?" He smirks.

"I think it's pretty obvious you're a pampered golden boy." I keep a straight face. "Or was it pretty little mama's boy?"

"You're an asshole," Anthony laughs.

I chuckle. "Guess that runs in our Devine blood as well."

"In all seriousness though, Tam-tam, when we were kids and I promised we'd find a way to make you immortal, I didn't mean for you to do *all* the ways. No need to show everyone up to become a vampire-werewolf-magic. One would have sufficed."

I know it's his way of saying he's glad I'm alive.

"I love you, too, brother," I answer.

As we approach the estate gates, our teasing fades and we both sit straighter in our seats. Something feels off. The spells along the borders are dimmer than usual. It's a bad sign in a house as security conscious as the Devine estate.

"Does this feel right to you?" I ask.

Anthony's grip tightens on the steering wheel. "No. I sense it too."

We cautiously pass through the gates. The house is eerily quiet. Zombies still lay on the lawn from earlier in the night. The broken front door is ajar. There are no lights in the windows. Even the fountain in the circular drive is silent.

"Did the electricity go out?" I frown. "Is that even possible?"

Anthony parks and Costin appears at my window before I can open the door. My leg and chest have already begun to heal. The vampire blood in my veins works its magic, but I'm still unsteady. He helps me from the car.

"Did something else happen after we left?" I ask Costin.

"I checked most of the house. I didn't find anyone inside," he answers. "No bodies beyond our little friends out here where we left them."

"Did Astrid sound worried when you talked to her?" I ask Anthony.

"She sounded like Astrid," he says. "Pissed at

Leviathan and Mortimer about the corpses on the lawn and the broken artwork. She was getting it cleaned up. I don't think she'd ever leave the house like this. Not willingly."

"Do you think Mortimer came back?" I suggest.

"No," Costin says, his voice tight. "This was Elizabeth."

My blood runs cold. "How do you know?"

"Her scent is everywhere. And this—" He holds up a ruby pendant. "She left it deliberately. She wants us to know it was her."

"Your sister?" Anthony frowns. "Why would Astrid go with her?"

I don't think she would. At least not willingly.

"Anthony, I need you to get Paul to safety." I grab my brother's hand and squeeze.

"What? No, I'm not—"

"Please, Anthony," I beg. "Take him and come back. We'll go see what Elizabeth wants."

Anthony takes my arm. "I don't trust her."

"That's because you're smart." I pat his hand. "Please. You're the only one I trust to handle this. We can't be in the sun."

He sighs and nods, going back around the car. "Just be safe."

Costin positions himself in front of me as we enter. Even though he said he didn't find anyone when he searched the house, he's tense and ready for attack.

The foyer is empty, but I can smell blood. I don't know if it was from our fight with the zombies or something else. I listen to the silence. Most of the staff had been sent away when they brought me back here, and three of the servants were murdered by zombies. It's possible the rest ran off from this house of terrors. I know I would have.

We move deeper into the home, following the scent of blood to the study. The door is splintered, hanging off its hinges. Inside, furniture is overturned, books scattered across the floor. Signs of a violent struggle are everywhere.

"This is where I found the pendant," Costin says.

But no bodies. No Astrid or Davis.

I pick up a broken chair leg. "But why would she do this? What does Elizabeth want?"

"What she's always wanted." Costin's expression darkens. "Power. Control. With the council in chaos over the unbalanced magic from her failed ceremony, she sees a power vacuum."

"And she's using my family as leverage?"

"Yes." Costin nods grimly, examining a smear of blood on the wall. "She'll want us to come for them. This is a message. She's been waiting for an opportunity, and while we were dealing with Leviathan, she seized it."

I move to the center of the room, closing my eyes. The new power I discovered in the crypt stirs inside me. Can I use it to find them? To sense where Elizabeth has taken them?

Nothing happens.

"What are you doing?" he asks.

"I honestly don't know," I whisper. I try a different approach. I think of Elizabeth's cold beauty, her calculating eyes, and her centuries of manipulation and control. I imagine the sire bond she shares with Costin, similar to the one I share with him but older, darker.

A flash of insight hits me. It's not a vision exactly, but a knowing.

"The underground city," I say, opening my eyes. "She's taken them to the vampire quarter."

Costin's eyebrows rise slightly. "How do you know?"

"I felt it in your sire bond," I say, unable to explain the certainty I feel.

He studies me for a moment, then nods. "It makes sense. It's the kind of theatrical gesture Elizabeth would appreciate."

I start for the door, but Costin catches my arm. "Wait. You need blood first. And we need a plan. Elizabeth has had centuries to perfect her cruelty. We can't just charge in."

The wolf in me bristles at the delay, but the

vampire acknowledges the wisdom in his words. "Fine. Blood first, then planning. But quickly."

He guides me to the pantry, where emergency blood supplies are kept in a hidden refrigerator. I gulp down a bottle, feeling strength return to my limbs as the rich liquid works its magic.

Costin watches me with an intensity that makes my skin tingle. When I finish, he takes the empty bottle from my hands and disposes of it. Then he's back in front of me, his movements so fast I barely register them.

"I thought I'd lost you today," he says again, his voice rough with emotion. "When the church collapsed, and I couldn't reach you through our bond for those first few moments..."

I place my hand over his heart, feeling it beat beneath my palm. "But you found me. You always find me."

His hands slide under my torn shirt, cool against my skin. It rests on the wound now healing over my chest. His eyes darken as he leans in, capturing my mouth in a kiss that steals my breath. There's desperation in it, a need born of fear and relief. I understand because I feel it too. The terror of almost losing each other.

My hands find their way under his shirt, tracing the hard planes of his chest. The kitchen counter presses against my back as he lifts me onto it, stepping between my legs. My body responds instantly, hybrid senses heightening every sensation.

"We shouldn't," I murmur against his lips, even as my legs wrap around his waist.

"Just a moment," he whispers, his mouth trailing down my neck. "Just one moment to remind ourselves we're alive."

I arch into him as his fangs graze my skin, not breaking it but threatening to. My own extend in response, the hybrid hunger rising. I want his blood, his body, the connection that only comes when we're joined completely.

He seems to read my thoughts, his hands tightening on my hips.

"When this is over," he promises, "when your family is safe, I'm going to take you to my home in the mountains. Just the two of us. No council, no Elizabeth, no one to interrupt. And I'm going to make love to you for centuries."

The image he paints makes me shiver with anticipation. "Promise?"

"I swear it," he says, sealing the vow with another kiss.

I believe him. Not because of the sire bond or vampire compulsion, but because in this moment, I trust him completely. Whatever comes next, we'll face it together.

The kiss deepens. This time neither of us pulls

back. There's no space for hesitation. His hands slide beneath the remnants of my shirt, lifting it over my head and tossing it aside without ceremony. I'm not gentle either, tugging his pants free, hungry to feel skin against skin. When our bodies meet, it's not just sex. It's need, raw and biting, sharpened by everything we almost lost today.

He sets me down on the counter. I barely register the hard surface. All I want is the slick slide of his skin against mine. He presses into me. His mouth claims every inch of mine like he's trying to imprint himself into memory. It's ridiculous because I'd never forget him.

We don't speak as we move. There's no need for words. I tilt my head, offering my throat without thought. His fangs brush the sensitive skin, teasing, threatening, worshiping, edged in hunger. My own pierce his shoulder and the blinding pleasure erupts in climax.

He buries his face in my neck, clamping down hard, and I feel him release with me. It's not gentle. It's not pretty. But it's real. It's us.

When we finally break apart, I feel more focused. The blood and Costin's touch have restored me, body and spirit. I slide off the counter, straightening my clothes.

"Let's go kick some ass," I say.

As we leave the kitchen, I feel something nudge

against my consciousness. A faint echo of the power I felt in the crypt. It whispers to me of danger, of change, of choices yet to be made.

Elizabeth is waiting for us, and she won't be alone. But neither will I.

I have Costin.

TWENTY

New York City...

Going to the underground city feels like descending into an old, familiar nightmare. The mausoleum entrance stands before us like a hungry mouth, eager to swallow us whole. The leering carved faces on the tombstones are judging me for coming back. I've been this way before, but never with such dread in my stomach. Strange, since I was mortal the first time.

If I listen, I can hear the city all around us. At first, it's car horns and the hum of engines stuck in traffic. Beneath that, I pick up pieces of random conversations. It's unsettling how much privacy humans don't have from supernaturals. I wonder how many of my conversations have been eaves-dropped on.

"Tamara?" Costin touches my shoulder. "What is it?"

The city has so many smells. Many of them unpleasant. Still, I take deep breaths, letting it overload my senses.

"Tamara?"

"I wasn't outside long when they took me from your underground palace to the estate. It's overwhelming, isn't it? All these people. So many lives. So many heartbeats."

"Do you need to feed again?" His hand becomes heavier as if he's preparing to stop me.

"I didn't say I wanted to *eat* all the people," I chuckle. Costin already made me gorge myself, and he gave me a canteen to carry as backup. He's worried that if I get too drained, I'll go feral like I did in the library. "I kept my wits when we fought the zombies. I've found balance. I'll be fine."

He frowns as he studies my face. I can tell he wants to warn me not to get too cocky, but I do feel fine.

He nods once.

Cold stone. Cracked door. The scent of damp limestone and magic lingers in the air like rot under fresh flowers. Yep, just like we left it. The vines haven't grown back over the entrance since Costin cleared them last time. That feels like a century ago, even though, technically, it was just a few months and several near-deaths ago.

I run my fingers along the edge of the door, remembering the way it *hummed* the first time we touched it together. A pulse of dark enchantment, ancient and alive. It doesn't do it now. Maybe because I'm different. Maybe because it recognizes me this time.

"The butterflies are gone," I whisper.

"What does that mean?"

"I used to see them everywhere, even here. I think they were Lorelai's magic guiding me when I was human. I just realized they're gone now."

"Lorelai doesn't have magic. She's human."

Why does he keep looking at me like he's analyzing everything I say for mistakes?

"Human magic. Charms, spells, a mother's love," I explain. "She kept an altar for me in her home."

He nods, but he's on high alert. The tension rolls through our bond.

"Home sweet hellmouth," I joke, turning toward the door.

Costin doesn't correct me because that's essentially what this place is. It's a gateway to the underground supernatural city, where all manner of goblins and ghoulies reside, a place that appears to have clawed its way through time just to prove it's still relevant. Still dangerous. Still here.

And we're going back in.

Costin moves silently beside me, his face a mask of control. As a human, I remember thinking that he must be emotionless, a cold-hearted predator. But there is a veritable sea of emotions hiding inside of him. The bond between us pulses with shared purpose, but beneath it runs a current of fear.

I'm scared of what I'll find. Astrid and my father would not have gone with Elizabeth willingly. Well, at least Astrid for sure.

"She'll expect us," Costin says as we approach the entrance. "Elizabeth never moves without planning several steps ahead."

"Good," I reply, flexing my fingers. "I'm tired of being surprised."

I feel him about to correct my bravado.

Pebbles skitter across the graveyard path and we both turn to look. Nothing is there.

The telekinetic power I discovered in the church crypt hums beneath my skin, new and unpredictable. I haven't told Costin exactly how it feels but it's like ice in my veins, spreading through me with each passing second. The vampire detachment grows stronger with it, making my emotions feel distant, almost academic, like I had expected his emotions to be.

I should be terrified for Astrid, but that fear begins to settle. Instead, I find myself calculating angles of attack, escape routes, and weaknesses to exploit. My heartbeat is steady and calm, and so loud it's like a metronome in my ears. The wolf in me still snarls with protective rage, but the vampire's cold logic is gaining traction.

We slip through the mausoleum, descending the spiral staircase into darkness. The first time I came here, I marveled at the hidden supernatural world. As a human, I needed an escort to get inside. Now the magical barrier recognizes me, and I move through it like I belong, another predator in a city of monsters.

Thump. Thump. Thump. Thump.

And the metronome remains steady.

The main plaza spreads before us, buzzing with supernatural activity. At our arrival, an eerie quiet spreads like a plague. The beings scatter like exposed bugs under a lifted rock. The walkway becomes clear.

The city's not silent, though. There's a low buzz beneath everything. A drip here, a scrape there. Somewhere, a creature giggles, and I don't want to know why.

"The vampire quarter is this way," Costin says, leading me down a narrower passage.

This is a path we hadn't been before. The few beings we pass give us a wide berth and avert their eyes whenever I look at them. I feel their unease. The wolf senses it in their smell. They know something has shifted in the social hierarchy.

From alcoves and archways, and broken balconies that hang over the underground alleyways like rotting teeth, they watch us. Some are perched on high beams. Others crawl or slither. A few hover in ways that defy human physics.

I can't name all the creatures. Some look like nightmares scribbled in the margins of a forgotten tome. I don't look away, and I have to admit, it feels awesome to have them scared of me for once.

Two men wear the shapes of people, but their skin doesn't quite fit, and their eyes are too black. Next to them are walking skeletons with no skin at all, just bone and sinew stitched together by old magic.

They don't speak.

Unlike the others, they just stare, like they're trying to decide if I'm prey, threat, or entertainment. Maybe all three.

Thump-thump. Thump-thump.

And the metronome goes a little faster.

"Elizabeth would take them to the central gathering hall." Costin moves like he owns the place. Of course he does. Master vampire. One of the elites. This city knows him. Fears him. "She's always had a flair for the dramatic. She'll expect us to arrive through my home, but I'm sure she'll have this route covered as well."

The architecture grows more ornate. I haven't been to the vampire section of the city before, but it looks exactly as I would have assumed. There is some predictability to the supernatural world. Gothic arches and elaborate ironwork are like the Old World transplanted from the Medieval period. If I had to guess, I'd say the vampires were living some kind of heyday back then, as desperate as they cling to that imagery as a whole. It's kind of pathetic, really. Like the football hero from high school who spends the next fifty years talking about that one touchdown from his bar stool soapbox.

Guards stand at the entrance, but they step aside at the sight of Costin. His status as master vampire still commands respect, even as his sister attempts to usurp his authority. I stare them in the eye when I pass, feeling that icy calm in my veins. They don't scare me, but I sure as hell frighten them. They lower their eyes to me.

The gathering hall lives up to its name. It's a vast chamber with high ceilings and blood-red banners hanging from the walls. Vampires line the periphery, some I recognize from my parent's country parties, others are strangers who watch us with hungry curiosity. I wonder if they will try to fight me.

I smile. I'd like them to try.

A tremor works over me, and a wooden table shakes a little, drawing my attention.

"Elizabeth," Costin states.

I whip my head around to the far center of the room. Elizabeth is seated on a throne of carved obsidian. I have to give it to her, she knows how to look the part. She is resplendent in crimson velvet with lipstick to match. Her dark hair is slicked against her head. She's the true picture of deadly beauty. Beside her throne, seated in less elaborate chairs, are Astrid and my father. Their arms are locked at their sides and they're not moving. Neither appears injured, but their postures are rigid with tension.

And standing at Elizabeth's right hand, looking smug despite his recent disgrace, is Uncle Mortimer. Costin tosses the pendant he found in the study at his sister. She catches it with one hand, not taking her gaze from him.

"Ah, brother," Elizabeth purrs. "And your lovely progeny. You got my invitation."

"Enough. Release them," Costin demands without preamble.

Elizabeth laughs, the sound like crystal shattering. "Who says they're not here willingly?"

Astrid's eyes dart to the side, but she doesn't move her head.

"Fine. I might have slipped a little something into her cocktail." Elizabeth waves her hand in dismissal.

"I said let them go," he orders. "As your master."

I flinch. Yeah, no woman wants to hear that bullshit coming out of a man's mouth.

"So direct. So boring." Elizabeth groans. "Where's your sense of occasion? I went to all this trouble."

I scan the room, assessing those gathered. There are at least thirty vampires, all likely loyal to Elizabeth. No werewolves. I doubt any of them are willing to back her up after she tore the heart out of the Alpha. Near the back wall, I spot Anthony being restrained by two hulking vampires, his magic apparently suppressed somehow.

The cold in my veins freezes. I've about had it with this bitch.

My eyes meet Astrid's. Her face betrays nothing, but I see the subtle blink she gives me. She has a plan. Of course she does. She's Astrid.

"What do you want, Elizabeth?" I ask, stepping forward to stand beside Costin.

"What everyone wants, darling." She smiles, all teeth. "Love. Understanding. A warm meal."

Her minions chuckle.

Elizabeth smirks and corrects herself. "Power. Security. A seat in the new order."

"New order?"

"The old ways are dying," she says. "The council is nothing but a bunch of lazy relics high on their own myths. Leviathan's attack exposed how vulnerable we truly are. He should never have been allowed to gain so much power. They should have known how many souls he collected over the centuries and what that would mean to a necromancer's magic."

She pauses as if she's waiting for me to argue. What can I say? The bitch has a point.

"The werewolves have a new Alpha. The magics are scattered and leaderless, for now, isn't that right, Mortimer?" She glances toward my uncle's smug face. "Change is coming, whether we embrace it or not."

"And you thought kidnapping my family was the way to convince me to embrace it?" I can't keep the skepticism from my voice. "I mean, Mortimer you can have. I could care less what betrayal you have in store for him. The other three are coming with me."

"I prefer to think of it as creating an opportunity for dialogue," she replies. "Your family is enjoying my hospitality while we discuss the future."

"Some hospitality," I mutter, noting a flash of subtle magical bindings around Astrid's wrists.

Elizabeth leans forward, her expression suddenly earnest. "Tamara, I've watched you since your transformation. You're something entirely new, a hybrid that shouldn't exist, yet does. Your power is growing, evolving. I can feel it from here. Your vampire blood is settling. You feel it too, don't you? That cool, perfect chill."

I say nothing, but inside, the ice spreads a little further. She's right. Whatever happened in the crypt with Conrad and the freed spirits has changed me.

Costin glances at me, frowning.

"You need guidance," Elizabeth continues. "Control. Understanding. Who better to help you than someone who's lived for centuries?"

I look at Costin.

"I could tell you stories about my brother's help," she says. "You need someone who knows both vampire and werewolf nature intimately? Someone who won't try to oppress you."

"You tried to kill me," I remind her.

She waves a dismissive hand. "Ancient history. Maybe I was just testing you, proving to you what you are capable of. The question is what we do now, moving forward."

"She's right about one thing," Mortimer interjects, his face alight with ambition. "The supernatural world is changing. Those who adapt will thrive. Those who cling to the old ways will perish."

"Like you adapted by making deals with necromancers?" I counter.

Mortimer's smile doesn't falter. "Leviathan

served his purpose. A necessary distraction while Elizabeth secured her position."

I know he's lying. It's so obvious. How am I the only one who appears to see it? He's an opportunistic prick. He probably has deals going with Leviathan, Elizabeth, Thane, and gods know who else.

"You want me to believe you two planned all this? You sent Leviathan after us so Elizabeth could make her move."

"Clever girl," Mortimer approves.

"Go fuck yourself, Morty," I answer, drawing laughter from some of our audience. "This is your backup-backup-backup plan. The Freemont betrothal failed. Your rebellion failed. Leviathan failed. Now you're here. It's pathetic."

"Tamara," my father states, standing. "That's enough. Let's keep things civil so we can come to an understanding."

It's then I realize he's not being held prisoner like the others. What a sad, pathetic man. How did I think so highly of him?

The cold creeps deeper. I'm so tired of this crap.

Elizabeth grins. "I wouldn't say planned. More like we seized an opportunity. When Mortimer found himself suddenly without allies, we discovered our interests aligned."

Costin puts a hand on my shoulder. "And what

exactly are those interests?" His voice is dangerously soft.

Elizabeth stands, descending the three steps from her throne to approach us. She moves with grace, every gesture formed of centuries of habit.

"A new hierarchy," she says. "One that acknowledges the changing balance of power. Vampires at the top, naturally. Werewolves will be offered their place as our martial force, guided by their new Alpha, who I understand has a certain fondness for our hybrid friend here." She gives me a knowing look. "Magics will retain their place as advisors and record-keepers. All under my leadership, of course."

"And where do I fit in this grand vision?" I ask.

"I thought you'd be Alpha. Imagine my surprise when you gave all that power to Sully." She leans closer. "We can undo that, if you wish?"

She points a nail at her neck and makes a slashing motion as she offers to kill Sully.

"Pass." I look at her, but my mind is tracking everyone in the gathering hall.

"So be it," Elizabeth says, clearly disappointed. She straightens and resumes her performance for the others. "As my protégé. I can teach you to control your growing powers, Tamara. To master them rather than be mastered by them."

I feel Costin tense beside me, though his face remains impassive.

"And what about him?" I nod toward Costin.

Elizabeth's smile turns cruel. "My brother has his uses. But his time as master vampire is over. He's grown soft like the others." She steps closer to Costin, her eyes flashing red. "Haven't you, my lord?"

I feel the sire bond between them twisting painfully. It's older and darker than the one I share with Costin.

"Kneel," Elizabeth commands, her voice layered with supernatural compulsion.

To my horror, Costin's body jerks, fighting the command but unable to resist completely. He drops his head forward and he bows, face contorted with the strain of resisting her will. Slowly he drops to a knee.

"You see?" Elizabeth turns to her gathering, triumphant. "This is the truth of the sire bond, Tamara. This is what awaits you if you follow him. You will never be free. You'll always be his, just as he is mine."

The ice in my veins spreads, crystallizing my thoughts. My heartbeat slows. I look at Costin, at the proud master vampire brought low by the bond he can't break. Is this my future? Eternally bound to his will, just as he is bound to Elizabeth's? Sure, he gives me free rein now, but what happens in ten years? A century? How long will love last?

"It doesn't have to be this way," Elizabeth continues, her voice softening. "Join me. I can help you break free of his influence. To control your own destiny."

For a moment, just a moment, I consider it. The vampire detachment makes Elizabeth's logic seem sound. Power. Freedom. Control over my own fate.

I also know the cost. The only way to be free of such control is to kill Costin. I can't do it, but Elizabeth can.

I look at Astrid, still watching me with those knowing eyes. At Anthony, struggling against his captors. At my father, who can't even meet my gaze. And at Costin, fighting Elizabeth's command with everything he has and failing.

Something shifts inside me. The cold calculation of the vampire and the protective instinct of the wolf realign, creating clarity.

I can see Elizabeth now, really see her. Not just her physical form, but the twisted soul beneath. Centuries of pain and rage and thwarted ambition, all channeled into an obsession with control. She doesn't want to help me. She wants to own me, just as she owns Costin.

I step forward, placing myself between Elizabeth and Costin.

"I've seen enough," I say, keeping my voice calm. "Release him."

Elizabeth laughs. "Or what, little hybrid? You'll throw a tantrum? You're powerful, yes, but untrained. Undisciplined."

"Perhaps," I agree. "But I'm learning."

I reach for the power that's been building inside me, the cold crystalline strength from the vampire, the primal ferocity of the wolf, and now this new force, born from the freed spirits. They flow together.

The chandeliers above us begin to sway. Glasses on side tables vibrate, then shatter. The vampires along the walls shift uneasily.

"What are you doing?" Elizabeth demands, taking a step back.

I don't answer. Instead, I direct my focus to the magical bindings around Astrid's wrists. They unravel like ribbon, falling harmlessly to the floor. I do the same for Anthony, freeing them without moving from my spot.

"Impossible," Mortimer whispers, his face pale. "She has no magic."

"She is magic," Astrid says, rising from her chair. "She always has been."

Elizabeth's expression hardens. "Stop this, Tamara. You don't understand the forces you're playing with."

"I understand enough," I reply. "I understand that you don't want to help me. You want to control me just like everyone else. I will not be Mortimer's magical broodmare for the Freemonts. I will not be Alpha. I will not be Leviathan's queen of the hybrid army. I will not be your puppet or your protégé. How many times do you people need to hear the word *no*?"

The sire bond between Elizabeth and Costin twists visibly now, a dark red thread connecting them. I reach for it with my mind, not to break it—*I don't have that power*—but to momentarily disrupt it.

Costin gasps as the pressure eases, rising to his feet. His eyes meet mine, filled with a mixture of pride and concern.

"This isn't over," Elizabeth hisses, backing toward her throne. "You have no idea what's coming. No idea what forces you've set in motion."

"Maybe not," I acknowledge. "But whatever comes, I'll face it on my terms."

Elizabeth's eyes dart around the room. The tide has turned. The vampires who moments ago seemed firmly under her control now look uncertain, some even fearful of the power I've displayed.

"Mortimer," she snaps. "We're leaving."

My uncle doesn't need to be told twice. He scurries to her side, all dignity forgotten in his haste to escape.

"This is merely a strategic retreat," Elizabeth says, her voice hard. "Remember that, brother. Remember who made you what you are."

"I remember everything," Costin replies. "Every moment of the past five hundred years. And I remember what you were before Marcus turned you. Before the darkness took root."

Something flashes across Elizabeth's face. Pain, perhaps? Or a fleeting memory of humanity long buried? Then it's gone, replaced by cold fury.

"This isn't over," she repeats, backing away. The vampires part for her, creating a path to the exit. "Not by a long shot."

She and Mortimer disappear through an archway, followed by their most loyal supporters. The remaining vampires look to Costin, then to me, uncertain where their allegiance should lie.

"Go," Costin commands, and they obey, filing out until only our family remains.

I rush to Astrid, checking her for injuries. "Are you hurt?"

"I'm fine," she says, straightening her already impeccable clothing. "Your uncle's betrayal is far more painful than anything Elizabeth could inflict."

My father finally looks at me, his expression unreadable. "That was..."

I arch a brow.

"...impressive," he finishes.

From him, it's high praise.

Anthony joins us, rubbing his wrists where the vampires had restrained him. "Remind me never to piss you off, sis. That was some serious power you just threw around."

I should feel relief. We faced Elizabeth and emerged victorious, at least for now. My family is safe. Costin is free of Elizabeth's immediate control.

So why does this hollow feeling persist? Why does part of me remain cold, detached, calculating the next move as if this were a chess game rather than my life?

"Tamara?" Costin's voice pulls me back. His hand touches my shoulder, warm despite his vampire nature. "Are you alright?"

I look into his eyes, trying to find my way back to the emotions that should be flooding me. Relief. Joy. Love. They're there, but muted, as if viewed through frosted glass.

"I'm fine," I lie, forcing a smile. "Just tired. It's been a long night."

He studies me, seeing more than I want him to. "We should return to the surface. Dawn is approaching."

We make our way back through the underground city, our strange family procession drawing curious looks from the few beings still about. Anthony supports our father, whose energy seems depleted by the ordeal. Astrid walks ahead, her posture betraying none of the stress she must feel.

Costin stays close to me, watching me with growing concern.

I feel it happening. The humanity in me recedes as the supernatural powers grow stronger. The ice spreads further with each step, making the world around me seem less real, more like a stage where I'm merely playing a part.

Is this what being a vampire is truly like? This detachment? This distance from human emotion? Or is it something else? Some side effect of whatever power I absorbed in the crypt?

As we reach the surface, the eastern sky is lightening with the first hint of dawn. Costin ushers us toward a waiting car. How he arranged it, I don't know or care to ask.

"The family penthouse may not be safe," Astrid says as we settle inside. "Elizabeth knows all our defenses."

"We'll go to my sanctuary," Costin decides. "It's warded against her specifically."

No one argues. We're all too exhausted, too shell-shocked by the night's events.

As the car pulls away, I stare out the window at the fading stars. The power inside me pulses in time with my heartbeat, growing stronger with each passing minute. I should be scared. I should be worried about what I'm becoming.

Instead, I find myself wondering how much stronger I can get. How much more power I can absorb. How many more battles I can win.

The thought should disturb me. It doesn't.

And that, more than anything, terrifies the small part of me that's still human.

TWENTY-ONE

I wake to nothingness.

No hunger. No thirst. No emotional residue from dreams. I just lie in a perfect stillness, as if my body has finally accepted that it has become a vessel for power rather than humanity. If my heart weren't beating, I'd think I was dead.

It's been like this for days, and each dusk when I open my eyes, it feels worse.

Or better, I guess, depending on how you look at it. There's comfort in not having to feel everything. Humans are full of emotions and doubt, worry and stress. It's an endless mess. I tell myself there is still a human part of me, but I don't think that's true anymore. The werewolf, vampire, and magic have crowded the human into a tiny space at the tip of my pinkie. I could cut it off and barely notice it was missing.

I lift my hand in the dark and trace my fingers with my eyes. I bend the pinkie down to consider it.

Costin's sanctuary is a modernist fortress hidden in plain sight. I honestly would never have guessed this was his. The penthouse apartment is in a building he owns, warded so heavily that even I can see the protective magic shimmering along the walls. The floor-to-ceiling windows are covered with blackout shades to make it safe for vampires. I live an existence suspended between dusk and dawn. We don't go out. I'm not sure if we're hiding from Elizabeth, or Costin is keeping me from the outside world.

I hear the shades gliding upward, marking that it's safe to go out. I slide from the silk sheets, leaving Costin still resting beside me. Even in sleep, he seems troubled, his brow furrowed as if he's fighting battles in his dreams. I know I'm the cause of his worry, but I can't seem to summon the appropriate concern. Maybe life has finally won. It's beaten all the emotion out of me. I've cracked.

I should care more.

It's kind of nice not giving a shit though.

My silk nightgown caresses my skin. I'll give my vampire lover one thing. He doesn't skimp on the details. He lives in rich comfort. I feel like a duchess.

I'd say queen, but that reminds me of Leviathan and his plan for me.

The marble floor feels pleasant beneath my bare feet as I move to the center of the spacious bedroom. It took me a moment to realize why certain creatures lean toward so much marble. The cleaning up. It's hard to get blood out of carpet. I don't want to kill anyone, but I suppose if I had to, I'd try to find a bad person. Someone the world would be better without.

I close my eyes, reaching for the power that now lives inside me like a constant companion. It responds instantly, a cold current flowing through my veins.

I focus on a heavy crystal sculpture on the dresser. The abstract piece must weigh twenty pounds. In the crypt, moving small stones required intense concentration. Now, the sculpture lifts effortlessly, hovering six feet off the ground with just a thought. I'm getting better at this.

I add the lamp. Then a book. Then the chair. Soon, a dozen objects orbit around me in a perfect celestial dance, requiring no more effort than breathing once did. The power hums through me, clean and precise, demanding nothing but my direction.

"Impressive."

Costin's voice doesn't startle me. I sensed him waking, felt his eyes on me before he spoke. I don't turn as he approaches, keeping the objects suspended with minimal concentration.

"It's getting easier," I say, my voice neutral. "Stronger."

"And how do you feel?" He steps into my field of vision, his expression carefully composed. He's wearing only sleep pants, his chest bare, hair tousled. He looks vulnerable. The sight should stir something in me, desire, tenderness, love. I remember feeling those things for him, but now they seem distant, like memories from someone else's life.

"Efficient," I answer honestly.

Something flickers across his face. Concern? Or perhaps disappointment? I gently lower the objects back to their places and turn to face him fully.

"You're worried about me," I state rather than ask. I feel it through our bond.

"Should I be?" His eyes search mine, looking for something I'm not sure is still there.

I consider lying, telling him what he wants to hear. But what would be the point?

"I'm changing," I admit. "The power is changing me. Hollowing me out."

He reaches for me, his hand cool against my cheek. "Tamara—"

"Don't." I step back, not wanting his touch to

cloud my thoughts. "I need to understand what's happening to me."

"I know what's happening," he says quietly. "I've seen it before. When a vampire first turns, there's often a period of emotional detachment. It's the mind's way of processing the transformation. But this is different. More extreme."

"Because I'm not just a vampire," I finish for him. "I'm something else entirely."

A monster.

A freak.

A hybrid.

Call it what you want.

I move to the window, looking out at the city below. My vision zooms in on them. People scurry along the sidewalks, going about their mortal lives, unaware of the supernatural dramas unfolding around them. I used to be one of them. Now I can barely remember what it felt like.

"I reached out to Sully for alliance against Elizabeth and Mortimer," he says.

I nod.

"He's coming tonight," Costin continues. "He asked how you were doing after the crypt."

This is Costin's newest way of bringing the subject up. He's tried several times.

"I told you that, when I was in the crypt and Conrad's spirit was freed along with all the others that Leviathan had trapped, some of their power transferred to me." I touch the window, tracing a distant building. "But it's not just the telekinesis. There is something else that's colder. I don't know what it is. There's no way to know who or what Leviathan was storing in the crypt. Spirits? Energy? Curses? Whatever it was, it changed me. Maybe I absorbed nothing. Maybe I absorbed everything."

Costin is careful not to touch me again. "Do you think it was necromantic energy? Death magic is known to dull emotions. Cold like the grave."

I study his face. "You're afraid I'm becoming like Elizabeth."

His expression tells me I've hit the mark. He blames himself for his sister. Just as he blames himself for me.

"I'm not," I assure him, though I'm not entirely convinced myself. "I just need to find balance again. I need to understand all the supernatural parts."

"Let me help you." This time when he reaches for me, I don't pull away. His hands frame my face, and I feel the sire bond between us pulse with something warm and alive. I feel his love for me. "Remember what it feels like to be connected."

His lips find mine. They start gentle but then become more insistent. I respond mechanically at first, but then a flicker of the passion we once shared stirs within me. My nerve endings fire after being numb for too long. The kiss sharpens. His fangs cut into my lip, so I bite him back. The coppery taste of him hits my bloodstream like fire. Blood flavors our mouths, and suddenly I remember how much I need him. No, how much I crave him. His growl vibrates through both our chests, and the bond between us tightens. I grasp at the feeling, wanting the warmth, needing our connection.

I push Costin back against the wall. My strength matches his now. He hits with a dull thud, and I'm on him before he can move. I pin him with my hips. The impact sends a picture frame clattering to the floor. His fingers dig into my ass as he pulls me tighter. Claws rip through all barriers until we're naked. There's nothing soft about the way we come together, not the way he touches me, not the way I take it. We're past tenderness.

He grins into the kiss, and I realize we're straddling the line between power and intimacy. My hybrid instincts roar that I need to dominate, consume, take. But underneath it, there's still me. Still us.

I urgently explore his body, not just for physical release but for emotional resurrection. His skin is cool, yet his touch melts the ice inside me. I rock my hips against him. The pressure builds. The pleasure is too fast, too much. It threatens to undo me.

My hands tremble as I drag my fingers over the

hard lines of his chest, down his ribs, needing to memorize the realness of him. His body responds before his mouth does. Muscles contract under my palms. A low sound escapes him, vibrating against my throat. I roll my hips in invitation.

Costin pulls me tighter. My fangs graze his throat. I don't bite, but I feel the flutter of his pulse beneath the skin. He tilts his head, offering his throat, daring me. I drag my tongue along the artery instead.

It's more temptation than I can resist. I clamp my mouth on his throat and drink.

When we come together, it's fierce and primal. It's not the violence of our early encounters, but a desperate search for humanity in each other's arms. When I sink down onto him, we move like we're made for this. For *each other*. His hands are on my hips, my nails drag down his chest. For a brief, reckless moment, as pleasure crests and breaks over us both, I can feel everything I've been missing. Love, fear, hope, despair, it all rushes back in a tidal wave of sensation.

A cry rips out of me, raw and unfiltered, as magic sparks beneath my skin. The violence of it makes me feel alive. My orgasm tears through me like I've been struck by lightning. My body arches against his, chasing every last flicker of sensation until I collapse into him, wrecked and finally awake.

We cling to each other. For those seconds, I'm not broken. I'm not magic. I'm not a Devine. I'm just *his*.

Then, slowly, the cold clarity returns, though not quite as absolute as before.

"Did that help?" Costin asks as we lie tangled naked together on the floor, his fingers tracing patterns on my skin as scraps of silk surround us.

"A little," I admit, resting my head on his chest. "It's like waking up briefly from a dream, only to slip back under."

"We'll find a way," he promises, pressing his lips to my forehead. "Whatever's happening to you, we'll figure it out together."

I want to believe him. Part of me still does. But the growing power inside me whispers that some battles can only be fought alone.

"The full moon rises tomorrow night," Sully says, his massive frame making Costin's living room furniture look oddly undersized. "Your first transformation will be intense, but the pack will be at our strongest."

Already? I look at the window. How long have we been in hiding? The days all blend together.

Anthony snorts from his position by the window. "Understatement of the century."

We've gathered for what can only be described as a war council. Astrid sits primly on a leather armchair, looking as composed as ever despite the events of the past. My father stands behind her, his hand resting on the back of her chair. Even now, he looms like a man still playing the part of devoted father and husband. In my cold assessment of him, I see the truth. I find him pathetic and weak. He traded our safety for his pride long ago. All he cares about is his own narcissistic vices. Why is he even here?

Anthony keeps watch by the window, though what threat he expects to spot from thirty stories up is beyond me. My brother succeeded in getting Paul to safety before Elizabeth grabbed him. At least one thing went right, even if I don't feel the relief I should.

Costin leans against the wall nearest me, giving me space while staying close.

And then there's Sully, Alpha of the werewolves, who arrived an hour ago.

"I need to know if you can control it," Sully continues, his golden eyes fixed on me. "A hybrid's first full moon is uncharted territory. If you lose control in the middle of battle..."

"I won't," I say with a confidence I don't entirely

feel. The cold logic inside me calculates the odds of maintaining control during my first transformation. It's not favorable, but not impossible either.

"You can't know that," Astrid interjects. Her voice is gentle but firm. "No one can. Which is why I suggest we delay confronting Elizabeth until after the full moon has passed."

"We may not have that luxury," Costin counters. "Elizabeth won't wait. She's gathering allies, consolidating power. The longer we wait, the stronger she becomes."

"And the stronger I become," I point out. All eyes turn to me. "Every day, my abilities grow. By the full moon, I may be strong enough to face Elizabeth regardless of the transformation."

"Or you might be completely out of control," my father says, speaking for the first time. "A liability rather than an asset."

The old me would have been hurt by his assessment.

"There's another factor to consider," Astrid says. "Mortimer. He's had contingency plans within contingency plans for years. He won't have allied himself with Elizabeth without some guarantee of protection."

"Speaking of Mortimer," Anthony pushes away from the window, "what exactly is his angle in all this? Elizabeth wants power, that's clear enough.

But Uncle Morty? What does he get out of backing her play? He never gave any indication he wanted to take over the Devine empire. Actually, quite the opposite. That whole thing with Tamara marrying Chester Freemont was to ensure the bloodline and create heirs to our line. It seems like he wants anything but to be in charge."

"Survival. He likes the power without the spotlight," I answer before anyone else can. "I think he fancies himself the true power behind the throne."

My father doesn't meet my direct gaze.

"And to punish those who exposed him," Astrid agrees, her eyes meeting mine. "Particularly me."

The thought of Mortimer harming Astrid sends a ripple of emotion through my cold detachment. The flash of protective rage feels refreshingly human. I cling to it, trying to fan it into a stronger flame.

"Yes, and revenge," I say. "Astrid humiliated him, and then the council stripped him of his position. He needs Elizabeth to regain what he's lost."

"Mortimer won't be a threat. I can talk to him," my father says.

Astrid arches a brow at him. "The time for talk is over."

"So we have a power-hungry vampire queen, a vengeful magic, the full moon, and a hybrid who's evolving in unpredictable ways," Sully summarizes.

"Sounds like a typical Tuesday night in the super-natural world."

His attempt at humor earns a smile from Anthony and a disapproving look from my father. I appreciate the effort, even if I can't quite feel the amusement.

"We need a plan," Costin says, bringing us back to the matter at hand. "Elizabeth will expect us to come to her. She'll have defenses in place, allies at the ready."

"Then we don't give her what she expects," I suggest. "We draw her out instead."

Sully leans forward, interested. "How?"

"With bait she can't resist." I look at Costin. "Her own greed."

His eyes narrow. "Explain."

"Elizabeth wants power, yes, but she also wants to prove herself superior to you. To finally break free of the bond that's connected you for centuries." I stand, moving to the center of the room where everyone can see me. "What if we convince her that you've found a way to sever the sire bond? That you've discovered some ancient ritual that could free not just you from her, but me from you?"

"She'd never believe it," my father dismisses.

"She might," Astrid counters. "If presented correctly. Elizabeth's greatest weakness has always been her ego. The idea that Constantine found something she couldn't, discovered a power that eluded her..."

"It would drive her mad," Costin finishes, understanding dawning on his face. "She'd have to stop it, to prove it impossible. Or to claim it for herself."

"And we'd be waiting," Sully adds, a predatory smile spreading across his face. "My pack, your vampires, the magics who remain loyal to the Devine family."

"It could work," Anthony agrees. "But we'd need to make it convincing. And we'd need a location that gives us the advantage, not her."

The discussion turns tactical. I listen as they debate the perfect spot for the trap, determining who can be trusted, and planning for all possibilities. I contribute where needed, my cold logic proving useful for strategic planning but little else. Part of me remains distant, observing rather than participating, as if I'm watching the scene unfold from outside my body.

As the others debate the finer points of magical barriers and attack formations, I find my attention drawn to the window. The city sprawls below, millions of lives intersecting, each with their own dramas and desires. From this height, they seem so insignificant, so fragile.

So tasty and fresh.

I try to hear their heartbeats.

Is this how Elizabeth feels? This detachment, this sense of being above it all? Is this why she sees nothing wrong with using others as pawns in her games of power?

The thought disturbs me enough to pull me back to the present. I don't want to be like Elizabeth. I don't want to lose what makes me human, even as I embrace what I have become.

"Tamara?" Costin's voice breaks through my thoughts. "What do you think?"

Their voices blur together like static. They're shadows of a world I'm slipping away from. But I can't afford to drift. Not now.

I realize everyone is looking at me expectantly. They've been discussing something, waiting for my input, but I haven't been listening.

"I'm sorry," I say, making an effort to reconnect. "What was the question?"

Concern flashes across multiple faces. Costin moves closer, lowering his voice though everyone in the room can still hear him. "Where did you go just now?"

"Nowhere," I lie. "I was just thinking."

He doesn't believe me. I can see it in his eyes, feel it through our bond. But he doesn't press the issue in front of the others.

"We were discussing your role in tomorrow's battle," Astrid explains, her tone carefully neutral.

"Given your evolving abilities and the full moon's approach."

"I'll do whatever needs to be done," I say simply.

Costin crosses to a bar and pours blood from a decanter. He brings the glass to me. It doesn't smell the freshest, but it's drinkable.

"We need more than that, Tam," Anthony says, frustration evident in his voice. "We need to know what you can do, what limitations you have, what we can count on."

"I don't know how to answer that," I admit, drinking the entire glass before handing it back to Costin. "The power keeps changing. Growing. I don't know where its limits are yet."

"Then perhaps we should find out," Astrid suggests. "Costin, would you mind showing them to the basement? Davis and I have things to discuss."

TWENTY-TWO

I feel magic brush against my skin before the elevator doors open. The shimmering barrier recognizes my supernatural nature and allows me to pass.

"We designed this level of the building to contain vampire strength and train young ones. The walls are reinforced with magical dampening fields to protect the structure from collateral damage," Costin explains. "But it's never been tested against a hybrid."

Sully and Anthony accompany us. My parents remain upstairs, finalizing plans for tomorrow's confrontation. I'm almost relieved to be away from their watchful eyes, especially my father's calculating gaze. I'm not sure we can trust him. I wonder if that is why Astrid kept him with her instead of coming down here.

The spacious chamber is impressive. Various training equipment is scattered throughout. Combat dummies, weapons racks, and what appears to be an obstacle course fill one half. The other half is open space, presumably for sparring or, in my case, power testing.

"How do we do this?" I ask, moving to the center of the open area.

"Start small," Costin suggests. "We need to establish a baseline. Use the telekinetic power to show them what you know you can do."

Anthony sets up a series of progressively larger objects along a table. "Move these one at a time. Let's see what you can handle."

I focus on the pencil first, lifting it easily. Then the book. A weight. A chair. A training dummy. Each object rises at my command, hovering steadily before returning to their place. Then, just because I can, I let the cold power flow through me and I lift them all at once, including the table. I let them dance in circles above our heads like a poltergeist.

"Show off," Anthony teases.

I set them back on the ground in no particular order.

"Good," Sully approves. "Now something more challenging. Anthony?"

My brother steps forward, a mischievous glint in

his eye. Blue magic wraps his hands, winding up his arms and down his waist and legs

"Try to lift me," he challenges.

I narrow my focus, directing the telekinetic force toward him. I feel his magic resisting mine. For a moment nothing happens, then he gasps as his feet leave the ground. I raise him three feet in the air, holding him steady despite the counterforce of his magic urging me to set him down.

"Holy shit," he breathes. "This is unnerving."

I set him down gently. "What else?"

"Distance," Sully suggests. "Can you affect things you can't see?"

They test my limits. I do what they ask, moving objects around corners, through walls, based solely on my awareness of their presence. The power stretches, adapting to each new challenge.

"Now defense," Costin says. He nods to Anthony, who raises his hands, blue magic coalescing between his fingers.

Before I can tell him I'm ready, a magical bolt flies toward me, fast as thought. Instinctively, I raise a hand, the power surging up to create a shield of pure force. The bolt splashes harmlessly against it, dissipating in a shower of blue sparks.

"Again," I say, feeling more confident. "Stronger this time."

Anthony doesn't hold back. The next bolt is brighter, faster, carrying enough magical energy to stun a vampire. It meets the same fate as the first, dissolving against my telekinetic barrier.

Sully whistles low. "Impressive."

We continue the tests, discovering my limits. I can deflect physical attacks as well as magical ones. I can affect multiple targets simultaneously. I can control the force with increasing precision, from a gentle touch to enough pressure to bend metal.

But with each demonstration, the cold detachment grows stronger. I feel myself slipping further away, the human part of me receding as the power expands. I don't like it. I want to tell them to stop, but I know I have to push through.

"One more test," Costin says finally. He looks to Sully, who nods in silent agreement.

They move to opposite sides of the room, circling me like predators. For the first time, I feel a flicker of unease. These are two of the strongest creatures I know.

"The goal is simple," Costin explains. "Stop us."

They attack simultaneously. Sully charges with werewolf speed while Costin blurs into vampire movement. The two supernatural predators converge on a single target. Me.

Time seems to slow. The power rises, not in a

controlled surge but in a tidal wave of fear. I don't think, don't plan, simply react. My hands extend, one toward each attacker.

The telekinetic blast catches them both midair, freezing them in place. Sully's eyes widen in shock. Costin's face shows a mixture of pride and concern. I hold them suspended, neither able to move forward or retreat.

The truth is I'm not sure how to turn it off.

My heart pounds. The power inside me shifts. The cold surges, not content to simply hold them suspended. It wants more. It wants to squeeze, to crush, to demonstrate complete dominance. A voice whispers to do it, to destroy everything, bring the building down, burn the city.

My fingers begin to curl inward. I feel the pressure around them increasing.

"Tamara," Costin warns, his voice strained. "Enough."

Sully coughs violently.

I don't release them. I can't. The power has taken over, flowing unchecked through my veins. My vision dims at the edges, turning red. I feel my fangs extend and my claws lengthen. The hybrid is emerging, driven by this new, cold force.

"Tamara!" Anthony's voice cuts through the haze. "Stop!"

I turn toward him, a snarl building in my throat.

He takes an involuntary step back, his hands raising defensively.

"This isn't you," he says, his voice steadier than his stance. "Control it."

But it is me. This is what I'm becoming. Power without conscience. Strength without humanity. The realization hits me like a physical blow, bringing me back to myself just enough to see what I'm doing.

"Anthony," I plead, not understanding how to stop it.

He charges at me, knocking me in the chest. I resist the urge to shove him back. We land hard on the ground. The impact makes me release the telekinetic hold. Costin and Sully drop to the ground, both landing in crouches, ready to defend themselves if necessary. Anthony rolls away from me, leaving me on the ground.

"I'm sorry," I whisper, staring at my hands as if they belong to someone else. Whatever I absorbed in the crypt, it's not just vampire coldness. It's darker. Hungrier. "I don't know what happened."

"I do," Costin says, straightening slowly. "The power is feeding on your emotions, or rather, your lack of them. Without humanity to temper it, it becomes pure force, unchecked by conscience or compassion."

Sully rubs his throat and breathes deeply. "That was unexpected."

"We need to be careful," Anthony says, looking between us. "If Tamara can't control this new ability—"

"I can," I interrupt, though I'm not entirely convinced. "I just need practice."

"No," Costin says firmly. "What you need is to reconnect with your humanity. The vampire detachment is natural, but it's being amplified by whatever power you absorbed in the crypt. If we don't find a way to balance it..."

He doesn't finish the thought. He doesn't need to. We all understand the implication. I could become something worse than Elizabeth.

"I'll help you," Anthony offers. "We could try some meditation techniques for grounding you."

"You should be around your pack members," Sully adds. "Being around werewolves might help strengthen that side of your nature. The wolf is emotional, instinctual, the opposite of what you're experiencing now."

I nod, grateful for their support even if I can't fully feel that gratitude.

"For now, I think that's enough testing," Costin says, his tone brooking no argument. "We should rejoin Astrid and Davis to finalize our plan for tomorrow."

As we return to the elevator, I catch Costin watching me with an expression I can't quite decipher. His concern is mixed with a deep fear. I wonder if he's scared of me or for me.

I should be upset by that. Instead, I find myself wondering if that fear is warranted. If I'm becoming something that should be feared.

The thought follows me on the elevator ride up, lingering as we rejoin the others. My father is gone. Astrid doesn't say to where and I don't ask. Costin brings me more blood and demands I drink it. The others tell Astrid what happened, and they fall back into their plans. I find myself drawn to the window overlooking the city. I want to float down there like a cold wind and wrap myself around the helpless people below.

When Astrid and Anthony finally leave for their own quarters within the building, and Sully leaves to gather the wolves, I find myself alone with Costin in the penthouse.

"You should rest," he says, watching me from across the room. "Tomorrow will be challenging without the added strain of exhaustion."

"Do vampires even get exhausted?" I ask, genuinely curious. "Or is that just one more human thing I'm supposed to outgrow?"

His expression softens. "We feel fatigue, yes. Not

in the same way as humans, but we can be depleted."

I nod, moving toward the bedroom. But at the threshold, I hesitate. "Costin?"

He looks up from the plans spread across the table. "Yes?"

"What if I can't come back from this? What if this is just what I am now?"

He crosses to me in three long strides, taking my face in his hands with a gentleness that belies his strength. "Then I will love you anyway," he says fiercely. "But I won't stop fighting for your humanity, Tamara. Not ever. The fact that you even ask me that tells me it's still there."

The intensity in his eyes stirs a flicker of warmth in the cold void. I grasp at it, desperate not to lose this last connection to what I was.

"Stay with me," I whisper. "Please."

He nods, following me into the bedroom. We don't speak as we prepare for sleep, moving around each other with the comfortable familiarity of lovers. When we slide beneath the sheets, his arms encircle me, pulling me against his chest as if he can physically prevent me from slipping further away.

I close my eyes, letting the rhythm of his heartbeat lull me toward unconsciousness. As sleep claims me, I feel the cold power recede just slightly, allowing me a moment of peace.

But peace doesn't last.

In my dreams, I stand in a vast, empty landscape. No horizon, no sky, no ground. There is just endless gray nothingness stretching in all directions. And I am not alone.

"Hello, Tam-tam."

Conrad stands before me, not as the vengeful ghost who haunted me, but as the brother I knew in life. His smile is the same smirk he always wore when he thought he knew something I didn't. Which, honestly, was always.

"This isn't real," I say, watching him warily. "You're gone. I freed you."

"Did you?" He circles me slowly, hands clasped behind his back. "Or did you just open a door to somewhere else? Somewhere I can see things more clearly now?"

"What do you want?"

He stops, studying me with an intensity that's unsettling. "What I've always wanted. To be seen. To be powerful. To matter." His smile turns bitter. "The things you were given without even trying."

"I never asked for any of this," I remind him.

"Didn't you?" He laughs, the sound hollow in the empty space. "You were always special, Tamara. Even as a mortal. Father's favorite. Anthony's precious sister. Astrid's pet. The dragon's chosen. Costin's obsession. My responsibility. Even the mother who gave you up did so out of love. Mine left me at a gas station so she could fuck some lowlife for crack."

There's no hiding the envy in his voice, or the resentment that festered for years until it erupted in betrayal and attempted murder.

"And now look at you," he continues, gesturing to me. "More powerful than any of us could have imagined. A hybrid with magic to boot. Everything I ever wanted."

"And it's destroying me," I say flatly. "Is that why you're here? To gloat?"

"No." He steps closer, his expression shifting to something more complex. "I'm here because we're still connected, you and me. Maybe we always will be."

"Connected how?"

"History. Shared experiences. Trauma bonds." He shrugs. "Take your pick. Or maybe it's simpler than that. Maybe I'm just what's left of your conscience, wearing a familiar face."

I don't know what to make of that possibility, so I ignore it.

"Is our deadbeat dad scrambling to protect his image? Or has he still not bothered to show up for more than two seconds?"

I don't answer and he laughs like he already knows.

"Seriously, you have to tell me. How does it feel to shove your superiority in Lady Astrid's smug bitch face?" Conrad asks. "Just between us. Admit it. It feels great, doesn't it?"

I frown.

"Don't pretend like you and Astrid are friends now," Conrad smirks. "You can't have forgotten the first twenty seven years of your life because mommy likes you now. Here, let me remind you. Listen."

Conrad cups his hand to his ear and pretends to listen.

"*What do you want me to do with it, Davis? It can die.*" Astrid's voice whispers from my childhood.

It. Not she. Not Tamara. She said it.

The sound is faint but clear. I've heard those words echoing in my head for decades. The memory stings.

I was five. Too young to understand what death really meant, but those words, and the way they were spoken, lodged deep in me anyway. They shaped everything. For most of my life, I was treated like a fragile butterfly that the supernatural world could crush for fun. Because that's what monsters do when they're bored. They break delicate things.

I was told to be careful. That I needed protection. That I couldn't survive on my own.

But I'm not that delicate mortal anymore.

The butterfly didn't get crushed. It evolved.

Now that I'm a hybrid, Astrid doesn't look at me like I might break. She watches me like I might break those around me. And it's not pity, it's pride that I see in her face. Like she's suddenly realized I'm not just her pretty family secret in a dress. I'm a Devine. Thane's blood. Vampire-marked. Dangerous.

"There it is," Conrad whispers. "I knew you remembered."

"Of course I remember," I snap. The coldness is back fueled by my childhood suffering.

"She used to pity you. Now she has to respect you. Make her fear you. You're not something that needs protecting anymore. You're what the monsters should be afraid of. It can die? No, Tamara. *They* can die."

"What do you want from me, Conrad?"

Even as I ask it, I think I know the answer. It's what he always wanted. Revenge. And I'm the only way he can get it where he's at.

"Nothing. For once in my miserable existence, I don't want anything from you." He looks almost surprised by this realization. Nearly as much as I am. "But I do have something to give you."

"What?"

"Information." His smile returns, tinged with malice. "About our dear uncle."

I find myself interested despite my suspicion. "Mortimer?"

"The very same. Did you know he's been studying you since you were a baby? Not just because you were human in a supernatural family. But because you were something else entirely."

"What do you mean?"

"I found his journals when I was going through the family papers after I framed you for the birthday fire. Fascinating reading." Conrad's eyes gleam with remembered satisfaction. "He called you a blank vessel because you could hold magic due to your blood, but did not naturally create your own. He made sure that you didn't absorb any. Then, after you got the amulet, that kept you from gaining power since Draakmar's magic took over and acted like a shield."

"Why would he do that?"

Conrad laughs. "Does it matter? Mortimer always has a scheme. First he was going to fill you with the magic he wanted. Then, when you got the amulet, he decided if you couldn't be magical on your own, he'd make you valuable in other ways. Hence all those suitors he paraded before you. Chester, Jasper, Rex, Leviathan..."

I remember Mortimer's constant attempts to marry me off to powerful supernatural families. Chester Freemont wasn't the first, just the latest and most persistent. Jasper Blackwood, my cheating liar of a college boyfriend, was on Mortimer's preapproved list. Jasper only dated me to get close to the Devine family and repeatedly asked me about shipping schedules and my access to family money. There were others, but they seemed to have left less of an impression.

"Rex?" I frown.

Conrad shrugs. "No clue."

It kind of makes sense now. If I'm a blank slate, he could use that to create whatever he wanted with my children. It also explains Leviathan's interest in me, how he knew I'd be able to survive as a hybrid.

So many failed plans for my life. None of them mine.

"But there was something else," Conrad continues. "Something he kept hidden even from our father. A ritual he developed, specifically designed to extract and transfer magical potential."

My blood runs cold. "Transfer to whom?"

"To himself, of course." Conrad looks positively gleeful. "Our uncle has been plotting to steal your power for decades, waiting for the right moment. And now that you've manifested abilities beyond what anyone expected, he's more determined than ever."

"That's why he allied with Elizabeth," I realize. "She's helping him get to me."

"Bingo." Conrad taps the tip of my nose, and I jerk my head back. "And here's the best part. None of them know. Leviathan thought he was making you his queen. Elizabeth thinks she's going to be some super villain."

"Huh. It's not a bad plan," I say, admiring the cunning it's taken to get Mortimer this far. "Why are you telling me this?"

"He's vulnerable during the ritual. Completely exposed. If you were to interrupt it at precisely the right moment..."

"He'd be defenseless," I finish. The tactical implications are immediately clear, even through the emotional distance that's become my new normal.

"One last thing before I go," Conrad says, almost fondly.

"You're leaving?"

"This is it, Tam-tam. My final curtain call." He spreads his arms. "I'm only here to deliver this message, one last 'fuck you' to dear Uncle Mortimer and the family. Consider it my parting gift. You can kill them all, Tamara. You have that power now. Our neglectful father who would rather fuck his way through Europe than protect his family. Our bitch mother who only cares about you now that you're special. Anthony is, well, Anthony. Spoiled little rich boy. I couldn't care less what you do to him."

"Why help me at all?" I ask, genuinely curious. "You tried to kill me. Multiple times."

Conrad's expression turns serious for perhaps

the first time since his death. "I owe you. You freed me when you could have left me to rot. And because in the end, I'd rather see you win than them." He smirks. "If anyone's going to bring down the Devines, it should be another Devine."

He begins to fade, and his form becomes translucent. "Goodbye, Tam-tam. Try not to suck at being supernatural, will you? Some of us never got the chance."

With those words, he's gone, leaving me alone in the endless gray. But as the dreamscape begins to dissolve around me, I feel something stirring in my chest that wasn't there before. Not love or forgiveness for Conrad, but something simpler, more human.

Understanding.

I wake with a gasp, sitting upright in bed. Costin is instantly alert beside me, his hand on my arm.

"Tamara? What is it?"

I turn to look at him, and for the first time in days, I feel tears prickling at my eyes. Real, human tears.

"I know what Mortimer is planning," I say, my voice thick with the emotion that I'd thought lost. "And I know how to stop him."

For the first time since the church collapsed around me, I feel like myself again.

Not a hybrid. Not a vampire or werewolf or magic vessel.

Tamara. Flawed, complicated, determined.

Ready.

He pulls me down on the bed beside him. "Tell me everything."

TWENTY-THREE

The full moon hangs low and bloated in the night sky, its silver light washing over the city. I feel it pulling at my blood, demanding transformation, but I hold it at bay through sheer force of will. There will be time for that later... if we survive.

Costin and I stand on the rooftop of what looks like the lovechild of an abandoned castle and an industrial building. It's one of the oldest buildings in the city. The location was my idea. It's near sacred ground which carries power that can be channeled. The high vantage point gives us clear sight lines in all directions. Most importantly, it's far from innocent bystanders.

"Are you certain about this?" Costin asks, his eyes scanning the horizon for any sign of our enemies.

I nod, feeling the cold power inside me stir in anticipation. After my dream of Conrad, something has shifted. The detachment remains, but it's now tempered with purpose. With humanity.

I doubt that is the gift Conrad meant to give me. I'm sure he fully believed he could talk me into killing our family. I guess he doesn't know me as well as he thought.

"Mortimer won't be able to resist," I say. "Not when he thinks he's finally going to get what he's wanted for decades. Elizabeth's ego will bring her."

Costin's expression tightens at his sister's name.

"The chance to publicly defeat you and prove her superiority once and for all." I turn to him, reaching for his hand. In the past he was unable to kill her. I get why now. The sire bond is a strong, real thing. Compound that with guilt and Costin would be physically unable to destroy his sister. "Are you ready to face her?"

His fingers intertwine with mine. "This confrontation has been coming for centuries."

I feel the sadness in him, and the guilt. When he looks at Elizabeth he still sees the human sister he married to a monster.

"I forgive you." I squeeze his hand. I don't want him carrying me around like a burden. "One way or another, this was my fate. I'm glad it was you who changed me. I wouldn't want anyone else to be my sire."

Red swirls into the whites of his eyes. His fingers brush my cheek. He looks like he wants to say more, but we hear Anthony's voice drifting toward us.

Behind us, the castle's flat roof has been transformed into a battlefield. Anthony and some of his friends have spent hours laying down protective spells. Sully and his most trusted pack members prowl the perimeter, their bodies already showing signs of the approaching transformation as the moon rises higher. Our childhood friend Peter is with them. Even Astrid is here, her usual composure replaced by the cold focus of a general preparing for war.

My father, unsurprisingly, chose to remain at a strategic distance. Yes, he actually called it a strategic distance. His absence barely registers as a disappointment anymore.

I hear someone climb the side of the building seconds before Sully lands next to us. He's half-shifted and breathing heavily as if he's reining the beast within.

"They're coming from the east," he growls, his eyes glowing amber in the rising moonlight.

I feel it too. There's a disturbance in the air. It prickles my skin with the threat of approaching danger.

"Everyone in position," Costin commands, his voice carrying across the rooftop without needing to shout.

The trap has been set. At the center of the roof, a complex ritual circle glows with faint blue light. It's the supposed sire-bond-breaking-ritual that we've circulated rumors of to reach Elizabeth. It's convincing enough to fool her, at least at first glance. Enough to draw her in.

I move to stand within the circle, my heart pounding with a mix of fear and anticipation. Costin takes his place opposite me, our eyes locked in silent communication. The plan relies on timing, on Elizabeth's predictability, on Mortimer's greed.

And on my ability to control the growing power inside me when the full moon finally triggers my first transformation.

Costin's head turns to the distance. A cold wind sweeps across the rooftop, carrying with it the scent of vampire. Elizabeth. And she's not alone.

They appear at the eastern edge of the roof like wraiths materializing from the darkness. Elizabeth leads, resplendent in crimson and black. I've seen her as a bat, but never like this. Behind her is a small army of vampires. Some of them had attacked me with her outside a gas station in my first timeline. The monsters look less scary now.

The air shifts direction with a sudden bite of cold. Frost laces the rooftop beneath Elizabeth's feet as Mortimer appears beside her, not so much stepping from shadows as pulling the darkness into himself to appear. He drags other magics with him, as if they ride in on his gravity. I always hated his transportation trick. It's unsettling. His suit is immaculate, but there's a tremor of violence in the way his magic hisses off his skin. He doesn't look at me. He doesn't need to. His presence alone is a promise of pain.

Mortimer's eyes narrow suspiciously as he looks at the magical markings on the roof and then glances up at the night sky. "What game are you playing?"

"No game," Costin says. "Just tired of the past controlling our future."

"Brother," Elizabeth calls, her voice carrying across the distance between us. "How thoughtful of you to make this so easy for me."

Costin steps forward, positioning himself between me and the newcomers. "Sister. I was beginning to think you wouldn't accept my invitation."

Elizabeth laughs, the sound like broken glass. "And miss your pathetic attempt to break our bond? I wouldn't dream of it." Her eyes shift to me. "Hello, little hybrid. Ready to be free of my brother's influence? Or has he convinced you this ritual will actually work?"

"It doesn't matter if it works, *grandma*," I reply.

She arches a brow and smirks. "Is that the best insult you've got?"

"Why would it be an insult? That's who you are to me, grandma sire." My hands begin to shake. I feel the moon's pull. It's hard to resist.

Elizabeth grins and spreads her arms wide. "Do you think you can break your bond to me?"

"I'm going to try."

"Give it a shot. Try to kill me, little one. I might not have turned you, but you're still bound by my blood." Elizabeth takes a step forward, then stops as she notices the protective circles surrounding our ritual space. "Clever. But not clever enough."

She gestures to her followers, who begin to spread out along the roof's edge. Others land behind her. I count at least twenty vampires and a dozen magics. More than we anticipated, but not enough to overwhelm us if our own allies hold.

"Hey, Uncle Mortimer, I'm curious," I call out, drawing his eyes so that he finally looks at me directly. "Did you tell Elizabeth about your plans for me? Or is she just another pawn in your game?"

Mortimer's smile falters slightly. "I don't know what you're talking about."

"No?" I step forward, feeling the power rise within me. "Not going to mention the ritual you've been designing for decades? The one specifically designed for someone like me? The one meant to extract and transfer magical ability from a blank slate?"

Elizabeth's head turns slowly toward Mortimer, her expression unreadable. "What is she talking about?"

"Nonsense," Mortimer dismisses, but there's a new tension in his posture. "The girl is trying to divide us."

"Am I?" I press. "Or am I just revealing what you've kept hidden? How many allies have you betrayed over the centuries, Uncle? How many schemes within schemes?"

"These markings won't sever the sire bond," Mortimer says. "I told you they were lying. It's half protection spell and half gibberish. And that bit," he gestures at a series of markings, "is to summon... chicken nuggets?"

"Enough," Elizabeth snaps, though her eyes linger on Mortimer with newfound suspicion. I've seen firsthand what Elizabeth does to partners who get in her way. I watched her tear Thane's heart out of his body. If I'm lucky, they'll tear each other apart and save us the trouble. "We didn't come here to talk."

She raises her hand, and her vampires surge forward. At the same moment, Sully lets out a howl that splits the night air. The werewolves emerge from their hiding places around the perimeter, their bodies already half-transformed under the moon's influence as they scale the side of the building.

Sully was right. I feel the pack's raw energy humming in my nerves. It invites me to join them.

Costin doesn't hesitate. He launches himself at Elizabeth. They crash in midair, twisting violently. A loud screech echoes out over the city.

Chaos erupts. Vampires and werewolves clash in a blur of supernatural speed and strength. The magics release balls of energy that illuminate the night sky with flashes of light. Anthony and his friends create temporary barriers to protect our allies.

Astrid fights with deadly precision, slashing through her opponents as if she's releasing centuries of pent-up frustrations. I wouldn't want to be on the receiving end of her lethal magic, as I watch it reduce vampires to dust.

And then there's Mortimer backing away from the front lines as if the chaos will provide the perfect cover. His calculating eyes fixate on me.

I step out of the fake ritual circle, moving to intercept him. The cold magic inside me surges, responding to the danger. It entwines with my vampire's natural tendencies. I embrace it but no longer allow it to control me. At the same time my predator reacts to the moon's pull and the werewolf battle raging around us. The primal urge starts to take over, fueled by the flashing lights of magic and the raw surge of emotions. It's fire to the cold.

"Hello, Uncle," I say, blocking his retreat. My gruff voice is not my own.

His face twists with rage. "You have no idea what you're dealing with, Tamara."

Oh, and there's hunger. The vampire and wolf want to hunt and feed. The need runs through me like lightning. It burns.

"Actually," I smile, feeling my fangs extend, "I think I do."

He throws a spell at me. It's dark and oily as it slithers through the air. I raise my hand, deflecting it with a telekinetic shield. The spell splatters against it, dissolving into black smoke.

Mortimer's eyes widen. "Impossible. Where did you get that?"

"You've been studying me my entire life," I say, advancing on him. I draw a breath. The vampire doesn't need it to live, but the wolf gains energy from it. "Did you really think I wouldn't figure it out eventually? That your precious blank vessel wouldn't fill itself with a power you never anticipated?"

Around us, the fight rages. I catch glimpses of Costin and Elizabeth locked in their own deadly dance, neither gaining the upper hand. Sully and his wolves are holding their own against the vampire forces, their full moon strength making them formidable opponents. Anthony and his magics continue to provide support, though I see them beginning to tire.

And above it all, the moon climbs higher, its pull on my blood growing stronger by the minute.

"How did you get that power?" He backs up, his hands working frantically as he prepares another spell.

"I picked up a few things when I killed your buddy, Leviathan. He had an extensive collection of souls." I deflect his next attack with a casual wave, the telekinetic force growing stronger with each use.

"He should not have had that power," Mortimer blusters. "I would have known."

The moonlight is too much. My pack mates howl. Their cracking bones echo over the roof as they shift completely. My leg jerks, the bone breaking. "I'm done being everyone's pawn."

Mortimer sees it too. His lips curl in a calculating smile. "You can't hold it back forever. When the moon reaches its zenith, you'll lose control. Just like every other monster. And I cage monsters."

"Maybe," I admit, feeling another wave of moon-pull wash over me. My arm breaks and fur sprouts over my chest. "But I'll still be more in control than you've ever been."

I reach out with my mind, grabbing him telekinetically before he can react. His body goes rigid as my invisible force wraps around him, lifting him slightly off the ground. It's hard to hold on to as another cracking bone brings me to my knees.

"What are you doing?" he gasps, fear finally breaking through his composure. He kicks his feet and waves his hands as if trying to grasp onto something solid.

"What I should have done a long time ago." I fall forward and crawl closer, maintaining my hold. "Ending your schemes once and for all."

His eyes dart around frantically, looking for escape or assistance. "You can't kill me. You're not a killer, Tamara. We're blood. We're family."

"I'm not the same person I was," I answer. "But you're right about one thing, I don't want to kill you."

Relief washes over his face, quickly replaced by confusion as I begin to pull at something within him. It's not his physical body, but something rooted much deeper. It flows toward me like the cold power already inside me, but twisted and corrupt.

"What—" he chokes out.

"There is still room in this blank vessel," I tell

him, focusing the telekinetic force inward. Fur runs along my back. I can't hold the wolf back much longer. I pull at the core of his magical essence. My growling voice comes out as a shout. "All the power you've hoarded, all the lives you've manipulated, all the schemes you've woven. It ends now."

His magic fights back, lashing out against my hold. It's slippery and dark. My hybrid strength gives me an edge he doesn't possess. Slowly, painfully, I begin to unravel the complex web of spells and bindings that make up his magical identity.

Mortimer screams, a sound of pure anguish that cuts through the noise of battle. Several heads turn, including Elizabeth's.

"What are you doing to him?" she demands, launching Costin off the side of the roof. Blood drips from her nose and I smell it calling me.

"Exactly what he planned to do to me," I reply, not breaking my concentration. "Stripping him of power he doesn't deserve."

Elizabeth's eyes narrow. She makes no move to interfere and help Mortimer. "You can do that?"

"Apparently."

Costin flies back onto the rooftop, renewing his attack with increased ferocity. There's something different in Elizabeth's movements now. She's not just fighting to win anymore. She's fighting to survive.

Mortimer's screams rise in pitch as more of his magic unravels. It flows into me.

"Please," Mortimer begs, his voice barely audible. "Stop."

He whimpers as the last of his stolen power flows out of him. I finally release him, and he collapses to the roof. He looks old and frail. The powerful magic that has sustained him for centuries is gone. He crawls on his stomach toward me, reaching out as if he can take back his power. His body stiffens and a breeze whips past, blowing him like snow into nothingness.

I didn't intend to kill him, but that's what's happened.

"Goodbye, Mortimer." I turn away from his final resting place, toward the larger battle still raging across the rooftop.

The last of my human form disappears into moonlight. Unlike the shifts I've experienced before, this is overwhelmingly inevitable. Bones continue to crack and reshape. Muscles tear and rebuild. Fur covers my skin. The pain is excruciating, but I don't fight it. I embrace it fully. My mouth elongates and a howl erupts from deep inside my chest. The sound is met by my pack, like locator beacons telling me where they're at.

A scream cuts through the night, sending me on high alert. Anthony. I charge toward my brother.

One of Elizabeth's vampires has him pinned against a chimney stack, fangs inches from his throat. Without thinking, I rip the vampire away with a large paw and fling him off the roof entirely. I hear him smack into something hard.

Sully runs past, brushing up against me before leaping off the roof after the vampire. Anthony stares at my wolf form and then gives me a shaky nod of thanks before rejoining the fight.

I assess the battlefield. Our forces are holding, but just barely. The werewolves' moon-strength gives them an advantage, but Elizabeth's vampires are ancient and skilled. The magics on both sides seem evenly matched. And at the center of it all, Costin and Elizabeth continue their deadly dance, neither able to gain the upper hand. I watch as they transform into bats and dive toward each other in the air.

Two vampires converge on me, and I feel fangs bite into my shoulder. I growl in anger and fling them off. I pounce on the one that lands closest to me. I rip his head from his neck. His heart still beats and I smash into his chest with a heavy paw. His companion looks at me in horror before disappearing into the night in retreat.

I need to end this. Now.

With Mortimer's power added to my own, I feel stronger than ever. The moon pulls at me, but it no longer feels like an irresistible force. It's just another part of what I am now.

Moving to the highest point of the roof, I fight the full shift and raise my hands. I stand, half human, half monster. The telekinetic power surges outward in a wave, separating combatants and holding them in place. Not permanently, but long enough to get their attention.

And not all combatants. I let Astrid, Anthony and Costin maintain their free will. Astrid doesn't hesitate to keep fighting and takes out her opponent.

"Enough!" My voice carries across the roof. "This ends now."

All eyes turn to me in fear and confusion.

"Elizabeth," I call. "Your ally has fallen. Your forces are matched. This battle will only end in mutual destruction."

Elizabeth yanks herself free of my telekinetic hold. Maybe it's the sire bond running through our line, but she's too powerful to be restrained for long. She glares at me. "You think I fear destruction? I've faced death for centuries."

"Then face it one more time," I challenge. "But not with them." I gesture to her followers. "Face it with me. One on one. Winner takes all."

Costin's head snaps toward me. "Tamara, no—"

"Yes," Elizabeth interrupts, a slow smile

spreading across her face. "The hybrid against the master vampire. How poetic."

"Tamara," Costin moves toward me, his eyes pleading. "You don't have to do this."

"I do," I tell him softly. "This is my fight now."

Elizabeth laughs, moving to stand opposite me in the cleared space my telekinetic wave has created. "So eager to die, little hybrid? Even with your new powers, you're no match for me. I've had centuries to perfect mine."

"Maybe," I agree. "But I have something you don't."

"And what's that?"

I smile, feeling the moon reaching its zenith above us. "Perfect timing."

The new transformation slams into me once more.

The werewolf emerges, but it doesn't consume me. The vampire and magic remain, cold and calculating. And beneath them both, the core of who I am holds them in balance. No one alive has seen this before. Three natures, one being.

I rise to my full height, a hybrid in true form at last. Not human, not vampire, not werewolf, but something new and terrible and beautiful. Elizabeth takes an involuntary step back, her composure cracking for the first time.

"What are you?" she whispers.

I don't answer. Words feel clumsy and inadequate in this form. Instead, I move, faster than she can react, my clawed hand closing around her throat. She fights back. Her nails tear at my fur, her fangs snap at my face, and her energy pushes against mine.

But the full moon sings in my blood, and Mortimer's stolen power amplifies my own. I hold her fast, resisting her struggles, until finally she goes still in my grasp.

"Do it," she hisses. "Kill me. Prove you're the monster they all fear."

I lean close, my muzzle next to her ear. "I'm not going to kill you, Elizabeth."

Confusion flashes across her face.

"I'm going to do something much worse," I continue. "I'm going to let you live. Live with the knowledge that you failed. That your brother is free of you. That the power you've sought for centuries will always be beyond your reach."

I release her throat but maintain my telekinetic hold on her body. "You're going to leave this city. You're going to stay away from Costin, from my family, from everyone I care about. If you ever return, if you ever threaten what's mine again, then I will kill you. And Elizabeth?" I lean closer still. "I'll enjoy it."

Fear, *real fear*, flashes in her eyes. She knows I mean every word.

I release her completely, stepping back. "Go."

For a moment, she doesn't move, as if she can't believe I'm actually letting her leave.

"I'm going to kill everything you love," she warns. "Starting with that human brat. This isn't over."

Then, with one last venomous glare, she turns to flee into the night. Costin steps into her path. For a second, I think he's just blocking her exit. But then I feel the bond between sire and sibling breaking like glass. This wasn't my mercy to give. It was his.

Costin's hand dives into his sister's chest.

Her eyes widen in surprise.

"I guess I can't be as forgiving of your many sins," he tells her as he pulls her against him.

Costin holds Elizabeth close, and they drop to the roof. I feel every emotion as it flows through him. Pain, regret, relief. It's all there.

He lovingly touches her face. As if in slow motion, Elizabeth's expression grays. I see pieces of ash floating in the air as she slowly dies. The wind picks up and carries her away. Costin lowers his head, remaining on his knees.

Elizabeth's remaining followers hesitate, then scatter into the night.

The silence that follows is deafening. I stand in

the center of the roof, still in my hybrid form. Around me, the wounded are being tended to.

Then Sully's howl echoes in victory and my head snaps in his direction.

"Go," Costin whispers, not looking up.

A howl erupts from deep inside and I let the moon take me. I fall to all fours and run blindly after my pack in celebration of our victory.

TWENTY-FOUR

The night belongs to us.

Or maybe we belong to the night.

My claws scrape against concrete as I race with the pack across New York City's rooftops. The urban jungle stretches below, a maze of lights and shadows that pulses with its own heartbeat. To anyone on the street, we'd be a blur in the night, some sense of déjà vu.

My new senses detect everything. I feel the rumble of subway trains beneath the streets, smell a cocktail of scents rising from restaurants and alleyways, and hear the electrical hum of power lines crisscrossing overhead.

I don't know where we are going, but I trust my pack to take me there safely. We leap from building to building, supernatural strength making impossible distances manageable. I catch my reflection in passing windows. I'm not fully wolf, not like the others bounding beside me. My hybrid form is larger, more powerful, with a posture that shifts effortlessly between four legs and two. Black fur covers my body, interspersed with streaks of silver that gleam in the moonlight. My snout is shorter than a pure werewolf's, and my teeth are more vampiric.

But the pack accepts me as I am. There's no judgment in their golden eyes, no fear of my differences. To them, I'm just another wolf running under the same moon, sharing in the primal joy of freedom.

Sully leads us, his massive form easily distinguishable as he vaults across a narrow gap between buildings. He stops near a water holding tank and throws his head back, howling at the moon that hangs impossibly large over the city skyline. The others join in, their voices creating a haunting harmony that echoes between skyscrapers.

I add my voice to theirs, feeling the power of it rise from my chest. My howl sounds different from theirs, part wolf's cry, part vampire's shriek, but it blends with the chorus. For these precious moments, I belong.

Even as my body revels in this newfound freedom, my mind can't fully surrender to it. Images from the battle flash through my thoughts. I killed my uncle. Mortimer dissolved into nothingness. I remember Elizabeth's face as Costin's hand plunged into her chest. The ash of her body carried away on the wind.

Costin.

I left him there, kneeling on that rooftop, surrounded by the aftermath of battle and the dust of his sister. I ran with the wolves without a backward glance, abandoning him in what might have been the most painful moment of his centuries-long existence.

The realization hits me like a physical blow. I stumble, nearly slipping off the edge of the roof. Sully notices immediately, padding over to nudge my flank with his muzzle. A question in his eyes.

I shake my massive head, trying to communicate without words. The guilt is a leaden weight in my chest, growing heavier with each passing moment. For the first time since I embraced the transformation, I feel the need to return to my human form, to process these emotions with words rather than instinct.

Sully seems to understand. He makes a soft whuffing sound and gestures with his head back toward the battle site. Permission. Understanding. The pack will continue without me.

I touch my muzzle to his in gratitude, then turn and sprint back the way we came. The city skyline blurs around me as I push my hybrid body to its limits, desperate to return to Costin. Buildings flash past, my powerful legs carrying me faster than I've ever moved before. Gradually, I find my bearings and know where I am.

Costin did what I couldn't bring myself to do. He ended Elizabeth's reign of terror once and for all. After centuries of being controlled by her, of being unable to break free from the sire bond's compulsions, he finally stood up against her. For me.

And I left him.

I reach the battle site in minutes, landing on the roof with barely a sound despite my size. The scene is quieter now. Most of the wounded have been taken away. Only a few figures remain, cleaning up evidence of the supernatural conflict before dawn brings human eyes.

I see him immediately, a solitary figure at the roof's edge, his back to me as he stares out over the city to where Elizabeth's ashes scattered on the wind. His hands are threaded behind his back.

The change comes upon me without conscious effort. My bones shift and reform, fur receding into skin, muzzle shortening into human features. The process is fluid now, almost painless compared to the first transformation. Within moments, I stand on two legs again, naked and vulnerable in the night air.

"Classy, Tam," Anthony drawls. He tosses a jacket in my direction. I hear it and catch it with one hand without turning to look. I put it on, grateful for the small dignity, and slowly approach Costin.

He knows I'm here. I can feel his awareness through our bond, a somber acknowledgment of my presence. But he doesn't turn, doesn't speak.

"Costin," I say softly, stopping a few feet behind him.

His shoulders are rigid, his posture unnaturally still even for a vampire. When he finally speaks, his voice is raw.

"Five hundred years," he says, flexing the hand that killed his sister as he brings it forward. "She was all I had for over five hundred years."

I move closer, the roof cold beneath my bare feet. "I'm sorry I left you. I shouldn't have—"

"No," he interrupts, finally turning to face me. His eyes are rimmed with red. Bloody tracks stain his cheeks. "You needed to run. The moon's energy needed to be released. It's why all wolves have the compulsion to run on the full moon."

The sight of his grief hits me harder than I expect it to. This is Costin. The immortal master vampire has seen civilizations rise and fall. To see him vulnerable breaks something open inside me.

His gaze returns to the horizon. "I had to do it."

"You killed her for me." It's not a question.

"For both of us." He drops his hand to his side, centuries of weariness in the movement. "As long as she lived, neither of us would ever truly be free."

I close the distance between us, letting the ends of the jacket slip open as I reach for his hand. Our fingers intertwine, cool skin against warm. The bond between us pulses, stronger than ever. The city lights cast his face in sharp relief, highlighting the ageless beauty and the very human pain etched there. I've never seen him like this, stripped of his careful control, his walls completely down.

"I never thought I could do it," he admits. "For centuries, I told myself it was the sire bond that prevented me from ending her reign of terror. But it was my own guilt. My own failure to protect her when we were human."

I squeeze his hand. "You didn't fail her, Costin."

"I arranged her marriage to Marcus." His voice is hollow. "I sold my sister to a monster because I was eager to advance our family's position."

His self-loathing cuts deeper than any blade. I can feel it resonating through our bond.

"You didn't know what Marcus was. How could you have? Most humans don't believe in our kind," I say softly. "And she turned you as revenge."

"As punishment. As a twisted form of keeping her family with her forever." He looks down at our joined hands. "I deserved it."

"No," I say firmly. "No one deserves what she did to you. What she tried to do to me. What she tried to do to all supernaturals when she tried to rebalance all the magic in the world. Elizabeth broke a long time ago. Some things you can't fix no matter how much you want to."

He stares into my eyes. "I feel empty. I expected to feel free."

"She's gone. Grief comes, even for the ones who hurt us. Give yourself time. We have plenty of it," I whisper. "She can't hurt anyone anymore."

He smiles sadly. "When did you become so wise?"

"I've had a good teacher." I step closer, letting the jacket fall down my shoulders. His eyes widen slightly, but he doesn't move as I place my hands on his chest. "You taught me that we're more than our natures, Costin. That we can choose who we become."

His hands frame my face. "And who have you chosen to become, Tamara Devine?"

"Someone who doesn't run away," I say, holding his gaze. "Someone who stays."

The bond between us vibrates with emotion, need and grief and hope all tangled together. I rise on my toes, pressing my lips to his in a kiss that's gentle at first, then deepens as he responds. His arms wrap around me, pulling me against him with a desperation that matches my own.

There's no violence in this embrace, no struggle for dominance or control. Just two beings finding solace in each other after the storm.

When we finally break apart, his eyes have shifted to their vampire red, but there's warmth in them now, replacing the hollow grief from before.

"I love you," I tell him, the words falling easily from my lips. "Not because of the sire bond. Not because I have to. *But* because I choose to."

There was a time I would've flinched at those words, when I believed every emotion I felt around him was just some magical compulsion, not real, not mine. I fought against him, against us, too afraid of losing control to admit I already had. But now? Every heartbeat, every choice, is mine.

He pulls me closer, burying his face in my hair. "And I love you," he whispers. "The human, the wolf, the vampire, *all of you.*"

A throat clears somewhere behind us, reminding me we're not alone on the rooftop. Anthony stands awkwardly by the stairwell door, pointedly looking anywhere but at my naked form.

"Um, Tam? Maybe save the romantic reunion for somewhere more private?"

I laugh, feeling lighter than I have in weeks.

Costin pulls the jacket back up my arms, his touch lingering longer than necessary.

"Your brother has a point," he says, though his eyes tell me he's in no hurry to be anywhere else.

"He usually does, the annoying know-it-all." I look over at Anthony, who rolls his eyes but can't hide his smile. "Is everyone okay?"

"Mostly. A few bad injuries, nothing fatal on our side." Anthony gestures toward the stairwell. "Astrid's arranging transport for the wounded. Our father suddenly appeared to fully support our efforts. I imagine he plans to take credit for the victory with the council. You know, the usual family dynamics."

I shake my head but can't find it in me to be angry. Davis Devine will always be Davis Devine. Some things never change.

I feel the first hints of dawn approaching, a subtle pressure against my skin that warns of the coming sunlight. Costin feels it too, his body tensing beside me.

"We should go," he says, his hand finding mine. "The night is ending."

I look at him, *really* look at him. The master vampire who became my reluctant guardian, my sire, my lover, and now something else entirely. Partner. Equal. He finally broke free of his own chains to stand with me.

"No," I correct him gently, squeezing his hand. "It's just beginning, my love."

His smile transforms his face. "Where to, then?"

"Somewhere with a very sturdy bed and excellent blackout curtains," I suggest, feeling heat rise in my cheeks despite everything we've been through together. "We have a lot to celebrate."

"Gross." Anthony makes a gagging noise. "And that's my cue to leave. Don't do anything I wouldn't do, which still leaves you plenty of options."

He disappears through the stairwell door, leaving us alone on the rooftop. The first pale light of dawn touches the eastern horizon, turning the sky from black to deep indigo.

Costin pulls me against him, his arms encircling my waist. "Are you sure about this? About us?" he asks, vulnerability still lingering in his eyes. "You're free now, Tamara. Free of Elizabeth's influence, free to choose your own path."

"I am," I agree, looking up at him. "And I'm choosing you. Not because of fate or prophecy or supernatural bonds, but because it's what I want. What I've always wanted, even when I was fighting against it."

His kiss is tender, reverent, a promise sealed in the growing light of a new day. When he pulls back, his smile holds centuries of patience finally rewarded.

"Let's go home," he says softly.

We leave the rooftop together. He carries me with him as we travel through the city toward his underground home. I feel the balance inside me settling into place. The vampire, the wolf, the magic, the human, all existing in harmony. I don't know what challenges tomorrow will bring, but for the first time since my death, I'm not afraid to face them.

I am Tamara Devine, survivor.

And I am, finally, completely, free.

TWENTY-FIVE

Power recognizes power.

I feel it the moment we enter the council's office building. Heads turn to watch me, all movement stopping as if their motions were merely a pretense to fool humans who might peek inside. I feel them assessing me, measuring the threat I represent. The council building appears unremarkable from the outside, just another glass skyscraper among many. Magical barriers shimmer like heat waves over the sides.

It has been three nights since I took Mortimer's magic and Costin turned his sister to ash. It only took one before the council summoned us to account for our actions. Their summons came in the form of a carded invitation. Though it looked polite, it was anything but. The supernatural world still buzzes with whispers of what we've done.

What I've become.

The elevator doors open as we near them. It's operated by a being that's more shadow than substance.

"State your business," it whispers.

"Council summons," Costin replies, handing over the ornate invitation.

The shadow-operator makes a sound like rustling leaves, then presses a button that wasn't there a moment before. He disappears.

Costin and I ascend in the glass elevator, traveling sixty floors above New York City.

"Ready?" Costin asks, adjusting his tie with the precise movements of someone who's attended a thousand such political gatherings. He's all in black except for a crimson pocket square. The dark waves of his hair are slicked back.

I study my charcoal pantsuit reflected in the elevator walls. I hate to admit I took a page out of Astrid's playbook when picking the outfit. My eyes still flash with hybrid power when I'm not careful. I watch them change, trying to control it. The silver threading catches the light and draws my gaze to the white gold butterfly brooch Costin gave me. He says it's a symbol of how far I've come.

"As I'll ever be," I finally answer as the elevator

doors open, depositing us in an opulent reception area. "Though I can think of better ways to spend the evening."

His lips twitch to suppress a smile. We've barely left his bed since the battle, finding solace in each other as we process everything that's happened. The loss of Elizabeth still weighs on him, but there's a new freedom in his movements, a lightness I've never seen before. The few times we do emerge it's to find his home has become our unofficial headquarters since the battle, with various allies coming and going.

The taste of victory is surprisingly bitter. I thought defeating Elizabeth and Mortimer would feel like freedom. Instead, as we walk toward the ornate doors of the supernatural council's conference room, it feels like trading one cage for another.

His hand brushes my cheek. "Be careful, Tamara. The council respects strength, but they fear chaos more."

"You think they'll still see me as the threat?"

"I think they'll see you as an opportunity," he corrects. "And in supernatural politics, that can be more dangerous."

We near the doors.

"The hybrid must be controlled." The words echo from inside before I even enter.

I pause outside the conference room, my

enhanced hearing picking up the heated debate within.

"This battle was not sanctioned," a man answers.

A woman laughs. "Since when are fights sanctioned in our world? Do you really want to have to regulate every supernatural dispute?"

Costin's eyes meet mine in silent question. I straighten my shoulders and nod. Under my breath, I say, "Let them question. We did them a favor."

I'm done being controlled.

"Come in," the woman calls as if sensing we're here.

"Elder Vasilisa?" I mouth to Costin. He nods that my guess is correct.

The sound of footsteps run behind us. I turn to find Anthony rushing to our side. His face bright with exertion. "Sorry I'm late."

I touch his shoulder, brushing a piece of lint from his jacket.

"You're not going to believe who just arrived," he says.

"Father?" I guess, already dreading the inevitable posturing.

"Better. Zephronis and he looked pissed," Anthony says. "He shimmered into the lobby. I blinked and he was gone again."

"The ancient wizard rarely involves himself

directly in council affairs," Costin says. "He's been showing himself a great deal lately."

"I think he might be a little sweet on Tamara," Anthony teases.

I elbow my brother in his ribs.

"We shouldn't keep them waiting." Costin pulls open the door.

Astrid and my father are already there. They block the way inside.

"There you are," Davis says, reaching to give me a polite hug. I stiffen at the surprise contact. "I was beginning to think you weren't coming."

"And miss your moment of glory?" I grumble under my breath, unable to keep the edge from my voice. "Wouldn't dream of it."

My father's expression tightens, but he says nothing as he reaches to shake hands with Costin. Beside him, Astrid studies me with those ice-blue eyes that see too much. She looks elegant as always in a silver dress that complements her pale blonde hair, but there's a tension in her posture.

"The council is ready for us," she says.

They step aside to escort us in. The round room is dominated by a half-circle table. Twelve seats line the curve, each occupied by a representative of a major supernatural faction. Not all factions, though. I see the werewolves are not represented.

Zephronis stands near the head of the table, his

ageless face impossible to read. He gestures for us to approach. We didn't see him pass us in the hall, but I'm not surprised he beat us into the room.

"The Devine family and Lord Constantine," announces a spectral voice. "As summoned."

We move forward as a group, though I notice my father positioning himself at the front. Some things never change.

"Lord Constantine," Vasilisa greets, holding his name in her mouth like a seduction. "Please, join me."

She motions to the empty chair next to her.

"I'm where I belong," he answers, staying beside me.

Vasilisa smirks. "Davis?"

I watch my father seat himself between Vasilisa and Elder Decimus, the same council member who questioned me during my first appearance. The image of him taking a seat of honor pisses me off, but Astrid catches my eye and gives a subtle shake of her head.

Decimus stands. "Davis Devine. You and your family have been called to account for the events of the full moon. The death of Lady Elizabeth and the disappearance of Mortimer Devine have caused significant upheaval in our community."

My father stands, his chin lifted with practiced confidence. "Elder Decimus, honorable council members, I stand before you to take full responsibility for the actions taken that night."

"You—" I start to protest, but Costin's hand on my arm stops me. His slight head shake tells me to wait.

"The threat posed by Lady Elizabeth had grown too great to ignore," my father continues. "Her alliance with my brother Mortimer represented a direct challenge to the established order. I had suspected and monitored my brother for years." He gives a dramatic shake of his head. "I didn't want to believe what he was capable of, but the proof became too great to ignore. As head of the Devine family and respected magic representative, I made the difficult decision to confront this threat head-on. It is my sad duty to report, Mortimer is not missing. He is dead. My son Anthony will be taking over his uncle's responsibilities."

Anthony takes a deep breath and lowers his head. He stares at the floor like he wants to set it on fire.

My father wasn't even present for the battle, yet here he is, claiming credit for our victory as if it was his master strategy all along.

"And what of the hybrid?" asks Madam Britannia, her gaze fixed on me. "Your daughter's evolution has not gone unnoticed."

"Tamara has proven herself a valuable asset to

our family," my father says smoothly. "Her unique abilities were instrumental in our success."

"Asset?" I can't help but interject. "Is that what I am now?"

Davis turns to me, a warning in his eyes. "Tamara, please. The council is addressing me."

"Actually," Zephronis says, speaking for the first time, "I believe it is Tamara Devine who should be addressing the council."

A murmur runs through the assembled elders. My father's face flushes with surprise and barely concealed annoyance.

"With all due respect," he begins, "as head of the Devine family—"

"The events of the full moon were not orchestrated by you, Davis Devine," Zephronis interrupts, his voice quiet but carrying absolute authority. "Nor were they merely family business. They represent a fundamental shift in the supernatural balance, one that requires an honest accounting."

He turns to me, his ancient eyes seeing far more than I'm comfortable with. "Tamara Devine. Please tell the council what truly happened."

All eyes turn to me. I feel Costin's silent support, Anthony's nervous energy, Astrid's careful attention. It's nothing compared to my father's growing discomfort.

I step forward. The hybrid inside me is calm,

centered. I am not the scared human girl who once stood before them, nor am I the unstable newborn monster they feared.

"Honorable council," I begin, keeping my voice steady. "The conflict with Elizabeth and my uncle was inevitable. They sought power at any cost. Elizabeth through vampire dominance. Mortimer through magical manipulation. Their alliance was one of convenience, not loyalty."

I recount the battle truthfully, leaving nothing out. The trap we set, the werewolves' aid under the full moon, the confrontation with Elizabeth, and Costin's final action against his sister. I even tell them of Mortimer's attempt to steal my power and how I turned his own plans against him.

"Elizabeth and Mortimer represented a threat not just to my family and to Lord Constantine, but to the balance this council is sworn to protect," I conclude. "We did what was necessary."

Silence falls over the chamber as the council members process my account. Some look troubled, others thoughtful. Zephronis gives me a subtle nod of approval.

Elder Decimus leans forward. "And what of your own transformation? The reports we've received suggest abilities beyond what any hybrid should possess."

"I am what circumstances have made me," I

reply simply. "A hybrid, yes, but one who has learned to balance my natures rather than let them tear me apart."

"And the telekinetic abilities?" Madam Britannia asks, her eyes narrowed. "Such power is rare."

I consider lying or at least minimizing the truth. But the time for half-measures is past. "When Leviathan was defeated, I absorbed some of the energy released by the freed spirits he had trapped. I can't tell you the source of the power."

Another murmur runs through the council.

"Demonstrated control or not, such concentration of power in one being is concerning." Elder Birch strokes his beard. "The potential for disruption—"

"Is no greater than the potential for stability," Zephronis interrupts. "Tamara Devine has done what no hybrid before her has accomplished. She has found balance. Not just between vampire and werewolf, but between power and restraint."

My father shifts uncomfortably. I can practically see his mind working, trying to calculate how to turn this situation to his advantage.

"The council must consider what this means for our future," Elder Decimus says cautiously. "The wolves are without an Alpha—"

"The wolves have chosen Sully as their Alpha," Anthony interjects. I look at him in surprise. His voice drops a little, like he wants to backtrack his sudden blurting. "He's proven himself loyal to the supernatural order."

"Sully is Alpha. He's completed the trials," I clarify. "The pack follows him willingly. I support him."

"And the vampire hierarchy?" Madam Britannia asks, looking at Costin. "With your sister gone, Lord Constantine, there will be a power vacuum."

Costin steps forward, commanding respect. "There is no vacuum. I maintain my position as master vampire. Those who followed Elizabeth have either pledged themselves to me or fled."

"And what of you two?" Elder Birch asks, looking between Costin and me. "The sire bond complicates matters. With control over her, the vampires will be too powerful. We can't ignore that fact."

"The sire bond exists," Costin acknowledges. "But it does not define our relationship or Tamara's choices."

"I am not anyone's puppet," I add, meeting Elder Birch's gaze steadily. "Not my sire's, not my father's, not this council's. I make my own choices."

Davis clears his throat. "What my daughter means—"

"Is exactly what she said," Astrid interrupts, stepping forward to stand beside me. "The time for speaking for Tamara is over. She has earned the right to speak for herself."

The look my father gives Astrid would wither a lesser being, but she merely lifts her chin, unmoved. In that moment, I see the steel beneath Astrid's perfect composure, the power she's wielded behind the scenes all these years.

"Lady Astrid speaks wisely," Zephronis says. "And it brings us to the purpose of this gathering. The events of the full moon have created an opportunity, not just for the Devine family or for Lord Constantine, but for our entire community."

He turns to address the full council. "For too long, we have clung to old divisions. Vampire versus werewolf. Magic versus creature. These artificial boundaries have made us vulnerable to those who would exploit our differences for their own gain."

"What are you suggesting?" Elder Decimus asks, though his tone suggests he already knows.

"A new council seat," Zephronis replies. "One that represents those who exist between our traditional factions. A voice for the hybrids, the cross bloods, the unconventional. And I nominate Tamara Devine to fill it."

The chamber erupts in chaos, everyone talking over each other. My father's face goes from shock to calculation in the span of a heartbeat. He stands and comes around the table to be near me. Anthony's mouth drops open. Astrid looks proud.

And me? I feel like the floor has dropped out from beneath my feet. "Wait, no, that's not—"

"Impossible," Elder Birch protests. "She's barely controlled her own nature, let alone—"

"She stood against two of the greatest threats our community has faced in centuries," Costin counters. "She has demonstrated not just power, but wisdom. She's fulfilled multiple prophecies."

Why is Costin fighting for this? I don't want to be on the council. That's worse than being named Alpha and having to be responsible for just the wolves.

"She is untested," Madam Britannia argues. "Too young—"

"She completed the labyrinth when she was still human," Anthony puts forth. "How many mortals do you know who would have made it through those trials?"

"Few have faced what she has and emerged stronger," Astrid interjects.

Through it all, Zephronis watches me, waiting for my response. He lifts his hands. The room falls silent, their arguments exhausted for the moment.

"Tamara Devine," Zephronis says into the quiet. "Will you accept this responsibility? Will you stand as voice for those who have none, as bridge between worlds that have too long been separate?"

My father steps closer, his voice dropping to a

whisper. "Think of what this means for the family, Tamara. The prestige, the influence. You must say yes. Don't you see what this could mean for us?"

I look at him, really look at him. My father, always calculating, always maneuvering. In his own way, he cares for me, but he will never understand what truly matters.

"I'll consider the nomination," I say finally, addressing the council rather than my father. "But I have conditions."

Elder Decimus raises an eyebrow. "Conditions? You presume much. This is an honor. Not a negotiation."

"I presume nothing," I reply evenly. "I simply know what I'm willing to accept."

"What conditions?" Vasilisa asks.

"Speak your terms," Zephronis encourages, ignoring the discomfort of some of the council members.

"First, my position will be entirely my own. Not an extension of the Devine family's influence, not a puppet seat controlled by others. I will speak with my own voice or not at all."

My father stiffens beside me. I continue without pausing.

"Second, I will work with Sully to ensure werewolf concerns are fairly represented. They have been relegated to the margins for too long. The werewolves will have a seat at the table."

Several council members shift uncomfortably, but none object outright.

"Third, I require time. Time to fully master my abilities, time to understand what I am and what I can be. I will not take a council seat until I am certain I can fulfill its responsibilities properly."

Zephronis nods, a glimmer of approval in his ancient eyes. "Reasonable terms, all. The council will consider them."

"There is no need for consideration," Madam Britannia says, surprising me. "I, for one, find these terms acceptable. Tamara Devine has shown wisdom in not grasping for power before she is ready. It speaks well of her judgment."

One by one, the other council members nod their agreement, even Elder Birch, though he does so reluctantly.

"Then it is settled," Zephronis announces. "Tamara Devine will join this council when she is ready, as representative of a new faction. A year should be enough time. We don't meet again until then, anyway. Until that time, she will be afforded the respect and protection due a council nominee."

A year? That's not exactly what I had in mind when I said I wanted time to master myself. Zephronis knows it too. I see it in his expression.

"It is decided," Zephronis states.

It's over so quickly I barely have time to process what's happened. The council moves on to other business, and we are dismissed with ceremonial courtesy. As we leave the conference room, I catch Anthony by the arm.

"What was all that about?" I whisper.

"What? You mean you being on the council?" He avoids my eyes.

"Don't what me. What was all that stammering about Sully? Are you guys...?" I'm interrupted as my father appears next to me. He grips me by my elbow and squeezes.

"You could have seized that seat immediately," he says, his voice low with displeasure. "Why delay? Why surrender the advantage? So much can happen in a year."

I gently but firmly remove his hand from my arm. "Because I'm not you. I don't want power for its own sake."

"Then what do you want?" he demands, genuinely perplexed.

I look past him to where Costin waits by the elevator, his eyes meeting mine with understanding and love. To Anthony, whose face shines with pride for his sister. To Astrid, who looks at me like an equal.

"Balance," I tell my father. "Freedom. The right

to define myself on my own terms. And I think I want to get married to Costin."

There was a time I didn't want magic in my life. I would've given anything to stay human. But everything changed. Now I finally get to decide what that change means.

His brow furrows. "That's not how our world works, Tamara. There are always obligations, allegiances, compromises."

"Maybe it's time our world changed," I reply. "Maybe that's what I'm here for."

I leave him standing there, speechless for once, and join the others. As the elevator carries us down, Anthony bursts into astonished laughter.

"A council seat? My baby sister, on the high council? That's..." he searches for words, "that's kind of hilarious."

I arch a brow at him, so he knows I'm not done asking about Sully.

"It's a target on her back," Costin says soberly. "There will be those who oppose this change, who see Tamara as a threat to the old order."

"What's new," I say, finding a confidence I never knew I possessed. "I've faced worse than politicians and bureaucrats."

Astrid studies me with those calm eyes, her expression inscrutable as always. But when she speaks, there's a warmth in her voice I've rarely heard before.

"You've surpassed every expectation I ever had for you, Tamara," she says. "Though I suspect that was always your intention."

I'm not quite sure how to respond to this praise. For so long, I've craved Astrid's approval while simultaneously resenting that I needed it at all.

"Old habits," I say finally, with a small shrug.

The hint of a smile touches her lips. "I look forward to seeing what new habits you form."

The elevator doors open to the lobby, and we step out together.

"So," Anthony says as we exit the building into the night air, "did you mean that part about marrying Costin, or was that just to shock our father into silence?" He chuckles. "I wish we could resurrect Mortimer just to see his face when you tell him there is going to be a vampire in the family."

I feel Costin go still beside me, his eyes suddenly intent on my face. The sire bond pulses between us, but it's not the bond that makes my heart race.

"I meant it," I say simply, holding Costin's gaze. "If he'll have me."

For a being who's lived centuries, Costin looks remarkably stunned. "Tamara…"

"Don't answer now," I tell him. "Take some time. Think it over. I'm not going anywhere."

The smile that spreads across his face transforms him. Not the careful, measured smile he shows the world, but something genuine and almost boyish.

"My answer is yes," he says, taking my hand and pulling me into his arms.

Anthony makes a gagging noise. "And that's my cue." He turns to Astrid. "Please tell me you have a car waiting."

"Of course," she replies, her eyes still on us. "Tamara, we'll speak tomorrow about the next steps. Costin, start thinking about a guest list."

I hear a motorcycle and feel the pull of my pack. I turn, knowing it's Sully before he pulls up.

"Never mind," Anthony says, winking at me. "I've got a ride."

Astrid looks at the Alpha and then her son. Her expression gives nothing away.

I lift a hand to Sully, giving a small wave. He nods.

Anthony joins him by the curb. There's a brief hesitation, and Sully reaches out, picking a stray hair from Anthony's shoulder. The touch is more tender than casual.

Anthony startles slightly, then glances back toward Astrid as if out of old habit. She's watching them, her mouth quirked in something between approval and amusement.

I go to my brother and Sully. "How did I miss this? How long has this been....?"

Anthony shrugs and gives me a slight smirk. "When you were trapped in the crypt, you told me to live my life. Guess I finally listened."

"You just liked how I looked fighting zombies." Sully chuckles low, and for the first time, some of Anthony's ever-present tension slips away. "Ready?"

"Always," Anthony says.

They don't kiss. They don't announce anything. But when my brother swings his leg over the back of Sully's bike and smiles at me, I can tell he's no longer holding onto that secret.

"I love you," I mouth to Anthony, happy for him.

"I know," he answers. "I'm very loveable."

They take off and I hear my brother's voice drifting back, "...my sister on the council and marrying the master vampire. My dad's going to have a coronary."

Astrid joins us on the curb. "It's not who I would have picked for him, but it's about time."

I look at her in surprise.

"He's my son. Of course I've known since he was a boy," Astrid said. Then to Costin, she says, "Get me that guest list."

She walks toward her waiting town car.

My focus returns to Costin. The rest of the world seems to fade around the edges.

"I can't believe I proposed to you in front of my family while arguing with my father," I admit to Costin once we're alone.

"I can," he says, pulling me closer. "You've never done anything the expected way. Why start now?"

His lips find mine. The future with all its complexities falls away. There will be time enough tomorrow to deal with council politics, with my new position, with whatever challenges come next.

Tonight belongs to us.

As we break apart, I notice the moon rising over the city skyline, no longer full but still luminous. I feel its gentle pull, a reminder of what I am now.

"Take me home," I tell Costin.

His eyes meet mine, understanding all I'm not saying.

Balance. Freedom. Love.

For the first time since my transformation, I'm excited to have all three.

TWENTY-SIX

I'm awake to watch the blackout shades rise to let the last rays of dusk filter through the windows of Costin's sanctuary penthouse. There is an almost gold to the light for the briefest of seconds before it turns dark. I stand watching the colors shift, remembering when sunshine was something I took for granted. Now it's a reminder of what I've lost and what I've gained.

"You're up early," Costin murmurs, his arms encircling my waist from behind as he finds me in the living room. He presses a kiss to my shoulder, and I lean into him, savoring the cool strength of him.

"Big night," I remind him. My stomach is in knots. "Paul and Diana are coming."

He tenses slightly but says nothing. After everything that's happened, he's still wary of my connection to Paul. Not jealous. We're beyond that now. But concerned about the pain reopening old wounds might cause.

"I need this closure," I say, answering his unspoken worry. I can't seem to stop pulling the humans into my orbit, but I have to say goodbye. A final-final-*final* goodbye. Hopefully one where no one tries to kill any of us. "We all do."

His lips find my neck and fangs tease my skin. "I know. I've arranged everything as you asked. There will be extra security. No one unauthorized in or out. Human snacks are prepared. They're on the dining table."

The penthouse apartment is neutral territory, not Costin's underground lair or my family's estate. Somewhere Paul and Diana will feel safe, where a child won't be overwhelmed by supernatural energy. Plus, there are no secret tunnels leading to the underground city. I'm not taking any chances that goblins might try to sneak in, or elves decide suddenly to revolt.

"Thank you," I say, turning in his arms to face him. "For understanding."

His smile is gentle. "I've had centuries to learn patience, Tamara. A few more hours are nothing."

"Is that what you tell yourself about the wedding?" I tease, referring to Astrid's insistence on planning what she calls, *"an appropriate ceremony befitting the Devine name and the master vampire."* Three weeks of preparation already, and she's talking about months more.

"I'd marry you tonight if you wanted," he says seriously. "No witnesses, no ceremony. Only us."

The intensity in his gaze makes me shiver. "Don't tempt me. Astrid would never forgive us."

He laughs, the sound still rare enough to feel like a gift. "Then we wait. After all, we have forever."

Forever. The word doesn't scare me anymore.

The doorbell rings, interrupting our moment. I feel a flutter of nervous anticipation. "They're early."

"Do you want me to stay?" Costin asks.

I shake my head. "This is something I need to do alone." I press a kiss to his lips and glance down his naked body. "Besides, I think you should probably put some clothes on before you greet guests."

He chuckles and nods in understanding.

"If you need me I'll hear you." He vanishes in a blur toward the back of the apartment as I move to answer the door.

Paul waits on the other side, Diana half-hidden behind him. He looks better than when I last saw him, though there are new shadows in his eyes. Diana peers around his leg, her face lighting up when she sees me.

"Tamara!" She breaks free of her father's protective stance and launches herself at me. A backpack drops on the floor behind her.

I catch her, careful of my strength, and hug her close. The amulet hangs around her neck, its magic a familiar vibration against my skin. "I've missed you."

"I missed you too. Did you know I got to see real wolves?" Her excitement bubbles over. "They were huge. And they let me pet them!"

I raise an eyebrow at Paul over her head. He shrugs as he lifts the backpack from the floor. "Sully and Anthony's idea. They know how important she is to you and thought she should understand that part of your world. Sully said something about the pack protecting their own."

So Sully had visited them? That's surprisingly sweet.

"Sully's funny," Diana says.

"Oh, uh, sorry, come in," I say, stepping back as I realize I'm blocking the entrance.

Paul hesitates at the threshold and glances at Diana "Is he...?"

"Giving us space," I tell him.

He nods and enters, his hand protectively on Diana's shoulder.

"Nice place," he says, taking in the modern furniture and floor-to-ceiling windows with their spectacular view of New York at twilight. Diana bounces ahead to explore the penthouse.

I don't want to tell him it's only one of many homes Costin owns. I honestly don't even know how many he has. I never thought to ask. "We like it."

"We," he repeats. His eyes find my antique engagement ring, a simple platinum band with a blood-red stone. "Anthony mentioned you're getting married."

"Yes."

An awkward silence falls between us. There's so much to say, and no easy place to start.

"I wanted to say—" I begin.

Diana breaks the tension, running back into the room.

"You can see the whole city from here." She tugs at Paul's hand. "Dad, come look!"

I let her lead us to the window. The three of us stand side by side, watching the city lights come alive as darkness falls.

"It's pretty here," Diana says. Then, with the directness only children possess, she asks, "Are you really a vampire now?"

Paul starts to object, but I stop him with a look. "Yes," I tell her honestly. "And a werewolf too. I'm something new."

Her eyes widen. "Cool! Can you turn into a bat?"

I laugh despite myself. "Not yet. Maybe someday."

"Can I pet you when you're a wolf? Sully says I can't just pet any wolf."

I nod. "Sully is right. Ask your dad before you do anything with the supernatural. That's important."

"Does this mean I'll be special someday too?" She touches the amulet.

I really hope not. "You're already special. The dragon needs you to be you."

"Can I see your fangs?" Her boundless curiosity is untainted by fear.

"Diana," Paul warns, but I shake my head.

"It's okay." I kneel to her level. "Are you sure? It might be scary."

She nods eagerly. I let my fangs extend slightly, just enough to be visible without being terrifying.

Instead of recoiling, she leans closer, fascinated. "They're cool. Dad, can I get fangs?"

I retract them, feeling a strange relief. Children see the world so differently.

"Absolutely not," Paul states.

"The amulet's keeping you safe?" I ask, touching the pendant at her throat. "Draakmar is behaving himself?"

She nods solemnly. "It gets warm sometimes when there's danger. Dad says that means it's working."

"Smart dad," I say, standing up again. "It'll always protect you, as long as you wear it."

"Draakmar gives me his dreams sometimes. He really likes fires," Diana says. "Did he do that to you too?"

I nod. Though, the visions the ancient dragon gave me were his fantasies of fire consuming the world as he destroyed it. I put a stop to that plan, and suspect it was the dragon's way of keeping his magic before Elizabeth and Thane tried to steal it. Hopefully, things will be easier for Diana. She doesn't seem afraid, and maybe that's the difference. Draakmar chose her. The dragon's connection to the girl seems strong. That's good.

Paul's expression has softened, watching our interaction. "Diana, why don't you go draw a picture for Tamara? I packed your markers."

He lifts the backpack. She needs no further encouragement as she grabs it, racing off to the dining table.

"Help yourself to the snacks," I call after her.

Alone with Paul, I feel the weight of our complicated history. I think of the timeline that was erased from when we were together, and the memories given back to us. I think of the dangers I've brought into his life, and the impossibility of what might have been.

"Anthony mentioned you're heading to Kansas City," I prompt quietly. I know his parents live there. They're good people.

He nods. "It's a fresh start, away from all of this. My business has gone under since I've been," he gestures vaguely, encompassing the supernatural world that's become my home, "away. Your brother and Sully have arranged protection for all of us. Discreet, he promised."

"He's good to his word," I assure him. "The pack will make sure you're both safe."

"And what about you?" he asks. "Will you be safe?"

After everything, his concern still touches me more than I expected. He still cares.

"I'm learning," I tell him honestly. "Every day gets a little easier. And I have people watching my back."

"The vampire," he says, as if not quite able to say Costin's name.

"Among others." I don't elaborate. Paul doesn't need to know about council politics or my newfound abilities. The less he knows, the safer he'll be.

He runs a hand through his hair, a familiar gesture that once made my heart race. Now it's just a memory, bittersweet but fading.

"I wanted to hate him," Paul admits. "For taking you away. For changing you. But when I saw how he fought to save you that night in the graveyard..." He shakes his head. "He loves you. I can't hate him for that."

"Thank you," I say softly. "That means more than you know to hear you say that."

"We had something real, didn't we?" he asks. "In that other timeline. Before everything reset. When you were human, we were real."

I nod, throat tight with emotion. I thought he could be my future, but he was just my waystation. "We did. It was beautiful, Paul. But it wasn't meant to be."

"Because of what you are."

"Because of what I've always been," I correct gently. "This was always my path. I just didn't see it. Even when I was human, I was never fully part of your world. I just didn't want to admit it. I wanted to be normal so badly."

Diana returns, proudly displaying a drawing of what appears to be a wolf standing next to a figure with fangs.

I take the picture, genuinely touched. "Thank you, sweetheart. It's perfect. I'll keep it forever."

And I mean it literally. Long after Diana has grown old and forgotten this night, I'll remember the little girl who saw the monster in me and called it cool. The idea of it makes tears fill my eyes. I don't like the thought of losing her.

"We should go," Paul says, checking his watch. He goes to retrieve her backpack. "Our flight leaves early tomorrow. I need to sign some papers with the realtor selling our house and do some packing."

I walk them to the door, knowing this is truly goodbye. Not just for now, but likely forever. It's better this way, safer for them, cleaner for all of us. But it still aches.

I kneel to hug Diana. "Have so much fun with your grandparents, and be good for your dad, okay? And remember, if the amulet ever gets warm, listen to it. Go close to your dad. It can protect you and him."

"Will you come visit us?" she asks.

"We'll see," Paul says. "Let's get settled first."

"If you ever need me, I'll be there," I promise her.

"Come on, sweetie." Paul nudges her to come with him.

She nods solemnly, then surprises me with a kiss on the cheek. "Bye, Tamara!"

Paul hesitates, then hugs me too, a brief embrace that carries the weight of what might have been in another life.

"Be happy," he whispers.

"You too," I reply. "Both of you."

I watch them walk down the hallway to the elevator, Diana's chatter fades as the doors close. Another chapter of my life, ending. But this time, it's a gentle closing, not a violent tearing.

I sense Costin before I see him, standing in the doorway behind me.

"You good?" he asks simply.

I nod, surprised to find it's true. "Yeah."

"How can I help?"

"I cost them so much. I uprooted their lives. He lost his business. They have to move." I sigh.

I know he can feel my guilt, just as I feel his concern.

"I want to buy his house above asking, enough to matter but not draw suspicion. Anonymously," I decide. That will give them help in the immediate future. "And I want to set up a trust fund for Diana. I never want her to have to worry. It's the least I owe them."

Costin doesn't even blink. "I'll call the lawyers. It will be done."

His arms enfold me, and I lean into his strength, grateful for his comfort. I feel our bond wrapping around us and we stand in silence for a long moment. He understands that some moments don't need words.

"Lorelai will be here soon," he reminds me after a while.

I sigh, sensing my mother's arrival. "Another goodbye."

"It doesn't have to be," he says. "California isn't that far."

"Are you saying you want to move to the golden state? Can't get enough sunshine here?" I tease, but I know what he means. Unlike Paul and Diana, my separation from Lorelai doesn't need to be permanent. She's part of the supernatural world, whether she wanted to be or not. It happened the second she had her affair with my father.

The doorbell rings again. This time, it's my birth mother who stands there. Her bohemian skirts swirl around her ankles, and her bracelets jingle on her wrists.

"Butterfly," she says, embracing me without hesitation. She smells of incense and essential oils.

I hug her back, careful of my strength. "Thanks for coming."

Costin excuses himself discreetly, giving us privacy. Lorelai moves into the apartment, her gaze taking in everything with the artist's eye.

"So this is where vampires live these days," she muses. "Much nicer than crypts and dungeons, I imagine."

I laugh. "Costin has those too. And apparently a place in the mountains. But this is more practical for New York."

She settles on the couch, patting the spot beside her. I join her, feeling a strange mix of comfort and awkwardness. Our relationship is still new, still finding its shape.

"The council has been in touch," she says without preamble.

I stiffen. "What? Why?"

"Apparently having a daughter who's about to join the supernatural high council makes me a person of interest." She smiles wryly. "They offered protection."

"Protection or surveillance?" I'm immediately suspicious.

"Both, probably." She shrugs. "I have to admit, I was surprised."

"Astrid's already making arrangements for my appointment," I say, half amused, half exasperated. "She's calling in favors I didn't know she had."

Lorelai chuckles. "That woman could outmaneuver a fae queen with one eyebrow raise."

"What did you say?" I ask.

"I declined. I have my own methods."

I frown. She should take the help. I'm going to make sure she has it whether she wants it or not. "Such as?"

"You'd be surprised what a lifetime of studying magic can teach you. Just because I'm human doesn't mean I'm helpless." Her eyes twinkle. She touches my cheek. "I was able to help protect you all those years. I think if the supernatural world wanted me dead, it would have happened by now."

All this time, she'd been watching over me in her

own way. I remember she'd bartered with trolls for the amulet Diana now wears. I think back to the butterflies that used to appear when I needed help. The strange coincidences that saved me more than once.

I put my hand over hers. "Thank you. For everything."

"I'm going back to California," she continues. "My life is there. But I want you to know you always have a place with me, if you want it. A mother always finds ways to help. We could be happy there, away from this city. I used to dream about you coming to live with me. You're different now, but it could still happen. We'll convert the basement. I'll make a deal with a blood bank. You'll be safe."

"Thank you," I say, meaning it. "But my place is here now."

"With him," she says, glancing toward where Costin had disappeared.

"With myself," I correct. "I fought for so long to be normal. Now I know I never really was. And that's okay. I know who I am now. What I can be."

She studies me, her eyes so like mine. "You've found your path."

"I'm getting there."

"That's all any of us can do." She takes my hands in hers. "I'm proud of you, butterfly. Not because of what you've become, but because of how you've faced it. With courage. With heart."

Tears prick at my eyes. All my life, I've wanted to hear those words from a parent who truly saw me. Not as an asset or a disappointment or a project, but as a person.

"Costin is very lucky to have you," she says. "Don't ever forget that. He's the lucky one."

I want to argue and tell her I'm the lucky one, but I don't. "I'd invite you to the wedding, but—"

"It'll be a supernatural affair," she finishes. "I understand."

"You should visit, though" I tell her. "After."

"Wild horses couldn't keep me away." She squeezes my hands. "Or vampires. Or werewolves."

We talk throughout the night, catching up on everything that's happened. I tell her about the battle, about finding balance between my natures, about the council's offer. She tells me about her art, her friends, her quiet life that somehow intersects with the supernatural world more than I ever realized.

When she finally leaves, it's with promises to call, to visit, to stay connected. Not a goodbye, but a beginning.

Costin finds me on the balcony afterward, watching the light shift over the city as dawn approaches. He wraps a blanket around my shoulders, though I no longer feel the cold the way I once did.

"How did it go?" he asks, handing me a glass of blood.

"Better than I expected," I admit. "I thought I'd be mad at her for leaving me as a baby, but I realized the past doesn't matter. Life is messy. We're all doing our best to make it work."

"It is good you spoke with her," he says, a smile in his voice. "Sully called while you were talking. I didn't want to interrupt. He wanted us to know that things are calm but not settled. His exact words were, 'there are always shadows after a storm.'"

"That feels like a next week problem." I lean back against him, savoring his presence. "Have you thought about where we'll live? After everything settles down."

"Wherever you want." His arms tighten around me. "New York. Romania. The moon. I don't care, as long as we're together."

I laugh. "The moon might be difficult, even for us."

"Give it a few centuries. Humans will build something there, and we'll follow." His tone is light but sincere. "That's the gift of immortality, Tamara. We have time to see it all, do it all."

Immortality. The word still feels strange, a concept too vast to fully comprehend. But with

Costin, it doesn't feel like a sentence. It feels like hope.

"I was thinking somewhere quieter," I say. "At least for a while. Somewhere we can just be, without council politics or family expectations."

"I know just the place," he murmurs against my hair. "A little estate in the Rocky Mountains of Colorado. Isolated. Beautiful. Room for wolves to run."

An image forms in my mind of snow-capped peaks, forests stretching for miles, open skies where stars blaze without city lights to dim them.

"Perfect," I say.

"There is a ghost town on the property that can be quite entertaining," he adds. "I've seen a ghost duel."

I chuckle. "No thanks. I might avoid that for the time being. I think I've had my fill of hauntings."

He turns me in his arms, his expression suddenly serious. "Are you sure about this, Tamara? About us? About everything?"

I know what he's really asking. Am I sure about binding my life to his for however many centuries we have?

"I'm sure," I tell him, holding his gaze. "It won't always be easy. But nothing worth having ever is."

His kiss is gentle, reverent, a promise that spans centuries. We make love with the city lights spread beneath us like fallen stars. Our clothing slips from our bodies, but I don't feel the night air. All I feel is our bond, drawing me closer.

There is no frantic rush to completion because we have all the time in the world. Every kiss, every caress feels like a promise, not one made in words, but through skin and blood and unspoken need. Costin's hands moves over me like he's rediscovering something sacred. I answer in kind, pressing my mouth to his chest, his throat, tracing his collarbone with my tongue until his control slips and he growls softly against my neck.

I feel his bite as he drinks me in. I arch into him, meeting him stroke for stroke. My senses come alive in a way I hadn't realized possible. This is not just sex. It's possession, a promise that we belong only to each other. It's identity and hope and perfection.

I bite him back, letting his taste fill me completely, strengthening our bond. There is no room for doubt, only raw pure emotion. Magic stirs beneath my skin, pulsing in time with our bodies, a low hum of electricity that wraps around us both and lights up the balcony with shades of blue. When we finally meet our release, there is a calmness between us, like the world has finally settled.

Dawn threatens, prickling my skin with warning. Costin sweeps me indoors to the safety of our bed as the blackout shades lower to protect us, and I find myself thinking about the long journey that brought me here. From the mortal girl who just wanted a normal life, to the hybrid who helped reshape the supernatural world's balance of power.

"What are you thinking?" Costin asks sleepily beside me.

"About destiny," I reply. "And choices. And how sometimes they're the same thing."

He props himself up on one elbow. "Philosophy at dawn? You really are becoming immortal."

I playfully swat his chest. "I'm serious. I spent so long fighting what I was meant to be, only to discover that embracing it was the key to finding myself."

"And are you happy with what you found?" he whispers against my temple.

I consider the question. Am I happy with what I've become? With the wolf blood in my veins, the vampire hunger in my heart, the magic at my fingertips? With the council seat waiting for me, the responsibilities that come with power, the eternity stretching before us?

"Yes," I say simply. "I am."

And it's true. For the first time in my life, or death, or whatever this existence is, I feel complete. Not perfect, not free from doubts or fears, but whole in a way I never was before.

I am Tamara Devine. Hybrid. Council member.

Bride-to-be of a master vampire. Friend to werewolves. Daughter of magic and mortality. Once broken, now whole.

Costin's arm tightens around me as a deep sleep claims him. I press a kiss to his chest, right above his heart. That heart has beaten for centuries, waiting for mine to find its rhythm alongside it.

I close my eyes, surrendering to the day's embrace. Tomorrow night will bring new challenges, new battles, new moments of joy and sorrow. But for the first time in my existence, I'm not afraid of what's coming. I'm ready.

I am Tamara Devine.

And I am finally, completely alive.

The End

MERELY MORTAL SERIES

Merely Mortal

Mostly Shattered

Barely Breathing

Nearly Dead

Visit MichellePillow.com for details!

About the Author
Michelle M. Pillow

New York Times* & *USA TODAY
Bestselling Author

Michelle loves to travel and try new things, whether it's a paranormal investigation of an old Vaudeville Theatre or climbing Mayan temples in Belize. She believes life is an adventure fueled by copious amounts of coffee.

Newly relocated to the American South, Michelle is involved in various film and documentary projects with her talented director husband. She is mom to a fantastic artist. And she's managed by a dog and cat who make sure she's meeting her deadlines.

For the most part she can be found wearing pajama pants and working in her office. There may or may not be dancing. It's all part of the creative process.

PLEASE REVIEW
THANK YOU FOR READING!

Please take a moment to share your thoughts by reviewing this book.

Thank you to all the wonderful readers who take the time to share your thoughts about the books you love. I can't begin to tell you how important you are when it comes to helping other readers discover the series!

Be sure to check out Michelle's other titles at www.MichellePillow.com

www.ingramcontent.com/pod-product-compliance
Lightning Source LLC
Chambersburg PA
CBHW071533120726
47907CB00014B/1543